THE YEAR OF SECRETS

a mystery novel

by Silvia Villalobos

Paperback ISBN: 979-8-218-29672-8

First paperback edition October 2023

Editor: Gwynn Rogers

Cover Design Get Cover Designs

https://silviatomasvillalobos.wordpress.com

Silvia Villalobos

a paperback original imprint

Dedication

To my readers, who breathe life into these pages.

THE YEAR OF SECRETS

Silvia Villalobos

CHAPTER 1

Los Angeles

It was cold enough to freeze Zoe's blood, but tonight her problem wasn't weather-related. She stepped out of the elevator and into the lobby, unease winding through her body. Silence filled the office. No late-night workers, no cleaning crews. No one but the stranger behind glass doors, his face unreadable in the falling light.

Zoe steeled herself, opened the door, and stepped inside the room.

"Ms. Sinclair." The stranger oozed poise in his charcoal suit and tie. His coal-black eyes held a hint of recognition hard to shake off.

She gave Power Suit a chance. "Have we met before?"

"Kip Pulaski. Old firm client."

Zoe sat at the end of the table, facing the window. The moon shone over Los Angeles, reflecting off buildings and foothills. A calming sight most nights. Tonight, one phone call had shattered the calm, forcing a late-night visit to the twentieth floor of Century City Tower One.

"You requested the wrong person, Mr. Pulaski. I no longer work old cases."

He took his seat. "I value candor, Ms. Sinclair, and yours is refreshing. Tells me I requested the right person."

An awkward pause lingered like a cloud over the room.

"Like you," he said. "I once killed a man. Shot him right in the head."

The twinge in Zoe's stomach threatened to blast into full-blown pain. She focused inward—she had never intended to kill, despite the distorted narrative out there.

"Not everyone can do it." He poked at her silence. "Only the mentally strong."

Traces of citrus cologne filled the air until it saturated every inch of the space.

She looked through the interior glass, into the lobby of the twentieth floor—one of the three Grunman and Forester Law occupied in the skyscraper known as Century City Tower One. A woman associate passed by, stealing glances at Zoe.

Not an empty office, after all.

Aware that her thoughts were painted on her face, Zoe masked them with a smile. "Bob Forester should be here soon." If only her boss could hear the drivel coming out of Power Suit's mouth. Why the hell did Bob insist she come here tonight?

"Trusting is hard," Pulaski said. He stood and strode to the window. "Do you trust your fiancé, Ms. Sinclair?" He peered into the night, then faced her.

The question hit like a punch to the face. Zoe's mind raced to process its true meaning.

"We did a background check with emphasis on the last year," he said. "Usual practice."

She considered Pulaski as an old firm client, but something didn't add up. She'd expected him to be older, not close to her age. Most of their clients were men in their sixties and seventies. Then, there were his questions. Why would a firm client do a personal background check? That was far from "usual practice."

"Your fiancé is linked to various dark web groups. Nothing illegal." He rushed his words. "Not upright either, roaming among hackers."

"Code writers are known for their curiosity." Zoe threw out a plausible guess. Leaned closer. "I don't see how this is your business."

"The problem with curiosity, Ms. Sinclair, is that people will do anything to protect their privacy."

A weak threat, but his question lingered. *Do you trust your fiancé*?

Thoughts of Sebastian tumbled through Zoe's mind. He'd been on edge. Snapped at her questions about a last-minute trip to Wyoming, only to apologize again and again. They blamed it on stress, on his move a year ago from Laramie to Los Angeles.

An excuse easy to reach for these days.

"If you have something to say, Mr. Pulaski, say it." Zoe forced herself to exhale.

Kip Pulaski turned to her with a probing gaze that spoke of questions born long ago. He was scanning through mental images, as if comparing the past and present.

Nonsense. She didn't know the man.

"We'd like to hire you, Ms. Sinclair." A beat of silence. "You, not the firm. For a sensitive matter involving a defunct operation."

"You don't know me." Her voice sounded disembodied. He obviously knew about her. "As a lawyer," she said. "You don't know me well as a lawyer."

And I don't want to know you.

"We know enough." He walked to the table, pulled two papers out of his briefcase. A matter-of-fact gesture. "It's confidential work." He slid the papers toward her. "This is our proposal."

Bob's words came to mind: "He insisted on meeting with you. No other lawyer." For his part, Pulaski had tackled the *why* with mentions of her past. He needed a lawyer with a measure of notoriety. A lawyer with something to use against, whatever his secret intentions.

"Tell me about my fiancé," Zoe said. "Your findings."

Pulaski set his card on the table and pointed to the papers. His business came first, and that was the price for answers. "Order is everything, Ms. Sinclair. We hire lawyers to keep order." A ballsy stare. "I'll be expecting your call."

Typical practice among Power Suits: intimidate, scare, demand surrender. Big Shot Power Suit had aimed for immediate surrender.

A moment later, only the waft of Pulaski's cologne lingered in the room.

Zoe grabbed the card and stared at the black letters. The meeting had reawakened emotions suppressed with antidepressants, memories she'd worked hard to bury: Wyoming, murder. A dead body on the frozen tundra. Blood, so much blood, but not enough to draw out her guilt.

The therapist's advice cut through: *You killed in self-defense. Get out of your mind.* Zoe took the required breaths. After months of counseling and weaning herself off medication, she was not going to crumble again.

On the side-desk computer, she typed Kip Pulaski's name into the database. Nothing.

Bob had asked her to meet an old client who was not in the firm's database.

She tried Google. Hundreds of links popped up, but nothing close to exact. No man named Pulaski associated with Grunman and Forester.

Why did Bob send her here this late? And what did Pulaski want with her, with Sebastian?

Theories emerged, a rush of conversation flashing by: Sebastian on the phone discussing dollars, meetings. Whatever Kip Pulaski's story, it must be about Sebastian's work—an intersection of code writers and breakers. That was the only explanation.

But one question needed immediate answers. Her boss and law mentor had begged her to take the late meeting, then never showed up.

Zoe pulled the phone from her pocket and punched a pre-programmed button. The generic voicemail came on.

Where the hell are you, Bob?

* * *

The Foresters' Tudor mansion sat on a quiet road in Hancock Park. A house hidden by climbing roses and palm trees. The inside—Zoe remembered from brief visits—rivaled the Gilded Age era with chandeliers and turn-of-the-century mahogany.

Tonight, Zoe's brakes shrieked in protest as she abruptly halted.

Police cars, fire engines, and a TV van crammed the asphalt, blocking driveways. Officers stood behind yellow crime-scene tape that blocked access to half the street.

Red lights flashed near Bob's house.

Zoe's heart flipped in her chest. This was more than she'd bargained for. She should've driven home for that bottle of Xanax.

The early-November wind picked up, the chill piercing her coat. Zoe slammed the car door and made a beeline for the peach-colored corner house. The homiest house on the extravagant street. The only one outside the yellow tape, with people standing in the driveway.

"What happened?" she asked the gray-haired lady in a robe and fuzzy slippers. Behind her, a hunched man, likely the husband, held a phone to his ear.

The lady took a moment, eying Zoe. "Do you live in the neighborhood?"

"Trying to reach the Forester house."

The husband pocketed his cell phone. "Are you family?"

"Lawyer in Bob Forester's office." Chills iced Zoe's spine.

Hovering neighbors had congregated, their whispers lifted by the wind. A police officer, clipboard in hand, made his way around collecting names.

Dread surged through Zoe's body.

"I'm sorry," the old man said.

The elderly woman shook her head at her husband. But whatever the secret, it burned inside the man.

"My son heard it on the police scanner," the old man said. "Mrs. Forester found her husband dead in his study. There's chatter about self-inflicted gun wounds, but it's hard to know."

The cell phone buzzed in Zoe's pocket. She ignored it. The dread, now filling her, made it hard to breathe.

She stepped back as the cold kept biting, her awareness slipping until a gnarly hand touched hers.

"Would you like some water?" The woman's soft voice made the cold recede.

Zoe mumbled something about work or home. She dashed to her car while a police officer rolled more yellow tape, including the peach-colored house in the scene.

CHAPTER 2

A sedan sped away from the curb, flying out of view.

LAPD Detective Jett Riker caught the color and shape—silver, possibly a Lexus.

Who drove like a maniac near a police scene?

Sure, the victim had blown out his brains, but every Tom, Dick, and Harry knew police work fell in a gray area until every proverbial stone was turned. Here, they'd only scratched the outer layer with preliminaries.

Riker radioed in a restricted be-on-the-lookout for the Lexus. No sense initiating a chase through Hancock Park and cause the leadership a collective stroke.

He walked past lawns lush enough to host PGA tournaments. Folks here lived the dream. Except dreams evaporated at the crack of dawn, leaving behind twisted scraps of memories.

In the Tudor mansion, Bob Forester must've come face to face with a reality he couldn't accept and pulled the trigger.

Riker needed a moment before going back inside. The cool air helped him think. And walking the perimeter helped organize mental details.

He had detected the metallic blood odor upon arrival. They'd found Bob Forester on the floor of his home office, face angled out of view behind his desk. Forensic evidence to be analyzed, he'd been told by the CSIs. The quarter-size head wound was an ugly sight, blood and brain matter splashed over the desk and rug. Extensive blood spatter. Meaning Bob Forester had bled to death.

Looking at a man as remains, the spark of life gone, never got easy.

The deceased's wife proved of no help, as expected. She nodded when asked if her husband's behavior had changed recently. Nodded when asked about his possible depression. The shock-stricken woman just nodded.

Riker halted, cataloging the houses, people, and vehicles. The sprawl of Hancock Park homes gave a detached vibe—massive houses on mounds, their windows peering down at the world like silent judges.

A distant sound droned on. Music at a far distance.

Life and death, coexisting.

He turned and trotted toward the Tudor mansion. Ready or not.

Crossing the endless yard, Riker stepped inside the vestibule. He zeroed in on Detective Neva Braxton, who stood at the base of the stairs, leafing through notes. "I'm listening."

Sporting an ensemble of baggy clothes, hair pulled into a bun and aversion to makeup on display, Neva had set her beauty-queen days behind her.

"Ever hear of Grunman and Forester?" Neva's frown deepened into a scowl.

"Lawyers. Our victim was a partner there."

"Top L.A. firm. They hire the best young minds, with preference to local schools' graduates. Work 'em to exhaustion until poor young minds take their brains elsewhere." She flipped a page in her notebook. "Massive hiring out of UCLA Law seven years ago."

Riker's extra sense kicked in hard, making him flinch, no doubt to Neva's satisfaction. She knew his family, his life. She was a part of it. "The point, Neva."

"You know the point."

"My brother works there? Don't think so."

"Okay, worked." Neva poked the paper with her pen.

Qin Young, the medical examiner, called from across the room, severing the brief silence. Riker held up his hand, asking Qin to wait.

"Man like this, blowing out his brains." Neva pointed upstairs where the victim's wife, a white-faced woman with red hair who had the ill-fated luck of finding her husband covered in blood, was being treated for shock. "Wife's a mess. Won't make sense for a while. Larson knew Bob Forester, and Larson's your Bro. He could help, maybe."

Neva knew better than to wait for an immediate answer. She left to search the scene anew, notepad and pen in hand.

Riker found Qin Young, a tall Chinese American who corrected everyone's pronunciation of his name—Chin not Kin—and preferred it to his surname.

"Take a good look at the victim, Qin?"

A slight nod. "Close shot to the right temple. No abrasion, midface exit wound, that's why the pool of blood." A pause. "We need an autopsy for more."

"I hear a *but* coming."

"The angle. Most suicide shots are angled slightly upward. Downward wounds, meaning the gun was pointed down from a higher position, are hard when suicide is the objective."

"And here?"

"Difference is almost negligible, less than a millimeter, but there appears to be a downward angle."

"Which you say is impossible when suicide is the objective."

"Hard. I said *hard* to accomplish."

Riker let out a sigh. "Is that enough to change things here?"

Qin mumbled something unintelligible while crime-scene techs passed by. When the chime of someone's phone sliced through, he said, "Scratches on the victim's left wrist."

"Scratches or cuts?" Riker knew that cuts weren't the typical suicide choice for men of Forester's age.

"Not deep enough for cuts, something shallow."

"You're saying there was a fight, and someone shot Bob Forester?"

“Not saying, Riker. That’s your job. Thought I’d give you a heads-up.”

Riker took in the room filled with a dozen techs, five or six more marching up and down the stairs. Thanks to Qin Young, dark thoughts flashed through Riker’s mind, heading for hostile destinations.

CHAPTER 3

Zoe pounded on the cabin door.

A pale light shone from the window, but no sounds of anyone inside. Only her breathing cut through the hum of the canyon. She rubbed her shoulders, warding off more than cold. After Hancock Park, she'd turned on Highland and weaved up Laurel Canyon, not ready for an empty apartment and the draw of sedatives.

She'd missed a call from Larson. Not Sebastian, as she'd hoped. Larson, the ex-boyfriend she'd avoided since Wyoming. Now, here she stood at the cabin of their past. With the property on the edge of the hill and neighbors three acres away, darkness concealed the outdoors.

The view from high up, the city displayed like a postcard below, cleared some mental space. There was something special about the canyon, a deep connection to intangible forces. A vibe.

She scuttled across the grass to the back door. The bungalow of their romantic dinners in law school was empty. Larson's hidden space, an inherited piece of undeveloped real estate in the Santa Monica Mountains.

Zoe used the key she'd kept with his tacit approval. One turn later, the door popped open.

"Larson?"

She stepped inside the room, which curved into a galley-style kitchen. The bungalow sat on a large lot with a back terrace. She'd suggested improvements, but Larson loved simplicity, a different world from his Studio City bachelor pad. Last they spoke, he said this was home.

Tonight, silence reigned. Zoe flipped the light switch and called out again, but only the echo of her voice bounced back.

Heaps of papers lay on the corner piano, all Larson's work. Books sat propped open with highlighted quotes from Justice Oliver Wendell Holmes, the poet turned judge. "A man is more careful of money than principle," one highlighted quote read. "This is a court of law, young man, not a court of justice."

A realist consumer of literature, Larson.

Zoe was rearranging the stack when the sound of a car engine broke the silence.

Heavy footsteps trotted near the entrance before the front door flew open, and Larson stormed inside.

"I saw your car." Two strides later, his arms were around her, a throwback to their nights of wine, love, and philosophy.

Her rigid posture forced him back a step. When silence led nowhere, Larson said, "A drink?" He disappeared into the kitchen, and after some popping and pouring, returned with two glasses of red.

"You called earlier." Zoe took the offered glass.

"Long workday reminded me of you," Larson said with a slight smile. "Thought I'd try again."

After a sip Zoe said, "Bob Forester is dead."

No change in Larson's posture, only a subtle nod. "My brother called on the drive up."

"Your brother?"

"Jett, the police detective, remember? He knows I used to work for Bob."

Zoe stared a load of questions at him, struggling through confusion.

"Wanted to know when I'd last seen Bob. Signs of trouble, changes in demeanor. That sort of thing."

She waited for a follow-up that didn't come. "The rumor is self-inflicted gun wound," she said. "Found by his wife. Bob adored his wife, worried about her."

Larson took a gulp of wine. "Sudden death leads to speculation."

"Doesn't sound like Bob."

"People change."

“Bob called today.” She pressed her thumb against the smooth glass surface. “Asked me to take a late meeting. Client knew too much about me, never mentioned what he really wanted, just that I was a good fit for his work. Why me?”

“The business world is full of rich eccentrics.”

“But not Bob.” She stopped at the sound of her cracked voice.

“We think we know people, but we don’t.” Larson gulped more wine. “You should talk to Jett. Want me to call him?”

“Tomorrow.” She set her glass on the edge of the piano. Wine and company had sounded good until the first sip and first exchange.

Larson’s stare cut through. “Are you back? I’m sure the firm would love to have you back full time.”

After Wyoming, she’d never spoken about work with anyone but Bob. He’d given her unlimited time off and a say about her work, until tonight. “I’ve done a few hours on select cases.” She shook her head. “But now ….”

Work would never be the same without Bob Forester.

The knowing look in Larson’s eyes made words pointless. He knew her soul. Intimacy opened hearts in strange ways over time.

“Glad you came,” Larson said. “It’s been too long. You look good … healthy.”

Zoe felt herself reddening. This was harder than she’d imagined. “Do you know a man named Kip Pulaski?”

The headshake was curt, the eye contact cutting. “Stay for dinner.” Larson flashed a dimpled smile. “Why go home and eat alone?”

The mere thought of food sent a drilling pain through Zoe’s stomach. “Next time?”

Larson reached for her hand and squeezed. The circles under his eyes, more pronounced now, dampened his Casanova smile.

They stood for a minute, listening to the vague sounds of the city below—the ambient buzz of millions of Angelinos packed together, laughing, loving.

Dying.

Outside, the wind hit Zoe like a brick, a hostile world awaiting her.

Zigzagging down Laurel Canyon, she spotted the bungalow in her rearview mirror. A fading dot.

She'd run from old emotions; from all she'd come to say, but hardly did. Not easy around Larson. After law school, Larson had moved on with someone else. It stung, so she began dating a corporate hardass until he mentioned matrimony. Then she and Larson joined Grunman and Forester. Spending late hours on legal cases sank them into familiar comforts. Accidental hand touches, furtive glances, none of it helped. Every night, she pulled away only to go home and feel alone.

When he took another job, they laughed away their relationship with awkward goodbyes. Weeks later, a birthday card landed in her mailbox—a lunch invitation scribbled in Larson's jumbled writing. A friendly routine emerged, one she'd come to love, until Wyoming.

Everything from her past, including Larson, became too painful to consider after Wyoming.

Tonight, she'd run away from the look in his eyes, the sympathy in his voice. From words spoken and unspoken.

The implication that …

A honk blared, and Zoe's foot tapped the accelerator. Until tonight, her communication with Larson had been through email. Sleep deprived and under the spell of sedatives, she must've gone on about Sebastian's moods, about his trip. How else would Larson know she'd have dinner alone?

Zoe put away Larson's parting words. Her mind had been a mess of thoughts. She couldn't be sure what she'd said or emailed—if reality or recollection.

After Wyoming, psychiatric drugs had erased most memories. Weaning herself off medication was a struggle. She often fell short.

She'd hoped visiting her ex would ease the pain of the tragic news. Larson had known Bob. And Larson had been a positive force before last winter. But revisiting her past bled Zoe's heart of peace, because taking a life was no easy way out. The cost of self-preservation kept growing, intent on devouring her soul.

Her psychiatrist called what she felt anxiety. Zoe imagined it was something stronger, like PTSD. Sebastian's love had helped, but a man's dead eyes remained imprinted on her memory.

Give it time and as much space as you give the sharp turns on this winding road.

She needed to cling to memories like those of Mother during happy times, and her best friend Lori welcoming Zoe to Pine Vale with eggnog and gossip. Lori, before she was killed.

Most days, Zoe dismissed doctors and therapists with half-smiles. Went home, popped pills, and pulled the covers over her head until Sebastian coaxed her out with fresh smoothies for a nerve-ravaged stomach and love for her soul. It had become a year-long routine, since his move to Los Angeles. Now he was a thousand miles away, and questions were eroding her fragile peace.

He wouldn't have allowed a year of secrets between them. Would he? It was hard to fathom a year had passed since they left Wyoming.

Leaning into a car turn, Zoe tried in vain to put away the images flashing before her eyes. Mother. Last winter. Pine Vale, Wyoming. A town so isolated, most state residents didn't know it existed. Then one man in that town went too far. Stepping in had forced Zoe to pull the trigger. The very act Kip Pulaski thought gutsy.

Lori had been the gutsy one. She'd uncovered the plan and paid with her life. But for a moment of lucidity, when self-preservation kicked in, Zoe would have met Lori's fate. Zoe had pulled the trigger, and Marshall Park's dead eyes would forever be with her.

Focus on tasks. She focused on the winding road taking her home.

CHAPTER 4

The dark living room blinded Zoe.

She reached for the light switch, stopped. Hints of an unfamiliar scent hung in the air, earthy with traces of vanilla. Faint, drifting away, but obvious. It could've wafted in through cracks and keyholes, but she'd lived here long enough to recognize the different odors in the building.

There were no signs of forced entry. Her Manhattan Beach neighborhood, steps from the ocean, had always been safe to the point of boredom.

Why the strange feeling then? This would not be the first time her internal sensors tripped off for no reason.

Holding her breath, Zoe turned on the light. Exhaled when nothing happened. She couldn't let paranoia prevail.

Nothing in the apartment looked out of place, thank God.

A car's headlights pierced the room. Bright enough to notice the phone headset lying on the carpet between sofa and wall.

Zoe picked up the receiver and set it in the cradle. Things tended to fall. Any rational person knew that.

She turned on the TV for background noise. Ten minutes until the top of the hour, when the news should be dominated by what happened in Hancock Park.

"Mystery in Skid Row," the newscaster droned on. "There is a spike in missing homeless people."

Some buildup to the top-of-the-hour headline in the City of Angels.

Rummaging under magazines spread over the table, she found the bottle of Xanax. Thought about popping one, then set the bottle aside. Not today. She needed to think clearly. So many questions circled through her mind, chased by bouncing answers, unable to settle down enough for Zoe to grasp.

The newscaster came back on: "Police are puzzled by the whereabouts of homeless people who'd lived near a downtown shelter named Helpers of the Needy. They seemed to have disappeared."

The announcer went on, teasing with the promise of breaking news, only to prolong the suspense and play with Zoe's fraying nerves. Anything to keep anticipation building.

Zoe gave the news story another ten seconds, then pushed the Off button. The media were getting lazy, throwing out verbal clickbait with no factual details.

So much for background noise.

She walked to the window, taking in the vastness of the Pacific. The roaring ocean crashed furiously onto the rocks, waves lifting high, sporadic and not long lasting.

What was she missing about tonight? Answers remained elusive.

In the bathroom, she avoided the Vicodin bottle. Her doctor had prescribed the meds for anxiety and pain, along with the Xanax. *Take as needed*, it read.

She turned on the tub and poured plant-extract soap, watching bubbles form. Ran her hand through, taking in the scent, uplifting and fresh.

A tentative sense of calm took hold. She'd take it after a day like today.

Looking in the mirror, Zoe unbuttoned her top. Felt the smooth silk of her bra. The last lingerie purchase had coincided with Sebastian's birthday three months back. A night of lovemaking, she recalled.

She slid shirt and bra off her shoulders. Let them fall to the floor. Examined her ivory skin, her breasts, and the outline of her thirty-seven-year-old body. Time had been good to her. At five feet nine, and the same weight since college, she used to see herself too tall and frail. But appreciative looks dispelled doubts when maturity brought confidence. Her light-brown hair, longer than ever, framed an angular face and big, brown eyes. Too big for her face, she once thought. Mother had insisted she'd grow into her own eyes.

The look, the touch, the bath perfume recalled feelings of

desire. She wrapped her palms around her breasts, caressing the skin, the nipples. Anything to transcend the pain. Soon, a sense of longing exuded. She slipped out of her slacks and silky underwear.

She'd been out of touch with her body, with her own sensuality for too long. Forgot to self-embrace.

She trailed her fingertips along her arms and stomach—a long, indulgent caress. Love, pain, pleasure—so many feelings our bodies gifted us.

Women could be soft and strong. She was surrounded by strong women in her family, at the office.

The thought lingered, overpowering.

The woman she saw at the office tonight. The only other person aside from Kip Pulaski. She was someone Zoe had seen before, someone of importance.

Zoe turned off the tub and dashed out of the bathroom.

CHAPTER 5

Manhattan Beach was an oasis of calm at night.

Hawke Ford hid behind a palm tree, steps from the beach, and watched the third-floor windows. The living room light had gone on five minutes ago, then the bathroom light. Hawke pictured Zoe Sinclair stripping naked, stepping into the shower. He felt himself harden and lit a cigarette, waiting for the sensation to pass.

Having watched her for the past week, Hawke discovered the woman was unpredictable. She stayed in for days, leaving only to return minutes later. Or she'd leave and not come back for hours. Never a discernible pattern with her, only a guessing game that kept Hawke engaged and, frankly, challenged him.

Entering Zoe Sinclair's apartment thirty minutes ago had been child's play. Then two messages lit up his phone, followed by a third. She was on her way back. Forced to abort, he'd snuck out, catlike, but remained riveted to her window.

He sucked on his cigarette, inhaled, and blew out smoke.

Zoe Sinclair had displayed erratic behavior in the past, but tonight she showed a hell of a deviation from the norm. When the tracker showed her driving to Laurel Canyon, he figured she'd fall into comfortable habits with her former amore, like all neglected women stricken with grief. But not Ms. Sinclair.

Hawke could smell and taste the ocean mist. Could stand here for hours and enjoy the broken moonlight glistening off Palos Verdes hills.

Nights like tonight reminded Hawke of his past.

He flicked the cigarette away and blew smoke toward the ocean. Night-shining clouds lit up the sky, offering a soul-soaring sight.

Maybe it was the view that reminded him of his past. The view brought back memories of his childhood, spent in a house like those on the hill, overlooking the Pacific. Well-off family, parents driven to succeed, smart genes inherited by the boatload. As an honor roll and gifted student, he whipped through academic acceleration courses, and graduated high school at fifteen. Too much, his older brother had said, suffering from puberty and a bighead. Jealous prick.

Now, ten years later, the occasional doubts intruded. How did he snap from gifted student to fleeing scenes to breaking and entering? The hum of the ocean seemed to answer: dull existence sucking away the thrill of living. That's how. Super-active minds weren't meant to float stagnantly. Life was to be challenged, limits tested. What was the point of moving from day to day and repeat?

Fuck that.

He looked up at Zoe Sinclair's windows again. The woman had forced him to flee before a thorough search.

They needed to know nothing damaging had passed from Bob Forester to Ms. Sinclair. The old man had been known to confide in his former pupil. Hawke had followed orders, but next time he might not be so generous. Next time, he might fucking snap.

He looked back on the past few months. At all the work demanded of him. Working as a law-firm courier at Grunman and Forester Law, and playing the roles of both lover and sidekick villain. That was a hell of an effort. He was pleased with the progress but looking forward to The End.

A few things along the way had surprised Hawke. His boss, changing the playbook midstride, had grown secretive, borderline obsessive.

"Focus on the masterpiece," Big Shot had said. "The ultimate success of our work requires sacrifice, direct or indirect. The cure is everything, and we're closer than ever."

Whatever you say, Boss.

He checked his phone again. No new messages.

Hawke lit another cigarette, searing away negative thoughts. He pulled the burner phone out of his pocket and dialed the number committed to memory.

Seconds later, the gruff voice answered. "Detective Riker."

"The vehicle you're looking for is a Lexus LX."

"Who's this?"

"Hill Road in Hancock Park, an hour ago." Hawke drew on his cigarette, blew out more smoke. "Car split before the scene was cordoned off. You've been looking for it."

"That was a closed-circuit APB, sent out over a secure police channel."

"Amazing, the devices a few hundred bucks will buy you off the Internet."

"Whose car?"

"Zoe Sinclair of Manhattan Beach."

"What makes you think I don't already have the info?"

"It's a direly overworked police force, Detective."

Jett Riker's silence rang unnaturally against the sound of the waves.

Hawke shouldn't have allowed for background noise, but the view held him captive. Tonight, it was beyond anything he'd seen. Below the mist, lingering clouds encircled as if searching for prey. For a second, Hawke closed his eyes and drank in the air, a mixture of ocean and fern.

"What do you want?" the detective demanded.

"A relationship for now." Hawke hated stupid games. More, he despised the police. But he needed an insurance policy, a plan dismissed far too long. Big Shot's unpredictable behavior as of late cemented the idea. He'd initiate contact for future negotiations, should the time arrive.

Hawke stared into the horizon when a sudden flash of light stung his eyes and pierced him like a blade. Burning. Cutting. Wind whizzed past his ears, intensifying in strength then fading. He swayed, waiting for more pain.

Had he been shot?

For a moment, he thought this was what death looked like, but something was wrong. The blinding light was directly in front of him. There for a split second, then gone. Caused by a far-away storm where clouds swirled, setting off a blaze of lightning.

On the phone, Detective Jett Riker was going through the motions: keep him on the line, push, cajole.

Hawke hung up. He slammed the phone to the ground, stomped on it, picked up the pieces, and threw them in a nearby trashcan. Detective Riker could go to hell for now.

Shivers cut through as the wind swept his hair. Hawke retreated to the thick callus of his heart, turning his attention back to the third-floor windows.

CHAPTER 6

Zoe rushed down the steps, two at a time, catching herself twice from slipping into a heap of flesh. Her apartment building stood like a tower of silence in the night. Nothing stirred. No one was coming or going.

She pulled her robe around her waist and tightened the string. That was all she threw on, and barely remembered the slippers. No patience for a civilized dress code. Once the thought hit, she dashed out the door.

There had been another person in the office during her meeting with the mysterious Kip Pulaski. Who and why?

In the basement, she took the last flight of steps into the garage. Chills cut through the terry cloth covering her. No turning back now.

She reached the storage cabinet assigned to her parking spot. Every tenant had one. Hers stood empty but for one box. She struggled with the cabinet key, hands shaking from the cold, before it snapped unlocked.

There it was—her souvenirs deposit. The box packed with mementos from places she'd traveled, old books, and medals from races she'd run with law-school friends. This was the in-between spot. Between her apartment and the trash.

Zoe set the box on the hood of her car. Any other day, she might have worried about scratches on the Lexus she was still paying for, but tonight the thought faded fast.

The picture taken at Bob's birthday lunch—the one his wife insisted on taking every year—had better be in the box. Zoe remembered seeing it, but not whether she'd gotten a copy. She'd found nothing upstairs. If the photo still existed, this was the only place it could be.

Books, insignia pens, more medals, and, stuck into a corner, an envelope.

Zoe took out the first shot and stared at the semicircle of friends: Bob, his secretary, a new associate, and herself. Four jovial faces, but Zoe fixated on the brunette to the far right. The same woman she saw tonight during her meeting with Kip Pulaski. The woman who passed by the glass wall, stealing glances at Zoe.

Clearly, Bob, or Pulaski, had wanted the meeting late enough for an empty office. Late enough that even the cleaners had finished their work. Yet the woman with shoulder-length dark hair and greenish eyes had been there.

Zoe racked her memory, trying to recall Pulaski's reaction. Had he turned to look? She hadn't given the moment enough importance to remember. Now, hours later, Zoe wondered if the woman being there was pure coincidence. Something told her no.

Damn, but the robe was no match for the night chill. She tensed and lifted her shoulders, still unable to move from the spot.

Okay, put the pieces together.

Zoe flipped the picture and caught the scribblings on the back. Date, occasion, and names listed from left to right.

Shila Diggs.

Now she remembered. Bob had introduced them at the first meeting.

"Shila, meet Zoe, and Zoe, this is Shila, our new associate. A friend of Mrs. Grunman." The last part played through Zoe's mind over and over.

A friend of Mrs. Grunman.

Cato Grunman, the firm's founder and named partner, was married to Asha—the antithesis of her husband, an outgoing young woman. A friend.

Zoe took out the second picture, a candid shot of Bob and his crew. A moment caught in the midst of laughter, while preparing to stand for another photo Bob's wife was taking. Everyone laughed except for Shila. Caught in an unguarded moment, Shila was giving the posers a look of stealth.

Zoe cautioned herself about reading too much into a photo. Shila could have been experiencing heartburn at that very moment. Who knew?

Still, that look—eyes narrowed, no hint of a smile during a celebratory time—said something about Shila Diggs, but Zoe didn't know what it meant.

She should do herself a favor and not overthink. A night like tonight came with too many questions to keep sane. But her attention went back to the face in the picture. *What's your story, Shila?* Only one way to find out.

* * *

Back in the apartment, Zoe's teeth stopped chattering and the brain fog lifted enough to think.

What did she remember about Bob's new associate?

Not a damn thing.

The woman didn't seem the ambitious type, who would do anything to become partner. Most would-be partners were hand-picked. Those who weren't came with determination to climb the ladder etched on their faces. Bob had called them the "driven lot," with some derision.

Shila wasn't the type. That much Zoe remembered, now that the mental gears were turning faster. Shila hadn't been showing off her knowledge, like the "driven lot." She had simply been there doing the work, a presence. Like tonight, when she'd been the only other person there during a pre-arranged meeting.

In retrospect, it was strange that Shila had been only a silent presence around Bob. Even the shy ones blabbered. They had to show something of themselves, discuss work, accomplishments. No one kept salary figures moving upward by keeping quiet.

A friend of Mrs. Grunman. Maybe a favor hiring. The law field was full of recommendations for entry-level associates fresh out of law school and in need of work to pay back student loans.

Zoe grabbed her phone, found the number and typed fast, then hit send. Prayed that Asha would blame the late-night text from her friend on shock, and answer back.

Going to bed would be sensible, but too many questions kept Zoe from hiding under the blanket and shutting out the world.

Kip Pulaski, to start with, had amassed damaging

information on her fiancé. Why? To force her hand at taking work Zoe would otherwise not consider? Pulaski had wanted a meeting with Zoe, a handpicked associate, in his long-time lawyer's office. Then his lawyer ended up dead by self-inflicted gunshot wound. In the meantime, Pulaski's name was not in the firm's database. How was that possible?

Zoe opened her laptop and brought up the State Business Division site. Typed Pulaski's name under Agents, then under Incorporators, and narrowed the search down by years. She pulled up a list of existing and defunct entities, altered the search to Similar Names. After the third try, the name Kipling P. popped up on a cancellation form for an entity named Specter Research Unlimited. Not a filed-stamped cancellation, meaning it had been withdrawn almost immediately after being filed, five years back.

Interesting. Pulaski would not do his own legal work but delegate to lawyers. Unless he was trying to hide something.

Whom would he call for legal work, Bob? Shila?

The name bounced through Zoe's head, over and over.

Shila Diggs. The newest associate at Grunman and Forester Law. A new hire by Bob Forester, the attorney of record for one Kip Pulaski who'd wanted a late meeting with Zoe in an almost empty office, tonight of all nights.

Outside her living room window, a car sat parked with the headlights on. The only car on the street. It could be anyone. While quiet, the street had some traffic, even late at night.

She waited, hidden in complete darkness. After a long while, the car drove away. No other movement, no sounds, nothing until the ding on her phone. A reply from Asha Grunman: *Shocked to hear about Bob. My God! And no, I don't know a Shila Diggs.*

CHAPTER 7

Zoe had grown accustomed to the dark.

She lay staring at the ceiling, watching the shadows dance. Pills would bring about sweet oblivion. That was the point, she knew, to feel nothing. Hard to tell what was worse, to hurt or feel nothing at all.

Some answers would ease her mind. There was one answer only the firm's private detective could dig up on a rush basis, but not at this hour. Was Shila Diggs an impostor, using Asha Grunman's name for employment gain?

A rap-tap cut through her thoughts.

At first, Zoe dismissed the sound. Must be nighttime noise traveling across the building—neighbors up for the odd reason people move around late at night. Sounds moved through space in a building with apartments separated by nothing but common walls.

The sound resonated again, more pronounced—like a knock on the door.

At this hour?

Zoe was in her bedroom, the farthest part of the apartment. Under the blanket, but awake. The lights were off, the blinds closed. As far as anyone could tell, she was either not home or asleep.

She sat up and pushed the blankets aside. Strained to listen closely.

There it was again, a soft rap of fingertips, not a knuckle tap.

She grabbed the phone and clutched it to her chest. Swung her legs off the bed and tiptoed on the carpet. Waited, holding her breath, then carefully exhaled.

She crept up around the wall and into the living room.

Nothing but silence reigned now, long and unsettling. But she'd heard the sound, clear in the night.

There was a distant shuffling of footsteps on cement. Someone going down the steps.

She ran to the window overlooking the entrance, hid to the side and waited.

A shadow appeared in the lamp-lit corner of the building. The lengthened shadow of a man, judging by the wide shoulders. But really, it could have been anyone. He stood there, hidden from view, still as the quiet night.

The phone in her hand started ringing.

Startled, Zoe covered her mouth. An unknown number. She glanced back out the window, but the man had disappeared. No shadows stretching anywhere.

Her phone beeped. Someone had left a message. Zoe hit the button and listened to Larson's voice. Strange, that he'd called from an unknown number. They'd spoken only a few hours earlier.

"Zoe, it's late, I know, but call when you get this. It's important. Don't worry about the hour, just call." Silence, then heavy breathing. "Be careful out there, Zo.'"

Zoe's finger hovered over the call-back button. She stopped, pulled up the contacts list, and found Larson's saved number. Read the two numbers to be sure. Larson had called from a downtown area-code. He'd always been a westside kind of guy.

Zoe dialed Larson's old number and waited through two rings, four, six. Then a click, and the call was forwarded to his answering service. She stared at the new number. No, she couldn't shake the feeling there might be something more to this change in Larson. Something best saved for a face-to-face talk.

She stared out the window, willing something to happen and reveal the answers to all her questions.

What about Larson's detective brother, Jett Riker?

Larson had wanted her to call Jett, a no-nonsense cop she'd met during family dinners, and talk to him about Bob and the late-night office meeting with Bob's eccentric client. She'd liked Jett—

a man easy to talk to, who loved joking about detectives solving cases with clue boards, like in the movies, with names connected by dots and arrows. *Crazy walls*, they were called.

Not his jam. But it could be hers.

She ran to her desk and shoved around magazines until she found her notebook. Tore out a page, grabbed a pen and sat. She needed events organized in her mind or she'd go crazy.

At the top, she wrote Kip Pulaski and next Bob Forester, with dots connecting the two names. Bob had insisted, almost begged, that she meet Pulaski. She'd have said *hell no* to anyone else.

Below Pulaski, she wrote Sebastian with a question mark between the two. What did Pulaski have on her fiancé? Why the veiled threat? She added Larson and, as an afterthought, his brother, the police detective. Someone she should call.

She added Shila Diggs' name. Whether by accident or some strange way these clue boards worked, Shila's name had landed between Bob's and Kip Pulaski's. Damn. If she stared at the paper long enough, she might start seeing cosmic connections. Maybe that was the reason detectives like Jett Riker said hell no to using *the crazy wall.*

CHAPTER 8

Good thing Riker knew where to find his brother, who had gone dark again.

It was busy on the streets of Sawtelle, a fifteen-mile drive from downtown, despite the cold. The place had grown into a magnet for hipsters and foodies, a world away from the days when streets lined with Japanese noodle shops were mostly bare.

Riker parked close to the intersection, ready to bounce when done. The new case demanded a chat with his brother, who was always busy.

Too bad, Bro.

It was here, in Sawtelle, that, forty years ago, a doctor and his pregnant wife from Oakland bought a ranch-style house. His real home, though nowadays visits were jolting. He loved his father and appreciated his stepmother, yet the heart never relinquished the what-ifs—had his own mother survived cancer all those years ago.

Today, the jolt faded fast. Shit storms abounded, coming at him from every direction. Larson's connection with Bob Forester had crawled under Riker's skin and stayed there. Same as his brother's refusal to return calls.

Then, there was the caller last night, whose info matched Riker's—Zoe Sinclair near his crime scene. The man's knowledge of guarded information piled on the questions. Why would Zoe be there shortly after her boss was found dead? And why floor it from the scene almost upon arrival? No one knew Zoe Sinclair better than Larson.

He reached his parents' house and snuck in through the side gate at the end of the lot. Hurried across the gravel rocks that formed a walkway through a garden full of multicolored plants.

Their brightness clashed with his mood. He'd spent the evening emailing Captain about conflict of interest because of Larson's work relationship with Forester. The department bosses didn't like detectives leading cases which involved family members, and for good reason. Hard to stay focused when grilling one's brother.

Budget cuts and severe personnel shortages gave Captain no choice—with the caveat to keep him in the loop at every step.

Just great. Being babysat like a rookie.

Riker had no choice but to paper the hell out of the case. Build protection against trial lawyers sure to invoke family bias, even if nothing material linked his brother to Bob Forester yet.

At the back of the garden, half hidden by a palm tree, Larson stood reading his phone. That was his favorite spot. Hardly a family dinner went by without Bro excusing himself to take work calls. But unlike his older brother, Larson was predictable, always here for dinners, for welcoming visiting relatives from Oakland. The kind of evening Riker would eat mud to escape.

"Hey, Bro."

Larson slid the phone into his pocket. "You scared the hell out of me." He threw out his hand for a handshake. "Didn't know you were coming."

Curious stares followed. Riker opened the file he'd brought and flipped the front side behind the back. No time for bullshit.

Pointing at the picture clipped onto the summary page, he handed Larson the file. "Your girlfriend was at my scene last night." He'd matched the anonymous caller's tip with the internal BOLO. Both turned up Zoe Sinclair's license plate.

A beat, then a head shake. "It's been over for ages, you know that. We were together in law school." Larson's voice went up an octave. He checked himself, dropped it. "She came to see me last night. Was shaken up about Bob Forester."

"Interesting."

Larson closed the file. "She worked for Forester, and legal work never stops. Like detective work."

They stood close enough for Riker to see tension in Larson's eyes. *Defensive of his former girlfriend, wasn't he?*

Mother had long joked about "the one who got away." Zoe Sinclair. One of the two women Larson had brought home to meet his family. He'd grown distant after they broke up, busy with work, the usual excuse. Mother had encouraged Riker to prod Larson about his love life, but Riker took a look and let it go. Larson wouldn't appreciate prodding.

Having become stepbrothers at age eight for Larson and ten for Riker, they were close, but an invisible curtain between them remained drawn. They had a good relationship, filled with playful moments, but mostly one of tolerance and respect for personal space.

But, again, this was different.

"When I called last night, you were driving and couldn't talk. Said you'd call back." Riker stared the next question at Larson.

"I got busy."

"Work, as usual."

A nod.

"No time for a five-minute call while waiting for Mother to finish dinner?"

Voices echoed inside the house. The Oakland cousin had arrived with someone, the latest flame. Shadows moved past the living room window. People hugging and laughing. The sounds grated on Riker's nerves.

"I was gonna call." Larson followed his gaze before their eyes met again.

"Soon?"

"You interrogating me?"

More laughter from inside the house, then the clinking of dishes. They were setting up the table. A child's voice rose above the racket.

Good God, Riker couldn't be around kids. His nerves would give out. Luckily, the trees hid them from view.

"You worked for Bob Forester." Riker pulled his thoughts together. "Zoe Sinclair, your law-school girlfriend who worked in the same office at the same time, was near his house, presumably about a case. Then she drove to see you, immediately after she left the crime scene, even though it's been over for ages between you two. Anything I should know?"

"Crime scene?" Color left Larson's face. "Not suicide? Are you saying --"

"Habit talk."

Mother was shouting about more chairs. Dad said something back.

Please stay inside the fucking house.

Larson turned toward the hedgerow. The term *crime scene* didn't agree with his stomach.

Their parents would be out, chide Riker for not saying hello, then freak out about Larson looking all pale. Thank God Bro kept his stomach contents where they belonged.

"Tell me about Bob Forester, Larson. Your former boss ended up with a gunshot wound in his head. Your former flame visited last night. Tell me. No detail is too small."

Larson glared. "You're overreacting about Zoe. I told you, she was shaken up."

"That why she came to see you?"

"You read the summary." Larson shook the file in the air. "The Wyoming story. She's been shaken up. This didn't help."

That was what brought Riker here, ready to ambush his brother: Zoe Sinclair had killed a man. Wyoming neighbor named Marshall Park had raped and killed Zoe's best friend and, soon after, killed the woman's boyfriend and buried him in the woods. In the end, it was Zoe or Marshall, and Zoe pulled the trigger. A victim turned assailant, who'd been in therapy and under psychiatric care since. Riker hated where his thoughts wandered, but as a detective investigating a possible homicide, there was no other choice. To what extreme would Zoe's past push her?

"I called to check on Zoe when she returned from Wyoming last year," Larson said. "Invited her for drinks. I learned she was engaged."

"Oh."

"Not the thing to do—visit an old boyfriend—when engaged. But last night, she came. Said Bob had called, asked her to take a new-client meeting, together I assume, but Bob never showed up. The whole thing seemed strange, so she tried to reach him. When he didn't answer, she drove to his house. It's how she found out."

Details easy to verify. Yet the mystery caller, who somehow knew about his BOLO, had pointed out Zoe at the scene. Why?

Larson's gaze moved past Riker. Whatever Larson was working up in his mind took monumental effort.

"I told Zoe to call you, go on record with everything." Larson lowered his voice. "She's been keeping a low profile since Wyoming. She'll come around."

It was always in the tone change and the deep look that more answers awaited. Nonverbal communication said more than a thousand words.

"That's all she knows, but what about you?" Riker said. "You know more?"

"Mom's going to come out any second." Larson pointed toward the house. "Wanna ruin dinner?"

Mom to Larson was Mother to Riker. What was in a name? Not much or a lot.

The back door cracked open, but no one came out.

"Anything else, Larson?"

Larson's gaze remained fixed on the back of the house, the screen door flipping in the wind. "Bob Forester called a month ago and asked me to meet him at his office, an unusually late meeting. Something about a case he needed outside counsel for. Big enough client, he'd want me to double my rate."

"Unusually late meeting?"

"Past ten o'clock. Had to use the back door."

"He'd never done that before?"

Larson shook his head. "Not with me."

"Why the office? Why not a coffee shop or home?"

"Bob hated moving files out of the office, insisted lawyers make work copies, and only copies of certain things, no confidential client information went home. A professional code of conduct thing."

"Why so late? Why not business hours?"

A squint followed by too large a smile. "Look," Larson said. "I've no freaking idea. Bob wanted to meet about a case he needed outside counsel for. That's all I know."

"And you said no?"

"Initially. Then I was intrigued. It wasn't the money, if that's what you're thinking."

"I'm not given to guessing."

"Nothing panned out. He called later and said it was a no-go. But … he sounded off. Distant, like we were strangers discussing a case. I used to be part of his team. Now, he apologized and wished me well in my endeavors."

"So, you were curious and pushed to learn more?"

Another bout of laughter followed eerie silence; then someone stood on the backdoor threshold. Two people talking. Mother and a tall figure Riker didn't recognize. One of the guests.

Riker moved a step back, behind the trees. Larson followed.

"When I called, his wife said it wasn't a good time, and that was that." Larson shook his head, impatient. "Then Zoe told me about the meeting last night. Bob not showing up, which was the reason she came to see me."

"Why would Forester have needed your help? What case was he talking about?"

"I'm guessing there was a conflict between Bob's law firm and the client. Bob's firm couldn't take the case."

"What case? Did he say what was it about?" Riker felt his patience melt.

"Something old … Look I don't …"

The back door slammed shut. Mother stood by the door, near the flowering bush.

"You never saw me." Riker grabbed the folder. He rushed between palm trees, toward the hedge that separated their property from the neighbor's. Jumped over the fence, cut through another yard, and reached the back alley.

* * *

Riker needed fresh air and coffee, and in that order.

He stepped out into the backyard of the house he shared with Neva, waiting for the promised fresh brew. They were coffeeholics by nature, irrespective of the hour. A woman after his own heart, Neva. Hard to imagine they'd have ever met if not for Larson.

Riker considered Larson. They grew up close for stepbrothers until Bro's senior year of high school, when a barrier went up. He spoke less and prioritized his friends over family.

Normal adolescence phase. Riker had experienced his own.

During and after college, news about Larson came mostly from Mother. She had hinted at Riker prodding Larson about life and dating, like an older brother would.

When Larson introduced Zoe to the family, Mother was ecstatic. When the romance ended, she was crushed.

Then Neva came along. An intuitive thinker, a cop, considering a legal career. The legal part brought Neva and Larson together, but it wasn't enough to last. Two months after Riker bumped into them at the local bar, it was over between the two.

Riker took a long breath of cold air and felt it in his lungs.

He remembered the day when one drink with Neva led to two, then three. Their shared profession made talking easy and brought them close, Riker told himself, but he knew better. The physical attraction had been immediate and overwhelming.

Larson had declared himself "fine" with the news of Neva, his former flame, and his brother dating. Same with his parents, though Riker had sometimes wondered. He blamed himself, Neva blamed herself, but Larson's distant demeanor was nothing new.

Riker should have prodded, like Mother had asked, about Larson's lovers, friends, and bosses. Maybe Larson would have shared something about his work, about Bob Forrester.

Neva stepped out and handed him a coffee mug. "Penny for your thoughts."

"Anything on Bob Forester's widow?" He knew Neva hated dividing roles by gender, but had agreed to question the grieving Mrs. Forester herself. Woman to woman.

"I'm making arrangements for her to come in. She wants no more cops in her house." Neva sipped her coffee.

"The scene didn't completely rule out murder."

"So far suicide sticks, even if like a wet bandage slowly peeling off," Neva said. "Neighbors said Forester's been withdrawing from life, missed golf games. Went from social butterfly to recluse for the first time in the last twenty years. Jives with being down and out."

"We'll need expert testimony. A chat with his doctors."

"His secretary said Bob Forester was working a lot. Too busy for golf."

"His partners?"

"They corroborated the secretary's statement but pointed to the main partner, Cato Grunman who knew Forester best. I left a message, got nothing back yet."

Aside from there being no suicide note, nothing at the scene screamed murder except for what Qin Young had said about the shot angle, a presumption at this point. They needed actionable facts, and statements from experts and those who knew Bob Forester well. Riker had hoped Larson would help piece together a good profile of Forester. But Larson had waffled. Something about his manner when pressed on Bob Forester and the recent legal cases wasn't what Riker had expected.

"Talk to your brother yet? Neva blew on her coffee. "They were close. Forester went from professor to boss."

A truth that bugged Riker, the fact that Larson had been close to a man who may have been murdered. "Larson pointed in one direction."

CHAPTER 9

Century City welcomed Riker with its usual nighttime buzz.

Tonight, they were in luck. With temperatures plummeting and frost making an appearance, notoriously jam-packed roads glistened, mostly devoid of traffic.

"Not so busy when it's like inside a freezer out there," Neva said.

From Santa Monica Boulevard, he hung a turn, crossed Constellation, and pulled in front of Tower One. His windshield LAPD sticker gave him the freedom to park anywhere.

Stepping out of the car, Riker took in the night air, ice-cold and foreboding.

Emerging from the other side of the cruiser, Neva looked like an Eskimo. The Caramel Macchiato in her hand, thick jacket, and scarf didn't seem a good buffer against the chill.

They mounted the steps to the entrance of Tower One, a forty-four-story building above one of the world's largest underground parking garages.

"There's a connection between the case and this location," Riker said.

"And it has to be made this late?"

Riker couldn't blame Neva. Once the cloud cover dispersed, the night chill rolled in like a moving train. Too damn cold out there.

At the top of the steps, Neva sipped her coffee, eyeing him.

"I take it Captain barked at your conflict of interest."

Riker nodded. The captain's email had been curt. "You're on the case, Riker. If it's not suicide, get the fucker fast."

Riker pushed the night button, and one of the security guards behind a counter of monitors hobbled toward them. A pudgy man of undetermined age, a scowl painted on his face. Riker showed his badge, and the scowl morphed into a watchful smile. The guard motioned to the fellow behind the counter. The doors hissed open.

"Detective Riker, LAPD, this is Detective Braxton." They stepped in but didn't move far past the threshold. "We have a few questions about a tenant."

The man, whose name tag read Duarte, said, "Have to call the chief." He strode away, fumbling with the radio mouthpiece.

Riker never dismissed hunches. Larson mentioning a late-night meeting at Forester's office needed one thing: a visit to get confirmation before any funny business happened, like someone forgetting to preserve video evidence. He'd seen worse.

After some garbled communication, Officer Duarte waddled back. They met him halfway.

"Chief is grabbing somethin' to eat. Be a few minutes."

"Okay if we look around?" Riker had to try, even if he knew the answer.

"Need the chief for that, and an escort. My partner's on patrol. Can't leave my post."

"How long have you been working here?" Neva rolled the Macchiato in her cup.

A grimace crossed Duarte's face. "Couple years." He turned to Riker. "Is there a problem, Detective?"

"Grunman and Forester, decent tenants?"

"Don't know the tenants. Just see them walk through the lobby."

"Any Grunman guests pop in at weird hours, need after-hour access?"

"Maybe, sometimes." Duarte's nervous tick came and went. "But that's a question for the chief."

Riker scanned the lobby, waiting for Duarte to sort out his nerves. He'd get nothing from the chief without a warrant and did not have enough probable cause for a non-warrant search, just Larson's story of late-night meetings. He was hoping for a guard persuaded by the badge and eager to help detectives with an investigation.

Some corporate types hurried between elevators, still on the money-making clock despite the hour.

Riker pointed upward to the general location of the Grunman and Forester offices. "Get any recent calls from Grunman to unlock doors after hours?"

"Not me. I'm on second shift, just covering a call-off today."

A non-answer.

"Someone else, then?" Neva asked, all smile.

A beat of silence. "We been told someone's been calling down here to let people in after hours. Might call again."

"When was this?" Riker pushed forward.

"Uhh … few weeks back."

"Weird business practice," Neva said. "Calling security for access during regular hours."

"It was a pass down from night to day shift."

Muddying the waters really well.

"So," Riker said, "the night shift was asked to open doors after hours? That normal at Grunman?"

"First I heard of. But I can't keep up with everybody."

"But someone did want a door unlocked late at night?" Riker re-confirmed. "For an after-hours meeting at Grunman and Forester Law."

"Yes, to the first part, the call to unlock a door." Duarte followed up fast, as if realizing he'd blabbered. "Lawyers. Different world."

"Who called? Must've been someone high up." Riker needed to establish if someone else in Forester's office had knowledge of his odd doings.

Duarte shook his head. Unclear whether he didn't know or didn't want to step on Chief's toes.

"You guys keep a log on those calls?" Neva's sweet voice again.

"In the computer. Whoever the guard taking the call, logs it in."

Riker pointed around. "Video recording all in good order?"

Duarte nodded.

A crackling came out of the radio. Chief was back. Dammit. Some security chiefs were worse than newly minted cops who memorized the Academy rules until life smacked them upside the head. He had looked up this particular one and seen the definition of a bureaucrat.

Duarte said, "Ten four," into his radio.

"Gotta go relieve my partner. Take the elevator to P2, Chief's office is on the right." Duarte turned, ready to stroll away.

"You doing rounds every night on the hour?"

"Two a shift."

"Every floor?"

"Gotta go." Duarte was no longer keen on the line of questioning.

Neva sipped her Macchiato, taking a second. "Wanna back during day shift?"

More people strolled by, the corporate world alive. Elevators opened and closed.

"Don't you have to use the bathroom?" Riker asked.

Neva gave him a look, all alert. He needed time in the lobby in ways that would make sense.

Neva threw her cup in the nearest trashcan and moseyed to the ladies' room near the entrance, motioning for him to wait.

The lobby smelled of forced ventilation and caffeine—a corporate place with an industrial feel.

Riker strolled near a painting of lines, a geometric creation that might've looked decent under better lighting. Hands deep in his coat pockets, he gave it a far look. Stepped backward, closer to the unmanned security counter. Duarte didn't seem concerned, leaving it unattended in the presence of cops.

Another step back, and Riker stood behind the counter. Monitors showed the lobby, outside the doors, and near the elevators. Two visitor logs took center stage.

Riker read the handwriting on the top log. Nothing alarming, not that he'd recognize red flags unless he saw them. He pushed the clipboard aside, thankful Neva was taking her time.

Steps echoed far down the hall.

Riker speed-read through the list of names, most entered by Levi Duarte, according to the record. On the bottom log, names had been crossed off. He memorized a few. The officer responsible for the writings, again Levi Duarte.

Riker halted. One crossed off name stood out: Sinclair, and another name entered instead. It could've been something else, but the crossed off scribbling read "Sinclair." Could be someone other than Zoe. Could be her. The name written on top read Shila Something. Could've been Biggs or Diggs.

"Excuse me." Duarte's voice echoed a few steps away. "Chief was called for an emergency next door. Not sure how long." He stood there, his face ashen.

Riker pointed at the logs. "There's one name in there that's been crossed off. That normal?"

"Sorry, that's a question for the chief."

The chief, who was no longer around for questioning.

Businesses rented office space at a premium here. Privacy reigned supreme in Century City unless there was a warrant, something security personnel were no doubt reminded of often.

Riker put out his hand. Pushing for more answers wouldn't help. "Good night, Officer Levi Duarte."

The man's face went from ashen to red. He'd never shared his first name. Riker had seen the log and wanted the implication out there. Every search started with a name.

He pulled out a business card. "The force appreciates good, honest people. Give me a call." Riker took two fingers to his forehead, hoping he'd both scared and piqued Duarte's curiosity.

CHAPTER 10

The morning air cut like a blade, the wind spinning leaves into a frenzy, as Riker stepped out of the car in front of the station.

After a sleepless night, fatigue drained his mental energy. He welcomed the blast of cold. A momentary break from having to think.

Rounding the entrance into the police station, he massaged away a headache.

He'd spent the night reading everything he could find about Bob Forester. By all accounts, a successful businessman, second-generation lawyer, married three times, but no animosity coming from two ex-wives after two divorces, and none after four decades of law practice, the last few spent working cases with Zoe Sinclair.

The Internet crawl on Zoe turned up a handful of social-media posts. No question she was a reluctant user. Except, sometime past midnight, he hit pay dirt. One last go through Zoe's list of *friends*, and one profile named LSD caught Riker's eye.

After he tracked the profile and clicked on the link, Riker felt the smile within. LSD stood for Levi S. Duarte, the Century City security guard. Social media filters must've worked overtime, making sense of initials associated with hallucinogenic drugs.

Zoe was friends with the guard who'd been uneasy noticing the visitor log had been moved. The same log with the name Sinclair written and crossed off, replaced with another name.

Bypassing his office, Riker turned toward the interview room.

Today was Betty Forester's day. Neva had offered to drive over for the interview, but Bob Forester's widow still refused police visits. She had come in instead. Riker could watch, Neva had said, but stay the hell out of her interview.

After a knock, he entered the colorless room.

Gritting her teeth, Neva turned to the pale woman. "Mrs. Forester, you remember Detective Riker. He'll sit in today."

Betty Forester stirred in silence. Thick makeup covered a gaunt face framed by red hair. Her bloodshot eyes told the story of a woman emotionally marred by her husband's sudden death.

Riker pulled a chair and sat in the corner. Out of the widow's sight.

"It was love at first sight." Betty Forester cut short Neva's preliminaries. "And nothing but love ever since. He could be stubborn, though, my Bob."

"How so?"

"His work. He'd complain about cases he found unwinnable, haunting. I'd urge him to drop them, but Bob never took my advice."

"Haunting cases?"

"Work that kept him up at night. Many times, it involved someone's loved one." She stared into a memory. Difficult, discussing loved ones who passed away.

"Did he mention a haunting case recently?"

The silence signaled dread flowing out of the woman. She knew what it meant to discuss her late husband's work, and wasn't comfortable breaching that trust.

"My Bob didn't kill himself." Betty Forester's voice trembled.

Neva let the woman work out what she meant.

"I know reporters imply that, but why would he? Bob had much to live for."

"You mentioned he was a different person lately," Neva said. "Missing golf games, dinners with friends."

"His work, that's why. It happened before." A long sigh.

"I've been telling him to slow down for years. Time to travel the world since we had no kids and grandkids to enjoy." The last comment brought the tremble back in her voice.

"Mr. Forester had children from a previous marriage."

"From his first two marriages." Betty Forester's shoulders straightened, and Riker imagined defiance. "They're adults and want nothing to do with him unless they need money."

"Any of his children call recently?"

Mrs. Forester shook her head, and nothing more needed to be said. Bob Forester's death had been splashed all over the media. Unless those children lived under a rock, they must've known. Yet, they hadn't called.

Riker held up a finger, and Neva got the hint. Or maybe she was on her way to asking. "How many children?"

Betty Forester's face turned toward the ceiling. "Two from his first marriage, one from the second one. The second wife moved to British Colombia, and communication ceased after that son turned eighteen. The son and daughter from the first marriage came to Bob's birthday party, asking for money. After, only the son, Tony, called to borrow money. Of course, he never paid back. Too bad Bob always gave in."

"Did Tony come to the house for the money?"

Neva was trying to establish if there was a pattern with Tony Forester. Visits, knowledge of the house, routine familiarity.

"He'd rush through sometimes. I would stay out of the way."

Not much of a pattern, but even one-off visits counted.

"When was the last time he visited?"

"Last summer. I wasn't there, but found Bob angry enough to imagine he must've had it. No more calls or visits from Tony since."

Through an increasing headache, Riker made a mental note to see about Tony Forester.

"As far as his work," Neva said in her best changing-the-subject tone. "Did Mr. Forester mention anything difficult or unusual about recent cases?"

"He was back to working his tail off, that's why the withdrawal from life." Silence followed. Riker looked at Neva for hints, but she gave nothing away. "People dramatize his absence now, but no one worked harder than Bob."

Neva nodded, waiting.

"He loved work. Said he was lucky to work with great people. Until that luck dried up."

"What do you mean?"

"A feeling. Bob never spoke ill of anyone."

Riker squirmed in his seat. Must've taken Neva every ounce of composure to keep from telling him off.

"People kept calling the house. I asked Bob to explain about business hours, but he accommodated everyone."

"Who called?"

"Cato Grunman, his partner, called the most. Late, near midnight. Bob said it was about a big case, or he wouldn't have answered."

"Did he say what case?"

"No, but I remember hearing him mention outside help. I don't think Cato Grunman approved because the young lawyer Bob wanted kept calling after Bob changed his mind about using him."

Something in Riker's mind stirred. He'd heard parts of this story from his brother's perspective. He tried catching Neva's attention, but she remained focused on the interview.

"And the name of the case?"

"Bob shared abstract bits about work. Not what went with which case or its name."

"Any other names on those calls?"

Betty Forester shook her head. She let out a long sigh, consulted her watch. She was shutting down. Neva would have to leave it here, even if she'd barely gotten going. She concluded by reserving the right to call with more questions.

When they stood, Riker stepped closer. "Mrs. Forester, one last thing, if I may."

Betty Forester seemed to have forgotten his presence. She allowed a smile.

"Did your husband take late office meetings? Unusually late? Did he mention names of whom he may have met?"

Betty Forester regarded Riker with an inquisitive stare, as if searching for a hidden meaning to his words. "I've wondered. No doubt he was tempted. All the young, beautiful women at the office."

Riker shook his head, not the answer he was looking for. But Betty Forester waved away interruptions. "Yes, Bob was late. More than once. He looked incredibly stressed. Something in his demeanor, I knew it was work related." She looked straight at Riker with newfound resolve. "If you're implying romantic entanglements led to what happened, take that off your list."

"Sorry… I …"

"We survived Bob's one indiscretion, a long time ago. Therapy and love got us through. One thing that kept from destroying Bob was that our marriage survived."

Riker made a mental note of Bob Forester having stepped out on his wife.

"You mentioned your husband had wanted to bring in outside counsel," Riker said. "Then he changed his mind. The young lawyer kept calling, even after his services were declined."

She frowned, perhaps pulling out a recollection. "Bob asked me to take the calls. I told the young man to understand and not call anymore. He must've heard the irritation in my voice and stopped pestering."

"Do you remember the young lawyer's name?"

She smiled. "One of Bob's protégés, part of the legal power couple, as he called them." She shook her head. "I felt bad being rude. It was something *son* name. Mason, maybe."

Riker thanked the woman, excused himself, and left the room.

* * *

In his office, Riker swallowed two pain pills he'd taken from the bottle in Neva's drawer. Paced, counted to ten. He did not need a headache today, not a real one that fogged his thinking.

Larson. The name Betty Forester had been looking for.

When the door opened, he sat and waited for Neva to get the door-slamming part out of the way. He'd rather keep the conversation quiet, for the sake of his headache but also out of anyone's earshot.

"Walking out on my witness like that is rude." Neva

smoothed her skirt and sat. A show of composure, even if pissed to her eyeballs. "I'm listening."

"Bob Forester wanted outside counsel, then rescinded the offer." Riker leaned back. "Larson told me Forester wanted a late-night office meeting to talk about it. Then Forester changed his mind, which made Larson curious. He called the house, and the wife told him Bob Forester was busy."

This was new information he hadn't yet shared. He waited for another bout of Neva's anger to pass.

"Did you ask Larson? What case did Forester want outside counsel for?"

Riker shook his head. "He didn't know much." The headache forced an economy of words.

"Well, what *did* Larson say?"

"Not a whole lot, and their stories differ." Riker checked his watch. "Betty Forester described a pestering Larson."

"Not jiving with what Larson said?"

"Do me a favor."

Neva squinted. "I have a ton of reports to write. What?"

"The affair."

"I'll follow up with the wife. Oh, joy."

"And Betty Forester mentioned the legal power couple."

"Zoe Sinclair and Larson?"

"Forester's protégés. Meaning they were tight. They know things about Forester they probably don't realize they know." He waited for another throbbing to pass. "I'll go look for my brother. It'll be good to know what the second half of the power couple is up to."

"Need the captain for a tail on Zoe Sinclair, or at least the lieutenant," Neva said.

"More paperwork? Someone must owe you favors 'round here. A quick look-see." Riker stood. "And we need to chat with Tony Forester, the son."

"Anything else?" Sarcasm dripped from Neva's voice.

She called out when Riker opened the door. "Larson is

probably jogging up in Laurel Canyon."

One of Larson's favorite pastimes.

Riker hurried away, trying to manage the concern nagging him like a bastard.

CHAPTER 11

Laurel Canyon welcomed Riker with traffic and killer views.

Roads curved forever, leading into the distant horizon. Houses sat perched in positions surely deemed unsafe in most other places. The farther up the drive, the larger the properties. Two to four acres of land between property lines, at least. Larson's bungalow, near a cliff, sat surrounded by three acres of rocky land with patches of grass.

The scenery did away with Riker's headache. From atop the steep incline, he could see far and wide, but no Larson jogging.

Damn you, Bro.

Riker parked and started walking toward Larson's usual running trail, up the hill from the cabin.

If his brother needed to be shaken for information, like a piggybank full of coins, then Riker was ready to shake. No more brotherly bullshit, no more handling with care for their parents' sake. *Time to spit it out, Larson. Everything you know about your former boss' cases, Zoe at the scene, late night office meetings, Forester's circle.* Clearly Larson knew Forester enough to be handpicked for late-night meetings, and mysterious legal cases.

Cursing his sore lungs, Riker made his way down the trail back to the bungalow. No car in the driveway. No way to see inside the windowless shack Larson called a garage.

Riker rattled the shack's double doors. Chain-locked, and reasonably tight. He gave a stronger rattle, hard enough to barely part the sides and take a peek inside. No vehicle, but the shack was stacked full of boxes.

Strange.

Back at the bungalow, he banged on the door without restraint.

Nothing but overwhelming silence all around.

Circling the structure, Riker stopped at the windows, cupping his hands around his eyes to look inside. The furnishings looked unchanged. But the bungalow had certainly been packed away. Old pieces of clothing had been thrown helter-skelter on chairs and the back of sofas. The papers and nick-knacks on the piano were gone. If Riker had to guess, the closet was empty and boxed away.

Where to, Bro?

* * *

Riker sped on shoulders and took every yellow light on his drive down to Studio City. Ran a couple of reds, too. Studio City was how out-of-towners imagined L.A. Wide boulevards lined with palm trees and shops, houses seen on TV sitcoms, and filming going on around every corner.

Most Angelinos would happily stay the hell away.

He turned onto Larson's tree-lined street at the base of Laurel Canyon Boulevard.

Questions pounded at Riker, carving holes in his heart. He cast doubts aside and called them brotherly worries. No go. Why would Larson pack up his bungalow? Not the mark of a person who wanted to stick around and answer questions from the police.

In front of the Studio City condo, Riker parked illegally, slammed the door and jogged to the second floor.

No amount of knocking brought Bro to the door.

"Larson!" Riker accompanied the banging with shouts.

A door squeaked open behind him, across the hall. The neighbor, a spectacled woman, poodle in her arms, stepped out but didn't come close.

Riker hurled out a story: out-of-town relative, stopped by unexpected. The neighbor wouldn't know the family relation given Riker's tendency to visit once every two years.

Poodle Lady hadn't seen his next-door neighbor in a week or two. Not a curious happening. People were busy in L.A. and kept to themselves.

Riker apologized for the racket. Joked about the wide time gap the woman provided—a week or two. Could she be more specific?

"Hmm, closer to two weeks," Poodle Lady said. "Hadn't heard sounds from there in a while. About two weeks ago, I saw the neighbor leave when Poppy went out late that night." The woman chuckled and patted her poodle.

"How late would you say? Nine, ten, later?"

"Past ten. Eleven maybe. Yeah." Poodle Lady stared at Riker; her curiosity triggered by the barrage of questions. "Everything okay?"

Riker tried reassuring words, but some days he left a trail of havoc in his wake.

Not unusual for Larson, leaving home Tuesday night at eleven. But he was a person of habit, annoyingly so. Early riser, jogger, then coffee and work. The first to arrive, worked late, jogged daily, then crashed early. Not a late-night person. One of the things Neva had shared about her time with Larson, his reluctance to have a life after dinner. One of the things they did not have in common.

"I tried saying hello, but he was in a deep phone conversation," Poodle Lady said. "I'm not one to get involved. Just tried to be neighborly, asked if everything's okay because he seemed unsettled." With that, the woman retreated into her apartment and shut the door.

The neighbor had confirmed Larson's odd behavior. Rushing out on a Tuesday night, unsettled, and deep in conversation. As if his packing up his cabin wasn't enough of an aberration.

In the car, Riker called Mother, cutting short the plethora of hellos and how-are-yous.

"I've spoken to Larson earlier," Mother said to his question. "Everything okay?"

God, he was beginning to hate that question.

"I've been thinking about joining you guys for dinner." Hell of a lie, but no time for regrets.

"I'm making your favorite calzone," Mother said into his ear. "Larson's coming. Dad and I would be thrilled to have you both over."

Bingo. "Let's make it a surprise then," he said. "Don't tell anyone I'm coming."

She laughed in conspiratorial short bursts. "You know how I love surprises."

Riker kept his answer to himself.

Most times they navigated the stepfamily road okay, but on occasion they fell into stereotypes hard to avoid—parent siding with biological child, or vice versa—by *forgetting* a little secret. With luck, his nonchalant request wouldn't register.

He hung up just as his phone beeped. A text from Neva. Tony Forester had arrived at the station.

I'll chat him up and record it for you, Neva wrote.

Turning toward the freeway on-ramp, Riker picked up speed, and startled a few pigeons. He needed more than a recording.

* * *

Inside Wilshire Station, the pandemonium felt oddly reassuring. Riker rushed through the lobby as phones were ringing and grievances were being aired. Another crazy day, its familiar chaos creating a controlled madness that set him right.

The office he shared with Neva occupied the rear corner of the station, with the door cracked open. With the phone squeezed between ear and shoulder, Neva pointed toward the interview room, while screaming into the receiver. She was giving or receiving an ass-chewing over late paperwork.

Ten seconds later, Riker came face to face with Tony Forester, who resembled a hobo more than a Forester progeny—thin frame, sunken eyes, long, washed-out blond hair knotted in places. Extra-large shirt that covered most of him.

"This waiting game is bull." Tony sat up straight.

"I'm Detective Riker. You must be Tony Forester."

Tony's grin showed crooked teeth stained by tobacco, or God knew what else. His gaze darted all over.

"I volunteered to come," Tony said. "What's the holdup?"

"Something came up for Detective Braxton." Riker sat,

leaned back. "Water, coffee?"

Tony fidgeted in place. "I'm good." He pointed toward the door. "The woman detective said it's about the old man. I thought he ate his gun, so what's this all about?"

"A formality. When was the last time you saw your father?"

Tony shook his head. "Shit, I don't remember. Spring, maybe summer."

"Long time."

"The last visit was a freaking mess. The old man blew a gasket. It's been the beginning of the end for him for a while."

"Beginning of the end?"

"He's been losing it, slowly but surely. Always blowing up about something. Why Ma finally said fuck this shit and filed."

"Are you saying your father had a temper?"

"Temper, borderline madness, who knows? Calm and cool on the surface. Put on a show for friends, business. But I knew the real man since way back."

Riker waited, letting Tony work through a bout of handwringing.

"Piled on the charm to cover up his control freak. Made Ma feel something was wrong with her. She never dressed right, never met his expectations. Smartest move she ever made was to get out."

"But you continued to visit, even after the divorce."

Tony shook his head. "By law, he wasn't obligated to support us past eighteen. So, when he called to make himself feel good about checking on us, we faked it. My sister didn't like the pretense, but me? Needed the fucking money, man, what can I say?"

"And he never said no."

"He had conditions. Come at this hour, act like this, look like this, talk like this. Be someone other than myself and make him look good. Insinuating I'm always strung up. I'm not. Drugs—that was a high-school stint. But he wouldn't fucking back off, so I said fuck the money."

"When did you find out about his death?"

A cough, then some throat clearing followed. "My sister called." The handwringing intensified, then, as if he realized it, Tony stopped fidgeting. Hid his hands under the table.

"Did you call the house when you heard?"

"And what, talk to that bitch?"

"Don't get along with your stepmother?"

"She's just like him, that's how they lasted. Fake smiles but can't wait to burn you to hell and back. She put shit in his head about us. I saw how she looked at me, like some bug to be squashed."

"What about his last will and testament? Did you ever ask?"

Tony laughed out loud. "He took Ma to court when she asked for more money. Had a prenup with the second wife and never paid a penny once his other kid turned eighteen. Only gave me money 'cause I bowed my head. And with the bitch riding him, she'll get everything, I'm sure."

An interesting picture of Bob Forester, if Tony were to be believed. Riker would ask a department psychologist to watch the tape. For now, it didn't take a degree in psychology to see that Tony's fidgeting increased—the result of a chemical reaction or internal nervousness as he talked about his father. Maybe both. Any shrink watching the tape would balk at pounding a man like Tony too hard.

Riker took a crack at verifying the affair story. "Do you know about any infidelity? Was he a loyal husband?"

"Pfft. He was like a pimply teen around women. Awkward as shit. Beats me how he found three wives. But he had money and power, so who the fuck knows how loyal he was?"

Interesting.

"Last thing, Tony. Do you know any people your father worked with, any clients? Work ever come up in conversations?"

Tony's eyes lit up for a fraction of a second. But he shook his head.

After the last set of formalities, Tony stood with effort even though his thin frame suggested ease of movement. Weighed down by something? Riker shook the frail man's hand, and watched him amble toward the door.

In the threshold, Tony halted and turned to Riker. "You really think there's money? You know, like inheritance?"

Silence.

"Been bouncing around for two years," Tony said. "Kinda sucks always crushing with friends. Shit's so expensive 'round here."

"Where do you live?"

"Anywhere I can. Palm Desert, down by the airport, back to the desert. Be nice to stay put. Money would help."

Money in his hands was the last thing Tony Forester needed. A shower, yes, another set of clothes and some decent grooming to start with. Then a series of healthy meals, and maybe therapy. Anything but money to spend on the next fix.

"I mean, we're his children, for fuck's sake," Tony said into the silence.

"Tony, if you need help, all you have to do is ask. Your stepmother's definition of help might just differ from yours, but it's still help."

Tony shook his head. "That's what the chick said at the old man's house. But reality is different, you know?"

"Chick at the old man's house?"

"Lawyer. She was there once when I stopped by. Walked out with me, offered a ride but I said no. Didn't need more speeches. Like I said, reality is different."

"Did she say her name? This lawyer."

"If she did, I didn't hear it."

"Describe her for me."

In colorful language, he described a woman who could've been Zoe Sinclair.

"Name Zoe Sinclair ring a bell?" As an afterthought, Riker added, "or Shila Biggs or Diggs?" Still needed to make sense of the name near Zoe's in the building security log.

Tony shook his head.

"Anyone else at your father's house when you went by?"

"You said that was the last question, man, like ten questions ago."

Riker pointed to the chair.

Tony looked away then back to Riker. "There was a tall, older guy. Looked like a ghost, skinny and pale. Got a kick out of his John Lennon glasses, though. He pulled for sophistication but looked like a fool. Conceited fucker, for sure." Tony shook his head. "Company the old man kept, what can I say?"

Riker gave Tony his business card. Watched him hurry away.

Money was one of the biggest crime motivators. Assuming Bob Forester's death was more than suicide, would Tony, angry and rejected, do something stupid?

If Tony were truthful and his description was right, Zoe had visited the Forester house. The woman popped out at every turn in the case.

Riker hated clue boards, but not today. He walked to the board and wrote the name *Bob Forester* at the top.

Then below: *Tall, skinny man with Lennon glasses.*

He added and *L* for Larson and *Z* for Zoe. Drew dots between the two and arrows from their initials to Forester.

Below he wrote *Shila Biggs or Diggs*, and to the bottom: *Tony Forester.*

CHAPTER 12

One moment Zoe was out cold, the next she jolted upright.

A distant cacophony came into focus bit by bit. Her cell phone on the stand was beeping. She wiped the sleep from her eyes and took the phone to her ear.

"Hello?"

"There you are. Finally."

Sebastian.

She'd popped two Xanax in the middle of the night, to rid her mind of questions, then thrown herself under the covers, turning off the world. Now, the unforgiving morning light cut through the curtains and into her brain.

"Where are you?" She coughed out the grogginess in her voice.

"Between meetings." The connection buzzed with static. "Don't have much time."

"When are you coming back? So much has happened."

Through the crackling noise, she heard, "Check your messages." Then the words she'd longed to hear.

"I love you, too," she said. Then the call dropped.

Same story—bad connection, no time.

In the bathroom, Zoe splashed water on her face again and again. Two tranquilizers, and she'd slept like a dead woman.

Dabbing her cheeks with the towel, she glanced in the mirror. Not too haggard looking. She shut her eyes for a second, willing depressing thoughts gone, but darkness triggered visual memories from last night when everything inside her broke. When she couldn't make sense of the clue board, and how the names connected. Or why Larson had called with a warning, then someone had knocked on her door. When the names Shila Diggs and Kip Pulaski would not leave her mind.

Her shrink had described detachment techniques: push the negative energy out through breathing—but in the end prescribed another antidepressant that knocked her out. Over time, she'd cut back to just Xanax at a lower dosage. Until last night.

Back in the living room, Zoe scrolled through the phone. Damn, the firm's private investigator hadn't called back. Two missed calls from Sebastian before the third call got through. She clicked on his voice message.

"My stay was extended." Silence, then Sebastian again, his voice thicker. "Why don't you take a long weekend and fly here? Miss you, babe."

Zoe squeezed the phone until her palm hurt. She had done everything to keep away from Wyoming, from memories. Now, Sebastian was asking her to return because, despite what had happened, he loved it there.

A whole year had passed since they left Wyoming—hard to imagine. A year of secrets, if Pulaski's implication about Sebastian was correct.

She touched a key, and the computer screen came to life showing the names Specter Research Unlimited and Kip Pulaski.

Her gaze fell on the business card. *Who the hell are you, Mr. Pulaski? Why did you really want to meet last night, of all nights?*

She dialed the number, and after one ring heard the now familiar voice.

* * *

Santa Monica was a city of extremes, where opposites existed in harmony. From Main Street's surf vibe to Pico's diversity, Wilshire's pomposity, and breezy Ocean Avenue, different styles welcomed visitors at every turn. In law school, Zoe had loved escaping the daily tedium for something uniquely Southern California.

Now, she once again fought her way through its unique traffic.

After three turns, she reached her destination—a French restaurant between the freeway overpass and a shabby graffitied building.

Not the fancy part of Santa Monica.

Inside *Bon Appétit*, Zoe was plunged into an ambience of visuals, smell, and music—all senses stimulated.

The tuxedoed maître d' looked Zoe up and down, his expression a sliver short of aversion. Her jeans and jacket over a turtleneck didn't match the style stressed by canvas art and white table linens.

A waiter led the way to a table occupied by Kip Pulaski.

"Ms. Sinclair." Pulaski stood, looking as though he invented the dress code himself—shirt and tie matching an indigo suit.

Her curiosity piqued, Zoe had agreed to meet, but downgraded his lunch invitation to coffee. Which meant nothing to Pulaski's choice of attire and locale.

Zoe sat, and the waiter fiddled with a pad and pen. "Something to drink?"

Pulaski took his seat.

"Coffee, black," Zoe said, and the waiter scurried away.

The smell of lilac lingered in a dining room empty of patrons. Somewhere, a violin played. Both music and scent reminded Zoe of a funeral home.

Looking at Pulaski, she was flushed with memories not fully formed. "Bob Forester --" She cleared her throat, looked straight at the man. "Last night was an interesting choice of time for a meeting."

Silence.

"How well did you know Mr. Forester?" She tried again. "Outside of the lawyer-client relationship?"

The waiter returned with a tray, her coffee and Pulaski's coffee martini. Obviously, Pulaski's order had already been placed.

After making a production of serving them, the waiter slipped away.

"Unfortunate news about Mr. Forester." Pulaski sipped his drink then set the glass on the table. A stark demarcation from the man Bob had described as a friend and important client. Cold. Inaccessible. Unwilling to answer questions.

After finding nothing in the firm's database, and only the handwritten filing on the Division of Corporations site, Zoe had opened accounts with two private detective search engines and ran Pulaski's name. He was involved with Specter Group, a research non-profit. A similar name to the one she'd found in the State site, yet different. Was Specter the old client, the group traveling to great lengths for privacy, as Pulaski had said, unhappy with Sebastian's *curious* tech friends? How the two connected, she had no idea.

"Your findings on my fiancé," Zoe said.

Pulaski stared, waiting. Not a man to set aside his priorities, of course.

Zoe reached inside her bag, took out the envelope and set it on the table. "The confidentiality agreement," she said. "Signed."

No mention of the money he'd offered for undefined work, or whether she'd take it.

Pulaski leaned back in his chair with forced nonchalance, his stare a mix of interest and familiarity. Same as when they first met. She didn't know the man, of that Zoe was sure.

He must've caught himself, or the question in her eyes. He opened the envelope, keeping his stare neutral.

With the contents inspected and tucked away, Pulaski pulled a file from atop his briefcase. "Your first legal case at Grunman and Forester," he said.

Zoe hid her surprise and let the quizzical look stand. She'd relegated early legal work to the dustbins of her mind.

"You may remember the client by its acronym," Pulaski said. "SRU, Specter Research Unlimited. Bulky name, changed and shortened to Specter Group."

She remembered, somewhat. Mostly with the help of last night's research. The name change explained why she'd found nothing in the firm's database.

"What does that have to do with my fiancé?"

Pulaski traced a line in the folder. "Says here, you worked on the Specter file your first year at Grunman and Forester."

As if she hadn't even spoken.

Zoe tried finding associations between her early work and Sebastian. Unless she missed something, she was the only link.

Pulaski stared, waiting. A man ideally suited for psychological games, interested in little outside answers to his questions.

Okay, her first case. Some company in ethical hot water after a representative made unverified comments to reporters. "I was part of a team," Zoe said. "First year out of law school. My work involved case summaries. The rest falls under attorney-client privilege."

"You were praised for having written winning pleadings." Pulaski traced another line in his folder. "For outstanding research."

Details escaped Zoe. "If that's what it says, then yes."

"You remember Specter was an up-and-coming research group, generating important studies that turned into big news stories."

She nodded, failing at her attempt to recall details.

"Soon after you were pulled from the case, Specter went dark," he said. "Completely dropped from sight."

"You seem to know everything."

The room fell into a hush.

Zoe pushed her cup to the side. "What do you want from me, Mr. Pulaski?"

Kip Pulaski drew to his full sitting height. "Specter was suspended, not closed. We needed time to reorganize, deal with the media, appease private donors."

"We?"

"I'm the client in the case. One of the clients."

More fucking games. The cancellation paper she'd found in the State database made sense. Pulaski had folded a faulty business, after having gone back and forth on the decision. He'd tried doing the paperwork himself, maybe a way to hide something, but, for some reason, had a change of heart and let his lawyer handle the dissolution of SRU.

"We're bringing back Specter." Pulaski's smile lacked warmth. "I'd like to offer you a position at the helm of the company."

The ridicule she felt within spilled into Zoe's words. "I have no media expertise, nor a business background. I'm a lawyer." She took advantage of the momentary silence. "Just a lawyer you asked to meet in a near-empty office the night Bob died."

She watched him closely. Did he know about Shila Diggs?

Pulaski smiled. "Just a lawyer? The media tried turning your story into a charade, but you maintained control."

He knew. Of course, he knew about Wyoming, about last year, when she'd pulled the trigger to save her life from a crazy neighbor. About the media going crazy on the story for months.

"Letting them trip over their stories hardly qualifies as my doing."

"Your legal expertise, and familiarity with Specter's old format are pluses. Knowledge and brilliance are rare qualities, irrespective of profession."

Flattery after a gut punch. The man had no interest in her questions. No boundaries. No shame.

"With the right person leading the effort," Pulaski said, "bringing back experts and funding wouldn't be a problem for us."

"Why should I care about your experts and funding?"

Pulaski fixed her with a stare. "Because we're changing the world, Ms. Sinclair. We're using cutting-edge research to find cures. Take our clinical trials of stem-cell therapy to improve blood flow in angina patients, for those who haven't responded or who aren't willing to undergo alternative procedures. Years of experimental work. Hard work."

He'd taken a direct hit at Zoe's emotion. In bringing up a disease prevalent in her family, Pulaski had revealed his hand. Or a piece of his game. Was there anything he didn't know about her?

His hard stare made it clear providing more information had

a cost: cooperation.

Zoe chased old memories. She'd been one cog in the wheel working the old Specter case, assigned research and writing summaries, little of which survived in her memory over the years. Ethics violations involving a representative had been the crux of the case. Wait, had it been a representative or expert? Yes, a medical expert, but key bits of information refused to resurface. It would make sense shutting down a business ensnarled in ethics violations, if that was what SRU had done.

Rapt in his bluster, and maybe stirred by her silence, Pulaski went on. "The medical procedure corrects an old method of delivering injections of stem cells to targeted sites into the heart muscle. Groundbreaking, but as stories go it's boring and that's all right. We don't want sensationalism. We want to quietly change the world."

Zoe looked away. Mother's coronary artery disease had weakened her heart beyond repair. Her death may have been delayed without the violence perpetrated on her by Marshall—the crazy neighbor—when he'd tied Mother up to keep her from coming to Zoe's rescue, while holding Zoe hostage.

But delayed for how long? The treatment used to dilate arterial blockage had only postponed the inevitable. Kip Pulaski's cure, if real, would've gone against Mother's wishes to "Go when my time comes. In my bed, at home. In peace."

Pulaski grabbed his folders. "A great man once said, 'Greatness is not where we stand, but in what direction we're moving.'"

Words to make one's mind snap. That quote, she'd heard those words before. Maybe not verbatim, but they belonged to someone important.

The waiter approached and pulled out Pulaski's chair at some unspoken command.

Seconds piled up before Pulaski, now standing, said, "My office will forward the first part of your payment together with answers," he said. "All answers, including about your fiancé."

Then Pulaski whirled away, buttoning his coat.

Zoe's thoughts ran straight to Sebastian. She should call him and demand answers to Pulaski's implications before secrets destroyed their relationship. Then again, the truth couldn't be forced out. It had to come willingly.

CHAPTER 13

The reply to Zoe's question was curt. "Not over the phone," Kim Snyder, the firm's private investigator, said. "Meet me same place as last time in twenty minutes."

They'd struck up a working relationship under Bob's tutelage, Zoe and the firm's PI. When Kim needed legal help in personal matters, Zoe lent a hand. But Kim's antisocial ways achieved the desired effect: distant friendship. To call them cell-phone chatting buddies would be an exaggeration. Yet, two big firsts happened today. One, Kim Snyder returned Zoe's call. Two, she wanted to discuss Bob Forester before entertaining Zoe's favor. "Something important and in strict confidence," was all she'd said.

Zoe took the two-mile drive that felt like an obstacle course through the congested streets and never-ending traffic lights.

Santa Monica College sat a stone's throw away from the beach and the 3rd Street Promenade. Between its location and reputation as the number one transfer school to Southern California Universities, the place was a constant madhouse.

Zoe pulled into a parking spot steps from the main entrance. She ignored Temporary Only signs, squeezed out of the car, and made a dash for the Sociology Department door. Parking blocks away appealed less than getting ticketed.

Few people enjoyed the same regard as Kim Snyder. She hardly spoke to anyone in the office and never returned calls. Until now. More, before hanging up, Kim had mentioned the late Bob Forester, whom she also wanted to discuss *in confidence*.

A sea of students surged through the main entrance, a panoply of sheer clothing, creative hair colors and piercings. Some students strode with purpose, like future leaders. Others appeared put upon, likely forced here by parents, brooding over the unfairness of it all.

A scene she'd have happily avoided if not for Kim Snyder.

Turning the corner, Zoe bumped into a hard chest. The contact sent her car keys and phone flying. A bulky fellow peppered Zoe with questions. Was she okay, did she need to sit. Zoe had heard schools hired retired cops for undercover protection, and this Hulk sure qualified. A muscled upper body like that was hardly the look of a student or professor.

She thanked Hulk and continued down the interminable hall, past students with buds stuck in their ears, glazed looks on their faces.

Kim Snyder taught criminal justice here. She'd lured Zoe out as guest speaker before, but this summon seemed different. Strange.

The wide-open door to Kim's class showed a room buzzing with students, but no professor. Zoe consulted her watch. Class was due to start in four minutes, yet Kim Snyder was not here. Zoe paced for a minute, two. Checked the time again.

Across the hall, students came pouring out of different lectures. Semi-open doors showed classes still in session. The only room without a professor was number 345.

More students rushed past—a few faces Zoe remembered from previous visits. They'd probed her about the fine points of lawyering, the prestige and money. Was it anything like Jack McCoy in *Law and Order*? She'd smiled. Soon, reality would drench them in ice-cold water. Let them dream a little.

But where the hell was Kim?

Students began to leave the class, some wandering down the hall undecided, some rushing toward the exit. Only a handful stuck around.

"Ms. Sinclair?" a soft voice said behind her. It belonged to a young girl with streaks of color in her hair. A walking rainbow. Tina or Mina, one of Kim's students, talkative and eager.

"Have you seen Professor Snyder?" Zoe glanced at her phone. No missed calls.

The girl wrapped her hand around the arm of a young man with trimmed, bleached hair. They both shrugged and shook their heads.

Zoe thanked the pair, smiled, and slipped past. She dialed Kim and kept a steady pace toward the exit, lest more students felt like chatting.

Kim Snyder's phone kept ringing and ringing.

* * *

Back on Pico Boulevard—named after the last governor under Mexican rule—Zoe envisioned the boulevard in 1820, during Don Pico's days. She imagined dirt roads and vacant land everywhere. Animals roaming free, few people, horse-drawn carriages.

When she finally climbed on to the freeway, daydreams couldn't compete with the overwhelming metal and fiberglass before her.

The mind was a dangerous place, taking us hundreds of years back or minutes away.

What the hell happened to Kim Snyder?

Zoe went through possibilities but nothing stuck. Worry ran cold fingers down her spine. Worry and fear, because Kim Snyder was nothing if not prompt and precise.

She couldn't go home. Not with Kim a no-show after mentioning Bob.

Zoe followed her instinct. She exited the 405 freeway, turned around and drove toward Century City. She needed the old Specter file. Not what Pulaski had given her, but law-firm amassed information. She needed to know why Specter had gone after Sebastian, and how well did Pulaski know Bob? Why did Pulaski ask for a meeting with one of Bob's associates precisely the night Bob was found dead? Too much of a damn coincidence for her comfort zone.

A part of her hoped for an encounter with Shila Diggs. For a good look into the woman's eyes, with the benefit of having seen the picture from Bob's birthday lunch. Shila had been there the night of Zoe's meeting with Kip Pulaski. Why?

Traffic on Olympic Boulevard started cooperating. Once parked, she avoided the suffocating elevator in favor of sidewalk and front entrance. Amazing, the difference the sky above her made to her psyche.

At the top of the steps to Tower One, she rushed through the revolving door, head down, avoiding groups milling about. The lobby swarmed with people, but there were gaps. The hour before lunch saw a slowdown, with deadlines upstairs. She'd hit such an hour.

Next elevator took a couple of deliverymen and business suits. When the third remained empty, Zoe hurried in and jabbed the twentieth-floor button.

Seconds later, she opted for the side entrance leading into the file room—her target and closer to Kim's and Shila Digg's offices.

The room was a labyrinth of shelves, dividers, stacks of boxes, and migraine-inducing cataloging systems. Zoe may have never found her way had she not worked as a clerk in college. As a lawyer, she'd often wandered back here and found more than folders. The hidden maze lent itself to lovers, unable to wait until after hours for kisses and gropes. Maybe she could hide as well.

Voices resonated opposite the main divider—clerks discussing a coworker—but they didn't turn her way.

Zoe waited. Best to limit face-to-face meetings.

Skipping parts of the alphabet, sections and subsections, she arrived at *Section S*. Flipped through, and in the back found a single folder marked SRU. The acronym for Specter Research Unlimited.

Legal work had been extensive. Hours of research, memoranda, and pleading writing. The folder held ten, fifteen papers at most. Had the rest been sent to storage? To Bob's office? No way she'd venture there.

Folder under arm, Zoe turned and made a beeline down the hall.

Conversation halted as she passed two secretaries.

Through the open door, it was easy to see Kim's empty office. No purse, bag, or laptop on the desk.

Where the hell are you, Ms. Snyder?

A group of people rounded the hallway corner, coming her way. Shila's office was between her and the group. Not today. Her encounter with Shila would have to wait.

Pushing the exit door open, Zoe dashed down the stairs, two steps at a time. Better than dealing with crowded elevators.

Downstairs, in the main lobby, a figure leapt in front of Zoe. Surprised and blinded by the explosion of light, she jumped back and let out a screech.

A man in uniform stood like a wall. From under a hat, dark eyes bore into hers.

Startled, Zoe dropped the folder. The man caught it midair.

"Sorry," he said, his voice familiar.

Levi Duarte.

Zoe remembered, granted she hadn't seen the security guard in years. Their buddy Levi would bring up food during nights she and Larson worked ungodly hours. Larson and Levi were chatty. At Larson's invitation Levi had joined them for dinner at times.

Zoe took the folder. "Levi, it's been a long time. How are you?"

He quelled a smile. "Everything okay?"

"Getting my exercise." What else was there to say?

"Glad I left the door unlocked. You woudda been stuck inside the stairwell."

A detail she hadn't considered. "Lucky me."

Sweat trickled down the sides of Levi's face. She filed that detail away where it met old memories: Levi's friendship with Larson. How Larson had grown in her eyes for finding time to friend everyone. Strange that such a memory projected now, as Levi seemed attached to the spot, staring and sweating.

Zoe stepped around him, said bye, and walked away. Heard the stairwell door shut, a key turned, then footsteps fading. She fought the urge to look back.

She glanced outside the lobby window, and pins shot through her skin.

Was that Hulk by the entrance steps? The man she'd bumped

into at Santa Monica College? A second later the man was gone. Or maybe he'd never been there.

Keep it together, Zoe.

The folder under her arm felt strangely reassuring. That she wasn't imagining.

On impulse, Zoe checked her phone again. No missed calls, no messages. Maybe Kim had lost her phone. Maybe she'd arrived late for class.

Zoe should call the college and inquire. Ask for the rainbow-haired student with blond boyfriend, see if she'd seen Professor Snyder. Stupid idea, she didn't even recall if the girl's name was Mina or Tina, nor the boyfriend's name.

CHAPTER 14

The news on TV irked Hawke to no end. The only positive was that the dot on his phone map was still marking his target's movements.

From the other room, Tina's jabbering on the phone cut through—something about a shopping trip with her girlfriends.

Pushing the door shut, Hawke returned his attention to the TV story: *Suicide in Hancock Park*, followed by: *Attorney Robert Forester, of Grunman and Forester, had committed suicide.*

Goddamn. This story had legs. As if Zoe Sinclair looking for Kim Snyder earlier wasn't enough to fuck up his day. Why hadn't Detective Riker put Zoe Sinclair in an interrogation room and kept her there? He'd given Riker reason to grill her for hours.

Hawke ran a hand through his close-cropped hair Tina had insisted on bleaching. Two days since everything went to shit and the story still marched on.

Breast Goddess, the hot lawyer who'd saved his ass from jail, was late with her phone call. She served as envoy and recruiter for the Big Man. Same as the other woman Hawke had only heard about. Big Shot liked to keep his women close but not too close, and only activate them when needed. One of his attributes in Hawke's eyes.

"Smart kid like you, Hawke, come on," Breast Goddess, Attorney at Law, had said. "You could be writing code for tech giants. Why resort to hacking?"

He'd swallowed back the answer and uttered the obligatory, "Yes, ma'am."

Two days later, she'd called: "How about I put you in touch with someone who needs a first-rate computer guy?"

Meeting Big Shot had been a money-spinning gig, so long as his conscience didn't interfere. How could it, after growing up in the perfect family? Career-driven parents who wrote the book on leniency after being blessed with the perfect firstborn, the doctor.

Except Hawke was nothing like his brother. If too much control turned kids against parents, indulgence fucked them up good.

Hawke looked out the window into the cold evening, not unlike the evening his adventure started, a year ago.

His job for Big Shot began with software updates, drive cleanup, seeing to hardware needs. Boring work until Hawke understood the man lived a double life. Disappeared for days, sometimes weeks, and returned looking like shit. Soon, the air of secrecy got thicker, harder to breathe. Big Shot limited Hawke's access to more and more files, a useless exercise for the most part.

Hawke found ways in and began putting together the story: Big Shot was screwing around on his wife. No big whoop, but that was only part of the secret. The other part was so well coded, Hawke could only access pieces.

Hawke started pacing to fire up his thinking.

Big Shot had a secret, one much bigger than a side piece. Something about a family health issue, from the bits Hawke put together. Since one of his kids' name and blood type appeared in the file, Hawke assumed the secret involved one of the children. Or maybe it ran through the lot of them. Who knew?

The man maintained the perfect family picture: a happy, fulfilled husband and father, blessed with nothing but fortune. A good-for-business appearance——a man untouched by the hand of fate, not susceptible to pity or blackmail. Pity chipped away at clout, making men appear human, not God-like. Add blackmail and the party was over.

The information Hawke had gathered was not enough to form a good picture. Only crumbs and guesswork. He needed the laptop Big Shot never let out of his sight. The one Hawke hadn't accessed yet. No doubt, the answers to Big Shot's vulnerabilities were there.

He had to work out the codes somehow and skim Big Shot's secret device, because a relationship where he put his ass on the line couldn't work with secrets. Hawke had followed orders, enrolled at Santa Monica College, endured the idiotic students, endured his target, Zoe Sinclair, who befriended his *friends*.

Zoe Sinclair's demeanor reminded Hawke of cops—appearing out of nowhere with that inquisitive stare in her eyes, and asking for the old woman sleuth, Kim Snyder.

Hawke switched off the T.V. Enough with depressing thoughts.

Striding into the next room, he grabbed Tina from behind.

Her surprise cry was followed by giggles. Tina excused herself to her friend, but Hawke seized the phone, pressed the Off button and threw it aside.

Between half-hearted protests, Tina turned to reprimand him.

He shoved her onto the bed.

* * *

Woken up with a start, Hawke didn't get it.

Why would Big Shot call to move the schedule up? The job was scheduled for tomorrow, during a moonless night. Why yank him from a warm bed and Tina smelling of sex.

He'd done everything by the book—observed, reported. Got close to his future victim. Put up with Goth-fashion airheads because they were Tina's friends. Tina, well, she fell on his lap like a gift from the God Eros, flirty and more than willing.

Now, he was given the order. Another fucking deviation from the norm.

Hawke grabbed the bag holding his Browning shotgun. His resistance over the phone had been met with, "Old Canyon in thirty minutes. Change of plans for tonight."

Then the line went dead.

Thank God he'd sneaked Tina the Mexican Valium. She'd be out cold till morning.

Hawke drove out of the garage through the back, more isolated gate.

Twenty minutes later, he exited the 101 freeway, hung a turn, took another left, and climbed onto a road leading to the opposite side of the hill. A little-known trail would take him to Old Canyon and his victim's route. He struggled to keep her name from demanding attention, but it pushed past mental barriers.

Kim Snyder.

For reasons unknown to him, she had decided to skip her lecture at Santa Monica College and was expected to drive on Old Canyon Road tonight. Big Shot must've bugged her well to trace plans, time, and location.

At the first intersection, Hawke pulled up to the curb. The small stretch of road glistened from a recent drizzle—enough to bring oil and grime to the surface, but not enough for muck to be washed down the sewers.

He crossed onto the dirt road and parked on a knoll behind a huge oak tree. Time to sit and wait, same as in Sunken City last month when Big Shot had given Hawke a job targeting hobos. Gave no reason. Hawke pushed that thought to the back of his mind. Sunken City had been a near disaster. At the last moment he'd found the hobos and hoped like hell never to go back.

He lit a cigarette and rolled down the window. This part of Mulholland, a road crisscrossing the canyon, lay mostly bare. Not a bad place to come get high sometimes.

When the purr of an engine cut through, Hawke tossed the cigarette out the window and reached for his bag. He'd altered the barrel, making the clip untraceable. But even if recovered through some miracle, it'd be nearly impossible matching the ammo to an unregistered firearm, or tracing anything to him or Big Shot.

The black Audi buzzed twenty yards from Hawke's spot. He pointed at the tire and fired. As the car skidded, he pumped the gun, chambered a fresh round, and fired at the driver's window, then the gas tank.

More skidding and spinning followed, then the Audi rolled down the hill, off the road and into the canyon.

The loudest crash followed. Another ten seconds and sparks came flying.

Hawke turned on the engine and drove back. Another job done, one more to go before the biggest payday of his life.

CHAPTER 15

Zoe's living room was a cluttered mess of Specter documents scattered all over. She sat crossed legged on the floor, as the morning sunlight pierced through the blinds, focused on finding clues. There wasn't enough to complete the enormous puzzle this case had become, but enough to maybe slide a few pieces in. She'd spent the night lying wide-eyed in bed, staring at the ceiling, trying to unravel the mystery surrounding Kip Pulaski's obsession with Sebastian's work, and his attempt to coerce her into doing his bidding.

She now had two goals in mind. First, unravel the secrecy around Specter, Pulaski and his motives. Second, understand if the meeting that took place on the same night Bob died was by design or coincidence.

She sifted through the papers, looking for something, anything that could bring answers. Settled on a one-paragraph memo she had written during the Specter scandal days. The summary of a phone call, lacking factual information. She focused on the last two sentences: *Not sufficient information provided. We need facts to mount a defense, should one be necessary, regarding the expert who spoke on behalf of the company.*

Damn. Specter had concealed the facts seven years ago, same as today. Hiding information in legal matters often paved the path to lying.

Frustrated, she stacked the papers and put them back in the blue folder. There was more information out there, at least a box full, but she didn't know where to find it.

Zoe searched through old memories, most faded by the passage of time and buried by new legal work. She'd been part of a legal team, alongside Larson and Bob. And she'd been too green to ask extensive questions, to wonder at the scarcity of facts. But Bob? A seasoned lawyer and firm partner, he should have caught the stench of lies.

What the hell have you done, Bob? Is it related to what happened to you?

She stared at the clue board with Shila's name prominently written on. Pulled open her laptop, brought up the State Bar site and searched for Shila's information. Nothing alarming. A second-year lawyer who'd graduated from law school at age thirty-five. Most Grunman and Forester associates, by comparison, were overachievers, out of law school before their frontal cortex was fully matured. That detail would not have made Shila the ideal associate, unless someone referred her.

Zoe picked up the phone and dialed the woman who had previously denied knowing Shila. To her surprise, Asha Grunman answered on the first ring.

* * *

"We missed you," Asha said the moment Zoe stepped inside the coffee shop.

The rich aroma of freshly brewed coffee mingling with the scent of baked goods and hum of conversations offered momentary comfort.

Asha's imposing six-foot figure and slim build made her hard to miss. Her olive complexion and long dark hair were accentuated by a ruffled sleeve blouse and long bandana skirt. "I love showing off my native Caribbean style," she had once told Zoe. "Watching people stare."

And indeed, everyone in the coffee shop was staring until the duo finished hugging and moved to a corner table where Mia was waiting.

Zoe sat between Mia and Asha, leaning in to give the young girl a hug. "My gosh, Mia, you're growing way too fast."

Mia's pink sweater and leggings mirrored the vivacity of her personality. Her smile put one on Zoe's face.

"She's fifteen, can you believe it?" Asha beamed a proud mother's smile.

"It's been less than a year since we saw Zoe, Mom, not ten." Mia's voice carried a hint of teen eye roll, even if it didn't materialize on her face.

"You look fabulous, young lady. How's high school?"

Asha scuffed and leaned back in her chair.

"Don't start, Mom." Mia turned to Zoe. "Don't listen to her."

"I'm not saying anything," Asha made a heart shape with her fingers.

"Love already?" Zoe said before she could take it back.

"He's a friend," Mia said, her face the color of her sweater. "Anyway, the paper I wrote on you, I can send it if you'd like to read it. Got an A plus. The teacher said my description of the subject was extraordinary, soft yet with tough edges, just as professional women in this competitive world should look."

"Don't you think that's too much from the teacher?" Asha asked Zoe.

"Well, it's a compliment." Zoe pointed at Mia. "Congratulations. Send it over when you can."

"Thank you for being a great subject and letting me write about you."

"Not that I could've stopped you." She grabbed and held Mia's hand. The young girl's affability had captured Zoe's heart since day one. Hard to imagine she was Cato Grunman's daughter. Asha must've worked overtime to shield Mia from the father's wooden personality.

"It made it easier for the muse that you agreed." Mia giggled. "I'm going to get my iced chai. Let you guys do your boring talk." Mia stood. "What can I get you, Zoe? Please, it's on me." She smiled big, and Zoe asked for plain coffee.

"She's going to be a great young woman, Asha. You've done a great job."

Asha watched her daughter walk to the counter as if she might not see her for a long while. The high spirits from a moment ago seemed to have dulled.

"You okay?"

A head shake, then Asha pulled herself back together. "Yeah, yeah. How are you? God, I'm so sorry about Bob."

The topic shift threw Zoe off for a second. "Hard to believe."

"I'm staying out of Cato's way. My husband can be harsh, but I know there's a soft side to him, one that must be sad about his law partner right now."

"What do you mean?" The question came out before Zoe could stop herself. She was asking the wife to talk about her husband, who was Zoe's boss.

Asha looked in the direction of the counter again, making sure her daughter was far enough. "It doesn't take special glasses to see my husband and I are made of different materials that doesn't stitch together well. He may have been better off with someone more like him, more inclined to accept certain things."

"Asha, you don't have to …"

"It's okay. Just usual marriage stuff, ups and downs. You caught me at a down time."

"You could've cancelled. No rush."

Asha shook her head. "Mia and I were excited to see you. What did you want to ask me about?"

"What?"

"I heard it in your voice, Zoe. And the weird text about someone at the office."

"Shila Diggs."

"I don't know the person. Why?"

Zoe felt a presence and turned to see Mia set a small coffee in front of her. She looked up and smiled, offered Mia a thankful nod.

"That's it?" Mia asked. "No milk, sugar, cinnamon?"

"Thank you, young lady. That's it."

Mia giggled at the thought of someone drinking plain, black coffee, while looking at her purple beverage topped with green whipped cream. "I'm going to step out, chat with my friends."

They watched Mia rush outside, sit on a bench and stick ear buds in her ears, already animated by the conversation with whoever answered at the other end.

"The boyfriend, you think?" Zoe asked.

A nod. "I married young. Mia's still much younger, but what

I want for her is to live life. Not even think about committing, or, worse, settling down, until her thirties."

All was not well with the Grunman spouses, by Asha's sour tone. But Zoe would not pry. She waited for Asha to finish her train of thought, got a long sigh instead.

"Who is Shila Diggs?" Asha asked.

A beat of silence. "Lawyer at Grunman and Forester."

"Why would I know her?"

"I was under the impression you had referred her for employment."

Asha's eyes cut through Zoe like a laser beam. Then she broke eye contact and laughed. "The wrong Grunman, I'm sure."

Zoe waited. She'd had trouble recalling memories lately. Cutting down on psychiatric drugs had helped, but there was the odd day when mind pops didn't line up as well as they should have. This memory was clear as day in her mind. Bob had said Mrs. Grunman had referred Shila Diggs. But Bob did not say if the request came directly from Asha, or through her husband.

"Is she beautiful?"

"Asha, I don't know what …"

"I didn't refer anyone, Zoe. If the name Grunman came up, it was my husband who did the referring." A sardonic smile followed by a faraway look. "It wouldn't be the first time. I fired two domestic ladies, excuse the stupid term, he hired in my absence."

Another story etched within the canon of infidelity. One as old as time. It didn't matter that Cato Grunman was married to a most-beautiful woman.

Zoe didn't know all the inner workings of their relationship. She'd read enough psychology to know cheating wasn't entirely about sex but about power, attention, obsession. She ached for Asha and for Mia, who deserved a better father.

* * *

Déjà vu.

Zoe was back in Century City, in the lobby she'd rushed through the day before. The rainmaker himself had called a meeting. Cato Grunman, the recluse. Had the message not arrived prior to her sit down with Grunman's wife, Zoe would've wondered if she'd crossed a line chatting up the boss' wife about family issues, and now had to explain herself.

They'd never exchanged more than a handful of words, Zoe and Cato Grunman. She'd connected with Asha, whom she had met at firm functions. Two kindred spirits, and what a relief. Younger than her husband, carefree, and exotic looking, Asha possessed unbridled joy. An adoring mother to young Mia. Unclear how adoring a wife, but Asha played the role. She stood by her man.

When Mia needed a model for her school paper—a young, professional woman—the trio agreed to meet for lunch. Talked, laughed, went shopping. Zoe learned of Asha's Caribbean heritage, and dancing background. Told Asha about her Wyoming roots.

Asha and Mia had presented Grunman in a different light—softer, almost human.

Now, Grunman wanted to meet.

The Grunman and Forester penthouse remained a little-known world within the firm, a place reserved for ultra-private meetings, accessible only through elevator code access. Cato Grunman had asked Zoe to meet up there, not in his office on the twenty-third floor, but in an exclusive space away from intrusions.

Stepping inside the only elevator connected to the forty-fifth floor, Zoe punched the key code. At once, the doors shut behind her. There was no sense of movement, but an invisible string pulled her stomach toward the ground.

All right. Relax.

Before the halt registered, the doors opened with a swoosh.

A circular entry curved into a high-ceiling space filled with natural light. Desk, chairs, and a T.V. comprised the décor, the sunlight and view, high above West Los Angeles, the main attraction.

Two men in suits stood in the back, hidden by blinding sunrays, their attention on the wall-mounted television set.

Zoe unbuttoned her jacket and stepped closer. Damn hot in here.

The taller man turned, his passing smile welcoming.

Larson, what was he doing here? He'd taken an obnoxious amount of money for a job elsewhere. Never looked back. And not once had he mentioned Grunman during her visit to the bungalow. His rigid posture stood in contrast to his usually relaxed manner; the old Larson no longer shining through.

Steps away, Cato Grunman leaned against the wall. He bore the features of a once attractive man, now older, excessively thin. Even his quality suit couldn't conceal the meagerness of his figure. His unshaven face contrasted with the polished appearance Zoe remembered well. Without his rimless glasses, Grunman's gaunt eyes harked back Zoe's impression of a forever sleep-deprived man. The ultimate workaholic.

Today, a man mourning his law partner.

"Hello," Zoe said.

Grunman shoved his eyeglasses back on, mouthing something that resembled a greeting. He gestured to wait a moment, his attention back to the television set.

Zoe stared at the screen. The news crew was still in Bob's neighborhood. A female reporter struggled to connect psychological problems with suicide, citing unconfirmed data. A news bar at the bottom of the screen repeated the homeless-disappearance story. Second time she'd seen that line in twenty-four hours.

Blowing air through her lips, Zoe tried to understand. According to neighbors, Bob hadn't been himself in weeks. Why hadn't anyone noticed in Bob's circles?

Cato Grunman peeled himself from the wall, arms folded. "I hear you're taking a leave of absence," he said to Zoe.

Her message for the managing partner had jumped directly to Grunman. A true know-it-all.

Zoe forced a smile. "Correct."

"How long?" Grunman's weak voice betrayed annoyance.

"A long weekend, a week at most. I should know soon."

Hours spent scouring the Internet produced two more write-ups on Kip Pulaski and Specter. One article announced the entity's existence. The second offered profile-raising drivel on Pulaski. For a figure associated with a reemerging research group, being kept outside the world-wide-web meant gobs of money had exchanged hands to delete or manipulate data.

Names and numbers in the blue firm folder needed looking into.

Sebastian had given Zoe a choice. Go to Wyoming. Let answers to her questions sort themselves out.

She could look into Specter and the mysterious Kip Pulaski in her own time.

But she had a burning question. "Do you know why Bob would've wanted me to meet an old client last night?"

"You worked for him. Wouldn't that be reason enough?"

She nodded. He rolled out the "you worked for him" words as if describing household help, not an associate attorney in his office.

"You have two pending cases." Grunman adjusted his glasses again.

She tried to meet Larson's eyes to no avail. Why was he here?

"One is on hold pending arbitration," Zoe said. "The second needs minimum legal work I can finish before leaving."

"No need." Grunman walked to the TV, lowered the volume. "Larson Fisher is taking over both."

Larson shrugged. "I'm returning on a temporary basis --"

"As a favor," Grunman said. "We need someone familiar with our practice."

Grunman's prolonged stare held Zoe in place. "I'd prefer not to keep your office tied up if you've decided to move on, Ms. Sinclair."

If Grunman threw out guesses, watching her reaction bordered on fixation.

Zoe imagined herself indispensable to the firm, but that did not hold in a post-Bob world. The friendly image presented by Grunman's family belonged to them alone.

"If you want my resignation, you have it." Zoe's words rushed out at wild speed. Letting go felt risky but liberating.

Grunman hid his surprise as well as a schoolboy. "Very well. Brief Mr. Fisher before you leave." He held up a finger, as if struck by an afterthought. "I'd like to keep Mr. Fisher's return in confidence for now."

A curt nod followed, Grunman's way to punctuate her dismissal. The shrill ringing of the desk phone cut through. Grunman staggered over to answer.

No more obligations. No legal work. Felt like her mind had been bled of toxins, ready for something wholesome and new.

She'd get away from L.A. Be with Sebastian—God, how she missed him. For all she'd lost in Pine Vale, when a madman raped and killed her friend and sent Mother to her grave prematurely, Wyoming was home. *The land of hard-working and good-hearted people, famous for more than Old Faithful and buffalo and bears, with wide-open sky as far as the eye could see.*

She needed to go make peace with the past before making sense of the present.

"I'll meet you downstairs, counselor," Zoe said, avoiding the questions in Larson's eyes.

One last look at the TV showed a split-screen shot—Bob's street and police activity on Mulholland—the homeless-disappearance story now gone. A vehicle had plunged into the canyon, the driver's body burned beyond recognition. Bob Forester's story had been eclipsed by someone else's tragic death.

* * *

On the twentieth floor, Zoe followed a strip of light between the elevator and firm's lobby. She hoped for a quick exit from the office she'd occupied for seven years. But hope was a fickle notion.

A gray-haired police officer guarded the entrance. Inside,

two uniforms blocked access to the criminal-law department, behind them a wall of yellow tape.

"Ma'am, I need to see your ID," the policeman said.

The dour-faced receptionist popped up from behind her desk. "Ms. Sinclair works here. And the managing partner is on his way."

The police had apparently moved in too fast for management to react. She wondered if Grunman had been alerted about the intrusion into his domain. Zoe motioned a quick "it's okay," and produced her ID.

"What happened here, Officer?"

The gray-haired cop checked her name against a list. "You can only access the right wing of the office, ma'am." He returned her ID and resumed the watchdog stance—feet apart, hands behind his back.

The receptionist turned to look at a large TV in the conference room. The same newsreel as in Cato Grunman's office played: car crash on Mulholland.

Zoe took in the scene. Why would the criminal-law section be closed? She hadn't set foot in that part of the office since … well, since yesterday's quick visit. Before that, not since she'd visited Kim Snyder, whose office was there. Zoe's mind raced with questions, ideas colliding.

The elevator doors beeped open and a wide-shouldered man in polo jacket and slacks, followed by a willowy woman, rushed in. Their swagger registered them as cops. The officers at the tape parted in a biblical manner for the man who halted, turned, and ambled back.

"Zoe Sinclair." His voice filled the space. The man's dark eyes and the mirthless smile on his angular face looked familiar.

Jett Riker, Larson's stepbrother. The police detective Larson had urged her to call. She came close to calling last night.

Zoe smiled back, recalling Jett's warmth during family gatherings—a carefree time a lifetime ago. Now, his eyes probed hers, formal and cool.

"This is Detective Braxton." Jett pointed to his partner.

No handshake was forthcoming from the woman with reddish-brown hair in a tight bun. Zoe nodded and earned an icy stare in response.

Something clouded the surprise in Jett's eyes, as if he'd given this moment previous consideration. "I understand you worked for Bob Forester," he said. "Knew his team well."

She nodded. Bob's *team* included a handful of associates and staff who worked on a range of cases. One case kept coming back to her, Specter, and by association one name: Kip Pulaski. Before doing the unthinkable, Bob resurrected Specter and brought Pulaski into her life. Then there was Shila. Zoe's intuition said she needed to tie up a few loose ends then share them with the detective.

But Jett was not here about Bob. The detective's sudden mention of Bob's team said as much. One thing she'd learned about detectives, they never threw out careless banter.

One step behind Jett, Detective Braxton kept a close watch. The whole scene had a charged feeling, like a theatre stage, moments before the drama reached its climax.

"I know Bob's team, yes," Zoe said.

"Then I need to ask you a few questions." Jett handed her a business card. "Come by the station. First thing tomorrow okay?"

Nudged by his stare, she nodded.

He offered a sad smile. Why, she couldn't tell although the words "Bob's team" stayed with Zoe like a bitter aftertaste. A tight team, which included …

"Jett … ahem … Detective," Zoe said when Jett turned away. She motioned behind the yellow tape. "This is about Kim Snyder, isn't it?"

Without a word, Jett offered a salute and walked past the uniforms.

Dear God. Kim Snyder had called to talk about Bob, in person. Then she missed the rendezvous.

Zoe massaged her forehead against dizzying thoughts. Kim had played a central role in "Bob's team." A unique figure: loyal, discrete. Their last phone call replayed in Zoe's mind, revealing nothing but Kim's urgent whisper of Bob's name.

There could be many reasons Kim hadn't shown up, but the yellow tape blocking access to a section where Kim's office was located, together with the police presence and the look in Jett's eyes, told a dark story.

In the conference room, the newsreel that had absorbed Cato Grunman's attention played on the split-screen with the caption: *Mulholland Drive—Car Plunges into Canyon.*

CHAPTER 16

Riker and Neva followed the office manager—a bowtie man with severe aversion to the sun—down an endless hall of doors, all shut. Riker was fascinated by how the mere presence of cops elicited unease, as though everyone harbored a guilty secret, or experienced abuse at the hands of law enforcement. Trust was a tricky matter.

Riker shoved his hands in his pockets. Yet another death, possibly connected to the Forester case, and the encounter with Zoe Sinclair stirred his thoughts. Larson had laid out an explanation for Zoe's presence at the scene, which did little to answer questions.

They reached an office at the west end. An unsuspecting passerby might have imagined it a cleaning closet, but the name on the door read Kimberly Snyder. No title.

"Thank you," Riker said to the manager as Neva stepped inside. "Now, the conference room please."

Kimberly Snyder's accident had inserted itself into the Forester case, providing ample cause for police presence. The manager scurried down the hall with Riker on his heels and arrived at an isolated conference room. The farthest place from all the other offices.

Through the glass door, Riker could see the back of a man facing the window. He thanked the manager and stared until the man hurried away.

Riker stepped inside the sparsely furnished room—a round table and two chairs. Not where one would expect to meet the firm's founder, but here they were.

Cato Grunman turned and nodded in silent greeting. He made no move to shake hands, remaining glued to the spot.

A tall man of lanky appearance. It wasn't what Riker had imagined the legal giant would look like. The well-tailored, oversized suit hid a scrawny body, but it couldn't hide a gaunt face and dark circles under his eyes.

"Detective." Another nod from Cato Grunman.

It looked like the main partner at Grunman and Forester hadn't slept well in some time. Understandable, given the reason for Riker's visit, but the thin body was a shock. If Cato Grunman was bothered by Riker's obvious one-over, he didn't show any signs.

"Mr. Grunman. Thank you for making time to meet with me."

"Time that is scarce, Detective. I'm in trial, and that comes with legal obligations. So, if we could get right to it."

Riker had read about Cato Grunman. Ivy League education, married, father of two, and, by all indications, successful at both, business and marriage. Grunman and Bob Forester went back thirty years, when Grunman had invited Forester to open the law firm together. The rest was a success story. Over three decades, the partners had built a fruitful business with a roster of clients ranging from celebrities to politicians and everything in between.

"What can you tell me about Bob Forester's work?"

Hands in his pockets, Grunman balanced from heels to toes. His partner's death explained the dark circles under his eyes. Riker had read about Grunman's workaholic ways, and attributed the man's meager look to stress and lack of rest. Building a successful law practice must've taken a lot out of Cato Grunman.

"I've been in back-to-back trials, Detective. Extensive legal preparation for the past year. I haven't been able to keep up with Bob's schedule. Regretfully, we'd fallen into a pattern of not keeping one another from our respective work."

"And if there were issues?"

Silence for a beat. "Everything office-related would go through the firm management. We have a system in place, and Bob liked that system." Grunman's voice quivered at the mention of his partner's name.

"Mr. Forester's secretary said he was very busy lately."

"I would think she knows best."

"His neighbors, some of them close friends, describe Bob Forester as withdrawn, not attending to life the way he used to. Missing get-togethers, golf games. A sudden and unexplained change."

Grunman simply nodded.

"You've known Bob Forester longer than the neighbors."

Another nod.

"Would you say it's possible Mr. Forester was suicidal?"

Cato Grunman looked at his shoes, then looked out the window for some time.

"Anything is possible." He turned to Riker. "I'm no expert on the matter, but the Bob I knew was a man with ups and downs, moments of ecstasy and agony. He'd gone through two marriages before his third one. Life can beat a man to a pulp."

Given Grunman's appearance, Riker wondered if the man was talking about Forester or projecting his own life into the "beating to a pulp" remark.

"I hope not," Grunman said, his voice weighed down by the gravity of the conversation, "but anything is possible."

"Mr. Forester's secretary deferred to you on his legal work. What was he working on?"

The corner of Grunman's mouth moved into a forced smile. It was the same question as the first, only reworded. "I don't know. I will tell you that our legal work is, for the most part, boring."

"For the most part," Riker said. "But we have to cover everything, Mr. Grunman. Just in case. There are attorney-client privilege exceptions, I understand. Do we need a court order to discuss this with you?"

Another nod, followed by a head shake. He did not need a court order and was ready to cooperate. Riker stifled a sigh of relief. Nothing slowed down a case like begging judges for warrants at every turn.

"I'd like to take a look at Bob Forester's files, his books. Question his secretary."

“I shall hope you give me some time, Detective, to set that in motion.”

“The sooner the better,” Riker said. “Not to change subjects, but regarding Kimberly Snyder.”

Grunman shook his head. “A human tragedy. Sorry to be useless, but I didn’t know her well.”

One thought ran through Riker’s mind. He’d seen businesses hide financial trouble that led to an executive offing himself. Did Grunman’s meager look and Forester’s death spell financial hardship at Grunman and Forester? He’d need a forensic accountant to look through the firm’s books.

“I need whatever your office can provide on Ms. Snyder.” Riker set his card on the table. And, as I said, the files and the books.”

“May I ask a question…” Grunman read the name off thecard. “Detective Riker?”

“More than one.”

“What do you think happened? Are there any … shall we say, leads?”

Riker tried a smile to keep from laughing in the face of the man asking him to discuss an ongoing case.

* * *

“What do you make of Larson’s former flame?” Neva asked, when Riker walked into Kim Snyder’s office.

Riker shrugged. “Nothing from her watcher?”

“I left him a message.” Gloved up, Neva stepped around the square desk. “Interesting that Ms. Sinclair happened by. I thought she worked mostly from home.”

Riker read the spines of legal books on the shelf. “She works for the firm. And we need access to more than their files.”

Neva stopped and looked up at Riker.

“Their financial books,” he said. “And the accountants.”

Neva opened and closed drawers, leafed through papers, then moved to the computer screen. Their techs had the hard-drive and were combing through it, but she pushed the On button anyway.

"There is a story behind every death, murder or suicide," Neva said. "I get the feeling we've missed a critical chapter here. One that will change everything."

Riker moved to the heap of papers on the corner of the desk.

"And that chapter involves the whole firm, including Zoe Sinclair and Larson." Neva clicked away without meeting Riker's gaze. Mention of his brother, she knew, would strike a nerve. But that was the fucking job.

"I'll talk to my brother. Alone."

Riker hated that Larson was involved—whatever *involved* meant in this case—more for his parents' sake. If the past were an indication, each time one parent felt compelled to stand with his or her biological child, the family had been shaken.

"And," Neva said, clicking and typing, "there is the possibility of an affair. Betty Forester wasn't well enough to talk again. So far, there is nothing anywhere about an affair."

"Keep digging."

When Neva no longer clicked, Riker straightened his back. "Nothing but legal crap here," he said.

"Talk about missing chapters." She pushed the computer screen toward Riker and looked up. "Our private detective lady liked taking screenshots. Take a look at this one."

Neva magnified a screen image on which three sets of numbers, broken in three lines, appeared one below the other. A simple addition or something else?

Clicking away, Neva found the image had only been minimized and not stored on the hard drive. Something an ordinary person might do, except Kim Snyder was a private eye who'd worked for Bob Forester. And they were both dead.

"Not being overly careful, or being careful not to save it?" Neva echoed his thoughts while jotting down the numbers.

Kim Snyder had definitely not done this for math. The addition total was wrong. The numbers signified something else, but Riker had no idea what. Phone numbers? Street address?

He grabbed the paper. "Call when you're done and check

with Zoe Sinclair's tail again."

He'd pay for pulling rank, but patience was a bitch.

* * *

In the lobby, the air conditioning blasted and barely competed with the elevated temperature. This despite the cold weather outside. Riker cringed at the smell of chemicals used to mask the odor of humanity.

Once outside, the mist of an enthusiastic breeze brushed moisture across his face.

He dialed Captain Caruso and left a message. The captain had wanted to be kept in the loop at every step. And he could push and shove and get a judge to sign off faster on an order for access to the law firm's database.

Riker hung up and dialed again. The first number, taken from Kim Snyder's computer, went nowhere. He listened to eight rings, nine, ten. No recording. The second offered *not a working number* message. The third clicked as if routed elsewhere. He texted all three numbers to the department tech with a *Rush ID* request, followed by, *On my way*.

Near the cruiser, pronounced footsteps tromped behind him. The window glass reflected a man in running gear, with a hoodie and sunglasses, some ten feet back. Vaguely familiar. But the hoodie made little sense for a real runner. When Riker turned, the man was swallowed by a group of pedestrians, then gone.

Another weirdo in Century City?

In the car, turning on Century Boulevard, Riker stopped for street crossers. An elusive thought nagged at him. More pedestrians rushed across—office workers, suits. A woman in a workout outfit moved fast. No one else seemed bent on exercising, and Riker couldn't be sure exercise was the woman's purpose either. Maybe a fast walker in comfortable clothes. Maybe …

Oh, hell.

He made an illegal U turn. The runner covered by hood and sunglasses—*that* was what nagged him. The man didn't belong because he wasn't a fucking runner. He was the security guard Riker had given his business card to, asking for a call.

Levi Duarte had come within feet, then halted. Out of uniform and covered by hood and sunglasses, Riker hadn't immediately recognized the man who called himself LSD on social media. Levi had come close then stopped, lowered his head and disappeared.

CHAPTER 17

Zoe drove up Mulholland through the Santa Monica Mountains. Few people knew the road was named after an Irish immigrant who left home at fifteen and later changed L.A.'s water usage with the Aqueduct. The name recalled nothing but scenic drives along crested mountains on a twisty stretch of a pure marvel road.

Driving up here sparked Zoe's imagination. Most times. Today, it only helped abate bleak feelings.

The traffic hour helped Zoe reach her target location in under an hour. At the third intersection up the road, she cut across several lanes past East Canyon, slowed at the first crossing, and pulled onto tire-eating gravel.

She squeezed her Lexus between two stacks of cones as close to Angelo Ranch Drive as possible. This would do for now. No doubt, LAPD's finest would track her down before long.

A call to Kim Snyder's friend—the man Kim had introduced as character witness when Zoe helped with Kim's tenant eviction case—explained Kim's disappearance. It did not explain the *why*, of course. Why was it that after summoning Zoe to Santa Monica College about Bob, Kim Snyder drove her car through guardrails and over a cliff? Here, at this intersection, on Mulholland Drive.

The thought brought Zoe physical pain. She banished it from her mind. It would no doubt return and fill her heart with sorrow, but not now.

Most scenes saw diminished activity once remains were bagged, the scene worked, and photos taken. Here, the police maintained close watch on the perimeter from a distance. The media, as usual, kept them company, but stayed out of the way.

The cool breeze welcomed Zoe when she stepped out of the car. All the commotion was down Angelo Ranch Drive. Access anywhere within the perimeter was monitored, albeit not closely.

She rushed up to the unmarked car, ignored the Do-Not-Enter cones, and hurried along the yellow tape.

News media called this an accident, but Kim's friend—another private investigator named Dick— said, "At this time doubt everything you hear."

The scenery—something out of a dream—made accepting death harder. The beauty of the mountains celebrated nature and life. A jolting contradiction of perception. The paved but not easily accessible part of the canyon where the breeze caressed treetops stood as a paradox—life and death coexisting yet clashing.

"Ma'am? Excuse me." A young police officer called out from behind Zoe.

Damn. Where did he come from?

She'd hoped the jaded policemen, like the media, had congregated elsewhere.

"Is Detective Riker here?" She handed the man a business card. "Zoe Sinclair."

"This official business, ma'am?"

Zoe couldn't bring herself to blurt out a lie. She shook her head.

"You have to call the office then."

"Detective Riker might want to see me." Zoe pointed to the officer's radio. "If he happens to be around."

If not a lie, maybe a delay would buy time to look around.

The man nodded, making a double chin. "Please wait here." Stepping away, he radioed in her name and request.

A gust of wind ripped through. Zoe braced against the wind tugging at her hair, tugging at her nerves. Any other day, she'd have loved gazing down the canyon, taking in the view.

Kim's car and what was left of her body had been hoisted up. Long gone. Turning in place, Zoe checked the winding road up Mulholland. Ahead, the road zigzagged but here, it was a narrow, straight drive. Not a dangerous part of the canyon compared with the twists and turns ahead, where mere seconds of distraction could spell disaster. Not so here. This was a regular downhill, maybe a little slippery when wet.

So, what led to Kim's losing control of the car?

Ten steps ahead, the officer's back stiffened. His voice, carried by the breeze, held tones of civility tinged with annoyance. Someone was barking orders at the other end of the radio. Not a good sign, judging by the officer's tense back. No sense waiting to be escorted outside the perimeter.

Zoe hurried back to her car. Seconds later, the officer appeared in her rearview mirror, a shrinking figure.

Once far enough away, she slowed to search for skid marks. Nothing to see, but she was at a distance from the crash scene. Countless vehicles had driven by, creating new marks.

With no traffic in the opposite direction, she drove across yellow double lines, pulled off the road, and drove up the dirt path. There was a vantage point—a boulder on an incline and a canopy tree. A serene place, if not for what had transpired down the ravine. Perfect location to pause and admire Mulholland and beyond.

She stopped near the tree. Paths wound on the opposite side of the hill. Miles away, the 101 freeway crisscrossed the pass into the valley.

Out of the car, Zoe turned to take in the view but the distance made it hard to see the ravine covered by vegetation.

Damn, she should've brought binoculars.

She wandered past the tree, trying to think. Why would Kim be driving down Mulholland at such a late hour, and how did she veer off the path into the canyon? So many things had to come together—losing control of the car, poor visibility, unsafe driving conditions, tank full of gas—to veer off and crash.

Zoe stepped on a rock for a straight-line view but found no better answers. Off the rock, she paced, stopping to think when facing the panorama of the Old Canyon.

Kim lived far, worked miles away. Did she have family in the vicinity? They hadn't been chummy enough to exchange family stories.

Zoe stopped, searching for clues that failed to show. No, if she knew Kim Snyder's secretively obsessive work ways, the firm's private eye turned to no one else. Then why Zoe?

Cursing the jagged rocks that pierced the soles of her shoes, Zoe halted. City footwear proved no match for rough terrain.

Something on the ground caught her attention: a rolled paper between rocks. A cigarette butt? Way out here? She searched around the dirt road, the immediate area. No other butts. Just one that looked clean and fresh. If this were a hangout spot for youths, a single smoker made no sense.

Climbing higher, Zoe walked around the tree. Found nothing else that didn't belong. Stepping carefully around the rocks, she circled the tree again. On the third round, a piece of plastic, or metal, shone under rays of sunshine cutting through clouds. Metal, half-covered by rocks, way out here where crawlers called home.

A casing? It couldn't be, yet there it was. A bullet casing steps away from a cigarette butt.

She stooped, leaning on her knuckles. The sun was going down, the light fading, but no doubt the two items hadn't been here long. Hardly a layer of dust coated them.

Standing, Zoe focused her attention downhill.

From this vantage point, Old Canyon was in direct line of sight. The tree and boulder were a good spot for someone hiding, perhaps smoking while waiting. It was close enough to see the road, particularly through the scope of a firearm.

CHAPTER 18

Hawke ran one hand through his cropped hair and kept one on the wheel.

A headache was pushing past his pain resistance. To get Tina to drink, he'd downed a couple shots. Watched her burn through a few.

That was what he liked about Tina—her docile nature. And the young body he could manipulate however he liked. But the manipulating ran too long. Now, Hawke was running late for the meeting with Big Shot.

What had started as profitable work last year was now a guessing game. Big Shot had become a different man. He looked stressed, not his usual kick-ass self.

Then, there were the ongoing mind games.

Hawke had access to all computers and networks. That was their understanding. Full access to monitor what needed *cleaning*. Hawke would not put his hacker signature on networks he couldn't keep an eye on. And access he had, except for one laptop.

Big Shot kept password-protected files with unique identifiers for that laptop. Why advertise its existence only to keep it out of Hawke's hands? And the big question: why choose him?

One reason came to mind. Hawke was green, untested, a geek to be used and discarded.

Breast Goddess Shila had skirted the question when he'd asked. "He and I think highly of you, Hawke," she'd said. "I don't recommend just anyone. You're a pro." The woman had no shame, massaging the ego of a former juvenile delinquent she'd represented in court.

Hawke had set virtual traps sure to catch something—the question was when?

Exiting the freeway past the Getty Center, he turned toward what looked like an old building. The meeting spot. He pulled up near the Town Car, stopped, and stepped out.

A razor-sharp chill blew in from the ocean. He inhaled the cold air, grinded his teeth. No time for a headache.

When the driver standing outside the Town Car opened the passenger door, Hawke climbed inside the back seat. Meetings were always private.

The car door shut, and Hawke waited, the interior heat overwhelming.

"Our work is larger than us," the familiar cracked voice from the back seat said. There were never greetings. "It's about purpose." After a short pause, Big Shot started again. "Purpose makes it impossible to merely exist. We must excel. Takes unimaginable work to excel."

Not an unusual speech, only short on details. Big Shot liked to say their work was about purpose, a grand design at work.

Hawke hadn't cared much, but after Hancock Park and Bob Forrester's death his focus had shifted.

He listened, hoping the computer network trap would soon ensnare prey. Give him access to the laptop, to real answers. Was Big Shot playing Hawke for a fool, setting him up to take the fall for something? If not, why so fucking enigmatic?

When the car door opened, signaling the meeting ended, Big Shot reached over Hawke's shoulder and handed him a note. Hawke read, then returned it to the hand still on his shoulder. Let no disappointment show.

Another assignment. His return to Tina's bed would be brief.

Hawke stepped out, said nothing. Hurrying to his car, he welcomed the wind whipping tree branches into a frenzy. Forcing him to brace.

He pulled out his phone, punched in numbers, and slid his thumb over several screens. A map opened; the familiar red dot named ZS blinking in the middle.

* * *

Hawke Ford poured two fingers and downed the liquor. Best scotch money could buy, warming him from inside out.

On the bed, Tina was out after a round of sex and more scotch. Her naked body glistened with sweat under the dim light. Hard leaving her sprawled on the bed like that. A young woman, desperate for commitment, the ultimate status among peers, had offered herself on a platter. For two months now, she'd been soothing his tired bones.

With some luck, he'd be back for the final round.

Grabbing his bag, Hawke slipped out of the apartment. Careful and quiet. Nosy neighbors abounded in the hundred-unit beach building, even after dark.

Baseball hat low to cover his face, he rushed down the stairs.

Nothing but the sound of the ocean broke the evening calm. He'd wondered how Tina could afford a place in Santa Monica, steps from the beach, until learning Daddy paid her rent. More reason for him to check out soon—Daddy was inquiring about the new boyfriend.

Hawke pushed the back gate and turned into the alley. Quiet reigned near the dumpsters at this hour, the reason he'd parked here. He opened the truck, threw his bag on the passenger seat, and, checking his surroundings, climbed inside.

A new restlessness was creeping in. Dreams of Costa Rica flashed through his mind. Never good being stationary too long. In the past, when jobs dragged on, he'd needed legal help. That was how he'd met Breast Goddess, Attorney at Law. A blessing and a curse, and not to be repeated. He'd get his money, one way or another, and bolt.

Another glance in the mirror, and Hawke rolled toward Main.

Two turns later, the ocean appeared in his rearview. Striking, the Pacific under moonlight. All that power out there, that sense of freedom.

The phone on the passenger seat lit up.

A text message from Big Shot: *On schedule?* Ahead of schedule, but Hawke kept the reply to: *All good.*

Thirty minutes later, Hawke parked near the palm-tree-encircled building in Manhattan Beach. At eight in the evening, the wealthy South Bay enclave was much calmer than Santa Monica.

One tenant's parking spot was empty. Zoe Sinclair wasn't home.

He grabbed the flashlight and knife from the bag and stepped into the cold breeze, letting it clear his head.

He'd orbited the place before, but only *visited* once. Aborted the plan, per orders, much as he'd have enjoyed an encounter with Ms. Sinclair. Today's mission: be sure she wasn't in possession of anything bound to lead authorities where they shouldn't be led.

"Remove anything incriminating," Big Shot had said, "but don't leave without the blue folder."

On the third floor, apartment 20C, Hawke used the pick. Three seconds later, the door opened.

Inside, moonlight cut through the curtain, filling the living room with light. Hawke closed the door. Waited for an all-clear silence, then started searching past sofas and cushions, through drawers and cabinets. Nothing different from his last *visit.*

The hallway led to an all-white bedroom, and a bathroom filled with the scent of oils. Neither was cluttered. No work-related items nor anything remotely incriminating lay around.

Back in the living room, Hawke mused upon the lack of color everywhere. It matched the rest of the place and the personality of the woman he'd studied, closed off and mysterious. Her drawers consisted mostly of black and white lingerie. Sexy, sure, but bland. Always smart to understand a target, and this one kept surprising. Thoughts of what he'd do to her, right here in her living room, roiled Hawke.

He went over everything again—end tables, cushions and throw pillows. In front of the sofa, the padding of the monochromatic gray rug felt thick under his foot. He lifted it, found nothing. Stepping around, Hawke smoothed the surface of the rug and straightened the fringe.

The closet door near the entrance drew his attention. Hawke had overlooked the spot when he first stepped in. A box corner stuck out and kept the door from completely shutting. Hawke pulled out the box and switched on the flashlight.

A blue folder sat atop stacks of magazines.

Flashlight between his teeth, Hawke opened the folder and read. A legal case going way back. Not much in terms of legal pleadings, just things one might call Exhibits. Numerical descriptions, lists of names, dates, events.

Confusing legal shit, but this was the blue folder.

"You'll know when you see it," Big Shot had said earlier tonight. Why so mysterious? And why was this file important?

In the corner of the box, two pictures sat wedged between magazines. In the first, Hawke recognized Shila Digs. She was at a party with a group of people, two of whom he'd studied well—the late Bob Forester and the woman herself, Zoe Sinclair. He didn't know the other two, but Shila's broad smile bothered Hawke. It looked genuine, as if she liked the people surrounding her.

He reached for the second picture when a sharp ring cut through the silence.

Hawke leaped to his feet.

What the fuck?

He pulled the phone out of his pocket. Hit the silencer. Communication took place via text message. No calls ever. Damn it, he'd left the stupid volume on.

Tina's name flashed on the screen. Not possible, Tina had ingested enough alcohol to be out for hours. He'd made sure of it.

Hawke hit the answer button. Took the phone to his ear and waited.

Tina's voice came on, "Baby?" Anxiety filled with a hint of panic.

Background shuffling cut through, followed by complete silence.

Then Tina again. "Hello?"

Someone had woken Tina and prompted her to call. And that someone was there, meaning the plan had gone to hell.

Hawke cut the call. Counted to five while listening for sounds. A door slammed somewhere on the bottom floor. Then silence.

He was not taking chances with the front door.

Folder in hand, Hawke climbed out the window, grabbed on

to the plant ladder for a handhold, and jumped. Hit the ground hard.

A buzzing sound filled his ears. He shook it off.

Keeping close to the ground, Hawke dashed behind the nearest palm tree. Counted to five, then hit the truck remote button, waiting to see if the beep brought anyone out of the shadows. Nothing.

He slammed the phone and squashed it with his foot. Buried it in the ground.

In the truck, driving, Hawke held his breath until the first stop sign. No suspicious activity behind him. No tail.

Three erratic turns later, Hawke began searching for the nearest convenience store. He had to make a phone call from an untraceable location.

CHAPTER 19

Feet propped on the desk, Riker read the stack of papers Neva had handed over.

A lawsuit. The Grunman and Forester Executive Committee was suing the city, asking a judge to delay access to the firm's database or pare down what the LAPD could look at, citing privacy concerns.

"This after Cato Grunman agreed to providing access," Riker said.

"It's the old, filthy rich who delay cases."

Neva paced for a while, then sat on the corner of the desk adjacent.

"So, Levi Duarte was tracking you down in Century City?"

Dragging him from one problem to another, his Neva. "He was there, then gone in seconds."

"I backchanneled for camera footage." Neva turned the computer screen toward Riker and pushed a button.

Riker set the papers on his desk and sat up when a grainy image appeared on the screen. Took a few seconds to pinpoint the figure with the hoodie and sunglasses.

Levi Duarte looked like a spooked man, his attention darting all around, making sure he hadn't been made. He joined a group of people, but it was clear he was trying to hide in plain sight. Then he broke away from the group and inched forward, hands deep in his pockets.

A few seconds later, the back of Riker's cruiser came into view and a shadow figure pulled open the door and stepped inside the vehicle. Riker, himself, unaware Levi was only a few steps behind. Levi's attention was clearly on Riker, even if it was impossible to see his eyes. He took a few tentative steps in Riker's direction, stopped, then turned and disappeared in the midst of a large group of pedestrians. The cruiser took off, and the image went black.

"He knows something about Grunman and Forester," Neva said, "and wants to talk to you about it, but chickened out last minute."

* * *

"A message from the precinct operator." Riker slammed the desk phone down. "And a damn puzzling one. Zoe Sinclair was looking for me at the scene of Kim Snyder's accident."

They'd spent the last hour scouring the database. Found pages of nonsense on the Grunman law firm, not even a speeding ticket on Levi Duarte.

Neva glared. "She gets around, our Ms. Sinclair. Highway Patrol still labeling the crash an accident?"

Another nod. Riker could've used some peace to hear himself think. But they shared a working space the size of a walk-in closet. No windows, no foot traffic. Since Neva was often gone, the office was mostly his. Riker had a desk up front in the bullpen, but reputation and longevity afforded him an extra space here in the quiet corner he preferred.

Neva read from her yellow notepad. "Kim Snyder was seen at a bar, not far from the crash site, hours before."

"By whom, and was she drinking?"

"Patrons who saw the news called through dispatch. The bartender confirmed it and became consternated by the drinking question. She wasn't drinking."

"*Consternated*, I like it. They teach you that in law school?"

Neva stared a fuck-off at him. She'd enrolled in evening law school classes after the bank robbery shooting six months ago. Something to fall back on in case detective work came close to killing her. But as far as he could tell, law school wasn't Neva's calling.

"Tire marks still being analyzed," Neva read on, back in detective form. "Recent rain didn't help preservation, but there wasn't much to suggest Snyder tried to stop."

"Not another suicide."

"Bob Forester's death still labeled 'suicide'?"

Neva was a pro at sprinting between questions.

Riker shrugged. He didn't have enough info, even if his instinct and Qin's words had just about erased the word 'suicide' from the case. "Why would Kim Snyder try to off herself?"

"Sometimes life just sucks." Neva's voice didn't carry assurance. "And she worked in Bob Forester's office. Maybe Levi Duarte wanted to talk to you about more than Bob Forester."

"What else from the bartender?"

"Crowded scene. Shaky memory. At one point, Kim Snyder sat next to a guy the bartender remembers saying was a doctor. Not a regular. The guy had said something about difficult patients, why he needed a drink, blah, blah."

"They look like they knew each other?"

"The bartender couldn't tell, only caught a glimpse of them."

Neva's phone beeped. Bouncing off the desk, she read from her phone then looked at Riker. "Ever heard of Sunken City?"

"San Pedro?"

"According to the scene report, a computer printout was found at the crash scene, in the canyon. Burned corners, but the rest is intact."

"And we assume it came from Kim Snyder's car."

She gave him a look. "Bottom of the canyon doesn't see traffic. And this paper, while burnt at the corners, is new, like it somehow escaped the car fire." Neva stopped to take in a mouthful of air, exhaled. Still a sucker for drama.

"Good work, Detective Braxton. What's on the paper?"

"Map of Sunken City with directions from Westside there. Date wasn't clear, but the IT team is looking into Kim Snyder's computer. My guess, Ms. Snyder printed this recently. Likely drove to Sunken City not long before she plunged to her death."

"Your guess?"

Neva rolled her eyes. "Okay, I sweet talked the lab guy into looking at the printout under ultraviolet equipment. Priority, of course."

"Of course."

"That was his finding." She stuck her phone back in the pocket. "San Pedro is a different jurisdiction. Don't know where they stand on the friendly, cooperative scale."

Their eye contact was short but telling. Riker's modus operandi was to visit every location that popped up in investigations. Immediately.

She shook her head, grabbed her keys and gun. He was on his own today.

"Gotta study for Constitutional Law class. Be careful out there." With a wink, she turned and strode away.

When the door shut behind Neva, he noted the time: 8:50. No sense driving to a dislocated piece of land called Sunken City in San Pedro where vagabonds and wannabe poets congregated. He could wait till sunlight to antagonize the precinct head of another jurisdiction.

Riker's cell phone buzzed—unknown number. In this work, all tips came from unknown numbers. Except this wasn't a tip. Larson had resurfaced, and he was calling asking for help on Zoe's behalf.

CHAPTER 20

Manhattan Beach had once been all sand dunes, then developers leveled the dunes and built a resort community. In 1902, a coin flip decided the name *Manhattan*, after the chief developer's hometown in New York City.

Tonight, the beach gem lay dormant, until Riker reached The Strand—a concrete path lined with restaurants and expensive real estate. Joggers trotted along the waterfront, even in the cold weather, while eateries burst with neon lights and lively patrons. The ocean glistened under broken moonlight.

Riker's kind of neighborhood—this corner of South Bay—near the ocean and close to freeways. A beach town without the tourism intrusion of Santa Monica or Venice. Quiet and clean, but a hellish drive from the Westside District.

Zoe Sinclair lived across the street from The Strand, within walking distance from the water and the quieter area of Manhattan Beach, in a three-story apartment complex walled off by palm trees. The best of both worlds—ocean proximity and peace.

Except someone had intruded into Zoe's peace tonight.

When Larson had called about a break-in at Zoe's, Riker took the drive. How could he not? Zoe kept popping up everywhere, albeit unwillingly. Then, there was Larson who'd all but disappeared until now.

A true mystery man, young Bro.

The familiar Range Rover sat in front of the building. Riker parked two cars behind Larson's Rover and stepped out, welcoming the refreshing ocean air.

Zoe and Larson, now that was a strange friendship. Riker would've erred on the side of pride. Let shit from the past go.

The evening chill slipped through Riker's jacket. For the past two weeks, winter had made a home in Southern California during late autumn, bent on sticking around. He didn't mind cold temperatures for short durations, but not this long.

He quickened his pace through the entrance, jogged up three flights of stairs, arriving in front of a wide-open door. Lights were on everywhere.

A stocky male cop stood in the middle of the living room, listening to Zoe and Larson. His partner, a dark-skinned woman, busied herself shining a flashlight in a corner, looking for clues.

Riker had liked Larson and Zoe together. Then again, if not for Larson's subsequent relationship with Neva, Riker would've never met the woman of his dreams. Bad as it sounded, dating his brother's ex, Larson had insisted he and Neva had never had a chance. Maybe, but on the odd day, Riker blamed himself for finding happiness on the heels of his brother's heartache.

Life, so fucking complicated.

After a nod to Larson, Riker approached the Manhattan Beach PD policewoman and showed his badge.

"LAPD Detective?" She gave him a long look. "This more than a break-in?"

"Relates to a case."

She seemed ambivalent but smiled. "Intruder didn't leave anything obvious behind." She nodded toward her partner. "Looks like he's done. We'll leave it to you, but share the report, please."

After some chitchat and promises to share findings, Riker closed the door behind the local cops.

"You didn't have to drive all the way here," Zoe said. "I'd already called the police."

Riker's gaze shifted from Zoe to Larson. He obviously hadn't told Zoe he'd called. Why was he here, anyway?

"I came to check on Zoe," Larson said, as if reading Riker. "Nearly took my head off when she opened the door." Joyless laughter followed, a way to fill the awkward moment.

"It's been a long day," Zoe said. "Now this." She and Larson exchanged a look.

Riker flashed back to the night of Forester's death, and Zoe's visit to Larson. She'd been distraught, in need of a friend. Tonight, Larson came to check on her. So much to probe into, and answers were never easy.

"Anything missing?" Riker looked from Larson to Zoe.

"That box." Zoe zoned in on the object as if possessed. "Was in there, not in the living room." She pointed to a small closet. "It holds documents, photos of my family, Sebastian."

"Sebastian?"

"My fiancé."

Riker threw Larson a glance. Got nothing back.

"There was a file in the box," Zoe said. "A blue, manila folder. It's gone."

"Sure you didn't put it elsewhere?"

She didn't seem sure but nodded.

"Important file?"

"Work. Old case."

She looked like she wanted to say more, her eyes two laser beams shifting all over the room.

"Important old case?"

Riker could tell an internal battle raged inside Zoe. An equal shit storm raged through Larson. "Old case Bob had been lead-attorney on." Zoe breathed out the words more than articulated them.

"Bob Forester?"

A nod from Zoe.

Near her, Larson shifted his weight from foot to foot. Impatient with the questions? Standing by his former flame, supportive? She appeared to be holding up fine on her own.

"Light was off when I walked in." Zoe moved toward the wall, switched off the lights.

Nothing but a sliver of moonlight cut through. Almost total darkness and silence.

"If you look there by the door." Zoe motioned and Riker followed. "You'll see several shoe imprints on the carpet. Ours and those left by the cops are now in the mix. When I got home and saw the box out of place, there was only one set of fresh prints. Larger than mine. And that area rug was out of place, the frills too straight, as if someone had cleaned up after stepping on them. I knew something was amiss. The carpet was recently vacuumed. Pattern should've been uniform."

Riker sensed her gaze on him and nodded.

"Now, if you look between the door, hallway, and window, you'll see one set of prints—likely the intruder's—move between the door, hallway, and the window, but never back to the door. See?"

Larson grumbled. Riker nodded again. Zoe Sinclair would make a hell of a detective. Maybe the reason she'd gone up Mulholland, to check into the Kim Snyder crash scene. He made a mental note to ask, privately.

She turned the lights back on.

"Strange," Larson said.

Riker shook his head. "Intruder heard a commotion and fled out the window?"

He moved to the window, looked out. Saw nothing amiss.

Made sense the intruder preferred fleeing. Of course, there was another theory, one Riker didn't voice. The intruder could've been casing the place for a planned return. If so, when? And *why* was the bigger question. He'd already taken a file, one tied to the late Bob Forester, no less.

"Can you tell me something about the missing file? The case?" He didn't turn as he spoke, giving Zoe space. Sensed movement from Larson. Bro didn't like the question.

"Nothing much in the folder." A beat of silence. "Old case."

Riker pressed a button on his phone, facing out into the night. When the operator answered, he recited the address. "I want a team to go over every square inch," he said.

Whispers drew his attention back to Zoe and Larson. He gesticulated. She vehemently shook her head. Then they both turned to Riker.

"A crime-scene team will be here soon." Riker pocketed his phone. "Is there somewhere you can stay tonight?"

Zoe rubbed her shoulders, looked around. "I'm okay here. I'll stay out of the way."

Stubborn woman.

When she turned toward Larson, volumes were said in silence. Larson, who seemed to become smaller, stepped back, reeling. He wasn't needed, and that hurt, Riker could see. He could also see that there was more to their communication. There was more to his brother's visit here. Stolen furtive glances suggested as much.

They needed to be sat down and grilled hard, both of them.

"Please stop by the station tomorrow morning." Riker set a business card on the table, the second he'd given Zoe today. "Bring a written description of the missing file."

* * *

Outside, icy air cut Riker's breath for a second.

He got behind the wheel, ready to wait for Larson. But five minutes later, nothing changed.

With a sigh, Riker reached for the file on the passenger seat. Flipped it to Zoe's picture. In between glances out the window, he settled into reading the story of a small Wyoming town named Pine Vale, an unwelcomed family, a sick mother, a dead best friend, and a man named Marshall Park. The murderer.

Riker had come across many Marshalls of the world—small-town nutcases addicted to anger that eventually grew into an uncontrollable beast they directed toward their neighbors. Marshall had set out to clean house, even if that required killing those who stood in the way, his own people. Pine Vale, for Marshall, was reserved for those who look the same, talk the same, with deep-rooted ties there. Likely that attitude drove many, like Zoe, out of clicky, insular places like Pine Vale. Riker couldn't imagine anyone he knew closely belonging anywhere hatred ran as reckless indulgence.

Still, Zoe remained a paradox. Tradition-loving and modern, patient with old customs and rational. She was a small-town girl, even if city converted. A woman interested in the interpretation of night dreams and their meaning. He'd thought it a joke when she'd spoken about dreams during family dinners, but no one had laughed. Not Zoe, anyway—the realist, and often the idealist.

He closed the file with a sigh. Looked out the window at the building's front door. *Where the hell are you, Larson?*

CHAPTER 21

Zoe's entire body was caked in a layer of sticky sweat. Her throat was tightening, as if squeezed by invisible hands. God, she was going to choke.

In the bathroom, she scooped up water with both hands. Drank fast. Deep coughs shook her until she started heaving. Zoe leaned over the toilet bowl, but nothing came from her body. She'd taken in nothing but the sleeping pill.

When she quieted down, she sat and curled into a ball.

She'd had a startling dream, followed by an anxiety attack. Which triggered which, no way to know, but Mother was back in her dreams. A blurry vision, but clearly Mother. She'd spoken words Zoe couldn't understand or couldn't remember. Fragments lingered—something about feelings and pain.

That ringing. What the hell? Zoe covered her ears. Waited for the internal alarm to stop. *Count, breathe, put it away. Come on.* She'd been free of panic attacks for a while. Life was slowly returning to normal. Now this.

Her thoughts settled, and it finally registered. The alarm clock was blaring, nothing internal. She waited, afraid any movements might trigger internal demons. When doors slammed down the hall, Zoe finally stirred and shut off the alarm clock. The blaring would piss off the entire floor and bring a mob to her door.

She padded into the living room and noticed Jett Riker's card on the table.

Last night, she'd wanted to tell Jett about Kim Snyder's phone call, about what she'd found at the scene, about Shila Diggs and Larson. But Larson had sworn that it hadn't been him knocking or sitting in a car parked outside. He'd called to check on her. Zoe didn't buy the welfare-check part, but she directed her anger toward the break-in. After the crime-scene techs left, she swallowed sleeping pills to quiet her thoughts.

Now, she had to go see Jett Riker

* * *

The autumn sun painted the sky in gold and brown hues, inviting the world to pause and marvel. Zoe would've loved to do just that, but the sight of the brick-and-stone police station steps away dampened her appetite for tranquility.

It was almost midday, and she was stricken with exhaustion, running on two, maybe three hours of sleep.

All right, try to forget.

No sense going on with inventories of her mind, or reflecting upon the unwanted visitor, the taken blue folder. If only she'd copied the contents of the folder someone stole from her apartment.

She hurried up the concrete steps to the police station door. Almost tripped. Her brain desperately needed coffee. The cup she'd managed to pour at home had gone flying all over the car, thanks to the driver in front of her. Why would anyone slam the brakes in the middle of the freeway for no reason? A miracle that she'd avoided collision and wasn't drenched in coffee.

Her haggard face in the glass door bore scars of a restless night. Life etched everything on our faces, good and bad.

Past her reflection, a truck rolled down the street. Same as the truck on the freeway, whose driver had slammed the brakes like a freak. Zoe spun in place, but SUVs blocked her full view. When traffic cleared, only the taillights were visible. A turn later, the truck was gone.

* * *

Jett Riker led Zoe into an interrogation room straight out of a T.V. show: metal table and chairs, green walls, acoustic tiles on the ceiling. After a few sitting formalities, he promised to return with coffee.

Aware she could be watched through the one-way mirror, Zoe sat casually. A familiar pain settled somewhere between her neck and shoulders. She dug in with her fingers, kneading hard. Kept her mind idle.

Five minutes later, Jett strode in, Styrofoam cup in hand,

steam curling off the top. The woman detective, Braxton if Zoe remembered correctly, closed the door, and leaned against the wall, the expression on her face unreadable.

"Sorry to keep you waiting." Jett set the cup before her. Pulling a folder from under his arm, he placed it on the table and sat.

His gaze was distant, as if they'd never shared family dinners and laughter when she'd dated Larson. A true professional, Jett Riker.

"This conversation is being recorded." He glanced at her. "You ready?"

No tape in sight, but the room was probably equipped with a wireless system. Modern-day conveniences.

Zoe pulled the cup closer to feel the warmth. Sipped a little, then nodded.

Jett recited her name, the date and time.

When he finished, Zoe heard herself say: "Anything new in Bob Forester's case?"

He took an extra moment, "Let's start with the time Bob Forester called you for a confidential meeting." No answer to her question.

"He called for a meeting, not a confidential one," Zoe said.

Jett stared, waiting. No doubt he could do that for hours.

"Bob mentioned a client he wanted me to meet," Zoe said. "To discuss potential new work."

Near the door, the woman detective stood stock-still. If only some alarm or a phone would go off and break the prolonged silence.

Jett riffled through the opened folder, moved papers around. "First time Bob Forester mentioned this client?"

Bob's voice was a blur, almost gone from her mind with the knowledge of his death. "Yes, I think so."

"Tell me exactly what happened that evening?"

Zoe shut her eyes, trying to recall events that seemed from ages ago. She'd been angry with Sebastian for abruptly leaving on a business trip. Had tried to nurse her heartache out on the balcony, looking at the ocean. That was when Bob called. She remembered not giving his request much thought, ready to refuse, but he came close to begging, so she relented. That's how friendship worked. She remembered arriving at the office to find no receptionist in the lobby, no Bob anywhere, only Kip Pulaski waiting in the conference room. She introduced herself. Then everything went off track.

"I keep a light caseload," Zoe continued. "Work from home. Only go to the office two or three times a month, early in the day. That was my arrangement with Bob."

Jett stared but said nothing.

"Bob asked me to take an unscheduled, late meeting. Just this once, he said."

"Why would he change the arrangement?"

"Important client, important case." Zoe's mouth went dry. She sipped the coffee.

"What's the client's name?"

"Kip Pulaski." Zoe's attention moved from Jett to the woman leaning against the wall, then back to Jett. Detective Braxton could have watched the proceedings from the hidden room behind the one-way glass. Her standing there, half hidden, must have been another police tactic. Dammit, for some reason she'd have preferred that only Jett be in the room.

Straightening her back, Zoe tried for a neutral tone. "I think attorney-client privilege prevents me from saying more." She didn't say *unless a crime was committed*, but by the look on Jett's face he understood.

"Give me generalities. Did you take the case?"

"During a follow-up meeting, Mr. Pulaski mentioned he wants us … wants me to work for him independent of the firm, to help bring back a defunct organization."

Jett lifted his eyebrows. He noted something in the file. "How well do you know Bob Forester?"

"Bob was a visiting professor when I was in law school. After, I was hired at his firm, and we worked multiple cases together."

"Do you know his family, his wife?"

"Betty, his wife."

"How would you describe his marriage? Any issues there?"

Zoe stared until Jett raised his eyebrows again. "Bob loved his wife. She was his world. And I'm sure she adored him."

"And Kip Pulaski?"

"I was made familiar with Mr. Pulaski again two days ago."

"So, you knew him from before. This Kip Pulaski."

"I had worked on his case, the Specter Group, years ago. An old firm client at the time, but new to me."

Jett moved papers through the folder, glancing at a few. Although he could've asked a plethora of questions about her follow-up meeting with Kip Pulaski, he didn't.

"Can you think back to Bob Forester's call. Word by word. What exactly did he say?"

"I remember his apologetic tone, his insistence that I should come in. Words like I came recommended, important client, important case."

"Specifics would be helpful. This only happened two days ago." Jett seemed to catch his testy tone. Smiled. "If you remember."

First, he'd wanted generalities, now specifics. Testing her memory, her mental capacity. No doubt, Jett was aware of her visits to a psychiatrist.

"I've been on anxiety medication for ten months." She'd better get in front of the story. "Been trying to cut down, so particulars aren't always easy to recall. Details are … sketchy." She looked toward the door where the woman detective stood. Glanced between Jett and the woman, then looked away. Whatever they were trying to accomplish as a tandem was as useful as a blindfold in a treasure hunt.

When she turned to Jett, his eyes bore into her. Then he smiled, stood, spoke with his partner for a few seconds, and took his seat again.

The woman left the room, letting the door close behind her with a click.

"More coffee?" Jett pointed to her cup, his voice softer.

Zoe shook her head, offered a thankful smile. Great detectives recognized the need for changes and made them. She'd worked with such detectives, won cases with their help. Jett Riker was one of the few.

After a pause and a deep breath, Jett said. "Did Bob Forester say who recommended you?"

"He didn't, but Mr. Pulaski was familiar with my work."

"And you said this Pulaski offered you work independent of the firm."

Zoe nodded then remembered the recording. "Yes." And after a pause. "I haven't agreed to anything."

"Did you call Bob Forester when you arrived, to ask why he wasn't there?"

A pang of guilt cut through Zoe. She should've called. "No," she said. "I did not. The meeting started right away, and the oddity of it all stumped me."

"Oddity?"

"Kip Pulaski brought up things from my personal life, said it was routine to check into the personal lives of lawyers he was looking to hire. Not something I've ever heard of. Clients look into lawyers' backgrounds, like law schools, experience, cases."

"But Pulaski had looked into your life."

"He knew I'm engaged and what my fiancé does for a living."

Jett waited, but Zoe wasn't ready to insert Sebastian and his dark-web workings into the interrogation. He had nothing to do with any of this.

"Did Bob Forester appear to behave differently over the past few weeks or days? Did he mention anything unusual before calling you about the meeting?"

Zoe felt her hands cold against the coffee cup. "No. But again, I was working from home. Didn't have much contact with him."

"Do you know anything about recent cases he was working on? Or any details about the firm, any problems … say things most people wouldn't know."

Zoe tried to read behind the meaning of the question. Jett let nothing more out. "I work on two lease disputes just about solved. Only doing part-time work, so I don't know about any other cases. The firm … nothing big comes to mind."

A shift in posture, then Jett leaned closer. "What did you do after the meeting?" A pause. "I have to ask, but if you …"

"It's okay." The question she dreaded. "I wasn't thrilled with the prospect of working with Kip Pulaski."

"His search into your life made you uncomfortable?"

"Made me unsettled with the prospect of working with him," Zoe said. "That's what I wanted to tell Bob."

Jett motioned for her to continue.

"After the meeting, I called Bob. When he didn't answer, I drove to his house." She swallowed hard. "One of the neighbors said he, or someone, heard on the police scanners that Bob was dead."

Silence. Long, excruciating silence while Jett read the file. The Century City building security had recorded her arrival and departure. Cameras with time stamps showed her entering and exiting. Likely the reason Jett wasn't probing for an alibi.

"And after?"

"I went to see a friend in Laurel Canyon." She waited for a beat. "Larson Fisher."

"For how long?"

"Twenty minutes at most."

"Care to share anything about your conversation there?"

"Larson had worked for the firm, knew Bob, his cases. I wondered if he knew the client I had just met, Kip Pulaski. If he could tell me anything about the man's strange ways. He said no, he knew nothing."

"What happened after?"

She'd wanted to pop pills, pull the blankets over her head, and turn off the world, but too many questions kept her mind going.

"I remembered there was someone else there during my meeting with Pulaski. A lawyer named Shila Diggs. Strange that there had only been one person in an otherwise empty office. She had started working for Bob not long ago. Later that night, I had a message from Larson."

"And?"

Zoe wondered if she sounded like a nutcase to Jett.

"Larson said to call him back, and to be safe out there, but … but he was calling from a different number. Said he was just doing a welfare check."

Jett made lots of notes.

"Tell me what you know about Bob Forester's team."

That question again. "You mean Kim Snyder."

"His entire team. People who worked on his cases."

"His support staff, myself and … Kim Snyder."

Jett waited.

Zoe struggled to remember details. If only she didn't feel so drained. "Bob held routine meetings. His clerk, law student, and his secretary were always there. Shila, the new associate, was introduced a few months ago. The others present were Kim Snyder, and … Larson Fisher, when he worked there."

At the mention of Larson, Jett met her gaze straight on. Narrowed his eyes, waited. She remembered tensions between the brothers in the past, a complicated relationship. One-ups and stare-downs. But she'd never seen that particular look, something close to animosity.

Seconds later, the look was gone. "Did anything seem different about Kim Snyder at the last meeting? Did she say anything out of character?"

"No, but …"

Jett leaned closer, staring, yet allowing her time. Zoe told him about Kim's call. About the invitation to Santa Monica College. Jett held up his hand, made a bunch of notes. Asked her to go over the Santa Monica College visit from the beginning. Down to every person she came across. Known or unknown. Faculty or non-faculty, students, employees. She detailed away and Jett wrote down like mad.

"That why you drove up to the crash scene?"

She stared at the cup and nodded, opened her purse and pulled out a plastic bag. “These were on a knoll, under a tree, some hundred feet from the scene. A cigarette butt and bullet casing. Looked fresh. Couldn’t have been there long.”

There was a twitch at the corner of Jett’s mouth. A stare sharp as a dagger. She couldn’t blame him. In the heat of the moment, she’d touched evidence.

Jett grabbed the bag and held it to the light for some time, then set it aside and wrote some more.

After a long pause, he again asked if she wanted more coffee. Zoe declined.

“The office building in Century City,” Jett said. “Aside from law-firm employees, do you have any other friends in the building?” He read from his notes while changing the subject.

“What do you mean?” Something stirred in Zoe, but she couldn’t say what.

“What I said. Do you have any other friends in the building?”

“Acquaintances. I move around the same people all the time.”

“But not close friends. Say people we consider close enough to ask favors of.”

“I’m not sure what --.”

He held up his hand. “That’s all right. Tell me about the blue folder taken from your apartment. Still the only thing missing?”

She handed him the written statement he’d asked for last night and nodded.

After exhausting the Santa Monica College inquiry, Jett scribbled more notes.

“Did Kim Snyder ever mention a place called Sunken City?”

Zoe searched through her memory. “No. What is it?”

When Jett looked up, his eyes remained unreadable. “Do you know a Levi Duarte?”

The same feeling from a moment ago stirred in Zoe. “Levi, yes. Levi Duarte, the building security guard. Why?”

The moment she asked, Zoe realized her folly. She was here

to be questioned, not the other way around. Maybe that explained the strange look in Levi's eyes. Had he been questioned about Zoe's comings and goings at the office?

Zoe felt drained, almost as if blood was leaving her veins. Empty.

A minute later, Jett closed the interview, reserving the possibility for another one soon. He led Zoe down the hall toward the exit. "Last night, after I left your apartment." He coughed in the uncomfortable way people do when broaching a difficult subject. "I waited for Larson for a long time."

"He left right after you."

An odd apprehension lit Jett's eye. A mixture of doubt and worry.

Jett looked around as if to make sure they were alone and handed her another business card. "Kip Pulaski sounds like a dubious fellow. Would you agree?"

Zoe nodded.

"From my read on Bob Forester, he was a strong, confident man. Not a push over by anyone, including those who tried to challenge him. Not one to implore people."

A flicker of understanding was breaking through Zoe's mind. "Yet Bob almost begged me to take the meeting, something he'd never done before." On the same night Bob was found dead. By the look in Jett's eyes, he was thinking the same.

"Kip Pulaski is one line of inquiry into Forester's death, one that might lead somewhere," he said. "Pulaski gave us an opening that can get us inside his operation, and that opening involves you."

Jett told her his plan.

CHAPTER 22

"A medical research company," Neva said, a folder that looked alarmingly thin in her hand. "Specter Group pushed for relevance six years ago. Ethics watchdog filed a complaint, and Specter retained Grunman and Forester Law. Bob Forester was listed as attorney of record."

Riker opened the file to everything that was not of public record. Six pages. "This is it?"

"Afraid so. After suspension, Specter disappeared, which means big money for big PR firms to manipulate data."

"Manipulate online information?"

"Search engines pick up content based on ranking," Neva said. "Clicks on popular articles sink old info. With blah articles written and repeatedly posted, Specter had enough to sink the past and announce its rebirth. The new beginning."

"Of what? And no one can disappear like that."

"Of what remains to be seen. Need authorization to dig on the disappearing act."

Neva walked to Riker's evidence-board paper wall. She picked up the red marker and spelled out Larson and Zoe, circled the names, added question marks, then wrote: *Specter, private meeting with Zoe Sinclair, hire independent of firm*, and added question marks.

"Lots of red," Riker said.

"The unknowns. Lots happened the night Bob Forester was found dead. Here's what we don't know: the real reason Bob Forester's old client wanted a meeting with Zoe Sinclair."

"Wanted to hire her independent of the firm."

"Here is what we know," Neva said. "Bob Forester called Ms. Sinclair, talked her into taking the meeting."

"Almost begged her."

Neva nodded. "Bob Forester implied he'd be there. She showed up, found Kip Pulaski alone. Went on with the meeting even if things went, as she said, "off track." After, she drove to Forester's house, learned he was dead."

"She was surprised when I asked about any problems at the firm," Riker said. "As far as the world knows, the law firm is doing great."

"Maybe they are."

"That's why they sued to stop us from examining their books?"

"Cranky old bastards want to rule the world."

Riker let the silence take care of the next few minutes, staring at the images forming in his mind. "The bag Zoe gave me from the Kim Snyder scene."

"Evidence in the possession of a civilian for hours, Jett."

"Chain of custody is fucked, but we gotta work with what we have." He drummed his fingers on the desk. "Pulaski is proving hard to track down. His number just rings and rings. The comms department is looking into it."

They stared at the paper with red all over, then Neva's voice cut through.

"Kip Pulaski and his group went dormant," she said. "Then, boom, they're back, and need legal help. Pulaski handpicks Zoe Sinclair, and Bob Forester directs her to the meeting. Not long ago, Forester had a different lawyer in mind. Larson. The second part of the "legal power couple, his protégés." An assumption but, we'll play along."

Riker felt a sigh in his chest but kept it there. He thought of his brother. How the hell had Larson slipped by him last night, outside Zoe's apartment? If he'd left right after, Larson would've used a different door. Had someone picked him up? Had he called a ride?

All that maneuvering to avoid him.

"The Century City guard, Levi Duarte," Neva said. "Obviously he knows Zoe Sinclair. They're social media friends, and his name struck a chord with her."

"Social media friends mean little. Strangers are *friends*."

"Warrants a look," Neva said. "Levi tried to approach you, changed his mind."

Silence.

"Zoe may or may not get into Kip Pulaski's world," Neva said. "His offer is an opportunity, but not without risk."

"No try, no win."

"In the meantime, we need more than six pages on Kip Pulaski and Specter Group. We need authorization to dig, and we need it an hour ago."

Riker stood. "I'll talk to the captain."

Neva set down the marker and cleared her throat.

He knew where she was heading, and God help him. Some things were better left off limits, even between detectives. Even between lovers.

As if probing the plumbs of his brain and reading his thoughts, Neva said. "Good, or I will."

As his partner, she had every right to push. But they were more than partners.

The captain had asked Riker if he was sure about their partnering. He wasn't sure. He'd fallen in love, and that sort of thing made men dumb. A moment of weakness, and he couldn't take back the answer. They worked well, ninety percent of the time, because they knew each other's limits, strengths.

Except now Neva was bent on fucking with his limits.

He faced her like she'd demanded to be faced. "What do you want?"

"To fight for that warrant like you've done before, politics be damned. To stop pretending Larson's name popping up everywhere means nothing. You can't even bring yourself to write his full name on that paper, only an L. To stop treating the relationship between Larson and Zoe Sinclair with too much care."

"Their relationship ended long ago. She's engaged to another man."

"Their friendship. They need to be persons of interest, top of the list. Larson needs to be pounded like nails on a two-by-four."

Yes, he should grind the hell out of his brother. Riker wasn't sure his family would look the same after. Something somewhere would give. He'd do what he had to. He'd been trusted to put aside feelings and do the damn work.

The desk phone rang, startling them. Riker pressed the speaker button, thankful for the interruption.

The department's forensics guy was calling about the numbers found in Kim Snyder's computer. He recited his findings like a machine.

Coat in hand, Neva was at the door. Riker thanked their man, hung up and grabbed his own coat.

CHAPTER 23

The cruiser's tires kicked up gravel as Riker climbed the winding road.

The first number in Kim Snyder's computer was an IP address in the Pacific Palisades. The second was a landline at the same address. Both had been disconnected for months, but their existence meant something.

Kim Snyder had manipulated those numbers to throw everyone off. Why? The property was a tear-down on three acres at the end of a long trail in the Palisades.

Records sent to Neva's phone showed the property had been purchased for three million dollars two years ago and title transferred into a Delaware limited liability company.

No activity since.

Records showed plumbing, electric, and roofing in disrepair. The condition of the house—a 1,700 square foot structure ready to collapse—should've affected the asking price. But it was bought for not one penny less.

Hard to imagine anyone living there, yet an IP address and phone line had popped up. Disconnected now, but the house hadn't been in any shape to offer proper domicile to anyone in need of phone and data lines.

Riker had removed the windshield police sticker and shoved the blue light out of view. Precisely the reason he drove versatile vehicles, to switch between police and regular guy at will.

Whatever the deal at 105 Sunset Canyon, not wise broadcasting his stripes.

At the fork in the road, he followed the sign and veered right. A narrow path led in the desired direction, but not before the trail narrowed again.

After a tight turn, a wooden booth came into view, boasting a sign that read *Private Property Keep Out*. Behind it, there was a chain-linked fence covered by overgrown weeds. Riker couldn't see a house behind the fence.

A chubby-faced man stepped out of the booth, walking toward them.

"Sorry," Riker said, easing to a stop. "Made a wrong turn or two. Do you know where Sunshine Canyon is?"

He'd seen Sunshine Canyon Road way back. Easy to miss for lost folks.

Chubby smiled broadly, sign they weren't the first turning the wrong way up this maze of a canyon. Taking a look in Neva's direction, Chubby smiled broader then launched into an explanation as to how to reach Sunshine Canyon Road.

When the man finished, he tapped the top of the cruiser, ready to say goodbye.

"Hey, thanks a lot." Riker pointed toward the distant fence. "Nice, having private security up here. Who can afford that kindda deal?"

Chubby's smile lost its warmth. He grew stiffer, waiting for Riker to go.

Pushing his luck would spook whoever hid behind the fence under security watch. He'd put the place under surveillance, formulate a better plan before barging in.

On the drive down, silence grew uncomfortable. Sign Neva didn't agree with his turning around.

Just when he readied to speak, his phone started to crackle. "Levi Duarte is on his way," the precinct operator blurted out over the speaker phone.

"Assignments are clear then," Neva said. "You at the station and I handle business here." She glanced in the side mirror.

No need to clarify. Neva would hike back up and find a way inside that property, security be damned.

Riker swallowed back a *be safe* speech. Neva was a cop, a first-class detective with a gun and years of training. She'd hate that comment.

* * *

With reporters swarming the precinct, Riker absorbed the attention while Levi Duarte was rushed through the back door.

Once word got out that "warrants to interrogate individuals of interest" had been issued, the media smelled blood in the water and came pounding. Reporters stood ready to incite riots, screaming out for answers. They shoved microphones and cameras at him. Insisted on the public's right to know, while whispering requests for exclusives and edited-to-his-whim deals.

The media were a bunch of articulate, well-dressed whores.

Bolting through the door, Riker made a straight line for his office.

Century City office logs had been seized, and a brief analysis performed by Forensics. On a rush basis. While experts were working on a full report, Riker knew from experience the main picture would remain. He picked up the report sitting on his desk.

Taking his time down the hall to Interrogation Room 2, Riker scanned the papers. Nodded at the duty cop who opened the door.

Inside, Levi Duarte stood, his back literally against the wall, trying hard for composure.

"Please." Riker pointed to the chair.

Dressed in black—jacket over turtleneck and jeans—Duarte was quite the depressing sight. The look on his face didn't help.

Riker pointed toward the chair again and took his seat, letting a smile play on his lips. Smile and ease of gesture helped. Duarte sat, back straight and eyes fixed on Riker, like a scared boy wanting to appear big.

"Mr. Duarte, we've invited you down here to ask a few questions."

"Do I need a lawyer?"

Scared but not stupid. "Do you feel you need a lawyer?"

"Depends on what you ask about."

"About your job at Tower One in Century City. Tenants, visitors, after-hour access, names entered then crossed off. We're matching fingerprints found on specific parts of logs, unless you tell me it's not necessary."

"It's not. I write on there every day, move papers around, file them."

"How about a specific log where a name was written then crossed off? Only one such occurrence."

"I wrote that name, then crossed it off. Part of the job sometimes."

"Quite forthcoming of you."

"It's not a crime to do my job, is it?"

"It's a crime, and a serious one, to withhold material information from the police."

"I'm not withholding nothing. Here I am. Showed up when called."

True and direct. Yet when Riker had visited the Tower, Duarte looked frustrated, uneasy when he noticed the changed order of logs. The only person close to those logs had been an LAPD Detective, after all.

Then there was Duarte's mention of "that" name in the log.

"What name were you talking about?" Riker asked.

"What?"

"When I mentioned names crossed off logs, your answer was, 'yes I crossed off that name.' Rather specific."

"Pretty sure I said *the* name."

"Would you like me to replay the tape?"

Duarte's eyes widened. An internal battle raged, one he struggled to keep from showing in his eyes.

"Well… I was going to get to that, so …"

"So might as well."

A period of silence was blissfully broken by a blaring phone somewhere.

"Look, Levi, truth is you're here to confirm what we already know." Riker laid his hand on the report. "Don't want to cause you problems, nor do I want to keep you longer than necessary."

Duarte's gaze flickered between the folder and Riker. Words locked within escaped slowly. "No one likes a talker. Not coworkers, bosses, not tenants I became friendly with over the years."

"Zoe Sinclair one of those tenants?" That would explain the social media friendship.

"I met her through Larson Fisher. Friendly young lawyer compared to others."

Riker hadn't expected Larson's name popping up already, fucking things up.

"The others pretty stuck up?"

"They're corporate types, lawyers, most Ivy Leaguers making good money, too busy for chitchats with security guards."

"But not Larson Fisher?"

"Started a few years back after Super Bowl with football talk. I took deliveries up, as a favor. Stopped by to say hello. Little things like that."

"And that name you were talking about earlier …"

"Our rule is to keep logs. But tenants have their own internal rules. They pay boatloads of money, want security, sure, but don't like us overstepping their rules and procedures. Diplomacy's important."

Riker remained silent when the man waited for approval.

"It's not my job to question tenants' policies, strange as they might seem," Duarte said.

"I'll need you to elaborate."

"Zoe Sinclair came in late a few nights ago. I noted her name in the limited-access, after-hours log."

"A few nights ago?"

"Monday … yeah, four days ago. Monday evening."

Riker had needed confirmation that was the same night, and the night of Bob Forester's death.

"Is that routine? Noting names in the log."

"We have limited and unlimited access, depending on tenant's policy. Camera time stamps everyone's arrival and departure, so the logs are mostly for tenants. Ms. Sinclair is on limited access. If she comes in after hours, her name goes on that log."

"Then what happened?"

“According to procedure, I called the office upstairs to let them know they had someone incoming after hours. A second later, I got the call telling me Ms. Sinclair had been moved to unlimited. I didn’t need to call or log her in or anything.”

“Were you told that last part, not to log her name, call or anything?”

“No, but the caller waited for confirmation. So, I said: ‘Okay, I’ll delete her name and note the status update.’ The caller thanked me and that was that. I made a note.”

“Who called about Zoe Sinclair’s status change?”

“Caller ID showed Grunman and Forester, so when he said, ‘calling from Grunman and Forester,’ that was enough.”

“Man’s voice.”

A curt nod, then, “Right.”

Someone had wanted Zoe’s name off the log. Why try to keep her name from showing on security papers?

“You must’ve thought the request strange, since her name was still readable. Crossing it off just attracted more attention.”

Duarte shrugged. “I don’t think the caller realized that. He may have thought it was a computerized log, which we used to have. If deleted soon after entry, the name would’ve been gone.”

The problem with trying to hide the truth was that it always resurfaced.

There were cameras in the lobby, and outside the door. Why worry about a damn log when the cameras had the date stamp and image? Riker didn’t like the implication that those too could be crossed off, so to speak.

“When and where did you last see Larson Fisher?” The dreaded question.

“Came in ‘bout a month ago.”

“You logged him in since he no longer worked for the firm. Right?”

A fake cough.

“Unless,” Riker said, “you got another call with status change.”

Levi nodded. "You asked if all this seemed strange. Okay, yes. But again, not my job to wonder, is it?"

Levi must've wondered when coming close to approaching Riker on the street.

"Tell me about the call on Larson Fisher's status change."

"Man's voice again, Grunman and Forester caller ID. Mr. Fisher's status was updated to unlimited. The only exception, the call came ahead of time, so I didn't log Larson Fisher's name to begin with. Just pinged upstairs."

"A month ago, you said."

"Approximately."

"When Larson Fisher went up, did anyone else go with or before him?"

"Bob Forester, just ten minutes beforehand. Obviously, he didn't need any logging or pinging.

"No one else went up before or after?"

"Not to the twentieth floor, but there had been penthouse access an hour prior, before my shift started. The penthouse is part of Grunman and Forester, but whoever goes up needs a special key code for the elevator. Few people have access."

Riker made a mental note to check who went up to the penthouse. From what he'd seen on reports, one person tended to use the penthouse more than most: Cato Grunman.

"How about when Zoe Sinclair went up Monday evening, when you got the call with her status change? Who else was there?"

"A lawyer and firm visitor. With a bunch of files."

"No one signed in?"

"The lawyer, Shila Diggs, had just been moved to unlimited access. She said the visitor was with her. In that case, we don't bother."

"That why Shila Diggs' name was on the log? Next to Zoe Sinclair's?"

"Yes. I didn't know about Shila Diggs' status change. It must've been something new."

Decisions made in haste were a great way to confuse people.

"Shila Diggs had a bunch of files, you said?"

"She was holding the pile, walking behind the visitor like the help."

"Did you see her leaving, the visitor?"

He shook his head. "It was after my shift, but … I heard they left the same way, files and all."

Interesting that a firm lawyer had escorted Kip Pulaski, hence functioning as a shield. Interesting that they knew each other.

Question was, who'd called security about access? And why? Camera footage would place Zoe in the Tower at that hour, so deleting names was an exercise in futility. Again, he didn't like where his thoughts led. Not the first time, or the last, camera footage would be manipulated to hide something.

"Anyone else at Grunman and Forester friends with security?"

Levi Duarte shook his head, his eyes questioning, then, "Not that I know."

Riker made a note for Neva to look into it. Whoever wanted names off security logs, most likely wanted other evidence gone and may have found someone for the job.

"Is all this going to get back to my work?" Duarte asked.

"Doesn't have to."

Duarte shook his head. He didn't like the answer, and Riker couldn't blame him.

"If it all checks, and if you're not leaving anything important out of your remarks, I'll leave you and your work alone. Okay?"

"Zoe Sinclair was there yesterday." Duarte blurted out.

"She works in the building."

"She actually quit."

Riker kept his cool. Why hadn't he known about this development?

"Also, day before Ms. Sinclair quit, she came in. Was upstairs for a few minutes. Took the emergency stairwell down, twenty stories, on foot. Not unheard of, but strange."

Riker waited.

"Came back down with a folder she almost dropped. I caught it. Read S something U. Couldn't make it all up."

"Blue folder?"

"Possible … not sure." Duarte ran a hand through his hair. "Yesterday, right before she quit, she took the elevator to the penthouse. It's rare that lawyers go up there; it's mostly for partners and clients. But she did, spent some thirty minutes, then went down to 20th floor, the firm's main floor. Then she was gone, no longer a firm employee."

The day Riker had run into her. "Who was in the penthouse when she went up?"

Duarte shook his head again but answered anyway. "Cato Grunman and Larson Fisher."

Larson, again. For a second, Riker debated turning the case over to Neva or telling the captain to get someone else to find and question his brother. But he already knew the captain's answer. Riker could not walk away, much as part of him wanted to do just that. He'd come too far, and Zoe was already on board with the plan.

CHAPTER 24

Wyoming

The Wyoming plains stretched for miles, narrowing only to broaden again. A familiar drive for Zoe, across the changing landscape, where the sun played peekaboo through misty clouds.

The cold and wind and rain never stopped. Neither did the infinite beauty.

Although she grew up here, Zoe was struck by the surreal panorama of prairies and wilderness and the rugged mountains in the distance. Good or bad weather, the view was something to behold.

She'd missed the rain, but more was on the way. Clouds swirled against the evening sky, tumbling like waves. The wind slammed against her rented Jeep. Whispering. *Welcome home, child.*

Mile after mile, she eased her grip on the wheel and pushed past anxiety. Past reawakened memories.

The gravel path unrolled like a carpet of rocks. She'd steered clear of Main Road, keeping a line of trees between herself and scattered traffic. Even when it was late and cold, news of arrivals spread like a blaze through Pine Vale. Not being seen for a while suited her fine.

The familiar road came up on her left. She took it. And there, past lines of pine trees, the old house loomed dark and empty. A frail figure would normally wait by the door, waving.

Mother.

Zoe allowed the image to play at the edge of her mind, but reality intruded.

Mother would never wait for her again.

She forced the mental image gone and drove behind the house, near the back gate. Outside, the wind, carrying the smell of approaching rain, hit hard. Here she was, back home, where memories turned to grief, and sorrow filled her lungs. She took three breaths and counted to five.

"Time to march on," Mother would say.

The back gate gave after a gentle push. Shielding her eyes against scattered sunrays, Zoe unlocked the back door.

Semi-darkness drew her in, engulfing then freeing.

Home, the place once filled with the aromas of baked pies, stood empty and cold. The place she'd known the happiest of times, where laughter still bounced off the walls, too joyous for restrain. Strangely, the darkness comforted Zoe now.

Be strong, my girl.

Pulling the window curtains open, Zoe let the warmth caress her skin. The setting sun lingered out west, filling the sky with streaks of purple and gold. In the distance, the woods she'd explored as a child clung to foliage soon to be stripped by another winter.

Zoe closed her eyes and took a deep breath. Her body had been hollow the last time she'd been here. Now, the feeling of something, anything, was a sensation to relish.

She opened her eyes and glanced left, at the Herod house—a secluded place occupied mostly by Daphne and Nick Herod, mother and son: foreigners in a town uninterested in inclusion. Sebastian's family. Nick's health was deteriorating, his neurologic condition accelerating his mania. He lived a medicated life under his mother's care. A tender-hearted young man who'd been dealt a bad hand by life.

Sebastian could be there, with his mother and brother, or could be driving back from Laramie. She'd planned to arrive alone, deal with the past on her terms. They had much to talk about, she and Sebastian, much to overcome. Yet despite her anger, she'd missed him to the point of pain.

The back door creaked.

Zoe spun, moving away from the window. An approaching shadow stretched against the floor before its owner turned the corner.

"Zoe? You here?"

Dread lifted off her shoulders at the sound of his voice.

Zoe ran for Sebastian. She jumped into his arms and screeched when he lifted her off the floor into a bear hug. She laughed and locked away the tears.

Sebastian put her down but didn't say a word. Just stared, caressing her face. His smile, hidden under days of unshaven scruff, brought a bigger smile to Zoe's face.

"A different welcome than usual," Zoe said. "But I'll take it."

Under his gaze, she broke down a little. "Mother was always waiting by the window." She pressed her palm over Sebastian's, still on her face. "No matter how late. Then she'd go on the porch and wave."

Zoe rested her head on Sebastian's chest, his arm solidly around her. She took in the feel, smell, and touch of him, holding on tight because Sebastian gave the kind of love people wrote novels about. The kind that healed.

* * *

Bundled up on the sofa, Zoe watched Sebastian light the fire. "I'm glad you heard the car," she said. "This silence would've killed me."

"You're home." He looked out the window. "Strange, isn't it? That somehow this also feels like home for me." He looked back to her. "I should want to run after what happened, and never look back, but something about this place pulls me in." He laughed. "Glutton for punishment and all."

"The rugged country sets us right."

"I lived in a city before my parents dragged us here. Never knew how much I wanted an escape laden with rocks and rubble and mountains."

They laughed. "Don't let it steal you away from me."

Nor let the year of secrets do that.

He took her hand. "It's a telecommute world. We can spend more time in L.A., but come visit often."

Zoe squeezed his hand, afraid to voice her thoughts. Sebastian's love affair with Wyoming, in spite of the hell this town had put his family through, scared her. She wanted nothing to do with living here again, and he was smitten with the quiet, slow life, with the scenery.

Love had better conquer all.

They'd only turned on one lamp. The scent of earth and smoke from the fire filled the room, the smell of home everywhere.

"Well," Sebastian said. "Welcome back."

She wasn't going to say it, but the words rolled out. "Had to happen. Can't stay away forever." In her chest, everything felt heavy.

"These feelings are normal." Sebastian's hand was hot on hers. She responded with a gentle rub. Smiled at the smile in his eyes. The same deep, brown eyes she fell for, more endearing than ever.

Despite the stubble on his chin, the kiss was soft.

Nothing felt hurried, nothing felt rushed. They had the entire night, longer if necessary. Every moment was to be savored. Every kiss and every touch fully enjoyed.

When he lay next to her, she shivered at the feel of his hand on her skin, higher and lower, exploring while stirring a wild desire. She slowly stripped off her clothes, felt his hand slide everywhere, scorching her skin, moving in circles and back, as if to an internal, secret melody.

Sometime later, the last thing Zoe remembered before sleep claimed her, was emotional and physical satisfaction. A new high.

* * *

When she awoke cradled in Sebastian's arms, darkness concealed the room, the gleam of dawn distant.

Zoe wiggled and stirred. Untangling from his embrace, she slipped off, threw on a robe, and tiptoed away.

A flip of the switch flooded the kitchen with light. She turned on the stove for tea. Sounds and smells triggered old emotions. She opened the top cabinet, and in the back sat Mother's favorite single malt. Best way to blackout runaway thoughts, if not for the subsequent headache. She took out a teacup instead.

The first light touched the horizon. Sunrise couldn't be far behind, thirty minutes or so. Standing in front of the window, Zoe absorbed the scant light, the vastness—beauty unlike Los Angeles. Unlike any place else.

Normally, Mother would sit here and say something to reach Zoe's heart. Make life better. But *normal* now belonged in the past.

She should call her sister before word of her arrival reached New York. Pregnant with child number three, Angela lived in a different universe; her worries centered on runny noses, play dates, and morning sickness.

Zoe had avoided her sister's world, yet sometimes wondered about its magic. Angela's life was free of dead bosses and strange clients, free of doubts about the man she loved.

She turned when slight movement entered her peripheral.

Sebastian, hair messy and eyes puffy, stood by the door. She tried to smile, but her thoughts must've been scrolling down her face.

His eyes pierced hers, as if trying to read her soul.

"I didn't mean to wake you." She poured water in the kettle and set it on the stove.

Sebastian sat on the kitchen stool. "I didn't want to start with the bad news, but I saw the thing in the paper." He gritted his teeth as if to brace for retort.

"The thing?"

He ran a hand through unruly hair, a hint of impatience in both gesture and voice. "Bob was a great man."

With mention of Bob's name, here in Mother's kitchen, the twitch in Zoe's abdomen became a painful ache. Two solid forces in her life were gone.

"Your work." Zoe opened the drawer, pulled out a tea box. "Still keeps you busy?" After a reunion celebrated with lovemaking, reality was bound to cut through with razor-point precision.

"We signed on two clients." He rolled his shoulders. "One based here in Wyoming. Second operates remotely."

Zoe's desire to broach what felt like a secretive hush proved greater than any need for diplomacy. She'd given him enough time.

"One of those clients … is it named Specter Group?"

The tension in Sebastian's jaw, the flicker in his eyes—she might have missed both if not staring straight at him.

"What do you know about Specter Group?" A rough tone slipped in his voice.

"What do you want me to know?"

He stood, a range of emotions playing in his eyes. "It's not funny, Zoe." The muscles on his face tightened. She'd never seen him so tense.

"Shouldn't you go first?"

"Tell me about Specter." He remained firm, impervious to questions.

"The client Bob had asked me to meet before he died. Man named Kip Pulaski."

Sebastian focused inward, as if running the name through his memory. "Don't know him."

Not the answer she expected. "He *is* Specter Group."

His gaze shifted all over, as if chasing elusive thoughts.

"What's going on?" She leaned against the cabinet, worn out. "Who is Specter Group? Why do they have a file on you?"

Without warning, he walked toward the door then turned back. A reserved look crossed his eyes.

"Correspondence I received last year, soon after moving to L.A.," he said. "Inquiry from some start-up company, some gibberish about looking to hire tech support. I set it aside. Then another envelope arrived by courier delivery. Computer-printed images. Me walking to work, me in the car, at the office. Me in Wyoming years back. The note said there was more."

Zoe stared, feeling her jaw lock.

He paced as he talked. "I met the sender a month later—doctor interested in my brother's illness as research project. He'd learned about the case through Nick's neurologist. Both doctors belong to a medical society where they meet monthly, exchange information. Study patients with comorbid conditions, like Nick's.

Changes in neurologic pathways, disorders feeding on one another, how they grow and expand. They'd wanted to know more, talk to Nick, do scans. A call to that effect had been placed years ago, my mother said no, end of story."

Zoe found her words. "What did they want with you?"

"The name of the medical society is Specter Group," Sebastian said. "Research into neurologic pathways is part of their work."

A period of silence came between them until Sebastian spoke again. "They're an underground organization. Among other things, they offer specialized medical care to those who can't afford it. People living far below the poverty rate, homeless. If they meet the criteria, the patients are referred for care that is never simple. The doctors, all volunteers, are specialists, surgeons. They call themselves 'Helpers of the Needy.' Nothing immoral."

Something clicked in Zoe's mind, a memory that needed sorting out and fast.

"Not immoral but illegal?" Zoe asked.

"They keep an obsessively low profile. Through IT hacks, I found some crumbs. Two doctors were involved in a scandal years ago, when tubes of cerebrospinal fluid were found in their office refrigerator."

Zoe turned off the stove, pulled out a chair and sat. "What does that mean?"

"Claims the fluid was extracted without consent were immediately squashed. Three of those patients, all homeless, died."

"That's a lot more than crumbs," Zoe said, but her thoughts were elsewhere, at a TV news program about disappearing homeless in L.A., a banner at the bottom of the screen that read … 'Helpers of the Needy.'

"Nothing's been proven, no charges brought," Sebastian was saying.

"Oh, dear God." She snapped her fingers. "There's been a side story in the news, in L.A. Homeless people disappearing, something about 'Helpers of the Needy,' but I paid no attention with everything going on."

He looked at her, eyes wide.

"What did the Specter representative say about the fluid?" Zoe asked.

"It was extracted with consent. Blamed the confusion on interns who found the tubes. Eventually, one intern corroborated the story."

"Eventually. And the dead patients?"

"The issue was dropped by the state," Sebastian said. "No relatives came forward. More of my *crumbs* indicated some patients suffered from schizophrenia combined with other mental illness. Like Nick. I could find nothing to substantiate this, because Specter is a private entity with a unique system of firewalls in place."

Zoe tried to make room in her mind for the cascade of information. "What did the man you met want?"

"The group kept a dormant file on Nick. For study and reference purposes. Then the Pine Vale murders happened last year. Our names were splashed all over the news. That brought the Herod family, Nick Herod particularly, back to Specter's attention, and the dormant file became active. This time they decided to dig deeper and use threats."

"They threatened you?"

Sebastian stepped closer and grabbed Zoe's shoulders, as if to keep her from running away. "When my father passed, it was with my help."

"What?" Zoe stirred, but he held tight.

"The heart attack left him on life support, mind gone, heart still beating. With no instructions left by my father, my mother wouldn't pull the plug. She forbade any mention."

Sebastian let go but remained close. "During visits, I became friends with the nurse, a grandmotherly type. She told her husband's story. Wished she'd pulled the plug before he became a devastating memory she'd carry to her grave. In my mother's absence one night, I did what the nurse had wished she'd done, with the nurse's help."

Zoe stared, unable to look away, unable to move.

Sebastian steeled himself and continued. "Time of death was noted, listed as natural, no other details. Our family requested no autopsy. End of story until my meeting with the Specter man."

Zoe couldn't speak. She moved away and this time he didn't object.

Too much, all of it was too much. "Think the homeless L.A. story is related? 'Helpers of the Needy'?"

He shook his head. "Same name."

"You didn't think to tell me about the meeting? About Specter?" She faced him. "Don't say you were protecting my fragile mind."

"My stupid pride insisted I could handle it, tell you after."

A whole year of secrets. The hints had been there, now she could see, in Sebastian's quiet moments, his sudden need to step out right after dinner or before breakfast.

She shook her head, more to her own thoughts than his words. He'd been different for too long. Sure, it was incumbent on him to speak, but she should've seen it, dammit, just like she should've seen Bob's behavior change.

Thoughts of Bob stopped her midstride. "Years back, I worked on the Specter file. They had a different name, an acronym. Bob must've dealt with Kip Pulaski then. On the phone, Bob said it was an old, important client he wanted me to meet." Still so much she had to tell Sebastian.

"I called in big favors among hacker friends," Sebastian said. "Used servers of ill repute. If the name Pulaski was there, it didn't hold enough importance to remember. Not a lot on Specter either, except for the so-called confusion on fluid tubes. Nonsense about *helping* the needy."

This explained Pulaski's mention of Sebastian's hacker friends subjecting those with money to high-tech curiosities.

"They went by SRU back then," Zoe said. "All filings were done under that acronym. Then SRU was dissolved, probably due to pending charges. Now, they want a fresh start under Specter Group. And Kip Pulaski did mention medical research as their focus, but he used glorifying terms."

Anger boiled inside Zoe, but something stronger pushed past anger. Bob was dead, and Kip Pulaski, whom Bob insisted she meet, was part of this monster entity, this secretive group hunting Sebastian.

She tried smiling to ease the tension. They'd have to move past anger for now. Later, they'd figure out if their relationship would survive the twists and turns.

CHAPTER 25

Pine Vale.

Too many feelings Zoe didn't want to feel awaited. Decades of memories she'd made on country roads. Sights and smells so familiar, they knocked her cold. Constant recollections washed past. Images cut in and out between now and then, a mishmash of daydreams and reality.

Climbing the dirt road toward the Herod house, Zoe fell two steps behind Sebastian, unable to shake up a haze of mental images in motion.

She *saw* her late friend Lori—her face translucent. Lori, glancing back with sadness in her eyes. Lori, trying yet unable to look forward, toward a future denied her.

She *saw* Mother smiling, her strong profile reminiscent of the anchor she'd been in Zoe's life.

Stay strong, my girl.

Then Zoe *saw* herself: a career, professionally and financially set but not fulfilled. Last year, fulfillment came close with Sebastian's arrival in her life. But then there were the psychiatric lapses. Life was mostly a numbing existence she'd accepted as routine.

Then something dark, but this Zoe couldn't *see*, only feel.

Something dark had been growing inside her since last winter. A *Gloom*. She'd allowed it, fed it medication, depressing thoughts. She visited a therapist who listened, asked questions, and took pages of notes. Visited a psychiatrist, who prescribed what Zoe needed. Together, doctors and patient spun a punishing wheel.

Pain is not eternal, my girl. Accepting help and love is strength not weakness.

For fear of losing Sebastian, she'd let him help. And help he did, with his usual charm and tenderness of heart. *Gloom* shrank a little. Then a little more.

Now, Sebastian slowed down and put his arm around her as they continued up the winding country road. However stupid, however cliché, love conquered all. And crippling pain, as Mother had said, would not be eternal.

Zoe sure hoped so.

* * *

They had a short visit with Daphne, Sebastian's mother, by far the shortest.

Disquiet crept into Zoe's heart as she watched Nick, Sebastian's younger brother, sit there, mental health declining. His face was a mask held together by medication. Flat, empty eyes.

Near him, Daphne's motherly smile had stopped shining. Doctor Knox helped her cope, but not much more than cope. With new knowledge of Mr. Herod's death, unease reached Zoe's heart, crowding the space. She could barely talk.

Better that way; the visits came easier if absorbed in short bursts.

Zoe and Sebastian left holding hands, flanked by their two hosts. On the edge of the woods, where the Herod house sat, the wind blew wilder than anywhere in Pine Vale. Zoe shivered and swayed a little from the impact of the gust. Sebastian held her hand tighter.

Past the main gate, they all hugged goodbye.

Zoe climbed in the Jeep, avoiding a glance across the road. She'd already said goodbye to her childhood home, despite Sebastian's dreams of dragging her back here again and again. Time to move on.

She focused on Daphne instead, grateful for a bond that had deepened over time. Same with her love for Nick, who'd risked his life when Marshall had held Zoe hostage. Nick, whose courage brought the police to the woods. Because of the way his brain was wired, and with the passage of time, Nick's battle had transformed him into a ghost of his former self.

Still, seeing him had done Zoe good. She knew his heart. In

Mother's words, we all have a song in our hearts. Nick's song thought sad was beautiful.

They slowly drove away.

Low, gray clouds framed the moment. The weather and landscape set the mood from harsh to soft, like a movie reel, then back to harsh. Fresh air aplenty blew through the window, the picturesque view of mountains a spirit riser.

At the final turn, two elderly figures appeared in the mirror, waving goodbye. Zoe allowed herself a smile. Sebastian's mother and Zoe's family doctor were quite the couple. Thank goodness they'd found each other—gentle companions in their old age.

Time passed in silence as Sebastian drove the twisty road.

Better that way. All it took was a reminder of the past for emotional scars to bleed. Time, the metaphorical healer of wounds, did no such thing. Time only created some space to breathe without hurting.

Zoe stole a glance at Sebastian. At his face, creased by wrinkles not evident last year, the lines that framed his face, dark eyes and alluring lips. Sebastian, her love. She'd fight for their future together, but only time would tell their story.

"Ready?" Sebastian asked, killing the silence.

They drove up the incline leading to Lori's farm. The change of direction demanded words.

Zoe nodded, glancing in the rearview mirror at all she left behind. Who knew when she'd be back? Daphne, with Angela's help from New York, would look after the old house.

Pine Vale did not need her.

The Jeep climbed the narrow road toward Lori's farm, grinding from the push.

Lori had lived happy days up here before Marshall—once a friend—had violated her trust with unspeakable acts. Now, the place sat empty, at the mercy of Lori's brother who visited whenever.

Sebastian slowed as he pulled into the large clearing. Came to a stop and killed the engine.

Clouds covered the entire sky now, rendering everything gloomy. Might as well.

Security lights lit the perimeter, but the rest of Lori's farm sat in semi-darkness.

Zoe opened the car door and stepped on dry leaves. She'd craved sunnier days for her visit back to Lori's farm, but it wasn't meant to be.

Sebastian walked beside her in silence. Another reason she loved him, his willingness to tune in to her thoughts, as she tuned in to his. If not for his support and love, she may have never made it back to Lori's farm, or to Pine Vale.

Now here they stood, where it all happened.

The police report had listed Lori's final hours as a brutal struggle—beating and rape. Strangulation. Zoe's overactive mind put the details in a horror film, the ending a question spurred by centuries-old superstitions, here in the land of irrational beliefs: did death come in threes? It had last year: Lori, her boyfriend Corey, Mother.

Zoe's rational mind understood the foolishness of such notion, but the thought persisted.

She cleared her throat. "Remember the police investigation last year?"

Sebastian slowed his pace to hers. "They took their time."

"Pine Vale had never dealt with homicide investigations, but County knew better and still screwed up."

"Screwed up worse, considering your request they step in," Sebastian said. "Had they intervened, Corey might be alive."

Lori's boyfriend, Corey, had been found buried in the woods. Difficult to predict a different outcome, considering Corey had suspected Marshall, but Zoe did request County investigators get involved. She should've forced their hand with legal action.

"Three people gone," Zoe said. "A chain of events started with one murder."

"L.A. is different." Sebastian took her hand in his. He knew where her train of thought was heading and tried to derail it. The Wyoming massacre had started with one murder, one death, not unlike Bob Forester in L.A.

Lori's house came into view, a small structure on an imposing piece of land. Lori's parents had insisted their kids live in a modest house on a large parcel. Enjoy the wild beauty of Wyoming. She'd spent summers running along too, laughing, riding horses with her friend. Living life with untamed passion.

The wind picked up, swirling leaves like toys, as if nature's plan to prepare the land for winter.

Zoe had been thinking about the plan Jett Riker shared with her before leaving L.A. Sebastian's Specter story, and the similarity with the L.A. homeless news story, turbocharged everything. Jett was right, Kip Pulaski had provided an opening with his offer. Today, at the first light of dawn, she'd slipped out of bed and called Jett. Now, she told Sebastian.

She was game for going inside Kip Pulaski's company as a mole.

CHAPTER 26

Los Angeles

Riker pulled the broken wire fence aside and stepped inside Sunken City, a sprawl of broken land on the edge of the Pacific.

If Neva's information was correct, Kim Snyder had visited here before driving off a cliff. Why visit a place claimed by homeless, wannabe artists, and defiant youth, then drive off a cliff?

Sunken City of San Pedro was a reminder of California's propensity for natural disasters. According to records, the landslide of 1929 had turned thousands of acres into a post-apocalyptic world, after the ground shifted eleven inches a day over an eight-year period. Slow enough for some residents to relocate. A few houses were dug out and moved, others fell into the ocean. So, Sunken City was born.

Cliffs, trails, and palm trees swaying in the breeze met Riker's eyes. Seagulls flew in circles. Pipes and broken glass littered the ground. While within the San Pedro city limits, part of greater Los Angeles, Sunken City lay secluded—a world apart from the hustle and bustle of the incorporated city.

Riker stepped over broken slabs of concrete.

Distant guitar strumming reached him, a soft, finger-style tune, pleasant to the ear.

He'd read that starving artists came here to experiment with more than music, while catching sight of dolphins and whales. San Pedro had erected a fence to stop graffiti artists and vagabonds, but soon holes appeared in that barricade. Accidental falls and suicides sent over the occasional patrol car. Most times, the police kept out until residents complained.

The clouds had washed away, leaving the sky clear. Even with the sun dangling in the early-afternoon sky, rain left a chill in the air, but still, a glorious day.

He turned in place. Was the music coming from behind the

boulder with peace symbols scrawled all over, some ten feet away on the knoll?

Circling closer, Riker waited, hoping whoever was there heard steps crunching dirt. No need to spook anyone.

A man in a trench coat circled the opposite way, holding a dented six stringer.

"Hello," Riker said.

The man startled, spun around to leave, then changed his mind. A short fellow, sporting an unkempt beard. Almost swallowed by his coat, he looked in need of a nourishing meal and shower.

His eyes stayed on Riker, alert. "Are you lost, sir?" A gentler voice than expected. "May I guide you on your way?"

The man's brown fingertips betrayed a love for unfiltered cigarettes. Riker dug out the pack of Marlboro he kept on hand just in case. Extra strength.

"You around here often?" Riker took out a cigarette. Tossed the pack to the man, watched him catch it and pull out a cigarette with hesitant fingers.

"Some." Large eyes, set against a dirty face, darted between Riker and the pack.

Sitting on the ground, Riker tossed him the lighter. "I'm Jett."

The man sat on the rock, guitar in his lap. After lighting his cigarette, he set the pack and lighter on the ground. "Felix," he said.

Riker pointed out to the ocean, inhaling tobacco and sea breeze. "Beautiful view you have here, Felix."

Waves tumbled onto rocks, breaking the silence, splashing all they could reach. No need for words out here; the ocean and the wind took care of that, except Riker hadn't come for the scenery.

A cloud of smoke swirled above Felix's head. "Paradise is what this is, a dream, a love song," he said, his gaze distant. "Rolling waves splashing on the beach, seagulls flying over the roaring sea."

The immediate silence unsettled the man, who coughed his shyness in the wind.

"You write that?"

Felix shook his head. "Poetry is one of my loves, but my

talent does not lie with the poetic word. I'm more a songwriter."

"It's the passion that counts."

Silence took care of five seconds.

"You a scribe, sir?" Felix asked.

"Nah. I read some Dylan and Hawkins back in the day. But as a kid, I spent far too much time playing sports." He turned to Felix. "Broke a few bones."

They shared a laugh, allowing the moments to pass.

"The poet once said, 'Law is our fate, Law is our State.'" Felix gave Riker a once over. "You're the law, aren't you, sir?"

Riker laughed. He liked the guy. "I hear good writers are observant."

"The world whispers to us all the time. We need only attend to her sounds."

"Something tells me you attend to the world's sounds carefully." Riker stubbed out the cigarette. "Can I ask you a question, Felix?"

A long sigh erupted from the man's chest. "I've tried shelters, campgrounds. Even a car once. Now, a grotto down near the water, provides temporary shelter." A beat of silence. "But I'll be on my way if the law says."

Riker shook his head. "Not on my account. My question is about a visitor, last week. A woman, five seven, about hundred fifty pounds. Grayish, short hair and big glasses. Likely carried herself with purpose, searching for something or someone. She probably didn't stay long. Not sure if she found what she was looking for, might have left empty handed."

Seconds of silence, then Felix's meek voice again. "I was right. You are the law." A beat later: "Is the law going to right the wrong of our missing people?"

Riker had heard talk of homeless people gone missing downtown, but not in other jurisdictions. "Someone gone missing 'round here?"

"Several and not only here."

"Tell me."

"They vanished, people like me just poof, gone." Sadness

shook Felix's voice. "I know no more." He looked away.

Riker made a mental note to check reports of transients gone missing.

"Tell me about the woman."

"This imaginary woman." Felix strummed his guitar chords. "I shall write a song about her." He turned to Riker. "Out here, sir, we don't talk about visitors because we don't see them. All we do is try to live. Create art and live."

"Call me Jett."

Silence.

"The woman, Felix. She's dead."

Felix's crusty face turned a dirty shade of pale.

"An accident, but the investigation is ongoing," Riker said.

The man's eyes grew distant. "But it wasn't an accident, was it? In the realm we roam, there is no humanity. No rectitude."

"I need you to tell me about her. Promise, I'll protect you."

Felix sucked at his cigarette as if it were oxygen. Took a moment to put out the butt with the sole of a worn boot. "You're right, she was here. You're also right about her looks and demeanor. You're correct about everything except the last part." Felix's gray eyes stayed on Riker's unblinking. "She didn't leave empty handed."

Riker let Felix work out the story at his pace.

"I stayed hidden," Felix said. "But I saw her walk up and down, looking for something, flailing her arms for balance. She went down the path, toward the ocean, stayed there ten minutes or so, climbed back and stopped to catch her breath. But not empty-handed. On her way out, she was holding a small brown bag."

"Wait. Backup --"

"It's all I know. All I saw."

A distant laughter spooked Felix. When Riker turned to search, it was all it took for Felix to be gone.

Goddamn.

From atop the bolder, Riker could see Felix zigzag down the path toward the beach below. He should give chase, but if the homeless man didn't want to be found, that'd be the end.

Riker got part of what he wanted—confirmation of Kim Snyder's visit here.

Urgent business awaited now, a meeting with Captain Caruso for talks around his plan with Zoe Sinclair.

Pulling a business card out of his coat pocket, he wrote then placed it snugly inside the cigarette pack. He stuck the pack under the bolder, allowing one corner to be visible. With some luck, the message would get through to Felix.

CHAPTER 27

With a hell of a caseload and the election year ending, politicians were running department bosses like Captain Caruso ragged with demands.

For Riker, the worst part about the meeting was the wait. Usually, he made up excuses and skipped meetings. His solve rate allowed that luxury.

Not today.

Captain Caruso pressed for immediate answers on Bob Forester. The victim's high-profile and 'inconclusive manner of death' fast-tracked the case. Officially, the police statement read 'we wait for facts, don't jump to conclusions.' Unofficially, the Bob Forester case was termed 'homicide.'

Summoned to the Police Administration Building, Riker spent the better part of the day waiting. At least the cappuccino machine was first class, the coffee superior to the burnt brew at the precinct.

The view from the top floor of the Police Administration on First Street, just south of City Hall, didn't disappoint either. The captain occupied an office here on a temporary basis—some political maneuvering by the police chief to alter the chain of command if gossip held true. Caruso was on fast track for the next chief job.

Riker didn't want to understand the political machinations. Didn't care.

Pacing in the waiting room adjacent to Captain's office, Riker looked out at the City Hall structure. A Great Hall, some called it, and sure it looked grand—a thirty-two-story building faced with gray California granite and terra cotta, the most popular façade materials in 1928, when erected. A building to be admired, decorated with a tower and beacon. Or to draw attention from the dirty political tricks going on within its walls.

Diplomacy, they called it, and today Riker had to display some. Speak a little, listen and agree a lot.

With the media not getting inside information, reporters force-rolled the story, slinging mud and pointing fingers at City Hall and an 'inept police force.'

When Riker called Caruso about the plan—which Zoe had found intriguing—the captain was in no rubber-stamping mood. He required endless explanations, in person, but could carve out no more than ten minutes between phone calls and meetings to listen. So, when given time, Riker spoke fast until Captain was whisked away. Then Riker waited, as told. Did some work via phone and waited some more.

With Neva unable to crack the Pacific Palisades guard, Riker had two choices. Storm the Palisades property, warrants ablaze, and lose the element of surprise, or wait and watch from afar while working the Zoe-Specter angle.

Riker refilled his coffee cup, recapping what he had so far.

Tony Forester had a weak alibi for the night his father had died. He was on camera bumming a cigarette at a gas station, thirty miles away. In theory, Tony could've gotten in a car, reached his old man's house, and entered without being caught on camera. Not impossible, but hell of a stretch. For now, that theory was on hold.

Riker had two other angles in the Bob Forester case. Get his hands on paperwork the Grumman and Forester firm didn't want seen, and lawyers were working on that, or work the Specter angle. Kip Pulaski asking for a meeting with Zoe the night of Forester's death was a hell of a coincidence—or not. Soon after the meeting, Pulaski pulled a fast one and disappeared. But he'd given them a gift by offering Zoe a job at Specter Group. One she wanted to take as a mole.

For that, Riker needed the captain.

When the chamber door flew open, Captain Caruso rushed out followed by a short man rumbling about political endorsements. Caruso marched into his office, motioned Riker in and held up a hand. The man halted his salvo and stared at the intruder.

From behind his desk, Caruso leveled his gaze at Riker. He'd put on more than a few pounds, but stress made his inset eyes appear malnourished. His dark skin accentuated the circles around his eyes. Although in a nice suit, freshly starched shirt and a haircut so short it looked penciled on his skull, Caruso appeared caught between this world and that of zombies. No sleep in his past, likely none in his near future.

"Listen, Riker," Caruso said. "Your plan is bad with a taste of awful." He seemed to agonize over his words. Shook his head. "But the Specter bunch, they sound awful with a taste of sickening. Picking between the two wasn't easy."

"I understand --" Riker said, or tried to.

"You don't. That's why I'm making the decision, and it's a tough one."

The silence pounded against Riker's temples. Specter Group had given them an opening. Too many dots connected Specter and Kip Pulaski to Bob Forester and Kim Snyder, the woman whose manner of death was under review, same as Bob Forester's.

The Grunman lawsuit challenged the validity of the court order, and the judge issued a stay, pending a look at papers LAPD wanted examined. A delay, but one he couldn't afford.

"You have forty-eight hours." Caruso's deep voice echoed a graveled rasp.

"Thank you, sir."

Caruso pressed both palms on his desk. "That's not a lot of time. Go out and make something happen because if you got nothing in that time frame, Zoe Sinclair gets pulled and deal's off. If it goes wrong, I'll spend days, maybe weeks, answering questions, but if it goes right, you're golden."

They would be golden.

Riker nodded and hurried out, but Caruso's baritone stopped him in the doorway.

"Riker, be sure Zoe Sinclair is protected, and do something about that house in Pacific Palisades."

Caruso's stare warned Riker against creating a mess. He'd apologized too many times for breaking rules on his way to solving cases. For letting Caruso bear the brunt of criticism from politicians and the media.

Riker almost felt sorry for the captain.

CHAPTER 28

The drizzle worried Hawke. The road kept winding deep into Pacific Palisades, his truck struggling on the steep drive. He could barely see in the darkness outside.

He forced his foot on the accelerator.

This was hardly his idea of the Palisades—more a retreat than urban town. He'd driven up before but on the other side, where Spanish Colonial Revivals and Mid-century modern masterpieces designed by who's who in architecture sat atop crests overlooking mountains and the ocean. This backbone road, climbing high into Topanga State Park, diverged from the place he knew. Still the Palisades, but remote. Secluded.

Hawke listened to sounds as he drove—the engine grunting from exertion, grating of tires, slush of wipers. Nothing out of the ordinary. On the positive side, darkness and isolation were his allies tonight.

He sure needed something on his side.

He was flying solo after calls to Big Shot went unanswered. The compromised job left one option: flee. Except a better option had presented itself.

Some time back, when left alone with Big Shot's mysterious laptop, Hawke had snuck in monitoring software. Remotely installed a keylogger and watched when Big Shot logged on, which was rare.

Big Shot was quick to sign off. But at long last, the keylogger had captured the coveted password. Tonight, it pinged. Hawke had to work fast during the short window when Big Shot was on, but he got inside the secretive laptop.

He'd discovered a file named *Hospes*.

His own copy made and saved, Hawke learned *hospes* could've meant *hospitality* or *stranger* in Latin. No image or name of any stranger in the file, only the picture of a dilapidated dwelling on a large parcel in the Palisades. A grainy image, and below it, information indicating a Delaware LLC owned the place. A local company served as agent for service of process. Nothing more.

Hawke was familiar with Big Shot's holdings. He'd checked. The man owned property in California under a trust. *Hospes* read like a scheme designed to cloak the true owner, with extra layers of documentation and complications in place. It was a Delaware LLC owned by a Colorado LLC owned by a Nevada LLC owned by a corporate trustee of a trust. Not an undiscoverable shell, should someone file a lawsuit, but difficult and costly to peel back ownership layers.

Which begged the question: Why go through all that trouble for a dilapidated structure on a neglected piece of land at the end of a winding, arduous-to-climb road in the Palisades?

A curiosity Hawke couldn't dismiss after Big Shot's strange behavior, and his increasingly stranger physical appearance.

The drizzle turned to mist. Hawke switched off the wipers, appreciating the silence.

Hospes was not a popular destination. Traffic had diminished miles back, then become nonexistent. Up ahead, a sign announced the road would narrow yet again.

Hawke checked the map taped to the dashboard, running his finger over the lines. He was on the right path. Continuing on would lead to his destination, but simply showing up defined stupidity.

He pulled off the trail. The drizzle had settled, and dirt turned to grime. Hiding the truck between oak trees, Hawke stepped out.

Time for a trek.

* * *

After a short climb using low branches as handholds, the slope tapered off to an even trail. Fog hung overhead, ready to descend and engulf Hawke.

The dim flashlight provided enough light for guidance, the knife in his backpack and Colt in his belt enough reassurance. Mind and eyes alert, Hawke continued along the zigzagging trail. An easy walk, even in the dark.

He'd spent many summers camping with his family. His father, an avid hiker and naturalist, had sought out remote areas along rough terrain. Or so it seemed to Hawke. He'd hated sleeping in tents, traveling for miles only to find another camping site. But his past had instilled precious navigation skills no book could teach, no GPS could substitute. Using path tracks, linear features, and a basic map proved enough to blend in to the woods.

No tracks ahead. He was alone out here. A run of the flashlight showed the trail continuing on in the fashion shown on the map, so Hawke kept on tracking, like in childhood. Only with a purpose.

Thinking back on those early years, no wonder he'd never grown close to his parents. They were an item, his mother and father, in love and into each other. Amazing they'd bothered having kids. Hawke and his brother were but secondary thoughts, two smaller beings that happened to live in the couple's proximity. His parents led their lives discussing nature, the making of the universe, their love. If the kids cut in, their random curiosities were dealt with expeditiously. More than once, Hawke had walked in on passionate kissing or joyful laughter cut short by his entrance.

His brother, eight years older, was more like an uncle than sibling. They had nothing in common. Had they been closer in age, they could've been best friends, but their parents hadn't bothered making that happen. Maybe they tried, who knew? Family conversations about anything consequential were nonexistent.

The dirt path narrowed, the tree line thinning. In the immediate distance, an opening came into view.

Hawke saw lights over a booth some fifty yards away. He couldn't see inside the booth, but given its existence and lights, he assumed someone was there. At least one guard, maybe two. More would not fit comfortably.

Not that it mattered. He wanted no encounters.

The blaring lights provided enough illumination to see barbwire twenty feet away. The perimeter of *Hospes*. And not far past, a shadowy outline—the dwelling from the grainy image.

No barking dogs came running. No alarm. Sign he hadn't been detected.

Crouching, Hawke watched near and far. No cameras anywhere he could see, no tripping wires. Barbwire and humans hardly seemed enough security. If more awaited, judging by the lax look so far, it wouldn't be much. The best security was the hidden, hard-to-find location.

He'd have to circle around and through thick bushes to avoid the guard booth. Only barbwire would then separate him from the dwelling.

Crouching lower, he followed the perimeter, away from the booth and security lights. Stopped only to refill his lungs with air. Continued. Again and again for a good hundred feet, until the booth was out of sight, light covered by foliage and distance.

At the next clearance, he sprinted to the barbwire. Retrieved the cutter from his backpack and sliced through.

Calculating every move, Hawke crossed in. Tentatively. Keeping to the ground. Past the wire, he took off running toward the building. Reached it fast.

Hawke pressed his back against the cold wall. Silence surrounded him, and the sound of his heartbeat. Ten seconds passed, then ten more.

He made his way to the first window. Shapes of furniture entered his eyesight. Corners, edges.

He switched the flashlight from low to medium. Caught sight of bunk beds. Rows of them, but nothing else. No sheets, no pillows, just thin covers. Judging by the protruding outlines there appeared to be curved, motionless bodies there.

Dead people?

A minute passed, or maybe longer, until he noted movement. No, not dead. One occupant stirred, then another. No one got up. No one kicked off the cover. No one cried loud enough to be heard.

What the hell was this place?

Hawke made his way around the building, searching for more windows, a better look inside. Found only a back door locked solid.

He circled to the front again. Something at the top of the building caught his attention. A sign. He flashed the light and read:

Gratissimum Hospitalitatem. And below it: *Welcome to Hospitality.*

Hell if anything felt remotely hospitable.

No other soul stirred around the property. No caretaker or watcher minding those poor souls locked in that nasty room, in this guarded ramshackle hidden behind barbwire at the end of a long, winding road on the wrong side of the Palisades. A piece of property buried beneath layers of title in Big Shot's computer, in a file called *hospes*—hospitality.

Some macabre joke.

Hawke sucked in cold air that made everything inside ache.

The lingering mist had long vanished. The November moon lit up the Southern California sky. Any night, he'd call the sudden atmospheric change new hope. But the world had shifted under his feet. The urge to find Big Shot and demand answers forced its way into Hawke's heart, too powerful to quash.

CHAPTER 29

Zoe stepped out of the cab, grateful for the sunny day. Malibu, a uniquely Southern California town named after the Himaliwu tribe, welcomed her with blue skies and warm sunshine. It was balm for the soul after Wyoming's twenty-degree temperature, and wind chill that made it feel like negative one.

The address on Kip Pulaski's business card belonged in Malibu, off Pacific Coast Highway and steps from the ocean. A world apart from the shabby side of Santa Monica where they had coffee. This was a glass-and-marble building in an affluent area.

No surprise. Pulaski's persona defined affluence. And shadiness. To her message, he'd simply replied with a time and place: today and this address.

The cabbie peeled away after she handed him three twenty-dollar bills. Driving on Pacific Coast Highway held no appeal. She was too old fashioned to download a ride app.

Now, here she stood with no one's blessing but Jett's. Sebastian didn't like the plan. Too dangerous, he'd said. Maybe, but she was a grown woman who made her own decisions. Trust was still a fragile bond, difficult to mend after a year of his secrets. But Sebastian had returned with her to Los Angeles. She'd promised herself to try and trust again

Past marble steps, the double doors seemed to sense her rush. A young woman stood in the middle of a circle-shaped granite counter. She smiled wide and pointed toward a golden elevator.

Above the girl, a sign read, *Gratissimum Hospitalitatem*. Beneath the large letters, in smaller script, the English version: *Welcome to Hospitality*.

Interesting name choice.

Ten seconds later, the elevator door opened to the third floor and a rectangular entryway adorned with paintings below spotlights.

Here she was, deep inside a brick-and-mortar company that

had somehow managed to leave hardly an existential footprint in the virtual world.

Specter Group.

She followed the signs to a corner office with 180-degree ocean views.

A woman, somewhere around middle age, stepped forward. "Welcome to Specter Group." A practiced smile. "My name is Gwen."

Tall and slim, with blonde locks falling down her back, Gwen wore a silk blouse over knee-length skirt. With no handshake forthcoming, Zoe nodded and forced a smile.

"You'll be using Kip Pulaski's office in his absence." Back ramrod straight, Gwen clasped her hands regal style. Her deliberate smile and speech were complemented by an inquisitive look, hinting at more brainpower than the blonde curls suggested.

"Nice view." Zoe motioned toward the window.

Gwen maintained her reserved stance, showing no interest in small talk. "The introductory file is on the desk," she said. "Information about the company and a list of telephone extensions. Read at your leisure. I'd be happy to answer questions before the meet-and-greet."

"With?"

"Mid-management."

Zoe wondered why not higher management but kept that thought to herself.

"Should you need anything," Gwen said, curiosity playing in her eyes, "please use the extension list and buzz me."

Gwen excused herself and sauntered away, pulling the door behind her.

So much for a warm welcome.

Zoe took in the imposing mahogany and leather clashing with the easy-breezy view out the window. No artwork adorned the walls. No personal effects or photos. Maybe they'd been removed before her arrival, the art hung elsewhere.

She turned toward the desk where the file sat waiting. Something caught her eye in the peripheral view. A bookshelf, empty of books, in the darkest corner. A framed photo pushed back that looked like the shot of a woman, cradling something. Difficult to say from the distance, but the woman's angular features and poker-straight hair reminded Zoe of a movie star. Not a studio shot, something spontaneous.

There was a reason the photo sat there, hidden from immediate view. But she'd heed Jett's advice, not appear curious. Best to strive for nonchalance, as if reporting for a job. Jett insisted she'd be monitored. Was probably being watched right now.

Sitting on the leather chair behind the desk, back straight as if to obliterate nerves, Zoe opened the file. A piece of paper slid out and fell to the floor. She reached for it and nudged the bottom drawer open. Nothing there, not even a speck of dust. The rest of the drawers looked the same. Cleaned out.

Nothing but pages of hype in the folder—Specter described as a fresh research organization ready to change the world with medical breakthroughs. The words *story* and *us,* appeared in every other sentence. Nothing about *objectivity, fairness*. No facts.

The Fundraising page drew her attention. It listed hundreds of thousands of dollars, totaling millions, without names of donors. She scanned through more pages until one paragraph stood out. It referenced *tube fluid*, then unintelligible technical terms.

Same words Sebastian had mentioned about Specter's past. The page read, *Questions re: origin of cerebrospinal fluid found in medical office refrigerator*. A developing story Specter Group was working on for publication, but no names of authors or sources. More hype followed, then lists of department extensions with three names, Gwen and two others.

She was being handled. Put on a leash.

Slamming the folder shut, Zoe jabbed the intercom. "I'm ready for the meeting."

* * *

Gwen stood in the doorway, a dour look on her face. "As a rule, I answer questions before we call meetings."

"New management, new rules." Zoe leaned back on the chair.

"Preparing you, Ms. Sinclair, is my responsibility."

"Gwen." Zoe tapped her right thumb on the edge of the desk. "Call the meeting or I will."

Silence moved over them. Clearly, Gwen didn't appreciate the tone.

"By the way, there are no names of donors here, and only three extension numbers." Zoe placed her palm on the file. "I'll need new lists within the hour."

"I'll have to run that by --" Then abrupt silence.

Zoe leaned forward. "If my request is unclear, let's call Kip Pulaski before we go further."

Gwen pushed back her shoulders.

Zoe would work with intransigence. Not the first time.

"Good, I'm glad we agree." Zoe leaned back. "The meeting starts in fifteen minutes."

Gwen opened her mouth to speak, but once again, thought better, turned and marched away.

Damn shame friendship was off the table. Having worked in a patriarchal culture her entire professional life, Zoe had always gravitated toward women in her field. May have been a simple case of survival, or appreciation for like-minded individuals who'd chosen to work in a mostly masculine environment.

Standing, Zoe pulled the hem of her waist jacket, a last moment addition over a V-neck shirt and black jeans. A semi-professional look Gwen would likely term casual. She pushed a few strands of hair off her forehead and headed out the door.

A beige door adorned the end of the hallway. The only other access point besides her office and the elevator.

Zoe reached the door and pushed it open. A risk, but she'd studied the blueprint and floor plans with Jett. Saw no cameras in hallways. Exploring Kip Pulaski's office, any office, would be a risk, but familiarizing herself with the rest of the place, one she was supposed to be running, in whatever form, well, she hoped that'd ring no alarm bells.

Past the beige door, a tunnel-like corridor opened up with bright carpet reminiscent of Vegas casinos. The hallway led uphill, like a ramp. It dead-ended at a set of double doors.

Away from the blue seascape scene of ocean waves, the space felt confining.

Zoe pushed past tension pooling in the pit of her stomach.

She turned and discovered an elevator. Or a freight lift. She pushed the Up button, and wheels ground somewhere within the building. A thud announced its arrival then doors opened inside a narrow, two-person elevator. Not a freight lift.

Relax now.

Inside, she took measured breaths to fend off the feeling of being trapped. A single button protruded from a metal panel. Of course, there was no Up, only Down. She pressed it, and the elevator dropped a tad then began descending.

Zoe took quick breaths as her ears popped. The main level shouldn't be more than a ten-second descent, but the elevator kept plunging into the bowels of the earth. There must be a garage, but she remembered cars parked at street level. No Stop or Emergency buttons. She wiped sweat off her forehead, searching for solutions, when the elevator halted with a thud.

The doors opened to a curved corridor. A slant of light spilled from around the corner.

More quick breaths and hesitant steps.

The stuffy air pressed against Zoe's lungs. There was a smell she couldn't quite place. Something heavy, like being at the dry cleaners—steam, solvent, and a myriad of things hard to identify.

She turned the corner and coughed. A semi-opened door twenty feet away slammed shut. Was it a draft that caused it to shut or a person? Hard to imagine a draft in this suffocating space.

With the source of light gone, darkness swamped everything.

A clicking sound reached her. A lock turning, but where? Someone behind the shut door would be the rational explanation, but the sound bounced off the walls, echoing, hard to pinpoint.

Stumbling toward the door, Zoe felt the wall for plaques. Found nothing listing what or who was on the other side.

The thick air spurred a cough hard to repress. After some air found its way back into her lungs, she closed her eyes.

Slowly, she stumbled through the dark, slanted corridor back to the elevator, and, in what felt like forever, she reached the top level.

* * *

The sun setting over the ocean splashed the sky with vibrant colors.

Zoe didn't have to look out the window to appreciate the show. It covered everything in the office.

The open space radiated with light—a welcomed sight after her basement journey.

From behind her new desk, she listened to the dark-skinned man named Dion. He sat facing her, his back to the window. The second man, an older, paler fellow who'd introduced himself as Lou, sat in the middle flanked by Dion and Gwen.

While Dion droned on about Specter Group turning a new leaf, Gwen stole glances at Zoe. When Dion stopped, Lou spoke about filing reinstatement papers for Specter. In less than twenty minutes, they said everything they came to say.

"Thank you, gentlemen," Zoe said. "Who can tell me what led to the company's suspension?"

Dion's lips stretched into the semblance of a smile. "It was before my time."

"That's a legal issue," Gwen said, "for lawyers to handle. They have the files."

Clearly, Kip Pulaski hadn't told Gwen the extent of Zoe's responsibilities. Or who she was.

"I know the file," Zoe said. "I *am* one of the lawyers who worked for Specter seven years ago. I'm interested in the non-legal aspect."

Gwen stared at Zoe with borderline aversion. She did not appreciate being blindsided.

Zoe fixed her gaze on Lou. After some shifting, Lou said, "As you know, it pertained to an ethical issue. One of Specter's representatives misspoke."

"Misspoke on an ethical matter," Zoe said, and Lou nodded.

"I don't see the relevance to what we're doing today," Gwen said.

"Was it a research expert, the person who misspoke?" Zoe ignored Gwen, and again Lou nodded.

The file Pulaski had given Zoe was empty of details. The Grunman and Forester files, sent to storage, were unavailable upon request. So, Zoe worked from what she'd gleamed off the stolen file, her shaky memory, Sebastian's story, and bits Jett Riker had pieced together.

Not much.

Gwen strolled to the window. "Can we return to the matter at hand, which is reorganizing Specter Group?"

"The research expert," Zoe continued, "was introduced as medical doctor, but upon inquiry, it came to light the so-called expert was no doctor at all."

Gwen stepped closer, stopping behind Lou.

Zoe pinned the man with a fierce look. "The so-called doctor had never finished medical school, never done residency, but was somehow brought on by Specter to discuss medical issues."

"Ms. Sinclair …" Gwen again.

"We're on the same team." Zoe took a moment for Gwen, before continuing with Lou. "The expert spoke about research on cerebral fluid. About being in possession of test tube fluid, possibly obtained illegally, something Specter had previously denied. If true, however, where would the cerebral fluid have come from? Million-dollar question. When pressed, the expert folded, and the story was amended. That about right?"

Complete silence.

Both men knew who the boss was, despite Zoe's sitting behind Kip Pulaski's desk. No one was willing to confirm the bits Sebastian had found about three dead-homeless and the possibility cerebral fluid had been extracted without their consent. The same fluid found by an intern who later withdrew the report.

Around here, that was closely guarded information.

"An error." Gwen's voice boomed through the room. "The

expert was working from defective data. After, Specter improved the expert-selection criteria."

Afterward, the original entity had been dissolved, fines paid plus hold time met, and a new entity was about to be born from the ashes. One meant to hide its predecessor's past.

Kip Pulaski had mentioned medical breakthroughs, stem cell research, but to what end? They could've folded and walked away, been done with the legal headaches. Instead, Specter was back in business again.

When the silence stretched longer than comfortable, Dion and Lou stood.

"I'll have the reinstatement papers ready for your review and signature," Dion said.

"Thank you, both." Gwen waved her hand, dismissing the men.

Zoe leaned back in the chair. Outside, the sun sunk into the ocean, and colors splashed on the horizon.

"Let's start again," Zoe said, after the door closed behind Dion and Lou. "I'm Zoe Sinclair. Please call me Zoe."

No words from Gwen. Only an assertive stance from a woman used to holding the upper hand. Her dominance had been on display all along.

Was she trying to figure out Zoe's game, or had Gwen simply bought Zoe's story?

With Jett's blessing, Zoe had accepted Kip Pulaski's offer to reorganize Specter Group and handle internal problems. In a show of gratitude, Pulaski had promised information on Sebastian's file, but nothing had come yet. Stonewalling, of course.

The real question was: why did Kip Pulaski really hire Zoe? Anyone could've reorganized Specter, a first or second-year lawyer after a good read through the file.

"You don't want me here, I understand," Zoe said. "I'm not crazy about being here either."

Gwen stepped in front of the window, the fading light illuminating her like an apparition.

"I was against an outsider coming in. You're right."

Zoe waited for the dam to breach.

"Kip insisted," Gwen said. "So here we are." Gwen clasped her hands in front of her.

Kip. Not Mr. Pulaski, nor Kip Pulaski. To Gwen, the man was Kip.

"Well, I'm here. Let's work together."

Gwen scoffed. "There are rules. Making selected information and management available is how it starts."

"Is that what you call Dion and Lou? Management."

"Excuse me?"

"They work under your watch, Gwen. Under *your* rules."

A cold smile spread across Gwen's lips. "On the subject of rules," she said. "The basement is off limits."

So, she knew. Like Jett said, there would be surveillance.

"Tell me about the basement room, Gwen. Is that a lab down there? Kip Pulaski mentioned clinical trials of stem-cell therapy research. And I read enough to come across damning information about illegally obtained cerebrospinal fluid."

"Rumors, trade envy." Another scoff. "No other comment, and that's final. While I had no choice but to agree with Kip, you're here to reorganize and bring Specter in good standing under the law. I'll provide information and put staff at your disposal, but only for that reason."

Zoe pointed to the desk phone. "Dial Kip Pulaski."

A storm raged in Gwen's eyes.

"Full access, full files, or I walk," Zoe said. She had to navigate the game with care. Not push too hard. Not be overly compliant. Creating tension might reveal some of Gwen's cards.

The storm in the pale blue eyes gave way to new light. "I don't think so. You want information on your fiancé, don't you? And we have part of your compensation ready for you."

Bribe and blackmail. Zoe would not touch their money.

Something stirred inside Zoe, but she pushed past it. "Kip Pulaski knows information on my fiancé is part of the deal."

Gwen stared with the look of the hunter trying to decide

whether to pounce. She'd been in control, just playing a scripted role. She'd never given her full name. Sat through the meeting with Dion and Lou. Signaled them when to talk, when to shut up. Played the disgruntled role. For all Zoe knew, she'd done exactly what Kip Pulaski wanted.

Gwen blocked the view—as if to say she controlled even what Zoe saw out the window—arms crossed, shoulders straight. Like a boss.

Zoe felt it. Nothing more than a gut feeling, but a strong one. Whoever Kip Pulaski was in this game, Gwen was either his superior or making a strong play for that role. In all likelihood, she *was* Specter Group.

CHAPTER 30

The paper Gwen set on the desk announced an event in two days.

"A soiree for donors and medical experts," Gwen said. "Specter's reinstatement will be announced during the soiree."

"Who will announce it to whom?"

"It will all be revealed in time."

"Where is Kip Pulaski?" Zoe asked. "What is your role here?" Pushing buttons, but she hadn't come for fun and games.

Gwen sighed. "Please make sure all paperwork is filed on a rush basis. After your review and approval, of course."

"What if the FCC denies reinstatement, particularly on a rush basis?"

"We met all reparations and hold times. No reason for denial."

Government regulators worked at different speed, requirements were adjusted. Of course, there were always back doors to everything.

"What am I, a front? Reputable firm lawyer, here to inspire confidence among rank and file, experts and donors?"

Gwen just stared.

Zoe stood, stepped behind the chair and pushed it back. Though the heels she wore hurt her feet like hell, she was glad to stand two inches taller than Gwen.

"Work relationships, Gwen, are based on trust. I don't mind operating as your cover under one condition."

No answer, just the piercing stare.

"You could've hired any lawyer. Could've picked from eager associates at Grunman and Forester. You've picked me, for whatever reason."

"Your knowledge with the case."

"Bullshit. Any lawyer could've gained that knowledge." Zoe crossed her arms. "I want to know who the expert who *misspoke* was and I want the file on my fiancé first thing tomorrow morning on this desk."

"Or what?"

The words rushed out before Zoe could pull them back. "Or I start digging into everything here. I'm trained and ready to do just that."

Conflict revealed people's hearts when the moment of truth arrived. The forced smile at the corner of Gwen's mouth never reached the rest of her face.

Then the look was gone, replaced by something softer.

CHAPTER 31

Riker felt a prickling sensation, an itch under his skin. Like a trigger had been squeezed inside his psyche.

Something was wrong.

Sitting in a café, steps from Malibu Surfrider Beach, he had the distinct impression someone was watching.

The Psychic Staring Effect came to mind. A psychological analogy on detection by extrasensory means: people in large crowds could *feel* someone staring at them from a distance. A theory explored in 1898, updated many times. Required reading in his profession, but not his cup of java.

Riker erred on the side of realism. But, hey, to each his own.

Today, however, he might have to eat crow. There were eyes on him.

Sipping his coffee in the Malibu café, Riker studied patrons above the rim of his sunglasses. A group of women in yoga pants. Youngsters sipping whipped cream beverages, laughing like people did when absorbed in their own shit. Couples meandering outside on the walkway, admiring the multicolored sun smudges above the water. Surfers in the distance. On the sand, a lanky man in tie-dye shirt chatting up a woman who looked high.

Nothing alarming, just beach tranquility. Maybe too tranquil a setting for a man used to mayhem. Maybe he was going nuts.

No. Something was wrong.

A text from Zoe lit up his phone. *Look up Gwent Stone. She's THE BOSS here.*

Riker dialed Zoe, who must be done with Specter.

"Change of plans," Riker said, when the phone clicked on. "Meet me at Zen Place in Malibu. Know where that is?"

Zoe answered in the affirmative. The connection fizzled then a masculine voice spoke in the background.

"Who's that?"

"Sebastian."

Larson's competition.

"I didn't drive today." Zoe explained Sebastian's presence.

"Zen Place in twenty minutes." Riker disconnected. Took time strolling to his Escape.

He'd donned beach attire—hoodie and cut-off jeans, cap and sunglasses. The outfit couldn't have given him away. Then what?

Reaching the Escape, he took his time opening the door. No suspicious faces or dubious activity. But that was the point of undercover work: don't be made out.

* * *

Riker hung a turn, then another, onto Pacific Coast Highway. He sped past two cars, changed lanes, then slowed to regular traffic speed.

A glance in the rearview mirror showed no tail. Yet, the sense of having been watched stayed with him.

He'd been killing time at Surfrider Café for the past hour. Arrived early, drove past Specter, then reached his rendezvous spot with Zoe. She was to meet him at the cafe to give a report.

Nothing to see at Specter, aside from a building and parking lot. Riker drove here earlier than planned to enjoy the scenery. Since he couldn't contact Zoe while on Specter premises, Riker allowed himself a few moments for coffee and relaxation. That was when he felt eyes on him, but no source.

Traffic on PCH slowed down.

On the opposite side, some hundred feet away, a jaywalker ran across the street.

An oncoming green truck swerved between lanes. Too fast and wide a swerve. Overdone, from Riker's vantage point. Would not regain control.

No fucking way.

The blast came fast. The green truck slammed into the car to its right. Hard. Another vehicle, rounding the curb some fifty miles per hour, crashed into the halted car, unable to stop.

Horns blared, glass shattered and tires squealed.

Chaos.

Then total stillness amidst chaos.

Seconds after impact, the offending green truck rolled away, veering past traffic, climbing on dividers. Fleeing the scene.

Riker craned his neck for a look, as the driver hauled ass in the opposite direction. A man's profile—young, angular features. Sunglasses and cap covered the rest.

Something caught Riker off guard. The look on the man's face. He was not wincing in pain. Not panicked. Even in profile, a reserved smile stretched the edge of his lips. That was the look of satisfaction, not of dread for fleeing a scene.

Riker dialed Zoe. The recorder came on, instructing him to leave a message.

Something heavy lodged in his chest. A hunch and, damn, how he hated hunches. Why wouldn't Zoe answer?

Hanging a tight turn, he dialed Neva.

One hand on the wheel, Riker spewed out everything Neva needed to know in a tone not to be questioned. Seconds later, turning in and out of lanes, oblivious to blaring horns, Riker sped after the green truck.

CHAPTER 32

The sirens came from every direction.

Zoe didn't understand what was happening. Had she nodded off?

Hard to imagine, but something clouded her mind. Numbness spread through her limbs, creating a sense of detachment from the world.

She waited as the sensation returned bit by bit.

One memory rose predominant, a bang. Then metal crumpling. A shower of broken glass.

Oh, goodness, she'd been in a car crash. A glance out the window eased her fears a little. The car was right side up. Good, but the air bag had deployed. A serious enough collision. Still, moving felt manageable.

She stirred in the seat. No pain. She could feel everything fine.

A wave of memories knocked the air out of her lungs. A pedestrian running across the street. She remembered screaming, the vehicle on the other lane swerving into her lane. She must've lost control of the car.

Zoe stared at her arms, at the broken glass. Odd. Why was she in the passenger seat?

She whirled and paid with dizzy spells.

Dear God, Sebastian had been driving. His head hung to the side, his face blue and purple.

Zoe struggled to unbuckle, but panic sent tremors down her fingertips.

A gentle knock on the window. She turned to see brown eyes below a helmet staring back. A firefighter, asking if she was okay.

* * *

Fervor swept around Zoe.

Voices spoke on radios. Commands were being screamed into phones. A triage-type scene in motion.

The helmeted firefighter had extracted her from the car. Someone wrapped a trauma blanket around Zoe and helped her sit on the bumper of an ambulance. Aware and in no pain, she could've done it herself, but he insisted.

Her request to be with Sebastian was flat-out denied. They'd strapped him in an ambulance and taken off.

When she pushed the blankets off and tried to stand, another first responder intervened, helping her back onto the bumper of the ambulance. The responder, a ridiculously young woman with soft eyes, was running through a list of questions and taking notes. Her colleague, a green-eyed woman, buzzed about checking Zoe's vitals. They had no answers to her questions, only gentle smiles.

She'd never been at an accident scene as a victim. And, dammit, it was painful not knowing Sebastian's fate. At least they didn't take him in a body bag, the rational side of her insisted. There was hope, and she'd hang on to hope.

When she refused to lie on a gurney, the responders covered her with more blankets that emanated warmth. They cleaned her face with a solution that didn't smell half bad, put lotion and dressing around her eye, took her vitals and communicated the preliminaries back and forth. They gave her something bland to drink, not water, and spoke with the gentleness of angels. Although they wouldn't answer questions, outside of "you were in a car crash," she cherished them.

Forever later, a familiar face popped up. It took Zoe a minute to identify Jett Riker. His face looked tired and gaunt, but he forced a smile.

"Sebastian?" Zoe spewed out before Jett could speak.

"At UCLA. Preliminaries show he'll be okay."

Sweet relief.

When she met Jett's eyes something in there didn't sit right, but exhaustion was kicking her butt. As long as Sebastian was okay, whatever other demons needed attention could wait.

Jett conferred with the EMT, but his request was denied. Something about a green truck, Jett insisted, and once again the EMT said “no,” followed by “she’s in no shape, the medicine has kicked in.”

More voices came from all over. Cop voices. Radio transmissions.

The EMTs helped Zoe into the back of the ambulance, laying her down. The overwhelming exhaustion prevented a peep of protest.

Before they shut the doors Zoe caught sight of Jett, and frissons cut through. His eyes told stories she didn’t want to hear. Dark stories.

She surrendered to sleep that took her away.

CHAPTER 33

At Riker's request, the crime-scene techs donning masks, booties and gloves arrived to preserve and work the scene. As if the earlier craziness hadn't contaminated enough evidence. Preserving was in their DNA.

With Zoe gone and the car impounded, officers formed a human wall around the perimeter while the techs worked.

He'd normally call the accident in and bolt the hell out. But having witnessed the crash and fleeing car—while Zoe was in the middle of an undercover stint nearby—made this feel like anything but an accident.

"Pertaining to a case," Riker told the Highway Patrol. Same good ol' refrain.

On PCH, Riker glanced in both directions. Nothing short of hell on earth when a portion of the highway was shut down, and it sure looked like hell today.

The green truck had vanished. Easy to imagine a turn down a pre-planned route, maybe a change of vehicle. Anger raged through Riker like fire. He had APBs out with LAPD, Sheriff's Department, and CHP.

Nothing so far.

It bothered him that the mystery caller was right—theirs were overworked police forces. Riker pondered the thought. How did the mystery caller fit in this crazy game? Was he the jaywalker? The truck driver?

The jaywalker proved difficult to describe. Aside from dark clothing, Riker and a handful of witnesses hadn't seen much. After a sketchy depiction communicated to rank and file, Riker settled for wait-and-see, hoping the jaywalker would be picked up at a traffic light.

He zoned in on the scattered pedestrians—lookie-loos, craning their necks. Nah, if the crash had been planned, the jaywalker would have bolted. Had probably changed clothes, hid. Who knew?

A click-clack of shoes behind him preceded Neva's voice. "One hell of a mess. What happened?"

A woman of details, his Neva. Riker gave her a run through.

"Someone wanted the party or parties incapacitated?"

Riker never articulated the words, but the implication was enough. "A working theory for now."

She gave him a yeah-right look but pushed no further. While resisting the pull of unsubstantiated facts, all detectives knew unverified details played a role in investigations. Theories were discarded if proven false, but not before.

"Any luck with the phone tapping warrant?" Riker asked.

"The judge agreed after I showed him Zoe's text to you about this Gwen woman and told him about the accident, but only for seventy-two hours. Warrant can be extended if you show good reason."

"Judges can do that?"

"Be sure we're bugging the right person. Full name is Gwendolyn Stone, and she's listed as executive officer."

"On my way there now."

"Then call Qin Young back," Neva said.

Riker's curiosity was piqued at mention of the medical examiner. "News?"

"You must've been joined at the hip in another life. He'll only talk to you."

"Keep an eye on the scene?" Riker turned to go, glanced back.

"Always do." She waved him away.

Riker dialed Qin Young. Settled for leaving a message.

The road before him was filled with cars and curious faces, yet empty of clues. A challenge. As if asking: "Whatcha gonna do, Riker?"

Pay a visit to the glass and marble building up the road, that's what.

* * *

Stepping out of the Escape, Riker marveled at the ocean views. Specter Group must be sitting on one hell of a bank account.

Despite the late hour, lights shone at windows. Quick glances confirmed cameras at every corner.

Riker stepped through the double doors, casual like. Once on the premises, eyes were no doubt watching and ears listening.

Marble and glass made for a great interior, save for a strange sign in plain view: *Gratissimum Hospitalitatem.* It didn't fit the interior. More like something in a church or museum of Roman architecture. The English version *Welcome to Hospitality* explained meaning but not reason for something so overbearing in a beach setting.

A beefy guard stood at attention behind a granite reception counter, his over-exercised shoulders dwarfing his head. Images of Meathead came to Riker's mind. The man's uninterested look was no doubt a put-on.

"The offices are closed," Meathead said.

Riker produced his credentials, and a light flickered in the man's eyes.

"LAPD. Who's the person in charge?"

"Gwendolyn Stone."

Riker nodded, and Meathead traced a line of names on a list, looking for an extension number. He mispronounced Riker's name over the phone, then, without another word, hung up, and took his seat.

Riker dropped the rage. Saved it for a better time.

The woman who sauntered down the steps was either a photo model or expert seductress. Or both. A sensual smile played at the edge of her lips. She swayed her hips just so, not in any way tasteless, enough for lines and curves to show.

Curled, blonde hair spilled down her shoulders. A soft-material shirt, top unbuttoned, hugged her bosom.

The woman approached, her hand outstretched. "Gwen Stone. To what do we owe the unexpected pleasure, Detective …?"

"Riker. Jett Riker. Is there a place we can speak?"

Turning the charm up a notch, she smiled bigger and pointed toward a pair of double doors. "This way, please."

Riker followed and found himself in a sizeable conference room, the back wall covered by velvet. Crystal chandeliers captured the light above a long table. Surprisingly larger room than the entrance let out. Elegantly imposing.

Taking a seat, Gwen Stone pointed a few chairs away. "Please, Detective."

Riker ignored her hand and sat directly across. Took his time, letting the seconds tick away. Much could be revealed in time lags, when minds turn to guessing.

When Gwen Stone lowered her head to brush a nonexistent piece of lint from her skirt, her smile dropped, the cultivated appearance gone for a fraction of a second. Not enough for close inspection, but plenty for later dissection. Without the smile, the face lost luminosity. By extension, the person no longer radiated an aura of allure.

Riker's curiosity only intensified.

They'd found little on Specter Group since Zoe had gone undercover. For medical specialists helping the needy, and a research group interested in medical breakthroughs, Specter sure didn't want to be found. It boggled the mind what hoops a detective jumped through for morsels of information.

"Nice place." Riker made a show of glancing around the room. "The view up there must be magnificent."

"Thank you." Gwen Stone cleared her throat. "We certainly enjoy it."

"The guard said you are the person in charge." *The boss*, as Zoe had said. Big words considering Specter's and Kip Pulaski's possible connection to Bob Forester.

She offered a barely perceptible nod.

Several ways Riker could play this. He settled for a test of sorts.

"I'm helping a colleague investigating an accident on PCH. Why I'm here."

She rolled the chair back and crossed a pair of endless legs. "An accident? I hope everyone is okay."

"Me too, but that didn't come up. What did come up, however, is this address."

A head tilt. "One of our employees was in an accident?"

Riker shook his head. "The offending vehicle, a green truck, fled the scene. A policeman chased after it."

He let that detail stand for a while, but her expression didn't change.

"Particulars regarding the green truck led to this address."

Ms. Stone's gaze darted from Riker to a blank spot between them, then back to Riker. "Not very specific. What does this vehicle have to do with us?"

Ah, she wanted details.

"Exactly what I said. But my colleague is reluctant to release info."

"Good for him. Not very professional pursuing unconfirmed leads." Her voice pulled apart the word "unconfirmed." A disguised admonition, as he was doing just that—pursuing unconfirmed leads.

"Her."

"Sorry?"

"The detective is a woman. So, yes, good for her."

Another swipe of her skirt. Gwen Stone waited, keeping a pleasant appearance even if the smile dimmed.

"This woman colleague of mine," Riker said, "she's a bit on the rigid side, if you ask me. I thought I'd preface her visit. Keep everything pleasant."

"We appreciate it, Detective," Gwen Stone said. "But without details, I'm not inclined to speculate."

Gwen Stone was definitely the boss, and likely not a pleasant one. She had the attitude and rigidity of someone employees would fear rather than want to follow.

"I understand." Riker leaned in.

Gwen Stone uncrossed her legs and rolled the chair closer.

"Just occurred to me," Riker said. "How long have you been at this address?"

"Not sure how that relates, Detective?" She rolled the chair back. Crossed her arms this time.

"Details found in the green truck could be about the previous tenant or owner."

He'd checked the ownership records. The building had been owned by a trust for the past decade. He'd called department lawyers and was waiting to hear back. Likely a shell holding. Likely to show Specter as true owner. Likely as intricate to untangle a web as the Pacific Palisades property.

"We're not a business in the defined sense." She rested her arms on the chair armrest. "We're a non-profit."

"Not on government dime, I hope, considering the swanky pad."

"Private."

"What type of non-profit, if you don't mind?"

"Detective, I'd love to help, but your inquiry is rather vague and borderline intrusive. I have very important matters to attend."

A simple question seen as borderline intrusive. "Then avoiding a mutually detrimental PR case is not in the cards today. Let me apologize in advance for Detective Braxton. One of our best, but she can be a bitch."

Gwen Stone cringed but forced a smile.

Riker stood and she followed.

"Detective." Gwen Stone's smile bordered on subdued now. "Tell me the reason for your visit again."

Oh, she was good. Turning the interrogation around on the interrogator. No wonder she was the person in charge.

"Ms. Stone … Gwen, can I call you Gwen?"

She nodded.

"Gwen. A green truck rammed into a sedan on PCH. Sent the car's occupants to the emergency room and the car to the junkyard. Moments after the impact, the truck fled the scene. There was a chase. Information, possibly incriminating, led to this address. To you, Gwen, since you're the person in charge of this non-profit."

Pallor settled on her face, but she recovered fast.

He'd moved from test to risk, pounding information that should give Gwen Stone the chills or make her laugh in his face. If the green truck was linked to Specter, the driver could've reached out after fleeing. Then she'd know the police found nothing.

Gwen Stone put on a good face but appeared far from sure on her feet, apprehension coming and going.

Riker set his business card on the table.

In the threshold, he offered his hand, and Gwen Stone took it. He gripped hard and shook firmly, pinning her down with a fleeting stare. Intrusive play, let her think that. Let her recoil inside. He had a seventy-two-hour access on her phone, on her movements. Needed her spooked enough to make a move and soon.

CHAPTER 34

Back in the Escape, Riker dialed Neva's number.

"She's the boss, all right. What can we get through the tapping?"

"Everything," Neva said. "Calls, incoming and outgoing, movements. Pray she makes them soon."

Someone in the background shouted Neva's name. She swore and hung up.

If something hot came via the tapping, it would go a long way toward explaining Specter and Zoe's accident. Toward helping with the Forester case.

When his phone rang, Riker stared at the flashing number. Not local, nor familiar. He hit Answer and immediately recognized the voice. Phone mics altered some speech inflictions, but not Felix's hesitant tone.

"I know what happened," Felix, the homeless man from Sunken City, said, his voice above a whisper. "But once bones are unearthed, there is no putting them back, Detective."

"Felix, where are you? I'll be right over."

A gurgle or a laugh followed. "Not wise since I'm unsure of the location myself."

"Are you okay?"

"There is no danger to my person, Detective. Not physical anyway, though sane ships may have long sailed." Felix was warming up to the chat, speaking louder, clearer.

The wind howled in the background.

He was outside, likely calling from a burner phone, hence the strange number. Must've scraped enough money together to buy the phone. Or stole one. Hopefully he'd just found it.

"Felix?"

"I'm on foot, sir, granting location remains unknown. But if signs are correct, I'll soon be home."

"Meet you at the entrance to Sunken City in thirty minutes."

Fat chance Riker could reach San Pedro that fast, but making it sound expeditious mattered to Felix, no doubt.

"Sir, if I may …"

More howling wind in the background.

"Felix, call me Jett."

Silence, then, "Jett, don't arrive looking like the law. It's unhelpful in my neighborhood."

The call cut off.

* * *

They met at the end of a broken fence between Sunken City and San Pedro. Felix's gaze darted around, showing his discomfort with the rendezvous.

Out here, snitching meant trouble.

Riker had thrown on an old sweater to assimilate, and still stuck out like a ten-foot man. Dreadlocks and dirty, ripped clothes were the norm in Sunken City.

The secluded corner offered a momentary safe spot for Felix. He'd wanted a face-to-face about the case. He didn't trust phones and technology.

"Thank you for leaving the pack of cigarettes behind," Felix said, "with your number inside."

Riker pulled out the pack he carried on him and handed it to Felix with a nod.

"It's a sad story," Felix said. "One about a friend gone missing. His home was a grotto down there by the water."

The sun gleamed off broken glass on the ground.

"What do you mean?" Riker hoped like hell this was about his case.

Shivers cut through Felix. "We tried to investigate it, me and my tech-savvy friends, but no go. Then there were stories of others gone but no one cared. The disappearance of the unsheltered doesn't matter to the world."

"Homeless people disappeared from here, is that what you're saying?"

"A cursory look at the news, and this is the state of our world. People like me have become prey, sought out and finished out."

"That's a big statement."

"Not big enough for the local police who have better things to do. We told them about the close-cropped hair man crouching in wait by the water. I saw his shape once, others saw more. The man with a gun, smoking, and waiting. Two days later, one of my friends was gone, never to return. Others say more have disappeared, same as downtown. They're picking us up, one by one. We have become target practice for someone, Jett."

The story was murky in Riker's mind. With everything going on, he'd only peripherally kept an eye on the homeless-disappearance story.

"The downtown division is handling the disappearances."

"Not here. Ain't nobody handling nothing."

"Who's the man with the gun, lying in wait by the water, Felix?"

"Damn if anyone knows. There once or twice, like a hunter looking for prey. Then the prey vanished." Felix made air quotes around the word "prey," his face contorted to show disgust at the idea of someone hunting humans.

No shit.

Felix glanced around, then continued. "We called, told the local police. No one bothered to come down, not a single soul, until the woman you mentioned arrived."

Riker decided in favor of patience.

Felix shielded his eyes with a dirty hand. "I thought she was the law, finally coming to look into the disappearance." Felix stared at Riker.

"Maybe she was."

Felix met Riker's eyes tentatively, then looked away. "There can only be one answer, she was or she wasn't."

"What did the local police say when you called?"

"That it's a complicated case. The human brain with a hundred billion neurons is complicated, but not this. People disappearing is a straight-forward police matter."

Riker tried to piece this shit together, make sense of the story.

"When the woman you described visited here," Felix said. "I told you she didn't leave empty handed."

Riker kept the response to a nod.

"Back-to-back strange events," Felix said. "A disappearance, then a woman in business attire, visiting. Never happened before. I wondered if the events were related."

Another nod.

"I followed her down by the water. Kept my distance. She picked something off the ground, near the spot the man was lying in wait. Then she went inside the cave, where I didn't dare follow. Left holding a small brown bag."

"Kim Snyder came here and found something she took in a brown bag?" Riker said mostly to himself, still trying to understand.

"That her name?"

Riker nodded. "Did she find cigarette butts?"

A light flickered in Felix's eyes. They were on the same wavelength.

"I searched around after. Never found anything, but people saw the man lying in wait smoking and holding a gun."

Cigarette butts and firearm casing. Good God, these were Zoe's findings all over again. Whoever had been here may have been the same person lying in wait up on Mulholland, near Kim Snyder's crash scene.

"What else did Kim Snyder find? Any idea?"

Felix shook his head fast, the distant look back in his eyes.

Riker opened his mouth, then checked himself. Would do no good pushing Felix.

"The man you saw lying in wait." Riker kept his voice measured. "Could you or anyone else describe him?"

"It was too dark and all I saw was a shadow. Maybe close-cropped hair, but not sure." Felix shook his head. "No one around here will talk anymore after the local police told us more or less to stick it."

Riker burned to ask if Felix could identify the man in a photo, not that he knew where he'd get one, or how to even go about such a plan. But he dropped the question.

Kim Snyder, he had to focus on her. She left with a brown bag holding evidence. Riker made a mental note to check the list of items found at the crash scene. Again.

Felix slumped his shoulders, making himself smaller, stealing glances around. "We are expendable. Grains of sand, washed away by wave after wave. That is why we trust no one. We are nothing to the world out there." He looked to Riker for answers in vain.

"Look, Felix, I can provide a place for you to stay. A safe, warm place."

The glare was immediate and cutting. "We live here because issues prevent us from living inside safe, warm places, Detective."

"You wouldn't have to share the space." Riker eased his voice.

Felix hugged himself. "This is home, whether I like it or not." He forced an apologetic smile, turned and scurried away before Riker could stop him.

There was no holding him back.

On the dirt trail to his car, Riker considered the new lead.

If Felix was a reliable witness, Kim Snyder had taken evidence, same as Zoe, items that may have belonged to the same person. Did the man lying in wait know of Kim Snyder's investigation? Was that why he went up Mulholland where Kim Snyder happened to drive one night? All good questions.

How that fit with Bob Forester's death, Zoe's undercover assignment, a man named Kip Pulaski who seemed to have disappeared after two meetings with Zoe, Specter Group and Gwendolyn Stone, he had zero clue.

But there was a connection.

A gusty wind whistled through, freezing the air. Riker glanced over his shoulder at the sinking land that had become home to those whose lives forced them here. Where were some of them disappearing? He stifled a shudder. Zoe's story about cerebrospinal fluid and homeless people came to mind. A story quashed by Specter Group.

He had to get Felix to talk again. But first, better confirm a story that, if true, it might open a world as dangerous to navigate as the falling land behind him.

CHAPTER 35

For a big man, San Pedro PD Lieutenant Garza cleared the corner fast. He led Riker to his office, shut the door, and plopped down in a leather chair. As an afterthought, he pointed to the other chair.

Riker remained standing.

"We never get LAPD visits down here," Garza said, his voice hoarse. "And you want to know about a homeless disappearance. That's interesting."

"That's an old story around here, I take it."

"Beats me how that case went to shit."

Riker waited for the man to make sense.

"We got a call, then another." Garza looked up. "Went checking, found nothing amiss at first."

They went and checked. A wrinkle in Felix's story?

"At first? Tell me, Lieutenant."

Garza avoided eye contact. Leaned back on his chair. "It's a long story."

"I'm in no hurry."

"Doesn't mean I'm not. Or that surprise visits and questions merit urgent answers."

Garza needed his curiosity fed, so Riker fed it a little. "Case on the news, you may have seen it. Rich lawyer, partner at big Century City firm, found dead in his home office. I'm looking to tie up some loose ends, you know how it is. Any help would be appreciated and reciprocated, should that time come. On expedited basis, discreetly if necessary. Sure there are things San Pedro PD would like expedited by Central Division."

"Your reach that deep with Central bosses?"

"Not saying either way, just standing by what I just said."

Riker smiled big.

"I don't know everything," Garza said, surrendering to either promises or charm. "Captain took over the whole thing. There were meetings. Lawyers going in and out. Then one day we were told there's nothing there. Just stories from crazy transients." Garza leaned forward, elbows on his desk. "Is it possible your case is removed from this one?"

"Captain, lawyer meetings? That's a lot more than nothing, Lieutenant."

Garza's edge softened. "Police brass are like politicians. They can't have negative opinion pieces written about their jurisdiction. So, they call lawyers."

Riker didn't like where this was going. Policing and politics never mixed well.

"I know what you're thinking." Like any good cop, Garza was reading Riker. "I tried. Called and asked Captain to let me take another look. They're people, after all, human beings."

Silence consumed a good five seconds. Riker thought better than to answer that. Then, he said. "Lieutenant, high-level meetings over homeless disappearances come with some implications."

Garza squinted, didn't seem crazy about Riker's tone. "Like?"

"Like what the hell is really going on?"

"Invcstigation lcd to somcthing, but I don't know what."

"*Something* is vague."

Behind Garza's eyes, wheels seemed to turn at dizzying speed. "How exactly is this involved in your investigation, Detective?"

"I've got two victims," Riker said. "Both accidental deaths, or so it appears. One is the lawyer, second one employed by the lawyer, visited Sunken City where someone was seen lying in wait, smoking and holding a gun. Then people went missing. I can help."

Garza waved his hand, sign he knew promises were meant to be broken.

"It started with the missing homeless. While digging up shit on that, someone came across something. And that something got the captain and lawyers involved. And don't ask me what that was. All I know is lawyers came and went, and shit hit the fan. Nothing more."

"Did you ask your captain?"

Garza pressed his palm against the desk. "There was a gag order. All Captain said was, 'those fucking lawyers.'"

"Name of the lawyers?"

"Don't know. Only that their office was in Century City. The place crawls with lawyers."

"The firm? Did he mention the firm? What building?"

Garza shook his head. "I already blabbered too much. Wife is right, I shouldn't screw with the end of a long career."

Meaning a nice retirement pension.

"Lieutenant--"

"That's all I know." Garza's stare was deep and unrelenting. Whatever bits he knew, they were bigger than him. So big, sharing would threaten his pension.

Riker pitied and envied cops like Garza who worked toward retirement goals. In a gun-on-the-heap profession—adrenaline inducing, criminal chasing world—retirement was a life one had to die in order to be reborn into. That or ask to be transferred, let the pounds accumulate and mind soften. Garza, once a lead detective, was now police lieutenant. Maybe the fire within had died.

Riker hoped his never did.

On his way out, Riker pulled up Neva's number and typed. *Disappearing homeless in San Pedro, Captain and lawyers involved. Need info asap, whatever limits and luck need pushing.*

Outside the wind picked up, howling in horror to an indifferent world.

* * *

"Pain in the ass to dig up all this," Neva said on the phone, clicking on the keyboard.

"Tell me." Riker was speeding back to the West side, and, for once, the freeways cooperated.

"There is confirmation of one homeless who disappeared from Sunken City a few weeks ago. I've been reading his ex-girlfriend's statement. She calls him K."

Riker could tell info was coming in as they spoke. Neva's voice held the familiar edgy tone of newscasters sharing breaking news.

"She was told K had vanished, asked if she knew anything, and she said no. But the ex said there was someone else who had inquired about K, not just the police. Via phone call and letter."

Riker swerved by a slow car and picked up speed.

"The caller asked about K's blood-related family members. She said none are still around. Caller asked what she knew about a rare skin disorder in K's family. Something called XP, or as I found out, *Xeroderma Pigmentosum.* Those affected are highly sensitive to sunlight, can never go out during the day. There could be serious organ damage resulting in death."

Riker picked up more speed, leaving San Pedro behind.

"My brief research says both parents must be carriers to pass it on to kids. The risk of having a child carrier is fifty percent. The chance for a child to receive normal genes from carrier parents, twenty-five percent. Don't know where K stood on this."

"And someone had questions about a genetic family disorder. Why?"

"Bet you wanna know where letter was sent from," Neva said. "Law firm in L.A. someplace. Girlfriend didn't keep it. Doesn't remember where in L.A, but nixed downtown. I threw out guesses. While not a hundred percent sure, she said Century City sounded 'bout right."

The power of suggestion, or had the letter been mailed from Century City?

"We need more on K's biological family, the genetic disorder, phone records. She received a phone call, not just the letter. And we need to know if there were any genetic disorders among the recent missing homeless downtown, or this is just a one off."

"Qin called again," Neva said. "You take that. I'll look into the call that might've come from Century City."

The phone clicked.

The lawyer in question, who made the phone call and wrote a letter, was based in Century City. One piece of the story Garza shared before clamming up. The place crawled with lawyers, but Riker's gut feeling said this was no coincidence.

It wasn't mere instinct, though tried and tested, but a well-known conjuncture. A detective needed to consider information and evidence. But after doing a job for years, one developed a great inside knowledge of the human mind. A natural feeling for connecting the dots.

Everything had to come together—theories, evidence, information and, hell yes, intuition or hunch. Whatever the order of combination, it forcibly pointed Riker toward a certain law office in Century City.

* * *

Qin Young, medical examiner and friend, reminded Riker there was life outside the precinct. Qin wanted to dissect the postmortem report during a walk. He was an autopsy nerd riveted by work. The requested chat-and-walk part came as a surprise.

They strolled by the water's edge in Venice Beach, not far from Qin's office. The influx of traffic not yet amassed, Venice emerged nothing like the usual tourist trap overrun by street performers and visitors. But for sporadic bikers, ten in the morning proved too early for craziness.

Stuck slicing corpses all day, Qin had insisted on a stroll. So, Riker took the drive.

Qin Young, a second-generation Asian American, was an encyclopedia of medical data and deductions. One of the sharpest minds Riker had encountered.

"Bob Forester's pathology results show no signs of drugs, legal or illegal," Qin said. "No antidepressants, before you ask. No alcohol, no signs of tumors, or any number of a thousand other things that might have caused Forester to pull the trigger."

Hands deep in his pockets, Riker looked out at the ocean. Seagulls flew high against a blue sky dotted with white clouds. The wind picked up a little, cold but gentle. It would get colder soon, but for now the sun kept the chill at bay.

Qin, gangly and tall, attracted a few glances from bikers. At six foot six, he towered over most people. Riker stood four inches shorter, not a world of difference, but conspicuous.

Years back, they'd become close during a PD basketball tournament when Qin warned Riker he couldn't play that well, don't be fooled by height, but would take care of rebounds and layups. He made good on his promise. They advanced and won in finals. The tournament ended. Their friendship endured. Like minds and all that.

"Forester had lived a clean life," Qin said. "Not overweight, no heart or major organ issue."

The medical examiner wasn't one for emotional conversation, so Riker didn't interrupt. Qin had ventured into risky territory for Riker's sake. No reason to push. His friend was rationally focused by nature. Took the corpse for what it was, resisting irrational suppositions. And Forester's corpse—save for the gunshot wound—was one of the cleanest, if not the cleanest Qin had seen in … well, forever.

To Riker's surprise, Qin made another exception. "I know what you're thinking," Qin said. "I read the file, heard the chatter about Forester's recent emotional state. Withdrawn from society, possible life slump. But depression manifests in a person's appearance with weight loss or gain. Affects the heart." He avoided Riker's stare. "Offing oneself due to depression when keeping in great health strains credulity."

Right-on logic, but Riker needed more. "That your professional opinion or do we have something concrete?"

"How about ballistics?"

"It was Forester's gun and ammo," Riker said. "Wife confirmed he owned firearms, and records show it legally purchased."

A trio of bikers zoomed past. Riker waited a beat, then said, "Wife agrees with you, Qin. She's adamant Forester didn't kill himself. There were issues with problematic cases and stress, but according to her, they had a lot to live for."

"Stress is a constant in this world," Qin said. "For everyone."

"Very philosophical this morning, aren't we?"

"Forensics will study photos and the body," Qin said. Meaning they'd have the final say, but Qin hadn't insisted upon this walk for nothing.

Some thirty feet away, near the sand, a couple of seagulls went after a crow carrying something in its stout beak. The crow fought the intruders, but it was outnumbered until two other crows arrived. A standoff ensued, until more bikers zoomed past, scaring the birds. The crow dropped whatever it was holding, and after some crowing, all birds flew away.

Humans, changing the outcome of what nature might have had in store.

"I told you about the gunshot wound," Qin said, once silence resumed.

"Suicide shots are angled upward or evenly, given victim holds the gun." Riker had the information memorized. "Here we have a slightly downward angle, meaning gun may have been held from a higher position, maybe someone standing. And there were scratches on Forester's left wrist. Fresh scratches if I recall."

Qin nodded with a smile. Before he spoke again, the smile vanished. "I've had cases in the past where mysterious deaths were pushed as suicide for some time."

No one was pushing anything here, but Riker kept that to himself.

"In those past cases, wounds didn't match suicide claims," Qin said. "Forensics agreed, so did lead detectives. They took another swipe at questioning those close to victims and cracks appeared."

"What happened in those cases?"

"Jealousy in some, money in others. In one case, the perpetrator had been studying for months how to make a wound appear as if it happened by suicide."

"Meaning?"

"The perpetrator watched videos bought on the black market, learned how. It was a crime of passion, if I recall."

Riker had heard of homicides disguised as suicide. He'd collaborated on some cases, knew the perps were always caught. Still, Qin's story chilled him.

The peaceful seascape stood in dissonance with their conversation. Riker let the silence stand for some time.

"In that example, the angle raised suspicion," Qin said. "Aim may have started angled fully upward, normal when the victim holds the gun, but it ended up even to vaguely downward. By fractions. Gush was wider than normal, indicating unstable aim. There are two explanations. The victim's hand slipped from the position, or it was not suicide."

The world was a crazy place.

"On my last homicide-staged-as-suicide case, the wound angle," Qin said, "was the same as Forester's."

People were beginning to trickle in—a street vendor, pushing his cart, couple of skaters. Peace was about over.

They turned toward the parking lot.

"Going to go out on a limb and say no one killed Forester on some jealousy rage," Riker said. "Like in your case."

"Probably right. Different story. Which makes the near-exact similarity of the angle curious, to say the least."

When Qin slowed his pace, Riker fell in step. They walked in silence, each with his own thoughts.

"By the way, how's the case progressing?" Qin threw out, maybe his way to dispel dark thoughts.

"Nothing big moved yet. Chasing leads."

"So, there are leads?"

Riker opened his mouth to answer, stopped. He'd known Qin long enough to be taken aback by his sudden curiosity.

"The file," Qin said hesitantly, "it's horrible, the whole story, but good case study. When medical advances fall in the wrong hands, and the end justifies the means for some … it's important we put humanity first."

Riker waited for Qin to make sense.

"The file looks like a mess, that's all," Qin said. "Was just wondering."

Maybe true. Or maybe Qin was backpedaling, although that made less sense.

When Qin stopped near his minivan, Riker said, "You drove

here? Minutes from your office?"

"Have an appointment to go to." Qin glanced past Riker. An expression of hesitation, of wanting to say more but deciding against it, crossed his eyes. Happened too fast to be sure.

"That all you wanted to hash out, Qin?"

Qin pushed Unlock on the remote and pulled open the door. "Get to work, Riker. Can't do it all for you." A smile stretched where a frown had been seconds ago, but not a definite smile.

Riker remained standing in Qin's exhaust fumes, working it all out. Clues floated just outside his grasp. Something important but couldn't say what. He tried again, but nothing stuck. Shit.

When his cell beeped, the department tech's number flashed on the screen. "Tell me you have something on the Gwen Stone tap," Riker said into the phone.

"Texted you the report." The call disconnected. Typical techs.

Riker scrolled to the top and clicked on the audio file.

A phone conversation between Gwen Stone and a distorted voice consisted of mostly screaming and a few words:

Gwen Stone: *Coming over now. It's my fucking place too.*

Silence, Static. The other person was speaking through a voice-distortion app on their phone.

Voice: *For good. Calling ….* Then nothing.

Gwen Stone screaming unintelligible words. Static, then the words: *I will kill you.* Clear as day.

Voice: *Fuck you.*

Gwen Stone: *I will find you and fucking kill you.*

Noise consistent with door slamming. The map showed her moving through the Specter building toward the exit.

Gwen Stone: *You will never take this away from me.*

A click. Then the call dropped.

Riker checked the map. The tapped phone never moved from the Malibu Specter location, meaning if Gwen Stone had left to carry out the threat, she did not take her cell phone with her.

I will kill you.

You will never take this away from me.

Who was she talking to, and what did it all mean?

* * *

In detective work, picking up clues from a prolonged silence, or from a choice of words, was about gut feeling, instinct, and sometimes about emotion.

Generally speaking.

Riker had learned long ago to holster his emotions. When the call came, he had to do just that.

The supervising physician at UCLA Medical Center, an acquaintance beholden to favors Riker once did, described a surreal scene over the phone: Zoe's fiancé had been discharged from UCLA against medical advice. Which meant he'd gone home with Zoe.

Sebastian Herod had signed all necessary paperwork and hobbled out the door.

Then Doc lowered his voice and told Riker to listen carefully.

When UCLA had requested the patient's records, calls were made, and records emailed from Wyoming. A memory triggered by the patient's name had snapped Doc's attention.

"Have time for a story?" Doc asked.

It was the pause before "story" that grabbed Riker's attention. His senses kicked into high gear. "All ears."

"A colleague approached me last year."

Doc went on about a well-regarded neurologist, member of a consortium—specialists in research and studies for medical cures. The consortium met twice a year for a Brain Trust conference. Doc had received an invite to last year's conference at a Wisconsin country club.

An old-fashioned atmosphere, to Doc's surprise. No young, fresh faces, as Doc had imagined the breakthrough research scientists would look, but all elderly doctors.

After dinner, they moved to a room for cigars. As smoke swirled, discussion veered to a non-profit group designed to help the less fortunate—homeless and throwaways. Specialists from across the medical profession volunteered. There'd been some problems, but the consortium had a good system in place, one speaker said. A way to process the patients, house them. No details were offered. Words like "research" popped up, "cure" and "subjects."

"Sounded as if the patients were subjected to experiments," Doc said.

Doc had wondered how the consortium would've secured permission. The dark side of his imagination visualized payments rendered to patients, maybe to families. Highly unethical. Doc didn't like it.

Next day, the neurologist acquaintance showed up at the hotel requesting an audience. They had coffee, talked about neurological research the consortium was undertaking. Doc had studied and written on the subject. The consortium wanted him to join. They had a patient in mind—Wyoming man suffering of comorbid neurological conditions. They had a file.

One problem. The Wyoming man didn't fit the *less fortunate* criteria. His family, particularly the older brother, had refused involvement but they'd found a way to convince the man. They'd approached him recently. Conversations were underway.

When *convince* the brother sounded more like *coerce*, Doc said, "no thank you." He wasn't interested.

"I should've reported this to the authorities," Doc said. "But had no proof. It would have been a *he said, she said* thing."

Riker didn't think so but dropped the thought.

"Who's the Wyoming man with comorbid neurological conditions?" Riker asked.

"Name is Nick Herod, and his brother is Sebastian Herod. Same as the patient who walked out of here an hour ago."

Doc begged for Riker's discretion. His career was on the line.

In Riker's work, promises were like snowballs. Easy to make, difficult to keep. He hoped he could keep this one.

Speeding past two cars, he took the freeway off ramp to Manhattan Beach while dialing Neva.

"Hold on a second," Neva's voice cut through the first ring. In the background phones were ringing and people were screaming.

Another day at the station.

"*Bugada syndrome*," Neva said when she came back on. "One homeless youth downtown had a rare genetic disorder called *Bugada syndrome*, a rare cardiovascular disorder that affects the electrical system of the heart."

"And he's among the ones gone missing?"

"One of eight," Neva said. "Have to go."

She hung up, and Riker considered what he'd just learned. Felix may have been right. There was a strong possibility that some of the unhoused and unsheltered with rare genetic disorders were being picked up by someone. A medical group was interested in people with rare genetic conditions. One was Sebastian Herod's brother, not unhoused but of interest. One was the Sunken City homeless, and his family's *Xeroderma Pigmentosum.* And now someone with a rare cardiovascular condition.

Was it the medical consortium in Doc's story? If so, who the fuck were they?

Riker recapped what he knew: A tube with spinal fluid had allegedly been found in the office of a medical research company, or consortium, associated with Specter Group. Homeless people had disappeared.

At a different time, a young patient, in a different state, with a different condition was of interest to the consortium. The young man's brother, who was Zoe's fiancé, had been drawn into the fray, and, by association so had Zoe Sinclair.

Then there was Bob Forester's death, followed by the death of his firm's private investigator, who seemed to have gone searching for the Sunken City homeless. Why?

Riker dialed the captain's office and left a message, once again asking about his access to Grunman and Forester documents. He needed facts, dammit, not only half facts, words and gut feelings.

CHAPTER 36

Zoe helped Sebastian up the flights of stairs, sucking in air.

When she'd rented on the top floor of a building with no elevator, she hadn't imagined this day. With her shitty luck, anticipating disasters should've been a given.

Doctors had insisted on a longer hospital stay for Sebastian. But cuts and bruises, a concussion, fractured ribs, and the loss of two back teeth fell outside such nonsense in Sebastian's eyes. Exasperated doctors piled on waivers for signature and released him.

On the landing, a silhouette came into her peripheral. Zoe's heart summersaulted until the man stepped forward.

"You could've coughed," Zoe said. "Announced your presence."

Jett Riker stared loaded questions but settled for a nod.

"Sebastian, meet Detective Riker." Zoe fumbled with the keys. "Jett Riker, this is my fiancé, Sebastian Herod."

Zoe didn't bother observing the greetings but sensed cold stares and nods.

She held the door open. Forcing his back straight, Sebastian limped inside. God forbid she helped while her ex's brother was watching.

Against her better judgment, Zoe invited Jett inside. Also because he'd never leave. His stare said as much. And she had her own questions.

"Any leads?" She'd told him everything about the night Bob died, agreed to help, but gotten nothing back.

Leaning against the wall, Sebastian watched the exchange while avoiding the recliner.

"Anything you'd like to add to our previous conversation?" Jett asked. "Forgotten details?"

"Forgotten" sounded like anything but coming from Jett. He

hadn't taken the drive down here to be delicate or satisfy her curiosity.

Anger flushed through Zoe, but conviction failed to materialize. No, she hadn't told Jett everything.

"I went undercover," she said. "For you."

Silence covered the echo of her words.

Zoe looked at Sebastian. Pallor erased whatever color he'd regained.

She still felt betrayed by his concealing the truth, but wanted nothing more than for him to be all right now.

Sebastian tilted his head toward Jett, as if to say, tell him everything or I will.

Zoe moved to feel motion in her legs. "Okay, I didn't just go in for you. I went in because clearly there is a connection between Bob, Pulaski, and Specter Group. Also, for myself." She turned to Jett. "But all that helps you."

Distant sounds reached the top floor—ocean waves, birds—belonging to a happy world from which she was removed.

"I'm listening," Jett stuck his hands deep in his pockets. Waited.

"Okay, then." Zoe took off her jacket, hung it on the back of the chair. "I suggest you both take a seat."

Sebastian looked close to fainting but remained standing.

"I'm good," Jett said.

Zoe laughed. They wouldn't give an inch and get comfortable.

She pulled up a chair and sat. "It's a long story."

* * *

Zoe had been on several trial teams, working with detectives. Admired them. Learned to read them before they finished talking. Tested their credibility during cross-examination. Her job required analyzing words, facial gestures, measuring verbal and nonverbal communication, finding gaps before the opposition pounced.

She could not read Jett Riker.

She watched him listen to Sebastian, who finally dropped on the recliner and took over the story but couldn't tell what went through Jett's mind while he paced, stopped, paced again.

Sebastian droned on about his brother's illness, treatment, and lack of progress. How Nick's condition had left the family emotionally drained. After a pause, he spewed out the finale—how letters arrived, how he'd ignored them at first, how the letters led to meeting the mystery man. Learning about Specter Group. Being blackmailed. Telling them to fuck off.

"And you traveled to Wyoming," Jett said, concluding Sebastian's story.

"To talk to my mother. Check on Nick."

"Did you tell your mother about the meeting, the mystery man?"

Sebastian shook his head. "I asked about Nick's medical treatment, his doctor."

"The neurologist who shared Nick's private information with Specter?" Jett filled in the blanks. "You planned on visiting the neurologist."

"Zoe showed up," Sebastian said. "She asked me to pause, since you guys had a plan." His voice dropped at "a plan," making clear he didn't much care for Jett's modus operandi.

Jett waited for more. He must've sensed or learned there was more.

Zoe wasn't ready for the grand finale. Sure, Mr. Herod Sr. was already dying. Sebastian simply hastened the departure. But the thought offered no comfort.

"Reason for blackmail will come up big," Jett said. "They won't go away."

Zoe shook her head at Sebastian in vain.

The rest of the story rushed out of him, a secret scorching his heart. Everything about his father's nurse "helping me help my father out of his suffering," to no one's knowledge, not even his mother's. Until Zoe, "the act" had been between him and the nurse, with one exception.

"Specter, whoever the fuck they are, knew," Sebastian said. "And they wanted to use it and force my hand at having my brother exposed to their tests." When done telling the story, Sebastian looked as good as a corpse.

Jett nodded. Not passing judgment. He looked out the window, his stare distant as if checking a mental list.

He walked to the door, ready to leave, then turned abruptly. "Green truck that rammed into you, Ford extra-large. Do you remember seeing it before?"

"I remember driving," Sebastian said. "Then I woke up in the hospital."

"Wait, green Ford truck?" Zoe snapped her fingers. "Really large type?"

To Jett's nod she said, "Similar truck halted in front of me on the freeway, on my way to the police station. I remember because my coffee flew all over when I slammed the brakes. Thought I saw the truck in front of the station again, but it turned the corner before I could be sure."

Jett waited until the silence became intolerable. He was weighing something in his mind, looking from Zoe to Sebastian then back to Zoe.

"Days before she drove off the cliff, Kim Snyder visited Sunken City," Jett said. "Left with the same things you found up in Mulholland, cigarette butt and bullet casing."

Zoe tried to refocus, thrown off by the change in topic. "Why would Kim Snyder visit Sunken City, and where is that?"

"San Pedro, semi-detached piece of land," Jett said. "She was searching for something having to do with Specter, however distantly. Must have come across information about people with certain disorders being of interest to the group."

Jett was pacing from the door to the window, stopping only to look at Zoe then continued.

"Means someone in Sunken City came to Specter's attention," Zoe said. "And Kim was investigating… but the same things I found … how?"

"Whoever visited the hill near Kim Snyder's crash site visited Sunken City. A smoker. The person gone missing was a carrier of a rare genetic mutation. A skin disorder that leads to organ failure. The information must've surfaced somehow, and the person must've become of interest to the medical group, or consortium."

Zoe felt a gut punch. By his flinching, so did Sebastian. A story similar to that of his family: someone interested in his brother's medical condition. For study? Research? And why go to such absurd lengths for access?

Jett read from his phone. "Specter's attorney was Bob Forester, his main client Kip Pulaski. While trying to look into the case of the missing Sunken City person, the local police discovered ties to another case handled by Grunman and Forester and the name Specter Group came up again." Jett looked at Zoe. "For some reason, Bob Forester re-introduced you to Specter."

"It's all related." Zoe stared at Jett, nodding while her mind drifted to memories. "Specter is the group who wanted access to Nick and to someone in Sunken City who suffered from a rare genetic disorder."

A plan long in the works had run parallel with their lives. A plan involving a medical group, the green truck, someone breaking into her apartment, leaving with her file. Prior to that, letters were sent to Sebastian. And along the way, there was Kim Snyder's investigation into a case having to do with Kip Pulaski and Specter.

"Here's what we're going to do." Jett halted at the warning in Sebastian's eyes. "What I propose we do," he said. "Zoe, return to Specter as if nothing happened. We'll be nearby. Sebastian, be ready, Specter may try to make contact." A short pause. "Please tell me if you have better ideas."

They did not.

When the door slammed behind Jett, silence took over, until Zoe broke it. "The green truck on PCH," she said. "I'm sure I saw it before."

They exchanged looks. Too much to process.

If the car crash was related to Specter and Pulaski—and Jett wouldn't have brought it up otherwise—someone willing to go that far would strike again.

CHAPTER 37

Hawke Ford hurried inside the parking garage, forcing confidence in his step.

He hated being stuck in L.A.—the zoo that was Century City—but they had his money. This garage was the drop spot.

Feeling the gun in his pocket alleviated some worries.

Depressing thoughts had kept him awake all night: the job going sideways, those poor bastards in the Palisades. Alive, but good as dead. He'd considered calling in an anonymous tip, but self-preservation killed that thought.

He'd tried the secret phone number again. When Shila, Breast Goddess Attorney at Law, answered and mentioned his money, Hawke took the drive to this closed-to-the-public garage. Nervous but determined. He'd risked too much to lose everything.

An empty utility vehicle was parked in the back. Some scattered cars filled the bottom levels, but not the rooftop garage where construction had just been finished. Here, it smelled of stale air. Stale humanity. The dark side of chasing dreams defined this place, with its proximity to Hollywood and Beverly Hills.

Hawke hoped his dreams stayed alive. Take him to Costa Rica.

He'd dumped the green truck under the freeway overpass, off of Spring Avenue. An area favored by homeys and hobos. One group or another would vandalize it soon. Make the truck unrecognizable. With some luck, it would take a while to find the left-over parts and the vehicle identification number.

By then, the game should be over, and he should be out of L.A.

Hawke turned when the elevator dinged. Breast Goddess—Shila, as she was called—stepped out. Not accompanied by Big Shot, as Hawke had hoped. Another woman sauntered behind Shila.

Hawke kept both hands in sight. Needed the women to approach. Shila halted out of reach. The bitch was a mind reader.

"Where is he?" Hawke asked, his voice relaxed.

The other woman, blonde, hair pulled back tight, wore sunglasses and a long trench. Was this the mystery woman he'd heard about? She stopped two steps behind Shila.

"I take it you disposed of the vehicle and removed the plates," Shila said.

Hawke nodded. "I asked a question."

Shila laughed a sonorous laugh. "Our mutual friend is not available."

Hawke listened for distant sounds, anything out of place. The city buzzed in the distance but nothing alarming nearby.

"Who is she?" Hawke squinted behind Shila.

"I have what you want." Shila dropped the playfulness in her voice. "All in the car." She pointed to what Hawke had thought was an unremarkable utility vehicle parked in the back lane. He tensed inward.

A strategically placed car. They'd one-upped him.

He glanced past Shila. "She can get the money."

The mystery woman stepped lateral. "Hello, Hawke. I'm Gwen Stone." She removed her sunglasses. A pair of striking blue eyes stared with razor-sharp focus. You may have heard my name mentioned in conversations."

He didn't know the name. But the voice was unmistakable. He'd never imagined Gwen Stone as more than another helper, like Shila. Not Big Shot's equal. Men like Big Shot put women on pedestals to keep them around for fucks.

"I've taken the liberty of increasing your compensation," Gwen Stone said. "For one last favor. Then we're never to see each other again."

"The car crash was my last job," Hawke said. "I'm here to collect."

Gwen Stone smiled in a way meant to be disarming. She sure didn't have the demeanor of just another fuck, not with that calculating look in her eyes.

"My money," Hawke said.

"I said a favor, Hawke," Gwen Stone said. "Not a job."

What happened next was a blur.

All Hawke heard was the bolt clicking back then the muffled pow. No crack. Nothing. Barely a sound.

When it was over, Shila dropped.

Gwen Stone had shot Shila in the side of the head with a silencer gun. Shila was dead before she hit the ground.

For a second, Hawke couldn't breathe.

Taking a tissue out of her pocket, Gwen Stone cleaned the handle, and, stepping near the dead woman, dropped the gun.

"To be added to your criminal charges," Gwen Stone said. "Or not, depending on your cooperation."

Fear grabbed hold of Hawke's heart. His hand inched toward his pocket.

"We're on the same team," Gwen Stone said. "Please don't."

Were they? She could've shot him, sure. Chose not to. The thought did not moderate his fear.

Hawke stood stock-still. Was Gwen Stone showing blind trust or was someone watching him?

She sauntered toward the car. "Follow me," she said. "I've got your money."

Hawke waited.

Gwen Stone moved toward the parked sedan with tinted windows, then glanced back.

Before Hawke reached her, the front passenger door opened. A bulky man with more muscle mass than head stepped out, but made no other move. Just stood there, feet apart.

Hawke halted four steps away, searching for escape routes.

"No need to run." Gwen Stone's voice snapped back his attention. She signaled, and Muscle opened the back door of the car. On the seat lay an unzipped bag filled with stashes of hundred-dollar bills. More money than Hawke had envisioned seeing in one place.

"A lot of money, isn't it, Hawke?" Gwen Stone smiled. "Please stop squirming. You'd be dead, had that been the goal. But you have something of importance to me—anonymity and skill—and I have what you want. This bag full of money."

"What do you want?"

"There is a gathering, a party of sorts, I need you to attend tomorrow," she said.

"For what?"

"Details to follow."

"What insurance do I have on the money?"

She smiled broader. Despite his anger, Hawke relaxed a little.

"Nothing would be enough, would it? Promises, more money, sparing your life." She glanced in the direction of Shila's body. "Would it, Hawke?"

Hawke didn't like where this was going.

"In anticipation of your reaction, I've taken a little insurance of my own."

A nod, and Muscle tossed a phone at Hawke.

"Watch the video," Gwen Stone said.

Forcing his hand steady, Hawke did as instructed.

A video began playing on the screen, and it took every ounce of strength not to throw up.

His parents and older brother sat on a cement floor, naked, bound and gagged, with terrifying looks on their faces. They'd been roughed up. His mother was sobbing. His father, though trying for stoic, failed miserably, and his brother—the fourth-degree black belt—shook like a lamb.

CHAPTER 38

Riker inched along Ventura Boulevard in San Fernando Valley.

Seemed humanity lived here, in their cars. Lights took forever or weren't synced, horns blared. Not good for the hurried man, but turning on sirens or lights would cause pandemonium.

An hour ago, one Pete Master's call had been routed to Neva. At the onset, Master wanted to lodge a complaint about "cops breaking into his daughter's Santa Monica apartment," but Neva pushed the right buttons. The emerging picture had Riker drive to Encino Hills, an affluent, hilly neighborhood overlooking San Fernando Valley.

Officer Max, the tail picked by Neva, had followed Zoe to Santa Monica College, where Zoe had only spoken with a young couple. When Max put the couple through the system, red flags popped up on the young man named Hawke Ford. Assault, breaking and entering charges. No time served. Lawyer got him off with probation. No address in the system, and no other info.

Max was an off-the-books tail because of his methods. He got things done, asked permission later. He'd pulled up the SMC girl's address, student named Tina Master, and taken a drive. Hung around the young woman's apartment building for a quick look-see.

When nothing transpired, Max went knocking on the door in vain. Eventually, he *let* himself into Tina's apartment. Found an open bottle of Scotch and two empty glasses on the table. Weed. For her part, Tina lay naked in a drunken slumber.

The scene didn't sit right with Max. Maybe it was the message coming through from Max's confidential source. There was a warrant out for Hawke Ford's arrest. He was wanted for questioning in a cyber hack that had compromised millions of identities. This after the first offense. Once out on probation, Hawke Ford had simply vanished.

"Apprehend on sight," the report read.

The police had never had a direct link—like Max had now—to Hawke Ford.

Max searched the apartment, found no one but the young woman knocked out, and tried to tiptoe out. But with his bulk and clumsiness, he made too much noise and woke up the young woman from her drunken slumber.

Once she covered up and calmed down, Max's badge got her answering some questions. She remembered going to school. Her second class, taught by Professor Snyder, had been cancelled. Zoe Sinclair? Yes, Tina knew Professor Snyder's guest lecturer. Yes, they'd bumped into Zoe Sinclair at SMC. Max asked about the boyfriend. About their background. Took a while, but Tina said that he, too, was enrolled in one class, Professor Snyder's. Maybe Max had pushed too hard because Tina started freaking out. She called Hawke. Someone answered then hung up. No callback.

With everything going on, Max's message to Neva has slipped through the cracks.

The captain would chew Riker's ass for potentially creating a lawsuit with an unauthorized tail, resulting in an officer of the law breaking into a student's apartment. Riker only wished he'd gotten Max's message sooner.

Fifteen minutes was all he had for Tina Master before driving over the hill for a face-to-face with his brother. A surprise, if Mother remembered her promise to tell no one.

At the second house off Encino Drive, Riker pulled onto the curb and jumped out. The door of the Mid-century-modern was yanked open before Riker fully crossed the lawn. A short man with thick gray hair stood in the doorframe.

"Mr. Master." Riker handed the man his business card and shook hands.

"My daughter's shaken up." Master led Riker inside a dayroom where floor-to-ceiling windows offered spectacular views of the valley. "But the lady cop mentioned a case, so I agreed to this. Like I said though, Tina's traumatized."

"It's okay, Dad." The weak voice shriveled out of a semi-dark hallway. A young woman with multicolored hair emerged.

"Hello." Tina Master stepped into the light and sat on the nearest sofa, hugging two pillows. Oversized blue overalls swallowed Tina whole, shrinking her appearance from young adult to child.

"Thanks for talking to me, Tina," Riker said, with the calm voice witnesses needed to hear. He sat close to the father, opposite the daughter.

"I overheard my father on the phone with the cops." Engulfed by pillows, Tina appeared yet smaller, her voice weaker. "He mentioned my boyfriend … well, ex now." She sniffed and wiped her nose.

Pete Master left the room and hastily returned with a box of tissues.

"The man who came into your apartment and asked about your ex, did he hurt you?" Riker needed formalities out of the way. Establish who the bad guy was.

Tina used a tissue then crumbled it in her hand. She shook her head.

"I'm sure it was scary, waking up and finding a stranger in your place. The department will deal with that."

Riker knew the department had already *dealt* with the issue and documented everything.

Before taking voluntary leave, Max, the retired spec ops officer described Tina's apartment in frightening detail. Open bottles, mint-smelling weed. Clothes littering the floor. Explicit photos of Tina. Tina naked on the bed, hair and makeup a mess. Small bruises on her body, suggesting rough sex. Not a picture to paint in front of a father.

Given the glances stolen Riker's way, Tina would appreciate Riker's discretion.

"I'd like to hear what happened." Riker looked at Master. "If that's okay."

Master opened both hands toward his daughter, leaving decisions to her.

"The cop had questions about Hawke." Tina cleared her

throat. "Something about an urgent police case. I called Hawke. He answered, but didn't talk. Then the call disconnected."

"Did Officer Max suggest you call?" Riker stressed *suggest* enough to clarify he'd already heard Max's version.

"He alarmed me with all the questions, but I wanted to call."

"That the last time you saw or heard from Hawke?"

She nodded.

The unexpected call must've alarmed Hawke, who chose to disappear.

She pulled another tissue from the box only to crumble it. "When I had time to think back, to recreate our time together, Hawke was different. Guess that's what attracted me to him. Tough and gentle at the same time. Smart. But there were gaps."

"Can you tell me about the gaps?"

"He'd show up at my place in the middle of the night, tense as an arrow. Sometimes, late at night, his work would call and he'd leave. In retrospect, none of this was normal."

"What kind of work did he do?"

"Courier for a law firm, which I thought below his potential."

"What law firm?"

She frowned. "He never said, and I never asked."

"What classes did he take at SMC?"

Tina's shoulders tensed. "I saw the news about Professor Snyder. So sad." Her body shook, and Riker waited a few seconds.

"He took Kim Snyder's class?"

"*Only* her class," Tina said. "He was obsessed with her. Seemed funny at the time, the way he'd take apart her investigative skills, her background, everything she taught."

"He'd looked into her background?"

"He knew everything about her. Where she went to college, jobs she'd had, papers she wrote, talks she gave. When I asked why, he said, 'A good investigator excels at research,' and he'd chosen her as study subject. She was teaching criminal justice, after all."

Silence took care of the next few minutes.

"Anything else unusual about Hawke?"

She stole glances at her father then fretted, her gaze darting all over the floor.

Riker caught Master's eye. "Would you mind giving us a few minutes?"

After Tina's nod, Master left, promising a quick return. It didn't take a shrink to understand much of her story couldn't be revealed in her father's presence.

Tina waited until Master's footsteps faded away. "Hawke had this fantasy." Her voice dropped to near inaudible.

Riker focused all his mental energy on listening.

"Once," she said. "He brought up a … um … threesome. He saw the look on my face, dropped it. A month later, it came up again. He called it a game, so I played along. In this hypothetical, the third person would be a woman named Zoe Sinclair. Professor Snyder's guest lecturer. Freaked me out because days earlier, on Wilshire Boulevard, we happened behind a car Hawke said was Zoe Sinclair's. I couldn't see inside, but Hawke insisted it was her."

The wheels were churning in Riker's mind. "What kind of car was it?"

"A sedan, but not sure what."

"How did he know it was Zoe Sinclair's car?"

Tina shrugged. "He changed the subject when I asked."

"Tina, what kind of vehicle does Hawke drive?"

She blinked, thrown by the question, but recovered. "Chevy truck. Why?"

"A green Chevy Colorado?"

"Washed out green, but yeah."

"Do you have pictures of Hawke? Recorded messages he may have left you? Pictures of his truck?"

Tina pulled a phone out of her front pocket.

Riker consulted his watch. He'd be late meeting his brother. While the girl scrolled through her phone, Riker sent Neva a text. Change of plans.

"Don't have his truck, but here's a picture of us." Tina handed Riker her phone. "And if you flip to the next screen, there's a message."

Riker weighed the appearance of the young man with a buzz haircut against memories of the mystery caller's voice—the man who'd called after the internal BOLO—with information on Zoe's car.

A smile cut across the hard face, probably one coaxed out by Tina. The hard look in his eyes remained; smile notwithstanding. Good girl falling for a bad boy, how typical. Then Riker listened to the gruff voice on the message, and a new picture emerged in his mind. He knew that voice.

"Tina." He returned the phone and leaned closer. "I need to ask you a question."

Tina tensed, and Riker gave her time while checking the hallway. Master maintained his distance, as promised.

Good, because at Riker's special request, Officer Max had let himself into Tina's apartment again in her absence. He'd found not only drugs but literature about homicide disguised as suicide with a list of films on the subject. Max had checked the TV play history; found two of the films had been played.

The similarities to Qin Young's story of homicide disguised as suicide were too close for comfort. He hated his mind wandering to Qin. But how could he—or anyone—explain the similarities between the two cases.

"Had you been using drugs before meeting Hawke?"

She shook her head.

"How about heavy drinking?"

Another headshake. Max had found her heavily inebriated.

"It all started with Hawke? The drugs, the booze."

"Gradually," she said, by way of excuse. "And we didn't do it all the time."

"What about watching movies about murder disguised as suicide?"

Something in her eyes darkened. "What does that have to do with the cop in my apartment, with you coming here and whatever investigation Dad mentioned?"

"Trying to find out."

Tina's attention snapped to the doorway where her father stood.

"Find what out?" Master looked from Riker to his daughter. "You still okay, honey?"

She didn't answer, just stared between two voids, maybe trying to figure out Riker's line of questioning.

"All right," Master said. "I think she's had enough, Detective."

"I'll let myself out." Riker stood, left business cards on the side table, and thanked both father and daughter.

As he stepped into the cool breeze, Tina called from the dimness of the foyer. "Where were you going with those questions, Detective?"

Turning, Riker saw the delicate girl hugging herself against the chill. Tina's eyes showed a range of emotions—curiosity, fear.

In all likelihood, her boyfriend had been the mystery caller giving Riker information on Zoe. Meaning Hawke had been trailing Zoe while out with Tina. Hawke likely broke into Zoe's apartment then forced Sebastian off the road, putting him in the hospital. The question was, at whose order? And, more, Hawke liked to play movies about murders disguised as suicide.

Whoever this guy was, he wasn't playing games.

Riker risked another question. "Tina, did Hawke ever mention the names Specter Group or Gwen Stone?"

Tina shook her head.

"What about Sunken City?"

Another head shake. "What is that and who are those people?

Riker handed Tina another card. "Call if you remember anything or hear from Hawke. And please, be safe."

He turned and left her in the doorway, shaking like a leaf.

* * *

Riker met Neva in front of his parents' house. "He's gone," Neva said. She'd missed Larson by minutes.

"Your parents are freaking out." Neva followed Riker past

the gate, into the single-family bungalow type house. "Larson hurried out, then here I was asking questions."

Voices rang from the kitchen, louder as Riker and Neva crossed the foyer.

Mother had forgotten their surprise plan. When she mentioned Riker was expected for dinner, Larson *remembered* an office appointment and bolted out.

"Smells like heaven in here." Riker called out. "What are you guys cooking?"

Dad rushed out with Mother on his heels.

They'd aged ten years since Riker's last visit, some five months back. And they were bickering, or maybe that never stopped.

As the oldest son, restoring peace had counted among Riker's talents, one born out of necessity. What had been hell for the boy had sure hardened the man.

Two minutes of explanations volleyed between Riker and Neva as to the unexpected visits, not being able to stay, and his folks relaxed. Mother rushed back to the kitchen while Dad poured drinks no one touched. They caught up on sports talk, exchanged meteorological information. Swift nonsense, just to fill in the silence. Their stolen glances did the talking.

How are things, Dad?

Same, getting old, Son. Waiting for you to come visit.

Nah, you look great, strong as a bull.

You're a good liar, Son, and you look short on sleep.

That obvious?

Mother hurried back with containers packed full of food. "We don't see you in months and you rush through like your brother."

The smell of sundry tomatoes, garlic and melted cheese knocked Riker into the pit of his stomach.

"Thank you for the delicious meal." Neva threw her arms around Mother, melting her reservations. Nothing like Neva hugs.

"What are the odds?" Dad accepted a hug. "Emergencies for you and Larson."

"We take them off the streets, lawyers put them away," Neva

said. "Win, win."

"You all have fun tonight," Mother said. "It's gonna be cold in Malibu by the beach, so bundle up."

Riker and Neva exchanged a look.

"Malibu…" Riker threw out, half question, half statement.

"Larson said you're going." Mother pointed between Riker and Neva. "Well, he didn't volunteer, but the ticket on his dashboard gave it away. *Fundraiser in Malibu: Specter Benefit by the Sea.* Odd choice of words." She laughed. "I said he should tell you, because you brothers need to spend time together. He said you're all going."

"Oh, yeah," Riker said. "That."

They all laughed, shaking their heads at his *forgetfulness.*

CHAPTER 39

Zoe's focus was a mess, all mental space occupied with thoughts of the event tonight.

Specter Group Benefit by the Sea.

She could bail—should bail, as Sebastian had insisted—but everything since Bob's death came down to tonight.

She needed answers. Craved answers. Owed Bob and Kim answers.

If Jett knew about tonight, he would bring out the cavalry. Tip off Gwen, who would shut everything down, or scale back. If Zoe attended as planned—pretending the PCH car crash had been a fluke—the dynamics would change. Specter's underbelly full of secrets could be exposed right in front of her.

The fire in the fireplace warmed up the apartment. The warmth helped Zoe sort her meandering thoughts while Sebastian napped. His recovery would take time, the doctors had said. Physical and psychological therapy might be needed.

Since the accident, he'd grown more demanding. Wanted her to leave L.A. with him. "Anywhere but here," he'd said, but she knew he wanted the simple life of Wyoming. Zoe couldn't live there again after having lost Mother and her best friend to a madman. Even if his family had been affected by the small-town mentality, Sebastian had forgotten and forgiven and wanted her to do the same.

Two years shy of turning forty, Zoe was too old to be given demands. Too set in her ways. She'd worked hard to be her own woman, a professional, dammit.

Love had a way of seeing things through. Maybe love could help them find a way.

She searched through the firewood. All too green to burn. Damn. She'd ordered downed wood and this was the opposite. There'd be no fire in the fireplace for much longer. Forced heat instead.

A presence came near. Limping over, Sebastian sat beside her on the cushions spread over the floor.

"Sleeping pill didn't knock you out?"

"Been delaying the drug. Makes me grumpy." He laughed and Zoe joined in.

The reality behind his words was different. He'd been delaying sleep oblivion in favor of being present, watching her like a hawk. To his half suggestion, half demand that she skip tonight's Malibu event, Zoe smiled. So, he remained on watch.

They looked out at the sunset colors. "Brilliant sky," Zoe said.

A few scattered clouds blocked the sunrays, the early colors swirling alive. So much beauty and ugliness coexisted in the world. Hearing the ocean waves and looking out at the sunset colors defined goodness, yet all that was repulsive existed parallel to natural beauty.

"What do you think happened?" Zoe heard herself ask out loud.

"To Bob?"

When she nodded, he said. "Maybe he wanted your opinion on the Specter Group man, that's why the meeting, but hell of a risk to put you in that position."

A beat of silence.

"Maybe Kim Snyder had shared her findings with Bob," Sebastian said.

"About the Sunken City person with a rare genetic disorder?"

"I've looked up Sunken City," he said. "A piece of semi-dislocated land in San Pedro. Homeless people make their homes there."

Sebastian's stare was cutting. "And one among them had this disorder." Silence, then Sebastian voiced her exact thoughts. "Specter Group is up to something bad. Then, there is the mix-up with your firm." He looked at her. "Best thing would be to pack up and go."

Another hour until total darkness. Two hours until the Specter event. Zoe closed her eyes and held them shut. She couldn't have this conversation again. Not now, not ever.

Sebastian reached out, his way to apologize maybe. Zoe fell into him.

His fingers tangled in her hair. When she looked up, he leaned in for a kiss. They fell back in a pile of moans and grunts, their hands pulling off clothes, exploring. Sebastian drew her closer, his hand sliding to her beating heart.

* * *

Zoe woke with a start, disoriented, cold, immersed in darkness.

Feeling around, she found her phone under clothes and gasped. Six-thirty. Good lord. Elation coursed through her body. Love. Satisfaction. That was what tired her, not sex, but feelings. Took a lot to feel, and to love.

Next to her, Sebastian was out cold, floating through medication-induced dreams. He'd finally taken his pills, maybe lulled into believing she'd go nowhere tonight.

Guilt surged through Zoe, because skipping *Specter's Benefit by the Sea* event wasn't an option, and because she should've been honest and stood her ground.

One hour until taking the stage as keynote speaker.

Throwing the blanket aside, Zoe dashed into the bedroom and pulled open the closet doors. She stood naked before an array of choices, mostly monochromatic colors with a few bright exceptions, none appealing. She yearned for the spot under the blanket next to Sebastian, but life was a mess.

Zoe pulled a black dress off its hanger and took a look in the mirror.

All right, big girl, time to get the show on the road.

CHAPTER 40

Hawke stared at the floor-to-ceiling windows that gave the appearance of glass walls. The building on Pacific Coast Highway, steps from Malibu Beach, sat in one heck of a location, smacking of elegance and money. Big Shot's money, most likely, or a large chunk.

All signs led to the side door, manned by security guards and a valet who directed him through double doors into a large room decorated for tonight's event.

Soft jazz played infusing a downtempo, relaxed atmosphere as people mingled. A sign on a round table read *Specter Benefit by the Sea*. Damned if he'd expected this, but the address on the invite matched the location.

He scanned halfway through the ballroom before he saw Gwen Stone.

There she was, embodying sophistication in a silver dress and black heels. Outward elegance, because her soul was a different story. Slithering through the room, she exchanged greetings and welcomed guests. No doubt she noticed all arrivals.

The ballroom, like the building, defined wealth. Chandeliers hung in triangular patterns, silk-covered tables overlooked the Pacific Ocean and Santa Monica Mountains. Floor-to-ceiling windows for the ambient drama. Nothing but the best of Malibu.

A podium on a velvet-decorated stage under spotlights awaited speakers.

Hawke's instructions were simple. During the keynote, slip out, hide and wait. Someone will take him to *the spot* where *he was to execute*. He knew little of the plan. "By design," Gwen Stone had said, "to protect everyone, including you." All he'd been told was that he was to scare Zoe Sinclair into obedience.

Maybe a lie. Easier to have him imagine not pulling the

trigger. The payoff would be his family back and his money, if the plan worked. He would not entertain negative thoughts of what might happen if it didn't.

Waving away another tray-holding waiter, he returned nods and smiles.

He'd dyed his hair brown. No point in attracting attention. The suit made his skin itch, but blending in was the game. A game Big Shot and Gwen Stone had changed on him. No problem. Hawke would adjust or end up like Shila. His mind operated at optimum speed when challenged.

He smiled as a shimmering blonde passed by, champaign flute in hand. Beauty everywhere, from décor to guests. Toned bodies in revealing dresses, and hardly a face over fifty. Either Specter was making a play for trust-fund wealth or advancements in plastic surgery had reached new heights.

Hawke pushed past carnal thoughts. Women were to be used not to rivet the mind.

When he'd demanded to hear from his family first, Gwen Stone's bodyguard, Muscle, had provided a live stream video. Her first mistake: trusting Muscle with the phone displaying sensitive information. He neglected turning off Incoming Location Settings before handing over the phone.

Hawke had proof of life *and* location.

Now here he stood, at ground zero. The place that housed everything he wanted: his family and Gwen Stone who owed him money. And as an added bonus, Zoe Sinclair.

* * *

The redhead in beige dress approached with sway in her hips.

"Dull parties tire me too." She handed Hawke one glass, kept the second. "Drinks and good company, that's the only way to survive."

Hawke accepted the glass. Hardly a guest stood around without one. He'd arrived early to observe. Memorized every detail, replayed the plan in his mind. But roaming around alone might attract unwanted attention. Conversing with the woman in skin-tight dress while holding a drink made sense.

She toasted, took a sip. "Not bad," she said. "Least they can do, considering the expected donations, is serve decent champagne." Her eyes glimmered shades of green, her lips a pale pink reminiscent of candy.

She took in the room and Hawke every detail about her. Reddish-brown hair past her shoulders, tall, athletic built and beyond attractive. Early to mid-thirties.

"How are you connected?" Hawke circled the glass around the room.

"To Specter Group?" She laughed. "Family obligations. Not my kind of shindig." She took another sip.

Hawke allowed himself a smile. A brief break.

"I'm not into fundraisers." She turned back to him. Beamed. "For medical research causes or any such trivialities. Guessing you're also trying to survive the evening."

Hawke sipped and nodded. He'd better stay alert. The redhead's playful eyes captivated in whole new ways.

At the podium, someone announced the first speaker, meaning thirty minutes until keynote address, then dinner will be served. Hawke scanned the room for Gwen Stone and Big Shot, but found no sign of either. The crowd had doubled in size, easy thirty guests.

A short, bald man took the stage—the warm-up speaker. Hawke's first warning. Five minutes until his move.

The redhead slid closer, her arm touching his. In other circumstances, he'd have gone for the feel, but not tonight. He leaned in and whispered an excuse.

When she turned, her eyes bore straight into his. "By the way," she said. "I'm Neva. What's your name?"

He told her, then turned and stepped away.

Hawke had his own strategy; Gwen Stone's plan be damned. The allotted time should be more than enough.

CHAPTER 41

Looking out the window at the Pacific under moonlight, Zoe pushed away doubts. With luck, she'd glean some tidbits, get the hell out, climb out of this tight dress, wash off her make up, and slip under the blanket next to Sebastian. With more luck and help from narcotics, he'd sleep through her adventure.

The clock in Kip Pulaski's office read seven ten. Twenty minutes until she was expected to take the stage, reassure experts and donors. Or so the story went.

The real goal, well, Gwen kept that to herself judging by her furtive glances and clipped words. But Zoe established her own goals: snap mental pictures, note prominent figures in attendance, and meet the faceless people behind Specter. Then turn the info over to Jett. Her secret goal: find Kip Pulaski, the man who'd compiled damning information on Sebastian and never shared. Pulaski, who left Zoe to Gwen Stone.

Gwen had proved a formidable actress. No mention of the car crash. But in unguarded moments, Zoe had glimpsed panic in Gwen's eyes.

One last phone check, followed by a deep breath.

The favor she'd called in with Kim Snyder's PI friend couldn't be discussed over the phone. Dick, the PI, proved quite the maven in all Gwen Stone matters.

Gwendolyn Stone and Bob Forester had met fifteen years ago, according to Dick. She was twenty-five then, Bob nearly fifty. She a media consultant, he a law-firm partner. She a sophisticated splendor, he a man riveted by beauty and brains.

When word of their dalliance leaked out, Bob ended the affair and begged his third wife for forgiveness. Couple therapy and love saved the marriage. While the affair ended, the fat lady hadn't quite sung.

During pillow talk, Bob had yammered, and the young

beauty had kept a file. She later married Kipling (Kip) Pulaski. The marriage didn't last, but Gwen and Kip's business partnership thrived. When the duo needed legal help, Gwen turned to her files. Why pick Bob Forester, Dick the detective couldn't tell, but no doubt there was a reason.

Two knocks on the door.

Glancing at her glass reflection, Zoe ran a hand through her free-flowing hair, then turned and said, "Come in."

The door opened, and Gwen Stone, her smile as big as the moon, stood in the threshold. A black shawl covered her silver dress. A long coat hung on her right shoulder, ready to be pulled over.

Zoe grabbed her coat. With a nod, she followed Gwen.

Dion, light shining on his dark skin, stood in the open elevator bundled up in a double-breasted overcoat. Nods were exchanged, and Dion pushed the button for the underground level. The same level Zoe had stumbled upon two days earlier, her first day in the Specter Group building. Another way out, according to Dion, where a car waited to take them to the real soiree. The affair in the ground-level ballroom was a diversion.

A short descent this time, and the doors opened.

Dion led the way through the semi-dark basement, with Zoe in the middle and Gwen bringing up the rear. Perfect time to be eliminated, were that the plan, but they kept moving toward the end of the hallway.

Zoe kept her attention away from the door she'd staggered upon before. The same door that someone in a white coat had slammed shut. She regulated her breaths, keeping anxiety in check. Fifteen more feet before stepping outside. Thirteen more.

The main event took place a short distance away, Dion had explained. Smart move, throwing off the scent with the fake gathering here, should the police have sniffed anything.

Sudden sounds drew near. When Gwen halted, Zoe and Dion whirled toward her. Not clear where the sounds came from, but the echo bounced off the walls.

Gwen and Dion exchanged a look. Shadows crossed Gwen's face. She waited, looking around. For what?

With a shaky smile, Gwen signaled them to move ahead while she fell behind. Surveying, perhaps. They walked on, but air was getting harder to breathe.

Zoe and Dion reached the double doors and stepped outside where a black SUV waited, driver in tow. Air rushed back into Zoe's lungs.

Opening the back door, Dion let Zoe climb in then took the seat near her. Gwen reappeared; cell phone glued to her ear. After muttering inaudible words, she climbed next to the driver, slammed the door shut, and pointed ahead.

* * *

El Matador State Beach, a little-known gem in Malibu, described splendor.

Zoe had driven by countless times, but only stopped once when she felt lonely after her sister's wedding. She'd flown back to Wyoming for the occasion, watched Angela get hitched, and somehow managed to dodge questions about her single status.

When she found herself in Malibu, Zoe stopped and enjoyed the hidden caves and rock formations of El Matador. Nothing like natural beauty to lift crushed spirits.

Tonight, the view captivated her heart, but Gwen's choice of locale felt like a trap. Only a few miles from the Specter building, this was a secluded corner of Malibu. Gwen had chosen a terrace, extending off a small restaurant. The terrace was buzzing with people.

Waiting with Dion near a table filled with appetizers, Zoe watched Gwen speak on stage. "Be brief," Gwen had said in the car, a departure from early plans. The basement sounds had shifted something in Gwen. Seemed to have altered the original plan, in which Zoe would give a thirty-minute detailed speech, take questions, then be driven back to the Specter building, even if no one said why.

Now, Gwen wanted the show moving faster.

Elderly men in suits and ties made up the crowd. The uniform of old money—pricey outfits tailored in unnoticeable fashion, same color and cut. They'd come to weigh the wisdom of their investment. None were lab rats and medical experts. Clearly the gathering had nothing to do with research, only with fortunes.

Gwen had given Zoe no names. Despite her efforts with Dion, she'd been given no list of donors, even in her supposed capacity as interim head of Specter Group.

When Zoe moseyed into the crowd, while Gwen warmed up the stage, Dion followed every step. Not that it mattered. No one seemed interested in chatting with the young lawyer here to tidy up legal matters.

Heaters had been placed in all terrace corners. A quietly elegant atmosphere infused the decor. White tablecloths sat on round tables no one occupied. Everyone stood in groups, drinks in hands. Watching and whispering.

The moon shone over the ocean. Sonorous waves cut through without overwhelming the ambiance.

When her name rang out, Zoe took the stage to moderate applause. She let a few seconds pass, looking at the bland faces, studying the crowd of twenty, maybe thirty men, with a few women sprinkled here and there. No one under sixty, if she had to guess.

Going over every face in the audience, Zoe began her speech. Judgmental eyes stared back, the tension palpable. No one stood out, and in a sea of sameness remembering details would prove difficult.

She listed the litany of documents filed on behalf of Specter, letters of good standing from various agencies. She laced the fluff and bluff with humor, got a few chuckles. No one had questions; no one cracked a smile as she spoke. They all stared, uninterested in easing the speaker's nerves.

She wondered why Kip Pulaski was not here. Why would he make such a grand appearance, on such a night, then disappear?

As she readied to close, Zoe sensed relaxation falling over the room. With a lawyer present, and legalities resolved, there would be good return on investments.

Slight movement by the door leading into the restaurant attracted Zoe's attention. The sole stirring in all the stillness. There was a man, standing in profile, in a semi-dark spot. She stopped, gave a slight cough. Reached for the glass of water and took a sip.

The man moved out of the shadow then withdrew from view. But that moment was enough to see the man was Larson.

CHAPTER 42

Hawke had confirmed the locations of the cameras upon arrival to the Specter Group event. There were four. Two in obvious corners of the ballroom and two obstructed by decorations, spying on unsuspecting guests.

After excusing himself to beautiful Neva, he had hugged the back wall, the only way to avoid surveillance. He'd moved behind the side curtain and pushed past the door, taking the stairs down.

Flashlight on, he'd followed twists and turns through a semi-dark hallway.

He'd studied the blueprints. The building had a subterranean refuge. And lo and behold, there was a door on the east side. The only plausible location to hold hostages.

Then, a surprise. Upon close inspection, another door stood five feet away from the base of the stairway. The blueprints he'd hacked out of the Institute of Architects site showed remodeling of the place years back. But the plan hadn't been updated to show that extra door. Neglect or bribes kept the door off blueprints.

On Muscle's phone, yesterday, Hawke had noticed more than his family's location. He saw a map with a dot flashing in a familiar location, Manhattan Beach.

He wasn't the only one tracking Zoe Sinclair. Instinct told Hawke that if she was around, Zoe Sinclair had been lured into a trap. At an opportune time, he would be asked to either scare or execute for final payment.

What happened minutes ago may have screwed up the plan. Now, Hawke was waiting, reassessing.

The sudden click of heels had startled him. He'd halted and killed the flashlight. Three people, by the sound pattern, had come from the elevator. Moved in his direction.

He'd rounded the corner and stepped behind a bunch of

brooms. Barely caught the falling flashlight. It scraped the wall but didn't fall. Fuck.

They must've heard him. Seconds passed before the walking resumed. The walkers were no longer moving in unison. Someone loomed behind.

There was nothing to do but wait. Attack if discovered.

Eventually, the click-clack of heels intensified until out of range.

Once silence reclaimed the place, Hawke stepped back around the corner. Pressed himself against the wall and inched ahead. Twenty feet away, a set of double doors led outside into a tunnel of sorts. Another remodeling feature kept off the blueprint. A secret exit.

A lone figure walked toward the exit: Gwen Stone. She stepped into an idle SUV. Through the open door, the interior light allowed a glance at the back seat, and there sat a black man and Zoe Sinclair.

The SUV sprung away.

Interesting. The trio were going someplace Zoe Sinclair was needed. She had not been the target. If not her then who? He was the only other person in the basement.

The thought chilled his heart.

CHAPTER 43

The Specter conference room was also a ballroom. The paneling Riker saw during his visit with Gwen Stone was gone, nifty trick. Now, the room revealed a bigger size. The address Mother had given Riker for the Specter event was here, steps from the beach. There were more scribblings on the paper in Larson's car, Mother had said, more numbers she couldn't recall, but this address was easy to remember.

Here they were, the event in full swing, and no Larson in sight. No Gwen Stone either. The thought of Larson being tangled with Specter Group and Gwen Stone riled him.

He caught Neva's eye, signaled, and met her at the back of the room.

"Feels wrong," he said. "We're missing something."

"We showed up." Neva motioned around. "There is an event. Guy at the door confirmed the Specter Group event."

"Everyone belongs," Riker said, looking around. "Except the guy we singled out. He seemed nervous. Where did he go?"

"Hawke. He went to make a phone call."

"Hawke?" Riker all but shouted the name. When a few faces turned to look, he nodded an apology.

"Tina Master's boyfriend is one Hawke Ford." Riker led the way to a corner. "Student obsessed with Professor Kim Snyder, tailing Zoe. Likely the mystery caller on Zoe's car."

Damn.

The crowd was thinning. The last speaker went back to the microphone. "Guests can peruse our website for donations," the speaker said. "Thank you."

They'd missed Hawke Ford. He had dyed his hair and dressed up, but Riker should've recognized some likeness to the man in Tina's photo.

And where the hell was Larson? Mother had mentioned Malibu, Specter, an event and Gwen Stone's address.

Riker's cell vibrated. He pulled it out and took it to his ear. "Jett Riker."

A familiar voice broke through, the connection fizzling. Riker made a beeline for the door, searching for a quiet place.

"She's not here," the voice said.

"Who's this? And who's not where?"

"This is Sebastian. Zoe's not here."

A few moments passed before the gravity of Sebastian's words hit Riker. Zoe wasn't home and Larson wasn't here.

"Maybe she went to the store?" Riker scanned the room for Neva.

"Her black dress and coat are gone. She used perfume and makeup."

Something in Sebastian's voice didn't sound right.

"Where do you think she went?"

Hesitation, but only for a second. "She promised not to go. Not a verbal promise, but the silence was enough."

"Tell me."

Sebastian gave Riker a scary summary.

Neva rushed toward him, something ominous in her step.

"I'll call you back." Riker hung up. Gave Neva a quick rundown.

Neva pointed to a velvet curtain across from the stage. "That curtain covers a metal door," she said. "Leads to a stairwell going to the basement."

"And?"

"Hawke walked in that direction. Moved the curtain, and disappeared from view."

"Let's go find out."

They moved opposite everyone else, parted the curtain and opened a metal door.

Without a word, Riker unbuttoned his jacket, undid his tie and descended the spiral staircase into near complete darkness. No need to look behind him to know Neva ditched her heels and was following closely.

CHAPTER 44

The distant clouds would soon obscure the moonlight illuminating El Metador Beach. Struggling to get her bearings, Zoe felt her mind as cloudy as the sky.

She accepted a few dry compliments and dashed to the bathroom.

What was Larson doing here? He didn't fit the demographic of those in attendance, nor the business association.

She halted near the bathroom door, glanced back, then changed directions and pushed open the men's bathroom door. Larson had two options: hide or flee. The bathroom would be a good spot to hide.

The men's room was empty. Goddammit, he'd run like a scared little boy.

In the vestibule leading back to the terrace, Zoe crashed into Dion.

"Ms. Sinclair." There was an edge to Dion's voice, a foreign look in his eyes.

"I'll be right over. Just need a little air in my lungs."

"You should leave."

"Excuse me?"

"My honest-to-God advice. Get out while you can." He leaned so close Zoe could smell something sour on his breath. "There." He pointed left to a side door. "Hurry. Find a cab, or call one, but keep moving. Forget about all this. Look at it as a bad dream."

"I can't do that."

"Ms. Sinclair, I'd hate to see you harmed."

"By whom?"

Zoe didn't think it possible, but Dion found a way to lean closer. "They're not playing games. Don't be a hero. It never ends well for whoever decides to play hero. Please, leave now."

"What's Gwen Stone's plan, Dion?"

Silence.

"Did Bob Forester play hero?"

A shadow crossed Dion's face. "Don't know what you're talking about."

"Why are you staying? What about Lou?"

Dion stepped back and shook his head, ready to turn on his heels.

Zoe grabbed his arm. "There was a young man back here. Suit and tie like everyone else but didn't belong. Short brown hair, round face. His name is Larson Fisher. Why was he here? Where did he go?"

"You have a chance if you leave now. Take it." With that, there was no stopping Dion. He whirled around and hurried away.

In the terrace, guests mingled, conversing in soft voices. No one ventured a look in her direction. Gwen Stone could be anywhere, holding court or watching.

Zoe stood steps from the side door Dion had pointed out. She could hurry out, but she'd never choose that route. She wouldn't leave or play hero, but rather call for help.

Pulling her cell out of her dress pocket, Zoe dialed. Then, she sensed movement.

The beefy man from Specter materialized and planted himself in front of her.

"Please follow me." He blocked her way toward the exit.

Zoe slid the phone back into her dress pocket and did as she was told.

CHAPTER 45

In the basement of the Specter Group building, Riker adjusted his vision and felt for his gun, keeping track of Neva behind him.

Darkness surrounded them. But there was more. He couldn't articulate what triggered the feeling, but years of detective work and chasing suspects through all sorts of places provoked a sense for danger.

Neva stiffened behind him. Sign she was feeling the same.

Something stirred, something flashed. And then he saw the reason.

Raising his hand to silence Neva, Riker drew the gun and shouted. "Police. Hands up."

The tall figure five steps ahead tensed. Silence for a few moments, then the figure came out of the shadow, hands up.

"Detective Jett Riker," the young man in suit and tie said. "We meet at last."

Deep-set blue eyes bore into Riker's, then turned to Neva. "Hello, Neva."

The voice struck Riker as familiar. The elongated words and deep tone. "You're Hawke, the mystery caller."

"That the code you assigned me?"

"Hawke Ford, if you prefer."

Hawke's shoulders dropped as if a weight lifted, the look in his eyes that of a man resigned to having been found. His eyes were empty of joy. A symptomatic problem among men on the run. They kept going until finally realizing that being caught was what they needed to turn their lives around.

"Hawke," Neva said. "That your real name?"

A nod and Hawke tilted his head to the right.

Riker glanced in the signaled direction. At the end of the labyrinth a pair of double doors led outside, or into a tunnel.

"They went out that way," Hawke said.

"They?"

"The people you're looking for. Gwen Stone, Zoe Sinclair. Black guy named Dion. They disappeared into an SUV. Bolted."

That explained Zoe, but what about Larson? And who was the black guy?

"How about a young man about your height, slim, short brown hair?"

Hawke shook his head, holding Riker's stare. Calculating.

"Turn around," Riker said. "And move."

"First, my family."

* * *

They opened the hidden door to a scene out of a horror movie. Three naked people bound and gagged on the floor, the woman and younger man barely alive, the older fellow out, no pulse.

Gun in hand, Neva stood guard near Hawke. But given his deflated look, Hawke needed no guarding. Riker called an ambulance, crime scene techs. The whole thing.

Three naked prisoners, lying in piles of bodily fluid and refuse brought Riker's breakfast to the edge of his throat. The woman and younger man oscillated between unconsciousness and death. Whatever drugs coursed through their bodies may have been what emptied their stomachs. Terror was just as likely.

Riker covered them as best he could.

In the corner, Hawke sobbed, unable to look at his folks. Remorseful. Guilty. At the end of an ugly road.

In less than twenty minutes, police swarmed the building. The few party guests left upstairs were seated and advised there would be questioning. Some demanded calls to lawyers. The sober ones anyway.

Once ambulances drove Hawke's folks away, Riker pulled a chair and sat facing the young man who preferred the floor.

"It's all fucked up," Hawke said.

"Tell me everything."

Hawke closed his eyes and mumbled something, rocking himself back and forth. When he looked up, tears pooled at the corners of his eyes. Tears that wouldn't fall.

"I was recruited by a lawyer. She helped me with a shoplifting case, years back. Woman who works … worked at Grunman and Forester. Same office as Zoe Sinclair, where Bob Forester was partner."

"What's her name? And she worked there, past tense?"

A slight headshake. "Shila Something. She's dead. Killed in cold blood by Gwen Stone, in a Century City parking garage."

Hawke recited the address and Neva made a call, sending a team to Century City.

"Why did Shila recruit you?" Riker asked.

"To work for the man I call Big Shot." A smirk. "Appropriate name for Cato Grunman."

"Bob Forester's partner?"

Hawke sniffled. "Forester didn't know his partner well."

"How so?"

"Man is knee deep in a lot of shit. I was hired as personal IT guy, posed as firm courier during the day."

"How do you know he's in a lot of shit?"

"Dug through Big Shot's computer, found curious stuff. Like his interest in Specter Group. Title of ownership to property in the Palisades." He turned to Neva. "You might want to send someone out there." He rattled out the Pacific Palisades address.

Neva nodded but didn't move. Their team was in the area.

"They have history." Hawke wiped his nose with his sleeve. "Cato Grunman and the couple. I wasn't able to piece it all together, but got enough to know their affiliation involves some medical research."

"The couple. Tell me about them."

"Gwen Stone and Kipling or Kip Pulaski. I didn't know their names at first. Just vague stuff about Big Shot's business associates. Last night, I looked into old servers."

Riker waited.

"You must've heard the names," Hawke said. "Gwen Stone has Pulaski all pussy whipped. Cato Grunman too. Now I see it."

"How?"

A headshake. "I thought she was another woman for Cato Grunman." Hawke glanced at Neva—his sagged shoulder an attempted apology for his language.

"Gwen Stone and Cato Grunman, or Gwen Stone and Kip Pulaski. Who's the couple?"

"Cato Grunman is married with kids. Gwen Stone was married to Kip Pulaski, divorced now. She gets around. In her youth, she boned the late Bob Forester. It's how she met Big Shot … Cato Grunman."

The emerging picture was a mess.

"Bob Forester," Riker said. "Tell me about --"

Riker's phone rang. He dug it out of his pocket, his attention focused on Hawke. "Jett Riker," he said into the phone.

Muffled sounds, distant voices. Riker pressed the phone to his ear.

Zoe's voice, but she wasn't talking to him. A man's voice, one he'd heard before but couldn't place. The man wasn't talking to Riker either.

Zoe said, "Okay, after you." More muffled sounds. Vague noise. As if the phone was being moved around.

Oh, shit. The phone was on but hidden.

Riker snapped his fingers, and Neva came closer. He showed her the phone, the number on the screen. Motioned that it was still on, but no one spoke.

Zoe wasn't calling to talk. She wanted Riker to listen, track her location.

He whispered into Neva's ear. She hurried away, summoning a nearby policeman.

CHAPTER 46

In the El Metador Beach terrace, waiters holding trays full of drinks moseyed around. Zoe declined, searching for the muscled guy, Beefy, but he'd disappeared.

The remaining guests chitchatted softly. Some were asking for their coats, ready for departure. Many had already left. No one came to speak with her. Although grateful to be left alone, Zoe found their disinterest strange. They stuck to one another, to who they knew. She was a stranger, hired only to clarify legal matters.

Dion had disappeared as well.

Odd.

Then she saw hurried movement out the window. Gwen Stone, in profile, followed by Beefy. Rushing away, disappearing into a car.

Where were they going in such a hurry?

Had Beefy stirred Zoe away from the exit so she wouldn't see them leave? If so, Gwen's plans had really gone to hell after the noise heard in the Specter basement. She must've been recalculating, regrouping, rushing away from everything and everyone.

Zoe felt for her phone. It had disconnected from Jett.

Just then, Zoe caught sight of Dion rushing toward the parking lot.

She hurried toward the exit. "Where to, Dion?" She stepped in front of him.

"I told you to leave."

"Told you I can't do that." She pointed out the door. "Where is Gwen Stone going in such a hurry?"

Dion jogged down the steps, and she followed. The night chill reminded Zoe she'd never stopped to get her coat.

He signaled a car valet, and an engine started.

"Dion." She held up her phone. Her connection with Jett had been cut, but he must've gotten a location. "I have a police detective at the other end of the line. Just a matter of time until he arrives." She stepped closer. "Leaving doesn't mean you're getting away."

"A mistake. They'll make you pay for it."

"Gwen Stone, you mean?"

A Chevy Suburban approached.

"They'll stop at nothing to get what they want. The project is everything."

"What project?"

He stared straight at her, looked away, then turned his attention back to her. "The project that started with unimaginable grief then led to greed. It became a drive for accumulation of wealth. Power. They're backed by the wealthy and powerful interested in cures and profits, long lives and money."

The group who disliked being "subjected to tech curiosities," as Kip Pulaski had said in their first meeting. Who stopped at nothing for protection.

"Whose unimaginable grief, Dion? And what group, what project?"

The Suburban was in front of them, and a valet stepped out.

"Good bye, Ms. Sinclair," Dion said. "I won't see you again. I hope you have contingency plans, and a way to disappear and never be found."

He stepped around Zoe, got in the car and sped away.

Memorizing the license plate would do nothing, but Zoe did anyway. In all likelihood, Dion would disappear into another life, away from Specter Group.

Rubbing the chill off her shoulders, Zoe turned, looking for someone, anyone, but as guests trickled away, the place was nearly empty. Town cars sped in the distance.

"The project is everything. Unimaginable grief led to greed." Dion's words. Whatever Gwen Stone and Kip Pulaski's plans, they were far from anything good.

Had Bob known? Had he been involved in "the project," until Gwen and Pulaski's greed turned unethical, illegal. What about

Larson?

Zoe looked toward the terrace. The party had ended sooner than expected, and Jett was taking his time. Maybe the connection cut too early.

The moonlight shone through the night clouds, illuminating the landscape below. The chill brought a stiff coolness to the air. She'd better get her coat and call a cab before getting sick.

Sick.

The word brought an avalanche of thoughts. An idea drifted in and out, just out of reach. Thoughts piled on top of one another demanding attention, one word dominating the rest—*sick.*

Specter, a medical research organization, had been accused of illegally extracting cerebral fluid from sick homeless. Zoe remembered the news stories about disappearing street people, and shivered at the thought. It couldn't be related, could it?

Illegally extracting cerebral fluid. For research. The charges had been dropped, but the connection couldn't be ignored. Kip Pulaski had mentioned medical cures during their conversation. Now Dion named "a project started out of grief." After losing someone to illness? Someone sick? Whatever the reason, it seemed "the project" had progressed into a monster of wealth and power.

Her phone beeped and Zoe saw she'd missed several calls: Sebastian and Jett.

A car engine started somewhere, covering all sounds. The noise came close until a vehicle stopped near. A familiar sports car.

Larson, a sad smile covering his face, sat behind the wheel. He pushed open the passenger door and Zoe climbed in, out of the freezing air.

CHAPTER 47

"Carve every word carefully before you let it fall," the quote above the dashboard read. A favorite of Larson's by Oliver Holmes.

They drove in silence for a while. Anyone looking in would've seen two friends, maybe a couple, cruising around Malibu on a cold autumn evening. They'd once been that couple, enjoying long drives, music and laughter. Study partners enjoying legal debates. When tired of law, they'd moved to wine and sex and poetry. Larson had introduced Zoe to Oliver Holmes—the judge poet.

One memory hit hard: Kip Pulaski quoting Holmes at *Bon Appetite*, a connection that escaped Zoe then. A line from the book Larson kept on his piano in Laurel Canyon. No one else she knew read Oliver Wendell Holmes Jr.

"Literature," Larson once said, "brings friends together more than anything."

"Did you introduce Kip Pulaski to Holmes?" Zoe broke the silence.

"The other way around," Larson said, his voice strained. "Kip introduced me one summer long ago."

Kip. A name said with incredible ease.

Memories from law-school parties filled with cigarette smoking and booze cut through Zoe's mental fog. They were young then, adventurous, their minds infused with alcohol. They told daring stories. Larson, mostly, told Zoe lots of stories.

She'd attended to his questions about her sexual past. About her partners, all men. He talked about his past, about once in his freshman college year, just once in his life, having been attracted to a man. "My lost summer," he'd called it, because that man had wanted to be nothing but friends and couldn't reciprocate. The man was married to a woman, in love and happy.

"Kip Pulaski is the man of your *lost summer*?"

A barely perceptible nod.

"It was a one-time thing," Larson had said about his lost summer. "An intense attraction, and it probably had more to do with his personality. The man is like a magnet, but now we're just good friends." Then law school ended and so did Zoe and Larson's relationship. They threw themselves into their fledgling careers with long hours of work. At Grunman and Forester, Larson had tested their enduring friendship with flirting. Zoe couldn't go back. After Wyoming he'd called, and she was engaged.

The things she should've seen could fill an ocean.

"You know Kip Pulaski's wife," Zoe said.

A nod from her peripheral. "He's been divorced for a while. A broken man who needed a friend."

Silence could sometimes be so loud.

"I'm sorry," Larson said, his voice quivering.

She let more silence fall between them, for Larson's sake. She no longer cared about the past, only sought to know how *a project of unimaginable grief led to greed.*

"Tell me, Larson."

"Kip is a good person. Appreciates life and literature, loves nature as a way of existence."

Another poetic line. *Nature as a way of existence.*

"Tell me about Kip Pulaski's big project," Zoe said.

"His ex-wife's idea. One Kip originally rejected."

Dick, the detective had been right. Kip Pulaski and Gwen Stone went from spouses to business partners. "The wife is Gwen Stone?" Zoe needed confirmation.

"Ex-wife."

"Tell me."

"Six months after their wedding, she gave birth to a baby girl. At the tender age of one, they lost the baby to a rare disorder affecting the central nervous system. The tragedy broke them, their marriage. Gwen became obsessed with finding a cure for babies like hers. She put together the funding for research, experts, lawyers. Kip was skeptical but agreed. Then everything went to hell and he called me for help. I tried to intervene. Threatened to call the police after the Palisades place."

They were driving toward Pacific Palisades.

"Where are we going?"

"*Hospes*," Larson said. "Kip gave me the access code without Gwen's knowledge. I made adjustments to the security system, ended the nightmare, but I want to show you *Hospes*."

* * *

The sign at the entrance read *Gratissimum Hospitalitatem*. Same as the sign at Specter. *Welcome to Hospitality.*

Oh, the irony.

When they stopped in the threshold of the ramshackle building on a large piece of land in the Palisades, Larson turned on a flashlight and Zoe felt ill. She swallowed back the bile in her throat, waited to regain equilibrium. She followed Larson inside what should've been called Hell.

"I came back to help a friend," Larson said, his voice faint. "Know that before I say what must be obvious. This place was a human experiment lab."

Zoe couldn't look at Larson. After this, she might never be able to again.

Steel rail bunk beds lay empty in a room smelling of rot, pain, and misery. Medical instruments sat on carts—syringes, tools. She could only imagine what they'd been used for.

She didn't want to imagine.

The place was empty now, but the smell of death painted a dark picture.

"Ever heard of *Lab Rat Horror*?" Zoe asked. "The film showing human experiments?"

"I've arranged for the patients to be moved," he said by way of excuse. "Paid for everything. Soon the authorities will take over."

Zoe turned away from the grotesque beds. So much inhumanity. She shut her eyes for a second, tried to manage her raw nerves.

"Let's start from the beginning," she said.

"Kip called me this past summer. Needed help. At the onset, it was about the cure." Larson blinked away a tear. "I didn't know about *Hospes* until last month."

Scenes of what may have taken place here played in Zoe's mind. She pushed past the images. Nodded for Larson to continue.

"Gwen welcomed me at first. When I tried to knock sense into Kip, she told me to fuck off. But Kip told me of Gwen's plan, and eventually of *Hospes*."

"What plan?"

He pointed all around, as if that answered it, then said. "Human subjects testing for research, at first, to find the cures desperately needed in the world, for life-sentence illnesses like that of their daughter. Then … then human testing for a profit."

Zoe waited through his silence.

"The subjects." He cleared his throat at the inhumane term. "They started out as volunteers given free meals, a free place to live, free medical exams. People in need."

Helpers of the Needy.

The homeless disappearance story reverberated through Zoe's mind. The downtown shelter was called *Helpers of the Needy*. Then there were the bits from Sebastian's story of test-tube fluid, and Jett's story of the Sunken City homeless who went missing. They must've all ended up here, poor souls.

"Where would they get volunteers?" Zoe asked just to confirm.

"They had people fan out through homeless communities or find those on the down and out with medical issues and rare disorders. People with no family members to be found. They'd tell them it was research for a cure, which was how it originally started. Gwen's plan."

"You mentioned your own plan earlier."

"To bring this place down, and start with getting everyone out."

"How?"

"I hired a business of ill repute. They move around anything from dead bodies to drugs for the right price."

"Where were the patients moved?"

"Place in East L.A. Cared for by semi-trained or self-trained folks. They have their own illegal facilities, home garages and such, where they perform everything from teeth extractions to abortions, but they preferred a neutral place. So, I rented one. Twenty-four-hour care, no questions asked, then they bail."

"Why not call the authorities?"

Larson reeled as if from a blow. "Judging is easy." The words seemed to come from a place of pain. Zoe waited.

"Kip doesn't deserve to go down," Larson said. "Gwen pushed her idea, appealed to the love of a father who never got to see his daughter grow up. There is evidence showing Gwen was the mastermind."

"Where is Kip Pulaski?" The wheels turned so fast in Zoe's head, she felt lightheaded. Dion's parting words resonated again: 'I hope you have a contingency plan.' Meaning: run and don't look back, like some of us.

"Kip needed …" Larson trailed off.

"Time to disappear. And you helped him with that."

"I gave him time, that's all. All evidence points to Gwen. You met her, saw the manipulator she is." A beat of silence. "Help the authorities see that. Please."

"You're crazy." Zoe scoffed. "You want me to help exonerate Kip Pulaski. Right now, you're an accomplice. Your best hope for leniency is a withholding-information charge on material evidence that could've saved lives. And you worry about Kip Pulaski?"

"Please, Zoe."

"Pulaski went after my fiancé to get access to his sick brother for medical research. For what? To bring him here and experiment on him? Pulaski was basically ready to use Sebastian's brother."

"Gwen pushed, threatened."

"Not a valid defense. Kip Pulaski knew what he was doing."

Larson shook his head. "She played upon his emotions. She pushed and threatened until he broke."

"Because she—or they—became greedy, right? The plan for

a cure soon became a moneymaking business." Zoe faked a laugh. "Human experiments, possible organ donation for a price, and who the hell knows what else."

Silence.

"What happened to Bob Forester, Larson?"

"You heard."

"Bullshit. Kip Pulaski convinced Bob to drag me to that meeting. Same night, Bob was found dead. What the hell happened?"

"They wanted a new lawyer."

"They?"

"Specter Group. Bob was wavering, making excuses, suggesting they should seek new representation. Bob asked me, then changed his mind."

Because Bob had found a link between Larson and Kip Pulaski, hence Specter Group and his former lover, Gwen Stone. A link discovered by the firm PI, Kim Snyder, who also ended up dead.

"I mentioned your name," Larson said, his voice barely audible.

"*You* mentioned my name? *You* set everything in motion?"

"It was your knowledge, your expertise. You're a great lawyer, Zoe."

"Well, shit, thank you. Ever cross your mind to ask me first? To warn me?"

"I tried that night, after you left my place. Called you, left a message."

"From an unknown number. One vague message is a warning?"

"I wanted to, but …"

Zoe started pacing to release the restlessness that had taken hold of her. "So, that *was* you knocking at my door right before the call."

In the silence, the unspoken words filled the void with their weight.

The gears were turning at dizzying speed in Zoe's mind, thoughts whirling around.

"The night Bob was found dead," Zoe said, "when I came to see you at the cabin. You asked me why go home and eat alone. How did you know I was alone, Larson?"

"Kip … had said they may have contacted your fiancé, and … I'm sorry Zoe."

She looked away to keep from scratching out his eyes. All this had unfolded in the shadow of her ignorance. The wheels of fate were being turned by puppet masters.

"*You* knew everything, and *you* helped send me into the lion's den," Zoe said. "Face to face with Gwen Stone pretending she didn't want an intruder. Handling me. She got you to play her sick game. Why? So, Pulaski could move to contingency plans and disappear? Good work, Larson. Good fucking work."

"I'm glad you approve." A disembodied voice cut in.

Gwen Stone stood in the doorway with Beefy, her guard, who held a gun.

"What are you doing here?" Larson stepped forward, but Beefy waved his gun.

Larson halted, put up his hands.

"I own the place, Larson, remember?" Gwen smiled big. "Thanks for arranging transportation for my patients. The transport has been diverted, of course, to a place of my choosing. Our business will be shut down, anyway. It's been attracting too much attention from hikers, I'm told." Her gaze cut across to Zoe.

"I just reinstated your business." Zoe's heart galloped in her chest.

"Specter will continue on, achieve miracles." She glared at Zoe. "*Hospes* will shut down. Thanks to you and Larson we can all resume our regular lives."

The tragic laughter Zoe felt inside filtered out. The line separating mirth and pain, comedy and tragedy, she'd crossed it.

"What's funny?" Gwen's smile faded.

"Go back to our regular lives? Amusing, Gwen."

"You might be partial to yours, but surely you care about other lives."

"I see you have a knack for threats, Gwen."

Gwen waited, her stare inviting Zoe to continue.

"Going after my fiancé by using his father's death. I imagine you would ruin his life, like you did with your ex. Why? Because you have the financial backing for what started as a grief project, then became a monster you can no longer control?"

Gwen's eyes turned menacing, but Zoe no longer cared. "Illegal experiments on innocent homeless people," Zoe said. "No amount of grief justifies that."

"Spare me the emotional speech. You don't know what it's like watching your child die while doctors keep expressing regret."

"All those lives destroyed. No suffering validates that."

Gwen's face went from pale to morbid. "Shut up." The scream rose from her core, eyes crazed and widened as if independent of her actions. "SHUT UP."

CHAPTER 48

When Riker's phone rang, the number on the screen preempted the conversation.

Qin Young's story, hidden in Riker's mind, had been slowly sliding into the open, gaining traction. He'd paid it little attention. Now, waiting in the basement of the Specter Group building when the call came in, Riker moved toward the exit for better reception.

"Say it, Qin," Riker said into the phone.

"First, Bob Forester was murdered. No full autopsy report yet, but --"

"And second?"

"The name Herod—saw it in the file—is not unknown to me."

"Let me guess. You were invited to join a non-profit medical research group. You discovered some rich old timers were in for profits at the expense of life. It didn't sit right. Something about how they processed people in need—more like cattle to slaughterhouse—so you bailed. But you heard the name Nick Herod. Not their preferred person in need, but ideal research subject. Problem was his family told the medical group to fuck off. So, they were forcing the brother, Sebastian Herod, on board, in some way that sounded awfully close to blackmail."

Silence was growing thick.

"That about right, Qin?"

"Partially. You knew all that and never told me?"

"I wasn't the one who needed to tell. And I didn't know, pieces are linking together as we speak." The UCLA doctor targeted by a medical group had reminded Riker of Qin, how he'd given hints but had never come clean, all that gab about research falling in the wrong hands, medical groups, humanity first.

Riker hated the prolonged silence.

"Was that story you told me—similar wound as Forester's—true or were you working up the courage to talk?"

"True story," Qin said. "Similarities in autopsies aren't rare, but verge on rare. Plus, the name in the file, the wound, the medical consortium's interest in Herod, I wondered what was going on."

Riker waited.

"Calling the police …" Qin tried then trailed off.

"Your word against theirs? Yeah, familiar story." Riker wasn't in the mood for concessions. Qin could've told him. Could've hashed it out quietly.

"I'll tell you everything," Qin said. "Twenty minutes, my office."

"It's gonna have to be now."

"I didn't bail." Qin's voice was barely a whisper.

Riker hoped, prayed, that he didn't hear correctly.

"My father died of a bad heart, rare form of cardiomyopathy. Treatable, but complicated disorder. No male in his family made it past the age of sixty. I'm at risk, of course. Did I fully buy into the consortium? No, but I've seen the research. Top cardiologists and scientists working on treatment for this complicated disorder."

Riker raised his hand, asking the policeman, in his face again, for one minute. With Neva gone to chase leads, the young cop put in charge while Riker took the call, could barely cope with whatever news lit up his phone.

"I've been in the background," Qin said in Riker's ear. "More an observer than contributor. They were okay with the arrangement, hoping to cultivate me for some day, when the time was right. After the Forester case, I sent my goodbye letter."

"What did you mean when you said it was murder, even if the Forester report isn't complete?"

"The wound." A beat. "Like in the story I told you about, these cases don't change. Hunches don't go away. And considering everything else going on here …"

Meaning Bob Forester's involvement with Specter, the group experimenting on needy people for profit.

"The goodbye letter. Who did you send it to?"

"Emailed to the address I've had. Said I'm done."

"Send me that info?"

Qin mumbled in the affirmative. "I'm sorry … Riker … I didn't --"

"The info, Qin," Riker said, and hung up.

First, the UCLA doctor, now a friend working in the department? Just how wide was Specter's reach, damn it. How wide?

* * *

Qin had to wait until Riker dealt with emergencies flying at him fast.

Neva's handpicked cop reported Zoe's call had cut too early. They couldn't pinpoint the exact location. Neva was casting a wide net from Memorial State Beach all the way down Encinal Canyon, both sides of Pacific Coast Highway. Lots of wasted time. And they'd found Shila's body in Century City.

Some progress, even if the morbid kind.

Now, Riker had Hawke Ford to himself. Riker pulled a chair and sat, palms on armrests, back relaxed, giving the impression of patience. Burning to grab and throw Hawke against the wall.

"Whose idea was it to make Forester's death look like suicide?"

The deflated young man remained silent.

"I can help you," Riker said, "but you'll have to talk to me."

When Hawke looked up, his eyes bore the age of an older man. "A mess is what you got, Detective, and I don't know everything." He shook his head.

"You knew about Shila Diggs. Cadaver dogs found her body. Family gets closure."

"Big whoop. She's still dead."

"Help me get the person who killed her."

A long silence. Riker stood, paced, and sat back.

"My family okay?" Hawke asked just when Riker readied to stand again.

"Your mother and brother. Doctors not sure about your father. Listed as critical."

A sob shook the young man's chest. "Wasn't supposed to be like this. Things went off the rails after Bob Forester started wavering. Then his people went digging."

"Kim Snyder, you mean?"

"She continued what Forester started. Couldn't leave shit alone."

"So, Forester had been digging. Found damning information on Specter and started to investigate. That why the kill order? Who gave the order? Who executed?"

Hawke offered a fixed stare. Trying to hide the truth made it more visible. Or did it? The way in which he shook his head said truth was crazier than any imagined story.

"The fucking bitch is crazy," Hawke said fast. "Going after anyone who stands in her way."

"Tell me."

"Gwen Stone had me fooled. She had everyone fooled. But looking back, connecting everything … it makes sense. All a game, and we were her pawns." A bout of laughter shook Hawke's body. "A bunch of guys with high opinions of ourselves, all her pawns." Another headshake. "But now I'm done."

"You're going to need court leniency, Hawke. Help me talk the judge into it."

"Not after Kim Snyder." He looked away.

"That was you? You killed Kim Snyder?" Riker wanted to punch him in the face.

Hawke shook his head. He wasn't going to say either way. "Gwen Stone," he said. "That's the name you're looking for. Took me a while to realize it."

Riker wasn't surprised, but he'd had enough games. "She didn't do all this alone, Hawke."

"I was recruited by Shila, the dead woman. She introduced me to Big Shot, aka Cato Grunman. I was hired by Grunman, paid, and given orders by him. But looking back, it was one big, masterful manipulation. It all started from there."

"Cato Grunman introduced you to Gwen Stone and Specter Group?"

"I found that in Grunman's computer. About Specter. Nothing mind-blowing, just there. Made to look harmless. Took time to piece it together. Gwen Stone was made to look like another helper, but …" Hawke laughed.

"Tell me about Bob Forester."

This time Hawke looked away. "Find Grunman and you'll find your answers." He looked at Riker, briefly. "The Palisades place, go free those poor bastards. That's my act of charity. Maybe enough for court mercy, maybe not. Send someone to free those people."

"What do you know about a Palisades place?

"Human lab on a large piece of land. My guess? Shit either has been or will be going down there."

Riker considered Hawke's words. With nothing to show for, the captain had pulled surveillance from the Palisades house. Neva had forwarded him the captain's text: *It's a hidden piece of land, almost impossible to get in or out. One patrolman per shift should do it, till we're ready to storm in.* Then something came up and even the one patrolman was pulled.

Dammit.

* * *

After reaching the top of the trail, Riker crept in from the rear. Hawke's description of the Palisades back hill was spot on. Luckily, the moonlight lit the way.

Riker stopped to get some oxygen in his lungs and survey.

Remarkable that Hawke had found this trail and hiked it at night. There was nothing up here but sage scrub, trees with broad canopies, and crooked trails that climbed straight up until this clearing. A better way to reach the place led to the opposite side, via a narrow road, but arriving undetected was the aim.

The gap in the perimeter fence confirmed the correct location. Another relic from Hawke's visit.

No alarms, Hawke had said. So, Riker crossed in catlike,

kept low to the ground, and dashed to the house. Lights bounced through the windows, their beams like those emanating from handheld flashlights.

Nothing was moving anywhere.

Having arrived through the back trail, Riker didn't have the luxury of knowing if the place sat empty. If anyone was here, they would have gotten in through the front entrance, by the security gate. He should've put together a unit, but that would've taken time and made a lot of noise. Hawke insisted the latest crumbs he found in some secret computer, were all about this place, and gave Riker the sure way in.

He circled slowly, waiting for a sign, or for instinct to propel him forward.

Sudden shouting from inside the building cut through the eerie silence.

"Shut up." A primal scream. "Shut up."

Gwen Stone.

Crouching, Riker inched forward. The front door was ajar. Steps away, Gwen Stone and Meathead, the security guy from Specter, had their backs turned to him.

Zoe stood a few feet left. No sight of Larson.

Please be alive, Bro.

In a flash, Gwen Stone seized something from Meathead's hand.

A gun.

Riker threw himself at the door and landed on the woman, but not before she pulled the trigger. Then the gun went flying.

A shadow jumped in front of the bullet. A second, two, and the shadow dropped with a thud. Larson, the hero, had jumped in front of Zoe and dropped to the floor, bleeding.

Riker lunged at the gun, grabbed it. Leapt to his feet.

Meathead stepped back, hands in the air.

Riker shed his jacket and threw it at Zoe. "Press it on Larson's wound." He grabbed his phone, eyes fixed on Meathead.

From his peripheral, he caught a shadow, then another, sprinting outside—Zoe chasing after Gwen Stone. Meathead, who clearly valued his life more than the two women, hadn't moved.

The flashlight had tumbled into a corner, bathing the room into an uneven wash of light, yet enough to see.

On the floor, Larson's eyes bulged out. Riker motioned for him to stay put.

He punched the key on the dial, hit speaker and set the phone on the floor.

"You move, you die," Riker told Meathead.

Pressing the jacket on Larson's chest wound, all Riker could do was listen to the phone ring, and pray it wasn't too late.

CHAPTER 49

Zoe forced the sports car into submission, oblivious to bumps and scratches on its expensive exterior. Thank God that, true to form, Larson had kept a key under the seat.

It became clear Gwen Stone hadn't driven the motorcycle up here herself. She swerved and bumped into tree roots, almost got thrown off the narrow road a few times. Yet she kept going, forcing the bike into speeding down the dark, treacherous road.

Zoe leaned into turn after turn, her foot firm on the accelerator. Gwen was not getting away. Fuck her contingency plans.

At long last, the road evened out, all pavement. An isolated section of Topanga, but she'll take pavement over dirt.

After the last turn, there was no sight of Gwen. She'd gone into the earth and disappeared. No sound of revving motorcycle anywhere, just unnerving silence.

Not for long. The roar of an engine came from the west.

Zoe turned in the opposite direction and hard pressed the accelerator. Although the car coming after Zoe was a dot in her rearview mirror, there was no mistaking the blonde hair framing the driver's face. Gwen had switched from motorcycle to a sedan. They must have arrived via car then changed to motorcycle.

Devious, but she would expect nothing less.

Now, Gwen was gassing it after Zoe. Instinctively, she picked up speed, working on a plan to lead Gwen to the nearest fire station. She'd seen one not far from here. But Gwen stayed on, edging closer. Too close.

The bump came soft at first. A warning. Then again, until it sent Zoe spinning.

Everything whirled around, faster and faster. Zoe felt herself rammed forward. The feeling was dizziness, then numbness, then everything began moving in slow motion.

Zoe made herself into a ball, protecting her head with her arms. Fighting to stay within, to remain aware.

Sometime later, motion halted. Everything stopped.

It took time to extract herself from Larson's car. Awareness rushed in sharply, like a drug. Adrenaline overload. Not long lasting, she knew. Better get out before the world crashed down on her.

Gwen's car was twenty feet away. They'd ended up near the edge of the canyon, somewhere desolate. The car doors were closed, the airbags deployed. The headlights engulfed everything in their glow.

The driver's door cracked open. Gwen stumbled out; her face covered by red spots.

Maniacal laughter filled the air. The adrenaline, likely surging through Gwen, resonated with fits and furies. Her eyes lit with something so potent, Zoe fought the urge to reel.

For the first time in her life, Zoe would give anything for a gun. Mental pictures of herself holding one zoomed in and out, a wish so real it hurt.

Slowly, Gwen's laughter morphed into tears. No sobs, no sounds of crying, only a cascade of tears. The death stare remained affixed on her face.

"You're good, I'll give you that." Gwen's voice rang thick with blood, phlegmy.

Zoe felt for her phone. Not in her pocket. "Tell me about Bob Forester, Gwen."

"Oh, is it confession time?" Gwen's laughter was now a gurgle. She spit out blood.

"Bob Forester wavered once he figured out your plan, didn't he?"

"Weak man, like Larson." Another bout of laughter. "He double-crossed me, that turncoat Larson. Pretended to play along while working Kip. Lucky for him, he mentioned you. Our original lawyer and in proximity to the Herods." More laughter, then Gwen steadied herself. "That family's selfishness … as if one person's privacy is more important than all those lives hanging in the balance."

The laughter turned to crying again.

"So you killed Bob Forester."

Gwen's smile bordered on madness. "Cato got worried, that's what happened to Bob Forester."

"Cato Grunman?"

"I could've talked to Bob, but Cato got worried. Bob knew too much. Knew Cato's secrets, his dirty laundry." More laughter. "Don't you love all those clichés?"

Zoe stood in shock. She tried a smile, but didn't think she managed.

"Bob would've used Cato's secrets, that was Cato's conclusion. Specter was all that mattered; we both needed Specter to go on. But fools came poking around."

Zoe put a lid on the rage boiling inside her. "Did Cato Grunman get nervous about Kim Snyder too?"

"Cato's mess to contain."

"Where's Kip Pulaski?"

Dark shadows crossed Gwen's eyes. She shook her head.

Zoe feared the worst. If Bob and Kim were Cato Grunman's mess to contain, whose mess was Kip Pulaski? He'd wanted out of his ex-wife's scheme at some point, according to Larson.

"Was Kip Pulaski your mess to contain?" Zoe asked. "Did you eliminate him?"

"He was all gung-ho in the beginning, even killed for the project."

"Like you, I once killed a man." Kip Pulaski's words came roaring in Zoe's mind.

Gwen's laughter was pure evil. "He killed the first doctor we hired when he tried to call the police on us. I helped him cover it up."

The look in Gwenn's eyes was that of a woman crossing into madness.

Then Zoe noticed Gwen was stepping backwards. Moving toward the edge of the cliff. Realization hit, despite the ringing in her head. "Stop," Zoe said. "Stop right there."

Too late. The anguish in Gwen's eyes was tempered with a hint of mania. She pivoted and plunged to her death.

CHAPTER 50

The helicopter landed with a thud. For such a graceful flying creature, it sure made a lot of noise and wind on the ground.

Zoe was rushed out with help from medical personnel. She'd refused a gurney. She could think, walk and talk on her own, thank you very much. She wouldn't be treated like a victim again. Aside from feeling bone tired, she'd never lost consciousness. She remembered everything.

Jett Riker stepped out of the helicopter behind her. He'd arrived soon after Gwen jumped to her death.

Flanked by medical personnel and the lead detective, Zoe was rushed into a sedan. Not an ambulance, thank God.

In the car, Jett's phone rang. He answered, then handed her the phone. "Sebastian," he said, tone solemn.

At the sound of her voice, Sebastian's cried happily. Then something in his tone changed, as if miles of distance sprung between them. Emotional distance. He was thrilled she was okay, but the thrill stopped with that simple knowledge. Even his declaration of love rang differently than before. Distant? Forced?

The crash, watching Gwen Stone fall to her death, must've screwed up Zoe's mind. Stress changed perception, the sound of people's voices. Zoe leaned her head against the window, closed her eyes, and turned off the world.

* * *

Dreams were as simple or as complicated as our state of mind.

In Zoe's dreams—or nightmares—bloody ghosts gave chase through back alleys, and all she did was run and run, like in a horror movie.

The only saving grace was that she knew it was a dream and tried to clear it from her mind. Slowly, darkness receded, and she came to in a twilight state.

She was on a hospital bed. Brain fog persisted thick as mist. She fought through the brain muddle, focusing on slivers of light cutting through. The mist dissolved a bit.

Her chest felt like a bruise, but pain backed off elsewhere, leaving behind exhaustion. That too, she knew, would resolve once off medication.

Whether she'd spent hours or days in the hospital, she didn't know.

A shape stood by the window partially covering the light. Jett Riker, illuminated like an apparition. Except he was real.

When she blinked fast, Jett stepped forward. "Hello."

"What's going on?" She was hooked up to an IV but no fluids dripped into her veins.

"You've been watched for delayed internal injuries. Making sure there's no bleeding from trauma."

"How long?"

Jett palmed his forehead. "Twenty-four hours."

Zoe struggled to pull herself up, but dizzy spells said hell no. She piled a second pillow under her head. Easier to see Jett. No dizzying spells this time.

Small steps.

A quick run of her memory, and it worked fine despite the drugs. She remembered the showdown with Gwen Stone, the chase down Topanga, Gwen jumping off the cliff, Jett arriving and calling in the cavalry.

Oh, God. "Larson?" She met Jett's eyes.

"Serious but stable. Doctors say recovery's gonna be a bitch."

Zoe gathered spit in her dry mouth and swallowed back the bitter taste. "Did you close the case?"

A headshake. "Need to hear what you know."

Zoe rattled out what Gwen had told her in short bursts. Felt like she'd run a race and needed air in her lungs.

Silence for a while.

"We lost Cato Grunman," Jett said. "Bob Forester's law partner," he added, to refresh her battered memory.

Zoe nodded. She remembered who Cato Grunman was.

"His wife said he left for a conference in Miami. We checked with the hotel and the conference organizers. Nothing. He hasn't used credit cards or phone. Just vanished without a trace. The wife filed a missing persons' report."

Asha Grunman, the wife and Zoe's good friend. An unreserved, good-hearted woman. Friendly and so different from her husband. And young Mia, the daughter, who elevated the father's image in everyone's eyes.

Zoe should reach out. Asha and Mia must be devastated.

Yet, no one disappeared unless murdered, body chopped up in pieces and hidden. Or unless he had contingency plans, like Dion.

Cold of Grunman to abandon family and business, but people were strange.

One thought bounced through Zoe's mind, one nagging question: Would Asha have known about her husband's duplicity? God, Zoe hoped not.

"If you can think of anything --" Jett was saying.

"Kip Pulaski. Did he disappear too?"

"We're treating it as a disappearance …"

"But know better?"

Jett held her gaze but said nothing.

"Gwen Stone killed him," Zoe said.

"We don't know that for sure."

"He'd been her mess to contain." Zoe said, remembering Gwen Stone's allusion. "She killed Kip Pulaski or had him killed."

Jett looked away, like a man who knew more than he was sharing. "We're working on Gwen Stone's bodyguard."

Medical alarms sounded, cutting the brief silence. Another critical case was arriving, or someone was dying.

"They killed Bob and Kim." Zoe heard herself say. "Bob had something big on his law partner. Something he was ready to use, force Grunman's hand. If Bob had found out about *Hospes*, he would have wanted the place shut down. Maybe Bob was pushing hard for Specter's demise. He had to be eliminated."

"Whatever the showdown between Bob Forester and his law partner, it was bigger than we know," Jett said. "Maybe Pulaski knew."

"Pulaski and Larson were friends." Zoe said, and Jett's eyes went wide. That was news to him.

"Doctors won't let me talk to Larson," Jett said. "Not yet."

Something connected in Zoe's head, though pain was pulling it apart. "Kip Pulaski killed someone."

"Like you, I killed a man. Shot him right in the head." Some of the first phrases Kip Pulaski had uttered when they first met.

Jett seemed reluctant to answer.

Painful aches cut through Zoe's chest. She'd been taken off medication for this visit and was feeling it more every minute. The pain focused her mind. This was not the only visit Zoe remembered. She'd been floating through fog during the last one, when voices cut in and out, distant. She searched the room, felt more pain at its emptiness.

"Sebastian came while you were out," Jett said, reading her.

Tears burned Zoe's eyes. Sebastian was not here, and that said everything. His tone last they spoke told stories she could no longer attribute to brain fog.

"He needs some time, that's all," Jett said.

Zoe closed her eyes and felt the sting of tears.

"I need some time, that's all." The distant but familiar voice of her dreams. "I'm leaving L.A. for a while," Sebastian had said while she floated between dream and reality.

"What were you saying about Kip Pulaski?" Jett asked, bringing her back to the moment. "That he killed someone?"

The door opened and two white coats burst through, doctor and nurse. Words were exchanged, but Zoe no longer paid attention. The nurse worked on Zoe's IV. The doctor poked and prodded. Darkness lingered at the edges of her consciousness before it took her away.

* * *

Mother and Lori came in Zoe's dream with soothing words

she couldn't hear. Their gentle faces suggested peaceful words. They stood near the bed, two translucent figures, ready to vanish like miasmas. The dead did that, came and went with messages Zoe didn't always understand.

Then, suddenly, Mother's expression hardened, and Zoe heard the words.

What are you going to do about it, baby girl? Lay there forever?

She'd been medicated to keep calm, to heal. Even in her dream, Zoe understood as much. Doctors kept taking her vitals, making notes. Nurses followed, adjusting the drip. Angela, Zoe's sister, was on route to L.A. Doctors had scared poor Angela into agreeing to extended observations. Back-to-back trauma and various scan tests gave medical personnel reason to pause. Now and then they lowered the drip, asked questions, made notes, then adjusted up again.

Mother and Lori disappeared from Zoe's dream now that she woke up, but Mother's question bounced through the room.

What are you going to do about it, baby girl?

Something had been sitting on Zoe's mind. A question, maybe an answer trying to connect. Sleep and trauma and brain daze had prevented the connection.

Until Mother's words slapped Zoe out of her daze.

That, and the drip must've been adjusted way down, making her functional. Now, a key was slowly turning in her mind, unlocking answers.

Zoe forced her eyes open and waited through the wave of nausea.

She was stable. She focused; slowly inched up. The nausea wasn't half bad. When she sat all the way up, the world cooperated.

Progress. Dear, sweet progress.

Holding a deep breath in, Zoe pulled the needles off her arm and let the tubes fall. When the monitoring alarm sounded, alerting the nurses, she exhaled and swung her feet off the bed.

CHAPTER 51

Riker couldn't understand.

"An ocean of existence," Zoe said into his ear when he answered the phone.

Hell, if he could follow. "You're well enough to chat and going crazy?"

"Partial quote by Oliver Wendell Holmes," she said. "Life as we call it, is nothing but an edge of the boundless ocean of existence."

Riker waited. Last time they had a short call, they'd spoken about his frustration with not finding Kip Pulaski. How a quote pertained to anything, Riker's unliterary brain couldn't figure out.

"Larson said if he ever lived by the beach, it would be across from the Malibu Pier. We met there for coffee and book chat sometimes. The spot came to be known as our 'ocean of existence,' after that quote. Once, he became serious about renting there, so I went with him to look at a studio. Too expensive for a basic room, great views though. We designed one in our imagination, a much nicer version. Now and then we laughed at our fixation with this imaginary place—the flat in our 'ocean of existence place.'"

Too damn poetic for Riker. And still not making sense.

"At Larson's bungalow, a book with the poet's quotes sat on the piano," Zoe said, "this one among them. Last I saw Larson he mentioned Kip Pulaski's love for nature, as a way of existence. Pulaski had money and had Larson a friend with ideas. If Pulaski were to hide while maybe planning a way out, what better place?"

Dots were finally connecting in Riker's tired mind.

"Go find Kip Pulaski." Zoe rattled out the exact Malibu flat location and hung up.

* * *

Muscle, the bodyguard, corroborated Zoe's story. He'd driven Gwen Stone and Kip Pulaski to a Malibu condo on separate occasions. Never stepped out of the car. Couldn't remember the exact address, just that it was across from the pier. Zoe's location sounded familiar enough.

Except Zoe's address was a studio rented to an elderly painter, white hair down to her hips, with no connection to Kip Pulaski or Gwen Stone. Longhair lady asked Riker to describe the two. After careful study of his LAPD credentials, she detailed seeing the man in Riker's description coming and going out of the condo next door.

"More like a visitor than a resident," Longhair lady said. "Too bad. It's a place with much better views."

"Anything else?"

"A few nights ago, I heard more activity than usual. Like the visitor came to stay."

She hadn't seen Gwen Stone, though.

"Was it the crib of an illicit affair?" Longhair lady wanted to know.

To which Riker smiled.

A break into the condo next door confirmed his fears.

Kip Pulaski had been dead for more than eight hours, but under twenty-four. Shot in the back. They were past the faint smell of decomposition.

Cadaverine smell reached past the room, into the entryway. Riker's eyes watered. One officer rushed out to vomit. The second all but followed his colleague, Riker's presence and composure the only thing keeping him in place.

Zoe's instructions had been almost dead on.

Gwen Stone couldn't let Pulaski drop out of their monstrous venture, not after everything they'd been through, after coaxing people in, forcing Bob Forester's hand, bringing Zoe aboard. The tapped phone call will put the second person on the call, Kip Pulaski, at this address, no doubt. The person Gwen Stone had screamed at and threatened her ex-husband. She'd left her cell phone behind, just in case, came here and took care of business.

Kip Pulaski, encouraged by Larson, had wanted out. Maybe he was hiding here, biding his time, preparing, as Zoe said, to disappear.

The couple whose heartache had set in motion an organization preying on homeless people, were both dead—one lying semi-decomposed, one having jumped off a cliff.

The first officer returned, diverting his attention from the corpse.

"Flat was rented by an out-of-state company," the officer said. "Will have the paperwork soon. And the techs are on their way."

Another shell company.

Riker nodded and looked out the window at a view in contradiction with the macabre scene inside. The cold had finally abated. The nice weather brought a sense of calm, one Riker knew was false. While much of the case was coming together—the bodyguard's drips, the confession Gwen Stone had given Zoe, the existence of *Hospes* and Specter—many unknown pieces remained.

Footsteps directed his attention to the doorway. Officer One handed Riker a phone. The stink of rot released by a decomposing body must've fogged up Riker's brain. He didn't feel his phone vibrate in his pocket.

"Good news," Neva said in his ear. "Hawke's attorney agreed to a plea deal. We have Hawke's story. Bad news, we have another problem."

Riker listened. Then without a word, he handed the officer his phone. Told him to finish cordoning off and wait for the techs and medical examiner.

Riker had an unplanned interview to conduct with Cato Grunman's wife.

* * *

Cato Grunman was missing and so was his fifteen-year-old daughter.

Mia, the youngest of two siblings, had gone out for lunch

break and never returned to class. No security cameras captured her movements. One friend saw Mia walk toward the corner of the building, in the direction of the bathrooms. Given repeated parental instructions to keep away from strangers, the theory was she'd gone with someone she knew. Someone lying in wait, familiar with the cameras' layout. Someone who'd signaled Mia, and she'd been happy to see. Her father.

Of course, a theory, but a damn good one.

Why would Grunman hide in wait and signal his daughter, who then disappeared?

No one knew, until Neva reached out to Grunman's wife, a strikingly beautiful middle-aged brunette. Tall, slender, with copper-toned skin and stunning albeit sad eyes, Asha Grunman resembled fashion model Iman. As if aware of such resemblance, she carried herself with the poise of a star.

According to her file, Asha's family moved to L.A. from the Bahamas when Asha, a gifted dancer, was thirteen. Although early signs pointed toward performing arts, young Asha, an outstanding student, had wanted to become a doctor.

It wasn't meant to be. At twenty, the young beauty met thirty-four-year-old Cato Grunman. Six months into the relationship, she dropped out of college and moved in with her boyfriend. Three months later, they were married. On their third wedding anniversary, the Grunmans were a family of four.

Now, seated before Riker, coffee cup in front of her, Asha Grunman began telling her story.

"Cato and I led separate lives for the past year. We'd considered divorce, but breaking apart the family and a mountain of financial dealings seemed more complicated than the pretense. We decided to wait, at least until the kids left for college."

She avoided Riker's eyes, as if judgment would be too much to bear.

"A five-thousand-square-foot house with separate wings makes living apart easy." Her dark eyes shone with traces of tears. "I kept telling myself, three more years. I could manage until both kids would be out of the house."

She squared her shoulders and evened her sitting height with his. "A few months ago, Cato came to me with his secret. He's very ill. I've known about his condition, but not about his declining health."

This time, Ms. Grunman looked straight at Riker. He nodded.

"Cato's mother had died of familial acute leukemia. Cato inherited the gene responsible for blood protein abnormality, which means risk for leukemia and susceptibility to dangerous levels of anemia. He'd been seeing his doctor routinely, continued to be monitored to satisfactory results. Supplements and regular blood transfusions seemed to work. But he had to stay on alert."

Ms. Grunman looked at but didn't touch her coffee.

"The reason for our separation is the well-worn cliché of infidelity." A sardonic laugh. "It's how I found his medical file, while digging for answers to my questions."

Silence claimed a good ten seconds.

"It was all there," Asha Grunman said. "Long ago, Cato had started making contingency plans for the eventuality he might need medical help."

"The possibility of a donor?"

She nodded. "It would work best if from the closest kin. Cato has no siblings, his parents have long passed on. That would leave his children."

A long beat of silence, then Mrs. Grunman continued. "Cato left nothing to chance and carefully selected the mother of his children. Early in our relationship, while sedated, and without my knowledge, I'd had blood drawn and tested. Sure, I wasn't the first but tested the best. Results for *autosomal genetic inheritance* or any possibility that my CEBPA gene, which provides vital cell protein, was remotely altered were negative."

She took another moment. "While inheriting leukemia is rare, people with genetic mutations are at high risk. That was Cato, and he needed a perfect, healthy mate match for his children. Free of inherited cell mutations, young, healthy, and from a varied genetic background of no concern, I was as close to perfect for the mother role as possible."

Another short pause, then she spoke again. "So, Detective, I was romanced into distraction by a handsome, older man for good reason."

Cato Grunman hadn't started a family. He'd taken out an insurance policy against his disorder. He was looking for future donors in his soon-to-be children, birthed by a woman with no health risk.

She cupped the Styrofoam cup with both hands, as if drawing emotional support.

"You confronted him," Riker said.

Her lips bore the tightest of smiles. "We remained civil for the kids."

She looked away, then back to Riker.

"Why keep his illness a secret, you might ask?" Her smile tightened. "If his clients, among them powerful lobbyists and politicians, learned the truth about their lawyer, that would not bode well for business. When he lost weight, regained some, lost again, it was easy to put it down to fads. With help from his doctor, Cato kept it quiet."

A doctor likely associated with Specter Group.

"Anyone else know? The children, family?"

Asha Grunman shook her head.

Riker didn't doubt her honesty. He also did not doubt that at least *one* other person knew. Bob Forester—Grunman's long-trusted law partner. May have been with Forester's blessing, and for the sake of business, that the secret remained. But when Forester learned of *Hospes*, he tried to use the secret against Grunman. Get him to stop the madness.

Bob Forester had to be eliminated.

"By now," Asha Grunman said, "Cato needed copious amounts of blood, platelets, and plasma transfusions. Considerably more helpful if donated by kin. The closer the match, the better."

Seeing it in Riker's eyes, she nodded. "Our daughter is the best match," she said. "But donors have to be eighteen and 120 pounds. Not only because eighteen is the legal age, but consideration must be given to weight, strength, development. Mia is fifteen, about ninety-five pounds, and not ready."

Ms. Grunman's voice shook. She took a moment.

"He couldn't wait?"

Another headshake. "He needed an urgent transfusion. It would buy time until Mia could donate bone marrow. No guarantees, but better than nothing. A chance at life."

The weight of painful revelations pushed down Asha Grunman's shoulders. She no longer sat tall. "The doctor offered no promises the procedure wouldn't seriously harm my daughter," she said. "He didn't think it would, but couldn't be sure. So, when Cato came to me about it yesterday, I said no."

Immediately after, young Mia disappeared.

Riker wanted to trust Cato Grunman would not hurt his daughter, but he'd seen crazed men do worse.

CHAPTER 52

Jett's call had changed everything for Zoe.

Mia Grunman was missing.

Zoe sat in the hospital parking garage, in a borrowed clunker of a vehicle. Damn thing didn't take on the first key turn, but good to go on the second. The hatchback was the best that Dick, the private eye, could do for a loaner.

She couldn't complain. Kim Snyder's friend had come through. Not only with transportation, but he was working overtime to find something, anything, on Mia. He'd hit the jackpot on Cato Grunman with information on his clients, lovers, employees. In some cases, the last two categories overlapped.

Zoe picked up the folder from the passenger seat and opened it.

Shila Diggs, Grunman and Forester's new lawyer, had interned for Cato Grunman fresh out of college. According to Dick, street-cam images of Shila's car near the Grunman house, when Mrs. Grunman and the kids were out of town, suggested romantic entanglements. How long had the affair been going on, Dick wasn't inclined to speculate. Years back, Shila had worked at *Bon Appetite* in Santa Monica. Kip Pulaski's restaurant of choice, and from what Dick underlined on the page, a place Cato Grunman had visited at least once. A place where he may have met Shila.

Shila graduated from Loyola Law two years back. She was hired at Grunman and Forester as referral by Ms. Grunman, the file said, but Zoe had heard Asha Grunman's story. Dick agreed. Shila had been hired to spy on Bob Forester.

Zoe's cell phone rang. She hit Answer and heard Dick's voice on speaker.

"You're in the car and read the file, I take it," Dick said.

"Great work. An interesting figure, Shila Diggs. Anything

else?"

"Nothing on Mia, yet."

More keyboard tapping, sighing, asking for a second, then Dick came back on. "Shila Diggs rents a condo in Westwood, four thousand a month, and … wait." Furious keyboard tapping. "Oh, God, there is a new article. One Shila Diggs' body was found in a Century City garage. Have to confirm it's the same person, but listen, you must promise me --"

Zoe promised she wouldn't end up like Kim and Shila.

The promises we make to be left alone. "Anything else?"

Dick typed away. "Shila frequented an underground bar named *Specter* in Santa Monica. Posted pictures on social media, deleted them. Problem with anything online, nothing gets deleted."

"A bar named *Specter*?"

"The picture is outside a place about ready to collapse, surrounded by overgrown weeds. You know it?"

"Tell me where."

Dick rattled off an address not far from *Bon Appetite.*

Zoe remembered the shabby building near the restaurant. The only other structure at the end of the street. She'd wondered how an elegant place like *Bon Appetite* found itself neighboring such a dilapidated structure near a freeway overpass. By design, that was how. Kip Pulaski may have been visiting the area for more than food and meetings. He'd had business dealings with Shila, who was in with Cato Grunman. And Shila had photographed herself in front of the shabby building and called it *Specter*—the-not-so-fancy extension of the Malibu building.

Zoe thanked Dick, hung up, and eased out of the parking spot. Behind her, the hospital loomed large.

What are you going to do about it, baby girl? Mother's words in Zoe's dream.

She had to find Mia.

Zoe remembered the schoolgirl from years ago, smart beyond her years and oozing affability. They saw each other at the firm's holiday party and the following picnic. They ended up on the cupcake-decorating team. When Mia was assigned a school paper on *Your Heroes and their Jobs*, she asked to include Zoe. A tentative friendship started—Zoe, Asha and Mia Grunman. Then, there was the Mia she saw days ago. A young woman, in love, and so happy.

Now, fifteen-year-old Mia was missing.

She may have gone willingly, but was she free to leave? Grunman was tied to Shila who was tied to Gwen Stone and Specter Group. Two murders—Kim and Bob—and the horror lab in the Palisades told Zoe there was more to Cato Grunman than met the eyes. He was no ordinary father.

Zoe could turn Dick's findings to the police, but they had their own leads. And she'd made that mistake in Wyoming. Waited for the police to intervene.

A kid, for God's sake. Mia was a kid.

The early nausea returned, hitting with dizzying force. Zoe forced air in her lungs. Forced deep breaths.

* * *

Zoe parked the battered hatchback as the day was folding into the earth. Clouds lingered in the distance, moving closer. She could smell the humidity in the air, the approaching rain.

With the wind blowing through the open window, a wave of realization swept over Zoe. No one but Dick knew her whereabouts. Should something go wrong, how long until Dick called the police? Not until she'd make the news.

Phone battery was at red—eight percent left. Enough for a quick call. She dialed Jett and went directly to voicemail. Maybe a bad cell-to-cell connection. Humidity particles in the air were weakening an already weak signal.

She found the station number under Recently Called and dialed. The duty officer said Detective Riker was out. Did she want to leave a message?

On a whim, Zoe asked for Detective Neva Braxton.

The voice that answered seemed at odds with the cold-eyed redhead Zoe had met. Concerned, accommodating.

Neva Braxton cut to the point. "I need you to tell me where you are, Zoe."

Zoe had disabled GPS location after leaving the hospital. Didn't want to be found and reminded she left without proper discharge, in no condition to be anywhere but medicated on a hospital bed.

She told Neva what she could, skipping over details. Then the call dropped.

With a long sigh, Zoe turned off the engine and stared at the shabby building not fifty feet away.

What are you going to do about it, baby girl?

* * *

Dick couldn't deliver a gun with the borrowed car, but he'd hidden a Sting Ring in the glove compartment.

"Illegal in California, so be careful," Dick had said.

He'd also provided a medium-sized flashlight. "Doubles as a weapon."

Zoe had learned self-defense hacks in a Korean-martial-arts class a lifetime ago. Anything one could throw or hit with worked.

She grabbed the sting ring. The main part fit in her palm, with the ring on her finger visible. Not easy to register as a weapon to unaware eyes. She turned on the small side button, verified that it worked, pressed the charge with her palm and heard the zing meant to sting an attacker upon contact.

Ring on her finger, and flashlight in coat pocket, Zoe stepped out of the car.

The no-sign *basement night club* at the end of the narrow street was on a vacant lot where weeds had taken over. Not far from the graffitied underpass on the other side.

It may have been a nightclub long ago, who knew? Looked dilapidated now. The paradox of Santa Monica—elegance and shabbiness in close proximity.

Past overgrown weeds, she could see tarps and shopping carts near the tunnel. A homeless camp where those adrift took cover.

She hurried past the *club* entrance. On a quick glance, the door didn't seem bolted or secured. Just closed and likely locked.

Looked like the building had long been falling in disrepair. Yellow, faded bricks and the back door made up the rear. The oddity was the lock-key, but she'd expected some measure of security despite efforts to have the place appear abandoned.

Circling back, Zoe glanced around. Nothing and no one. She lifted the keypad cover. How convenient, or foolish. She entered the code written on the inside cover. Heard no sound, no click, nothing to indicate the door unlocked.

Holding a deep breath in, she tried the door anyway. It budged.

Moment of truth, Zoe.

She exhaled.

With the Palisades property in police custody and no leads, this was all she had. The only lead on Mia Grunman.

Zoe inched open the door and stepped inside a round space, at its center a spiral stairwell going into a basement. No time for doubt. She descended the stairs, slowly, carefully, Sting Ring gripped tight.

Nothing but darkness until she circled down the stairs. At the bottom, a single light and a humming sound. She would be covered by darkness but not for long. Not if she stepped forward.

Zoe stood on the cusp of a decision she didn't know if she wanted to make. The faint sounds behind what looked like a rubber divider came awfully close to hospital machine sound.

She held her breath and heard faint voices. Two people going back and forth, their words unintelligible.

One life, if she could save one life.

She inched down. One step, then one more.

A light blared, followed by a short-lived alarm sound.

A large fellow in all black rushed out from behind the rubber divider. Behind him, a short, wiry man in blue garb hurried in, gaze darting up the steps.

Zoe flung the flashlight at the man in black. It made enough contact to disorient him. Palm on the Sting Ring, she quickly covered the distance and aimed at the man's face.

The hundred volts zapped, and Zoe watched him faint.

Silence, followed by clicking sounds from behind the rubber divider. The wiry man in blue was dialing for help.

Zoe rushed in, the Sting Ring pointed at the man. The fellow raised his hands in surrender, the mind behind the eyes clearly calculating his next move.

"Hang up and drop the phone."

When he did nothing, she stepped closer and let him see the ring up close.

"Do it, or I'll zap you like your friend in black."

Blue-garb man touched a button and let the phone fall.

"Mia Grunman," Zoe said. "Where is she?"

He tilted his head toward a curtain.

"Open it. Hands up the whole time."

He did, revealing a mobile hospital room, in its middle a table. The patient, covered with an oxygen mask, lay hooked up to an IV.

Mia, looking pale, not one bit of color on her face. Good God. She didn't appear fully asleep, her eyelids fluttering.

"Not fully sedated?"

"Twilight sedation," Blue-garb said. "Sleepy but somewhat alert."

Moans came from the bed.

"Her father?"

A fixated stare.

Zoe wedged the ring closer.

"Sorry … I was brought to help with a one-hour procedure. It was supposed to be somewhere else, but was changed at the last minute… I'm not supposed to be here. It's …."

"Illegal, I know. Where is the patient in desperate need of his daughter's plasma?"

Blue-garb stole furtive glances behind a curtain Zoe hadn't noticed. Eyes on him, she stepped back and pulled the curtain. A man on a raised bed, so pale and gaunt, he'd look dead if not for the tubes and whisper of a breath.

Cato Grunman.

“Wake her.” Zoe motioned toward Mia. “I know there are drugs that reverse sedation.”

After opening and shutting drawers, Blue-garb pulled out a few vials of fluid and hooked them to Mia’s IV.

“How long?” Zoe asked.

“One to three minutes. She’ll be dizzy, not ready to move fast.”

The young girl moaned.

“Get up, Mia.” Zoe uncovered her. “We gotta go.”

Something shattered on the wall, inches from Zoe’s head. A glass.

The second she looked at Mia, Blue-garb had thrown a glass that missed Zoe. Then he dashed behind the divider, up the steps and was gone.

Zoe thanked her lucky stars. At least she didn’t get hit, and the sound woke Mia who took a palm to her forehead.

“What’s …” She looked at Zoe, blinked fast. Then she took in the room and began sobbing. “Where’s my mom?”

“We have to go, Mia.”

Another alarm had gone off. Blue-garb, causing all kinds of havoc.

“We gotta get out. Now. Come on.”

The girl swung her legs over the bed and tried to stand, but swayed. Zoe pulled Mia’s arm around her shoulders. Propped her up. “Hang tight.”

The girl held on, her fingers shaky. Limping and wavering, they made it around the fellow in black on the floor, and up the steps. The alarm had stopped, but whomever it alerted couldn’t be far.

When they stepped outside, Zoe half waited to be whacked by someone lying in wait. Nothing happened. But in the distance, turning on the freeway off-ramp, a black sedan was coming their way, lights off.

They—whatever that meant—were coming.

Mia had seen the car too. Some three hundred feet was all that separated them from the pursuers.

“We have to run, Mia. Toward that tunnel.” Zoe pointed in

the opposite direction. “We’re gonna make it. Ready?”

Zoe and Mia moved fast. Not a run, but they were moving.

They had to get to the blue tarps. Zoe could distinguish human shapes, the transients taking refuge in the tunnel as raindrops began falling in the semi-darkness.

Dragging Mia, she waved and screamed for help.

Two shapes emerged from under the tunnel, then one more. A man and a woman moved toward Zoe. Their darting eyes said they’d put two and two together. Someone was chasing after the screaming woman, nearly dragging a girl.

They motioned Zoe into the tunnel.

A dirty-faced woman came out of nowhere and signaled Zoe under a tarp. Out of breath, her knees almost buckling, Zoe obliged. Just then she remembered her phone, but it was out of battery.

“You okay, hon?” The homeless woman asked.

“Do you have a phone?”

The woman shook her head and smiled. “I don’t but Ace got knives. He gonna scare them away, love.”

Ace must’ve been the man standing like a wall outside, ready to take on intruders.

Zoe felt nauseous. Lightheaded. She was in no shape to run, but couldn’t think about that now. She had to focus, dammit.

She looked at Mia. “Can you walk?”

Despite the chill and rain beginning to fall harder, Mia was sweating. The sedation reversal drug had been too much for her young self.

“No, hun, she look like she can’t stand, forget walk.” The homeless woman coughed, and a waft of tobacco hit Zoe. She stared at the ground to regain her composure.

Screams echoed outside. The woman opened one side of her tarp, covered her mouth, and closed the tent.

A shot rang out. The woman stared straight at Zoe. “You gotta keep still, hon. Don’t know who out there, but they ain’t playing.”

When another shot rang, Zoe sucked in air.

No other sounds but the wind for a good five seconds then a

familiar voice.

Neva Braxton was out there. Zoe almost cried.

"She ain't looking good, love." The woman pointed at Mia, whose color had gone from pale to blue.

CHAPTER 53

Riker walked into a scene that looked like an urban warzone. Blood, bodies, ambulances, men and women in uniform.

So far, only the bad guys were out—both in grave condition. The homeless man who had come to Zoe's rescue had suffered a shoulder gunshot wound, but the prognosis was fair. Or as fair as anyone with such a wound could be expected to be.

Neva got here on time. Not before the first shot was fired, but close enough. Now, Neva was directing the bloody scene, which included the dilapidated building some fifty feet away, with two people inside—Cato Grunman and a man dressed in black.

The rain was gently washing away the blood on the ground.

In the distance, homeless tents stood erected haphazardly. People in ripped clothes were huddled in groups, checking out the commotion.

Neva was gesticulating, stopping to give orders to uniforms. Moving between points again and again.

Among the transients, two stood not ten feet away—a dirty-faced woman talking to a man whose back, although turned to Riker, had a familiar bent under a heavy coat.

Felix. Riker's Sunken City buddy. How did Felix make it from San Pedro to West L.A.? And why was he here?

Felix turned and Riker saw recognition in his eyes, then a tentative smile.

"Detective," Felix said as Riker walked over. "A pleasure." He waved between the woman and Riker. "This is Sage. We just met."

Sage's face and smile revealed years of hard usage. "For once in my life," she said, "I'm happy to see the police."

They laughed. Or Felix and Sage did. Riker allowed a moment, then motioned Felix aside.

"Please explain." Riker led Felix away, hands deep in his pockets. He took in the scene, Neva in the distance, then stopped and fixed his attention on Felix.

"The explanation is long and complicated, Detective."

"Summarize."

A long sigh, then Felix said. "I conducted my own investigation after your visits. Through friends with knowledge." A cough. "Computer knowledge."

"Hackers."

"The friend who disappeared was like a brother," Felix said, as if to explain. "And we have our own …"

"What?"

"Hacker network. You may have heard the homeless hacker story a few years back, of one transient coder turned hacker. Truth is there are more like him out there. Not many, but enough."

Felix waited for acknowledgment or maybe approval. When none came, he continued. "When I mentioned the San Pedro police, I figured you might visit them."

"You followed me?"

"From a distance, Detective. You evidently remained unaware of my presence."

"I drove there, Felix. You couldn't have …." Then it dawned on Riker.

Felix waited, then said. "Indeed. I did not follow in the sense of the expression, by shadowing you."

"You waited near the San Pedro police station."

"I hid nearby."

Riker had been a fool. "You sent me there, then went and waited."

"'Sent you' sounds harsh, as if manipulation was involved. I simply shared my story, which you asked that I share. After, I –"

"Never mind, Felix. What happened next, how the hell did you get here?"

"As I said, Detective, there is an entire network of us adrift folks. Not just the hacker types. There is an underground of sorts, and we know each other. After your visit with Lt. Garza, I called upon a *network* friend. Someone good with computers. This friend, who shall remain unnamed, entered some circuits, as I believe he called them, and certain things revealed themselves to him."

"Like what?"

"Names of lawyers orbiting my friend's disappearance case. Who among the lawyers might be good and bad. Other *network* friends with expertise interpreted the findings for me. The name Zoe Sinclair came up among the good lawyers. Her story also came up, and her involvement. Finally, one *network* friend helped with transportation."

Riker shook his head. "You had Garza's computer hacked and followed Zoe Sinclair until she led you here."

"I did not say that Detective." A shy look. "You did."

"When did you start following her?"

"Ms. Sinclair entered our radar—my friend's term—day before yesterday. But she was difficult to locate. Finally, she turned up at Providence St. John's Hospital."

A brittle silence stretched through the air for a while.

"Will you report me, Detective?"

"Jett. Call me Jett, dammit."

Silence again.

"I'll be lenient, if you cooperate." Riker tried to hide both anger and amusement. "Your punishment may involve a place to visit and use as base camp from time to time, for showers, clean clothes, food. But only if you share your findings with me."

"I shall never give up my friends, Jett. Please don't ask me to do that."

'Get with the times and solve the crimes,' was Captain Caruso's favorite line.

"We'll work something out, Felix." Riker put out his hand and Felix took it. "Like friends."

Although hesitant, Felix nodded. "When the dust settles, friendships are special."

Riker took Felix's shoulder and led him to the car for a short debrief. Nothing like breaking rules and breaking new ground. Having a homeless man, or a *network* of people adrift, as new confidential informants fell squarely in the new-ground category.

Because "when the dust settles, friendships are special."

CHAPTER 54

"When the dust settles," rung like too optimistic a view.

It assumed difficulties were solved and a better future beckoned. Part of it may have been true in Riker's now closed case. The other, however, remained a near impossibility for survivors.

Riker walked into the kitchen, wine bottle in hand, and let the morbid thought fall victim to the smell of homemade food.

Neva, hair pulled back and apron on, was finishing up a creamy pasta sauce. Noodles simmered on the stovetop. A waft of olive oil, garlic, and herbs mixed with the aroma of baked bread emanated from the oven. A bowl of salad, every color present and parmesan cheese aplenty, sat in the middle of the table.

Neva hardly ever cooked. But when she did, she went all out. The process lit up her face, erasing all tension accumulated over the past week. Accentuating her beauty. If she weren't dashing between pans, Riker would've planted a kiss on her scrumptious, red lips that unleashed crazy desires.

Soon enough.

"Wine?" she asked while turning off the stove and oven.

Riker set the open bottle on the table. "Need help?"

"Sit down and pour."

The pep in Neva's step was no doubt propelled by a rush of adrenaline from having put their case to sleep. One second, she drained the pasta. The next, she arranged it neatly in a dish and added the right amount of sauce. Almost without pause, she plopped in a serving fork and set the dish on the table. Then, taking off her apron, she grabbed a towel, pulled the bread rolls from the oven, piled them on a tray and set the addition on the table.

"Let's eat while it's warm." She sat down, smiled, and clicked her wine glass to his. For that moment, her smile set everything right.

Riker served Neva then himself. Dumped a generous amount of cheese on his plate and let his taste buds dance with joy.

"Delicious," he said, at last, through a mouthful of pasta.

"Zoe?" Neva asked after a few seconds of silence.

A true anchor, Neva, firmly attached to reality.

"She's better. Needs one more day in the hospital."

"I'll take the morning visit while you finish with Captain Caruso."

They ate and drank. Life seemed almost normal.

Early in their relationship, they'd discussed life together. A relief, learning Neva wasn't burdened by thoughts of marriage and children. A former beauty queen, she'd come to detest *feminine chores*, as she called the predicament of women lives. Detested having been put in pageants by her former beauty-queen mother. Detested the idea that women were little more than baby factories on a timer. She wanted no such life. Riker would have surrendered to matrimony and family, had that been Neva's desire, but was thrilled no alterations to life were needed.

"I like Felix," Neva said. "Glad he agreed to the motel arrangement."

"As a base camp to visit for food and change of clothes from time to time."

"Maybe he'll like it and decide on fulltime help. If anyone needs our help, he's right up there, top of the list."

No sense spoiling the mood.

There was more to Felix's homelessness than lack of resources. In a city with shelters and organizations galore, people like Felix had long fallen into a mental chasm from which they might never recover, help notwithstanding. They'd help him mitigate his circumstances, but likely not much more.

"Great hacker, Felix's friend." Neva added more sauce to her plate. "We'd have had to jump through hoops to access Cato Grunman's private computer. Grunman must've expected this day would come. Not much he stored on regular home and office computers."

She looked up when Riker remained silent.

"It all started at Grunman and Forester," Riker said.

Normally, they did a case recap in some food joint. But Neva had insisted on a home-cooked meal in their newly renovated, state-of-the-art kitchen.

"So, Cato Grunman went to his partner about his illness?" She pointed at her glass and Riker poured.

"Either that or Bob Forester sensed something and confronted Grunman. They agreed to keep it from senior partners, even from their wives."

"The wife thing is risky," Neva said. "Like JK Rolling's story. The Harry Potter author adopted a nom de plume she wanted kept secret. New novel, new name. Partner at lawyer's office told his wife, who confided in the hairdresser, who spilled the secret. Remember?"

"No, but I'll take your word for it."

Riker grabbed another bread roll. "Anyway, it had to be kept between the two partners, Grunman and Forester, to protect the bottom line."

"Then Bob Forester dug deeper."

Riker ate the last forkful of pasta. Cleaned the sauce with a piece of bread and washed it all down with merlot.

Another serving sounded good, but he took a moment.

"As we now know, Cato Grunman, who was in with Specter Group, wanted Zoe on board," he said. "Larson didn't help by singing Zoe's praises as a lawyer."

"Her knowledge of the case and proximity to Sebastian Herod whose brother was of interest to Specter."

"Grunman got his partner to enlist Zoe. She trusted Bob Forester, so she took the meeting with Kip Pulaski. Long before that, Grunman had Hawke Ford trail Zoe and Kim Snyder. Shila functioned as recruiter and spy in Bob Forester's camp. They learned that, at Bob Forester's request, the firm's private investigator was digging."

"When Specter Group's dealings came to light," Neva said, "Bob Forester demanded Grunman pull the plug on *Hospes*, even Specter. Accept his fate, health wise."

"Cato Grunman wouldn't accept that." Riker sipped his wine. "Neither would Gwen Stone and their investors. Bob Forester had to be eliminated."

Years of detective work and recapping the story after closing a case—looking deep into the dark minds of criminals—still bothered Riker.

"Cato Grunman had one last visit with his partner," Riker said. "He didn't use the front door, so at first no one saw him. He knew the Foresters' home-surveillance layout, avoided the cameras under the cover of darkness. If not for the hidden camera Betty Forester had placed above the shed in the back, we'd have never known."

"If not for the friend who referred the camera installer," Neva said. "Betty Forester completely forgot. When she called me at near midnight, it was right after her friend's call. Betty Forester suspected the family's gardener of steeling tools they stored there. She had the camera installed two months ago. The recordings were fed into a cloud storage. When the gardener died of a heart attack, she forgot all about the hidden surveillance."

"We saw Cato Grunman sneaking in then out thirty minutes later the night of the murder."

"Talk about cameras," Neva said. "Crazy that Grunman had the Century City building security chief tamper with the recorded video."

"Cato Grunman was one desperate man with enough money to bribe anyone who could be bribed. He didn't want names shown on logs, people appearing on cameras."

"And there is Hawke Ford, who filled in the rest of what we know," Neva said. "Another lost soul, that Hawke." She leaned back and sipped her wine.

"The plan was to make it look like suicide," Riker said. "Hawke was delegated to studying the process Cato Grunman would later have his partner follow or do himself to make it look like suicide."

Neva shook her head in disbelief. "The two partners argued and fought that night. Bob Forester didn't go down easy."

"In the end, Cato Grunman made it look like suicide."

"Almost," Neva said.

"Then Kim Snyder had to be eliminated and that task fell to Hawke."

"She discovered Hawke's name in Shila Diggs' file. Was getting to the bottom of doctors associated with Specter. Had gone to meet one doctor the night of her murder, right after visiting Sunken City. Matter of time until she'd have called us."

Silence descended for a few seconds while they processed their thoughts. Nothing they could've done to have saved Kim Snyder. Any consolation, besides reaching a conclusion, lay in knowing *Hospes* had been shut down and Specter Group would be dismantled. Larson will eventually be all right, even if wheelchair-bound for some time.

"Zoe Sinclair proved of great help," Neva said. "She'd make a hell of a detective. Strong woman." Neva coughed a knowing cough, side-eyeing Riker.

"What?"

"I called her," Neva said. "Threw the offer out there, see if it sticks."

It took Riker a second. "You did not."

"She laughed at first. Said her ribs were hurting from the laugh. But I caught something in her voice."

"Neva, she can't. She's a lawyer and worked in the office of a man who got killed."

"Private eyes come in many forms," she said. "Anyway, she didn't commit to anything. Didn't even let me finish explaining myself. But, like I said, I caught something in her voice. She's not completely uninterested in being a private eye."

Silence for a beat, then Neva again. "She's a strong woman. Be a hell of a detective at large. Think you can ask her?"

Zoe was strong, indeed. Riker knew that as fact. He also knew best not to spoil Neva's excitement. "Maybe another time."

Neva grabbed the bottle and poured. "To quote Caruso, 'case closed, amigos, we move on.'"

Because in the end, the dust had to settle whether they liked it or not.

CHAPTER 55

As the morning sun illuminated the sky and threw a different light across yesterday's events, Zoe suppressed her feelings. She needed time to reflect over the past week, not hurt again. In the hospital, pain could easily be dealt with, but she'd rather do it without relying on medication.

Zoe needed to be alone, now that she'd sent her sister back to her family. She pulled the blanket, wrapped herself in it, and looked out the window.

An hour earlier, she'd moved from bed to reclining chair by the window. For the fall view out there, and to see something other than images from two days ago her mind played on repeat: Mia fainting, the fear of losing her, guilt. People dropping. Neva Braxton, phone glued to her ear, taking charge of the scene with commands, and calls for reinforcements. Neva feeling for Mia's pulse, telling Zoe to hang in there.

The first ambulance had taken Mia to the hospital, the second Ace—the man who'd come to their rescue. Both pursuers confronted by Ace lay on the ground, not in good shape. The third ambulance took Zoe, but not before she told Neva about the patient inside *Specter Club*.

Later that night, she'd learned Ace was stable but critical. He'd been shot, but the bullet missed important organs and arteries. The second bullet never made it out of the pursuer's gun, because Neva fired first. The hired killers were both in critical conditions but expected to pull through.

Although grateful to be alive, the knowledge of yet more death did nothing to sooth Zoe's heart. Barely anything was left to be salvaged from the wreckage of one group's pain and ambition.

Looking out the window, Zoe recognized the feelings encroaching upon her, but pushed back. *Fight baby girl.* Mother's voice seemed to ring in the room. *Look at all the good you've done.*

Fight for peace of mind for it is a precious gift.

A gift she'd like to give herself and others, to new friends and old ones.

Detective Neva Braxton was becoming a friend, coming over to talk, then encouraging Zoe to sleep. She did, but not before Neva told her everything about Cato Grunman's race to find a cure at any cost. About Bob having stood in the way. About Cato Grunman's connection to Gwen Stone and Kip Pulaski and Shila Diggs. With help from the FBI, they'd busted Specter Group.

When she'd found Zoe awake, Neva pulled up a chair and sat with her, silent when running out of words. That simple act did Zoe more good than any medication. Eventually, Neva was called somewhere. She touched Zoe's hand and promised to return.

Something interesting happened that night, a conversation that still put a smile on Zoe's face. Neva made an offer. "Join the team off the books. You'd make a hell of an at-large detective." She described how that would work. They would just run things by her for insights.

Zoe could almost imagine herself working with Detective Neva Braxton.

Then she put the thought away, unable to fit it in her overwhelmed mind.

Now, Zoe sat physically and emotionally drained. No medication though. She chose to feel instead. If she wanted to continue on, she had better go back to feeling.

Bob was gone. A man with much to offer was no more, and so was Kim Snyder.

Although she hadn't known Kip Pulaski and Gwen Stone well, their untimely deaths felt heavy on Zoe's heart. All those people in the Palisades, the suffering.

No humanity.

Zoe picked up the falling blanket and wrapped it back around her to dispel negative thoughts. She didn't want to think about Larson's betrayal. Only that he'd made it alive.

Angela, like a good sister, had come and gone. Zoe insisted Angela go home to her husband and children. Aside from doctors and an army of dotting nurses, Zoe had Neva and Jett, who took turns checking on her.

Not Sebastian. He'd called, but she shortened their conversation, blaming exhaustion. The thought hurt like knives piercing through her heart, but even in the midst of that pain, she knew she had to face the hurt head-on.

She took a deep breath and squared her shoulders. In wanting to keep her safe, Sebastian had taken to giving ultimatums, something she couldn't accept. Pretending to be someone she wasn't would ultimately cost too much, break them apart. Maybe time would change things, because not having him around was agony, but being handled hurt the same. She'd wanted a partner, an equal she could love and be loved by. Not a handler.

The door creaked open. A nurse pushed a wheelchair carrying Mia, whose smile brightened Zoe's disposition.

"You look good, Mia. How are you feeling?"

The young girl rolled her eyes but smiled big. "I'm in this chair because Mom and the nurse insisted."

"Better safe than sorry, you know what they say."

Mia's smile dimmed. "That's what my mom said about never leaving school. Don't do it, better safe than sorry."

"You trusted your father, Mia. Nothing wrong with that."

Cato Grunman, Jett had told Zoe, didn't make it. The biggest insurance policy he'd ever taken hadn't paid up.

"My mother is gonna want to talk to you," Mia said.

"She already thanked me."

"Not just that." Mia glanced at the door, then whispered. "The firm wants to offer you some deal. Something like a boss."

Zoe shook her head mostly to herself. Kip Pulaski had offered her work Mia may have termed 'something like a boss.' Asha Grunman likely had noble intentions, but Zoe was not interested.

The door opened, the sound echoing through the room. Asha looked in on them, a smile spread over her whole face. The kind of smile that came from deep within, from a place of deep relief. The smile of a happy mother.

Zoe motioned her in.

They went through small talk, marveled at how good Mia looked, considering. Zoe accepted and soon deflected comments about her own state. Smiled, cracked jokes.

At last, she squeezed Mia's hand goodbye, and watched the nurse push the wheelchair out of the room.

Silence crowded the space for a few uncomfortable seconds. Then Asha pulled up a chair and sat in front of Zoe.

"Can I get you anything?"

Zoe declined and watched Asha cross one leg over the other, looking out the window, into the distant sky, then back to Zoe.

"I don't know about you, Zoe, but I've spent my adult life wanting to make a difference in the world, however small."

"You have." Zoe pointed at the door.

"Suppose I've done that to a small degree through my children. Through charity work. Now the kids are grown, and I'm left with time, means, and a stake in a successful law partnership. I could sell but would much rather have someone like you, a smart woman, take on an important role. Help me turn a portion of the law partnership into something charitable."

A moment ago, Zoe thought she wished nothing more to do with that place, but her curiosity lingered. "The main partners are gone, and other partners are ready to take over, Asha. I'm guessing a charitable direction would not be their vision of the future."

Asha smiled. "So, you accept?"

The pleading in Asha's eyes burned the space between them.

Zoe was ready. Something had shifted within her after the past week, something that had been there, dormant, and ready to explode out into the open. Dammit, Zoe was ready for something, whether for Neva's offer or Asha's invitation.

She'd been looking for fulfilling work her entire professional life. Even before. She'd imagined law as fulfilling, exciting. To a point it was, and one must work to pay bills. But was that all there was to life?

She could throw herself into work with the backing of friends—a police detective and a wealthy woman willing to finance the way.

For the first time in a long time, Zoe felt ready for work.

The answer must've been in her eyes but she said a tentative, "Maybe."

Zoe had lost enough—a thought that hurt so much she had to banish it.

That's why it's called heartbreak, baby girl, because the pain is real.

Yes, Mom. That's why.

She'd gained something too, a new appreciation for life, for work. She'd gained friendships, old and new.

In the calm moments after Asha's embrace, in the absolute silence that followed, Zoe thought of Mother's words: *Live life, baby girl. Live life.*

Thank you for reading The Year of Secrets,
a Zoe Sinclair mystery novel.

I would be delighted to hear from you.

Please visit and chat with me at:
https://silviatomasvillalobos.wordpress.com

To stay in the loop about my latest releases, follow me on Amazon:
https://www.amazon.com/stores/Silvia-Villalobos/author/B00U8AB0QK?ref=ap_rdr&store_ref=ap_rdr&isDramIntegrated=true&shoppingPortalEnabled=true

Facebook:
https://www.facebook.com/SilviaWrites01

Your comments and reviews are the fuel that keeps my writing engine running.
Your engagement means the world to me.

Acknowledgments

Thank you to those who accompanied me on the captivating journey of completing The Year of Secrets. Special thanks to editor Gwynn Rogers, and to the dedicated early readers who helped me shape this book into what it is today, JR Stone, Liv Sparks. I owe a debt of thanks to those who generously shared their invaluable insights on various research aspects, Miriam Garcia, Fanny Drae. Big thanks to my beta readers, Virginia Anderson, Bob White, Robin Pope Cain. My friend Noelle Granger, who offered a priceless final read and made it all better – thank you. Also, to the L.A. native Tracy Sullivan whose L.A. expertise complemented mine. To my wonderful writing groups, in person and online, your feedback and unwavering support have been invaluable.

Thank you to my family for their constant encouragement.

Above all, my warmest thanks go out to you, my readers. Your engagement makes this journey wildly interesting and worth the while.

Made in the USA
Middletown, DE
05 November 2023